SCREAM
AND
SCREAM
AGAIN!

Mystery Writers of America
Presents

R.L. STINE

PRESENTS

SCREAM
AND
SCREAM
AGAIN!

SPOOKY STORIES FROM
MYSTERY WRITERS OF AMERICA

Edited by R.L. Stine

HARPER
An Imprint of HarperCollins Publishers

Library of Congress Control Number: 2017942897
ISBN 978-0-06-249569-3

Typography by Joe Merkel
18 19 20 21 22 PC/LSCH 10 9 8 7 6 5 4 3 2 1
❖
First Edition

TABLE OF CONTENTS

INTRODUCTION
BY R.L. STINE

Y **AAAAAAIIIIIII!**

That scream is to kick off an entire book of screams, and howls, and mystery, and horror, and frantic suspense, and cries in the night.

When you read a book, do you enjoy a cold tingle of fear at the back of your neck? A tense feeling that tightens every muscle in your body and makes you suddenly breathless?

You've come to the right place.

We call this book *Scream and Scream Again* because every story begins or ends with a scream. And trust me, there are plenty of screams in between.

Here are twenty scary stories by twenty different authors. Some of them you know, and some of them will be scaring you for the first time. I promise every story will be a *scream*.

For example:

"The Platform" by Peter Lerangis begins with a girl falling onto the subway tracks as a speeding train approaches. Our hero, Justin Blonsky, dives to rescue her. The terror and screams build from there.

In "Cat Got Your Tongue" by Wendy Corsi Staub, kids start hearing

1

screams in the night. Are they the cries of bobcats? Or has something more terrifying moved into the woods?

Chris Grabenstein takes us back in history in "The Unknown Patriot." In this story a field trip to Colonial Williamsburg takes a boy time traveling to a frightening night nearly three hundred years ago.

In Emmy Laybourne's story "Bricks and Bones," Ben and Jamal, two skateboarding dudes, decide to skate in a place they never should have entered—and may never escape.

Who can create the most terrifying Halloween haunted house? A competition to see who can scare people the most goes badly out of control in Bruce Hale's shivery nightmare of a story "Raw Head and Bloody Bones."

And much, much more. Twenty stories. Twenty authors. All waiting to give you the shivers and shakes. So . . . what are you waiting for?

Let the screams begin!

THE BEST REVENGE

BY R.L. STINE

THIS STORY STARTS WITH SCREAMS, but don't worry—they are screams of delight. Freddy, twelve, and Teddy, his eleven-year-old sister, had been wanting new bikes for ages. And now the two kids stood at the door to their garage as Mr. Hardwick, their grinning father, waved a hand at the bikes, shining in the afternoon sunlight against the back wall.

Freddy recognized his bike immediately—a black-and-green Razor high-roller BMX bike: sleek and hot and very sporty. Dad explained that Teddy's bike was a bright blue single-speed. She instantly loved the whitewall tires with their purple rims.

Mr. Hardwick enjoyed their happy screams as they raced across the garage, grabbed handlebars, and ran their hands over the smooth leather seats. "Check them out," he said. "See if we need to adjust the seats or anything."

Freddy was already out of the garage and halfway down the driveway. Teddy, the more cautious one, was still admiring the shiny-smooth fenders and just the *newness* of her treasure.

"Let's take them down Millstone Hill!" Freddy shouted. "See how speedy they are. *Fast and Furious Ten*!" Freddy was a movie fan.

Teddy struggled with her balance. She leaned forward, testing the handlebars as she glided out of the garage. "Awesome, Dad!" she called as she sailed past him, pedaling harder to catch up to her brother. "Totally awesome!"

A giddy, gleeful moment.

Purple afternoon shadows danced around puddles of sunlight. The air splashed their faces, cool and sweet-smelling.

Of course, they had no idea they would soon run into the nasty Darrow brothers. Or that Harry and Cletus Darrow would make sure to spoil their fun. In fact, spoil their day.

In winter Millstone Hill was the perfect sledding hill because it slanted steep and straight. The hill seemed to go down a mile, and then you could bounce safely into the empty field at the bottom.

In summer it was crowded with neighborhood kids on all kinds of boards—skateboards, roller boards, even Hoverboards. If you had the need for speed in Mt. Sterling Village, you headed for Millstone Hill.

The hill was deserted when Freddy and Teddy arrived. They gazed down the sloping pavement, imagining it to be a mountainside. They were side by side when they slid their hands away from the brakes, leaned over the handlebars, assuming their best racing pose, and began to pedal. And side by side they flew down the hill, screaming at the top of their lungs, wind rushing at them like a storm. At the bottom, the new bikes glided along the pavement, smooth and fast. And both kids realized their hearts were pounding, and they were laughing, heads tossed back, laughing at the thrill of it.

They walked their bikes back up, keeping to the tall grass at the side of the road. A few cars came down the hill, picking up speed as they descended. But there was never much traffic in this quiet part of town.

"Let's race," Freddy suggested when they reached the top. He was the competitive one; not really a show-off but generally wanting to be the best.

Teddy started to protest. She didn't want to turn it into a contest. She just wanted to enjoy the feel of her new bike. But Freddy had already started pedaling downhill.

"Cheater!" she shouted. "That's not fair! I'm not racing!"

She watched as Freddy rocketed down. She heard the squeal of his brakes as he started to stop at the bottom. And then she cried out in alarm as his bike stopped too fast. Freddy wasn't used to those brakes. And he went sailing up from the seat and over the handlebars.

He made a hard *crunch* as he landed on the pavement. Teddy saw his body bounce once. And then the bike fell on top of him. And she was pedaling without even realizing it, hurrying down the hill. Not gleefully this time, but with a heavy feeling in the pit of her stomach.

She slowed to a stop and climbed off the bike. "Freddy?"

He shoved the bike tire off his chest, rolled over with a groan, and slowly climbed to his feet, shaking his head. Then he pulled the bike up by the seat and handlebars and inspected it for damages. "Not a scratch," he reported.

"But . . . are *you* okay?" Teddy demanded, eyeing the long dirt patch scraped along the leg of his jeans.

"Of *course* I'm okay," he replied.

Freddy couldn't be hurt. He was *invincible*. That's the word he always used, and he believed it.

"Now let's race," he said.

Teddy didn't want to argue. She followed him up the hill, feeling the late-afternoon sun on her back, listening to the soft *thrum* of the

7

new tires against the pavement.

Then the Darrow brothers appeared at the top of the hill; just appeared the way they often did. Floating in silently like a dark cloud.

They were tall and big for their ages—thirteen and eleven. They had scrubby brown hair—very straight and falling over their eyes—and tight pale faces, with dark angry eyes like wolf eyes.

They were mean boys and proud of it. Sometimes they acted like your friend, and that was when they were the meanest.

They never got in much trouble. They seemed to know how to hurt you—how to bump you hard enough to knock you into a wall, dig their knuckles into your side, or swing a punch that made you flinch—without being caught.

And so here came the Darrows, walking with that peculiar strut, their wolf eyes unblinking, trained on the bikes. Freddy and Teddy watched them draw near, and tightened their hands on their handlebars and felt the fear sweep up from their stomachs, knotting all their muscles. The kind of dread they always felt when a Darrow brother approached.

"Hey, are those new?" Cletus Darrow had a hoarse voice that sounded like he was gargling.

Freddy and Teddy didn't answer.

"New bikes. We *love* new bikes," Harry said. When he grinned, you could see how crooked his front teeth were; big crocodile teeth.

"We have to get home," Freddy said.

"Not till we test out your bikes," Harry said. "It's a thing we do. We test out new bikes."

"Kind of warm them up for you," his mangy brother added. His grin was just as ugly as Harry's.

"No. We just got them," Teddy said. "We have to go now."

"I don't think so," Cletus croaked.

And then there was some shoving and pushing. And Freddy and Teddy found themselves standing hunched at the side of the road, watching Harry and Cletus settle themselves on the two bikes.

"Give them back," Freddy said, tight fists at his sides. "Those are our new bikes. If you steal them . . ."

"We don't steal bikes," Harry said, wrapping and unwrapping his dirty paws over the clean handlebars. "We break them in."

"You should thank us," Cletus added, and both boys hee-hawed like donkeys.

And without a signal, they took off together, pedaling furiously, then letting the bikes shoot down the steep hill. Shouting, laughing, they raised their hands from the handlebars and squealed straight down, as if they were on a roller coaster.

When they reached the bottom, the Darrows were going light speed. Freddy and Teddy squinted into the dying sun—and both gasped as the howling brothers turned the wheels and crashed the bikes into the wide trunk of an ancient sassafras tree.

The high whine of crumpling metal made Freddy think his ears would bleed. Teddy covered her face. Her whole body trembled.

When she uncovered her eyes, she saw the damage. Saw the mangled, ruined bikes. The wheels bent like flattened soda cans. Saw Cletus and Harry leap off and do a wild, clumsy dance.

"Hey! Hey!" Freddy was shouting. "Hey! Hey!" Like that was the only word he could get out.

"Your bikes are no good," Harry yelled up at them. "You can have them back!"

And then the Darrow brothers were running away, slapping each other on the shoulders, hee-hawing and hooting. They flew through the knee-high grass and disappeared.

It took a long time to walk their twisted bikes back home. They dropped them in the front yard and hurried inside to tell their dad their sad saga.

Mr. Hardwick shook his head, as if he didn't believe it. He gazed at the fallen bikes through the living room window. "That Darrow family is trouble," he murmured.

"We have to pay them back, Dad," Freddy said. His voice caught in his throat.

Teddy was afraid her brother might cry. She felt more angry than sad. "Revenge," she muttered. "It's only fair, Dad. Freddy and I . . . We need to take our revenge."

Mr. Hardwick turned away from the window. His face was covered in shadow, but they knew his expression was serious. "That's not the way I brought you up," he said, his voice just above a whisper.

"But, Dad—" Freddy started to protest.

Mr. Hardwick raised a hand to silence him. "No more. We've talked about this many times. We must be patient with people like the Darrow brothers. Show no anger. We don't believe in revenge."

That night, Freddy tossed and turned in his bed. It felt like a stone slab beneath him. He stared at the shifting shadows on the ceiling and tried to count sheep. But he didn't see sheep. He saw his bike. He saw Cletus Darrow bouncing on the bike seat, laughing like a maniac as he drove the front wheel into the fat tree.

Freddy's throat felt as dry as sandpaper. He wanted to scream. His anger made his chest burn.

He was just drifting off into a restless sleep when a sound woke him. He sat up, listening, and heard a soft shuffling. A scrape. A footstep?

The air seemed to ring in his ears. The hairs prickled on the back of his neck.

He heard a muffled cough. His body shuddered and stiffened in sudden fright. Freddy's eyes went to the bedroom window. It was wide open. But he had shut it before he climbed into bed.

His room was on the first floor. So easy . . . so easy for someone to climb through the window. Another soft scrape. Yes. Yes. He wasn't alone. He was sure of it now.

A cold shiver lingered over his shoulders. He tried to swallow, but his mouth was still too dry.

"Who are you? What do you want?" His voice came out in a scratchy whisper, so faint, so soft and frightened.

He heard the shuffle of feet now. By his closet on the other side of the room?

"Who are you? I know you're in here." Another choked whisper.

Freddy took a deep breath. He shoved his hands behind him and used them to push himself up. The light switch seemed a mile away.

He heard another cough, followed by a soft laugh. And then a scrambling shadow darted across the room. A clump of shoes thudded on his carpet. The big shadow rumbled past him, big and heavy, plodding like a dark rhinoceros.

A ball of darkness—it pounded over the floor—bent forward and dove out the open window.

Freddy was on his feet now, legs trembling like rubber bands. His breaths came out wheezy and rapid, his chest heaving up and down beneath his pajama top.

He darted to the window. Grabbed the ledge with both hands. Peered into the yellow light from a streetlamp at the curb. And saw Harry Darrow running, head lowered like a running back, big shoes clomping across the front lawn, his dark hair tossing in the wind.

"Harry Darrow. In my room," Freddy murmured.

He spun and stumbled to the light switch. Blinking in the bright light from the ceiling, he saw a sheet of paper on the rug at the foot of his bed.

A note? Yes. He lifted it with a trembling hand. Squinting against the bright light, Freddy read the note, scribbled in black marker—half printed, half written—words tilting across the page:

IF YOU TELL ABOUT THE BIKES, YOU'RE DEAD.

A simple message, but Freddy read it three times. The words pulsed in his eyes. With a groan of disgust, he crinkled the note in his fist and tossed it back to the floor.

"My room. He was in my room." The words escaped Freddy's mouth in a voice he barely recognized.

I'm not safe in my own room.

He untwisted his pajama bottoms. Shook his head hard, as if shaking his fear and anger away. And bolted across his room and through the open door into the blackness of the hall.

Dark as a tomb. The air cool and heavy. His bare feet scratching against the carpet as he trotted toward his father's room.

Not safe in my room. Harry Darrow was in my room. Dad will know what to do. He will have to deal with this now. We will have to send a strong message to Harry.

"Huh?" Freddy uttered a soft cry. And stopped. His shoulder

bumped the wall. His eyes widened but couldn't focus in the total blanket of darkness.

He heard the creak of the floor beneath the hall carpet. He saw blackness slide over blackness. A figure. So near. So close in front of him.

It must be the other Darrow brother, he realized. *Cletus Darrow. They've both invaded our house. They're here to frighten us.*

Against the inky black, Freddy saw red. A wave of anger swept over him. *"Gotcha!"* he screamed. He plunged forward and pounced, grabbing the Darrow brother with both hands.

A scream. A struggle.

A light flashed on.

Freddy found himself gripping Teddy by the shoulders. She spun around. "What's *wrong* with you? Are you crazy?"

He stumbled back. Nearly knocked over a flower vase on the small hall table. "I—I thought . . ." He could only stammer.

Teddy brought her angry face close to his. "You thought *what*?"

"I thought . . . you were Cletus Darrow," he managed to say.

"Do I *look* like Cletus Darrow?"

"It was pitch-black. I couldn't see."

And then Mr. Hardwick was in the hall, rubbing the sleep from his eyes, the belt dangling from his robe. "What on Earth—"

Freddy and Teddy both started talking at once. But Freddy was the one with the story to tell. The words rushed out like a waterfall as he told his dad about Harry Darrow breaking into his room to scare him and leave a threatening message.

His dad pressed both hands on Freddy's shoulders, trying to calm him. But Freddy wouldn't be calmed.

"I have to pay him back, Dad. He was in my room. He . . . he threatened me."

"He'll get tired of scaring you," Mr. Hardwick said softly. "The Darrows will move on. They will get bored with you and move on."

Teddy stepped between them. She tossed back her dark hair. Her eyes were wide and angry. She could feel the anger burn her throat. "It isn't right, Dad. They have to be punished. We can't let them get away with this."

"And look at our bikes," Freddy added, his voice high and shrill. "Wrecked. They wrecked our bikes."

"Revenge," Teddy said. "Revenge, Dad. We need a plan to pay them back."

Mr. Hardwick shook his head. His eyes became narrow slits. "No. That's not the way to go. We've talked about this many times. That's not our way, and you know it."

"But, Dad—" Freddy started to protest.

"Give it time," Mr. Hardwick said. "Give it time. You'll see that I'm right." He turned and walked back to his room. The discussion was over.

The tall brick wall behind the school was perfect for hitting a tennis ball against. Teddy loved to play tennis, but her forearm was weak. She knew the only solution was to practice. Many afternoons—while Freddy was at his fencing lessons or cruising the neighborhood on his skateboard or at home playing video games—she slammed a ball against that wall again and again until the racket felt like part of her arm.

She liked the *thump* the tennis ball made as it hit high on the brick wall. And she liked trying to be in position to hit it when the ball came sailing down. It was almost as much fun as playing against an opponent. On good days, it was better.

Today wasn't a good day. Cletus Darrow appeared after she had been hitting the ball for only ten minutes. She didn't see him at first. She was concentrating on her game. But a shadow slid over her, and the shadow felt cold, so she knew a Darrow was near.

Teddy turned, instantly angry. "What do *you* want?" she snapped. The ball bounced through her hand, and she had to chase it.

"Something wrong with your racket?" Cletus said, wolf eyes peering out at her from behind a thick strand of dark hair.

"No way," Teddy shot back. "Go away. I'm serious."

"I'm serious too," Cletus said with a sneer. A sneer was his natural expression. "You have a hole in your racket."

"You're crazy. Go away."

"Let me see it." Cletus shot his arm forward and snatched the racket from Teddy's hand. He tugged it so hard she nearly fell over.

"Give it!" she cried, sticking out her hand.

Too late. Cletus pulled a pocketknife from his pocket—and cut through the center of the netting. "See? I told you. A big hole in your racket." He laughed and tossed the racket to the grass.

Freddy wasn't popular with girls. Maybe it was because he had so many interests of his own, and things he liked to do by himself, that he had no time for girls.

But the next day during lunch period, he was surrounded by a group of girls from his class. And they were actually interested in the story he was telling them, the story of how his family had lived on a cattle ranch and the time four big cows somehow had gotten into the house and refused to be moved.

It was one of those rare moments. Freddy being the center of attention, and the girls laughing at his story and enjoying hanging with him, and maybe noticing him for the first time since he'd started at the school.

Of course, the moment was spoiled when Harry Darrow crept up behind Freddy and pantsed him. Harry yanked Freddy's jeans down to his ankles. And the girls got hysterical because Freddy was wearing the *Hello Kitty* underpants his grandmother had sent him since it was the only clean pair he had.

So Freddy was double embarrassed because of the underpants. And because of the wild laughter that poured up from the girls like a bubbling fountain.

And then Freddy, struggling to pull up his jeans, saw Cletus across the room with his phone raised. And of course, Cletus was making a video of the whole thing and telling everyone about how great it would look when he put it up on YouTube.

Freddy wanted to kill *kill* KILL.

The rage shot through him till he thought his whole body would explode.

But later at home, Dad still insisted that revenge was not the way to go.

"Revenge never works out the way we want," he explained calmly, speaking in a low, soft voice, his eyes moving from Freddy to Teddy.

Both kids protested, shouting at once, insisting they couldn't take it anymore. "We have to pay them back, Dad," Teddy pleaded. "If we don't, they'll just keep on torturing us forever."

"They embarrassed me in front of *the whole school*!" Freddy said.

"How can I have any friends if they keep making me look like a total loser?"

"Patience," Dad said, raising a hand to signal that the kids should calm down. "Patience. All good things come to those who wait. Have you ever heard that advice?"

"No," Teddy grumbled. "And it's stupid."

"We don't want good things to come to anyone," Freddy muttered. "We want revenge."

"I'm warning you one last time," their father said. "Don't look for trouble."

They didn't look for trouble, but it found them.

Twice a week after school, they both took a lifesaving class at the town rec center. It was a stormy day, with strong gusts of wind blowing rain in all directions, so the instructor moved the class to the indoor pool.

Because of the dark skies and sheets of rain that cascaded down, Freddy and Teddy were the only students who showed up for class. They lowered themselves into the sparkling pool, which was heated and smelled delightfully of chlorine, and blinking under the bright white lights, waited for the instructor to appear.

Freddy suggested they do a few laps because he never could stay still, even in water. He kicked off from the pool wall and began to do a furious breaststroke. He always liked to be first.

Teddy began to swim after him. Her stroke was as graceful as his was frantic and choppy. They both loved the water. *How great would it be to be a seal, and swim whenever you wanted?* Freddy had once asked.

Freddy touched the far wall, turned, and started back. When

something grabbed his ankles, he thought at first he had bumped the wall. But when he felt strong hands tighten around his legs and hold him back, he began to kick furiously.

"Hey! Let go! Hey!"

He struggled to twist around and see who—or what—was gripping his legs, holding him in place. But he couldn't turn all the way. He felt a strong tug, and with a hard splash, his head slid under.

Spluttering and coughing, he pulled himself up above the water—and saw his sister struggling at the other side of the pool. She was splashing and thrashing and screaming, unable to move.

Was someone holding her legs too?

"*Let GO!*" Freddy managed to scream before another tug pulled him under the surface again. The hands squeezed so tightly, pain shot up and down his legs. Freddy squirmed and twisted, unable to free himself.

Someone's holding me down! Trying to drown me!

From under the water, he heard Teddy scream. The scream was cut off sharply. The water all around him churned.

Let go. Let GO!

He bucked and kicked. The water suddenly felt so hot. How long could he stay under?

As his panic swelled, his body went limp. Fear made his muscles give out. Fear choked him, paralyzed him, ended him. He gave up the struggle and gazed wide-eyed into the blue-green water as it bubbled and swirled.

And then the grip on his ankles loosened. He felt his legs go free. Freddy swung his arms up and floated to the surface. His head rose over the water. He choked and coughed, the taste of chlorine filling his mouth.

Shaking water from his hair, he spun around—and gaped at the grinning face of Harry Darrow. Harry pushed out his lips and spat a stream of water into Freddy's face. He giggled. "Scare you?"

Freddy opened his mouth to protest, but anger choked his voice. "You . . . You . . ."

Harry tossed back his head and laughed up at the bright lights. "You're so pitiful and lame, Freddy," he said, shaking his head. "You're no fun to scare. It's too easy."

He gave Freddy a shove, turned, and started toward the pool ladder.

Across the pool, Teddy was shouting at Cletus Darrow. "Did you really want to drown me? Are you both *crazy*? Did you think that was funny? You creep. You stupid creep!" Water dribbled down her chin as the angry words poured from her mouth.

The Darrow brothers climbed out of the pool and headed to the locker room, laughing, fist-bumping, and congratulating each other.

Freddy narrowed his eyes to slits and stared at Teddy, who stared back at him, still shivering, still shaking off water. Neither one said a word, but they were both thinking the same thing.

"They tried to drown us."

"They really wanted to hurt us. It wasn't a joke."

"They're getting meaner and meaner, Dad. They aren't backing off or getting bored."

"They held us underwater. They wanted to *kill* us."

Mr. Hardwick tossed up both hands. "Okay, okay. I surrender."

"Surrender?" Freddy asked. "What does that mean?"

"You can have your revenge," his father replied. "Go ahead. They asked for it. You've been very patient."

19

Freddy and Teddy both studied him. "You really mean it?" Teddy demanded.

He nodded. "Invite them to the house. I'm sure we can convince them to stop."

Both kids giggled at that. "I'm sure we can," Freddy said.

The Darrows appeared uncomfortable as Freddy and Teddy led them into the den. Cletus had a mouthful of pink bubble gum that he kept popping loudly. Harry had his hair down over his eyes, and he kept curling his hands into fists, as if he wanted to punch something.

"Nice dump," Cletus said. He dropped down onto the green leather couch and propped his big, muddy shoes on the coffee table.

"Why did you two losers call us over?" Harry demanded, eyeing Freddy and Teddy suspiciously through his thick strands of hair. "Did you want to apologize for being such crybaby wimps?"

Teddy couldn't keep a grin from spreading across her face. "We want to show you something," she said.

"What if we don't want to see it?" Cletus snarled, just showing off how tough he was.

"You losers don't have anything to show us," Harry said. He sat down on the coffee table, propping his hands behind him.

"You might want to see this," Freddy said. He raised his hand to his nose and poked two fingers into a nostril. Pinching his fingers together, he began pulling something from his nose.

"Ewww. What is that?" Cletus leaned forward on the couch.

"A worm," Freddy said. "Watch." He tugged the fat brown worm out of his nose and dropped it onto the carpet. Then he reached into his other nostril and pulled out an even longer worm.

"Whoa!" Harry jumped to his feet. He swept back his hair, and his eyes were wide with shock.

Freddy pulled another worm from his nose and tossed it at Cletus.

"Watch *me*," Teddy said, stepping in front of her brother. She opened her mouth wide and stuck out her tongue. Wriggling black insects covered her tongue. Spiders. They spilled over her tongue and tumbled onto the floor.

"Gross!" Cletus cried. "Ohhhh, that's *sick*." Both brothers were on their feet now. The pink gum fell from Cletus's open mouth and dropped onto his shirt.

Teddy spat out another dozen spiders.

"Have you seen *this* trick?" Freddy demanded. He had a large hammer in one hand and a long nail in the other. He placed his hand flat on the table, palm down, poked the nail into the back of his hand, and hammered the nail all the way in.

"No way!" Harry screamed.

Cletus let out a high shriek.

Freddy tugged out the nail. "No blood," he said. "And it doesn't hurt. Know why?"

The Darrow brothers were too shocked and horrified to answer.

"That's because we're dead," Teddy answered the question for them.

"You picked on the wrong kids," Freddy said. He pounded the nail through his hand again, just showing off. "You tried to drown the wrong kids. We can't be drowned. We're dead."

The Darrows were frozen like statues as Mr. Hardwick entered the den. He studied the quivering, pale, frightened brothers for a long moment and then turned to Freddy and Teddy. "You showed them?"

Both kids nodded. Teddy spat a spider from her mouth.

Their dad sighed. "Guess we'll have to move again. That's the problem with getting revenge. Now we can't stay here. This isn't a place for civilized zombies."

Teddy tugged her dad's sleeve. "But can we eat their flesh? Please?"

"We haven't had flesh for so long!" Freddy exclaimed, starting to drool. "Please, Dad? Please?"

"Well. . . ." Mr. Hardwick hesitated. "Okay. Go ahead, kids. But don't spoil your appetite for dinner."

And that brings our story to an end. This story started with screams of delight, and now it ends with a different kind of scream.

The last things we hear are the screams of the *tasty* Darrow brothers.

RAW HEAD AND BLOODY BONES

BY BRUCE HALE

SCREAMS RIPPED THE SUBURBAN OCTOBER afternoon in two like a construction paper pumpkin. *"AAAHH!"* A cluster of kids burst from the de la Vega family's garage, blowing right past twins Tally and Gabriel Soto, who stood in the driveway.

The kids screamed their way down the street, eyes bulging and mouths gaping in terror. But Tally and Gabe didn't join their panic. Actually, the twins were annoyed by it.

"Dang," said Gabriel. "He's done it again."

Tally grimaced. "That stinker."

For the past two years, Luis de la Vega had run the scariest neighborhood haunted house in San Lorenzo, scarier by far than the one the twins ran. The difference between the two was like that between a sock puppet monkey and King Kong.

Tally and Gabe suspected Luis was using his mom's Hollywood connections to spice up his scares with special effects and makeup from movies she'd worked on. But no one could confirm it. All the twins knew was that their sixth-grade classmates called the Sotos' House of Terror babyish by comparison. And the result was that Luis had raised

23

his admission fee to two dollars and was banking some serious bucks.

Meanwhile, the twins were stuck with the leftovers—broke kids, or those too young to know a good scare.

Jamming his hands into his jeans pockets, Gabriel scowled. "Come on." He jerked his head toward the now-silent garage. "Might as well get this over with."

Tally, short for Natalia, pulled her wild black hair into a ponytail and slipped a scrunchie around it. "We have to know our enemy," she said. "Otherwise, how will we beat him?" Her jaw tightened. Tally really didn't like to lose. Enough was enough. "Luis's reign ends today. Agreed?"

"Agreed," said Gabriel.

Together, they marched up the flagstone walkway to the garage's side door. A sign above it read "Enter at Your Own Risk" in dripping monster letters, and beneath that, "Admission $2." Somewhere, a hidden sound system played creepy organ music.

Nice touch, thought Tally.

Gabe turned the doorknob and pushed. When he saw what was inside, he gasped involuntarily, and they both took a step back. But it wasn't due to Luis's skill with frights.

A wild-eyed teen loomed close, staring at them, like she'd just seen a ghost. Her tan face had gone all chalky. Blood stained her T-shirt, and her hands dripped red.

Tally recovered first. She dug into her bag. "Very scary, I'm sure. Here's our four bucks."

The older girl seemed dazed. "What?"

"The admission fee?" said Gabriel. "To see Luis's crummy haunted house?"

Gory Teen's hand clutched her chest, adding more red smears to her T-shirt. "He's not— We're, uh, not open." Her lips quivered, as if she was trying to suppress some strong emotion.

"Great acting," said Tally. "Really. I'm sure you'll get cast on *American Horror Story*." She held out the bills. "Now take this, so we can go inside."

The girl glared at the twins with angry puzzlement, like they were insulting her in Norwegian. "He's gone, don't you get it? We're *closed!*"

Bam! The door slammed in their faces.

"Oh, our money's not good enough?" Gabriel twisted the doorknob, but Gory Teen had locked it from the other side.

As Gabe fumed, a pensive Tally led him back down the walkway.

"I can't believe how far he'll go to keep us from getting the edge," he said. "Turning down paying customers?"

"What if she's not kidding?" Tally mused.

Gabe scoffed. "Of course she's kidding. Luis saw us coming, then told her not to let us in."

"I dunno." Tally loved her brother, but even she had to acknowledge that he often missed the subtle stuff. Gory Teen's blood may have been fake, but the shock in her eyes was real.

Gabe cast a dark look back at the silent garage. "Never mind. Tomorrow we'll track down one of those kids who ran, get the inside story. De la Vega's not beating us this year."

"No way, no how," agreed Tally.

But the next day at school, when they went looking for Connor, one of the screaming kids, he was nowhere to be found. "I think he stayed home sick," said Omar, a mutual friend.

"*I* heard they had to take him to the funny farm," said Ebony, widening her eyes knowingly.

Oddly enough, Gabe and Tally got the same result for both of the other kids they'd recognized at the haunted house. Missing, presumed wacko.

Strange. But not enough to stop the twins.

They regrouped at the playground's edge as lunch period drew to a close. "It's like they're conspiring to keep us from learning about his haunted house," said Gabriel. He kicked at a tuft of grass with the toe of his sneaker.

"Don't you worry," said his sister. "We were born the day before Halloween. We own this holiday."

"But Halloween's nine days away, and our haunted house has to open soon. If we can't find out what Luis is up to, what can we do?" asked Gabriel.

She arched an eyebrow. "We get creative."

It turned out that creativity involved talking to a kid from their neighborhood, who attended Luis's fancy private school across town. Right after they got home, the twins dumped their book bags in the kitchen and headed down the street to Josh Johnson's house. He was shooting baskets in his driveway.

"Hey, Josh," said Tally. "What's the deal with your classmate?"

Their neighbor sank a swish. "Which one?"

"Luis de la Vega," said Gabriel, retrieving the ball. "We tried going to his haunted house yesterday, but some girl said it was closed."

"His sister, maybe," said Josh. "Older girl? A little scary-looking?"

"That's the one," said Tally. "She wouldn't let us in. Said Luis wasn't home."

Josh caught the pass from Gabe. "Maybe he wasn't," he said.

"Oh, come on," said Gabriel. "A bunch of kids ran screaming out of there just as we were walking up. And you think he wasn't home?"

Josh shrugged and then tried another shot. The ball bounced off the rim. "There were rumors today at school."

"Rumors?" said Tally.

Josh cleared his throat. "That Luis had disappeared, leaving only a puddle of blood behind. Or that he'd been eaten by some kind of monster."

Tally rolled her eyes. "Right. Because that kind of rumor wouldn't help his haunted house business much at all."

Their neighbor shrugged again. "Dunno. That's what I heard."

Gabriel took a shot from behind a red Toyota, and the ball clanged off the rim. "Well, do you know anything about where he gets his special effects?"

"The Halloween Store?" Josh rescued the ball from the bushes. "I'm not sure. I only know that Luis takes his scares really seriously."

"So do we," said Tally. "So do we."

Ten minutes later she and Gabriel were riding their bikes toward San Lorenzo's lone Halloween store. Like a rare night-blooming flower, the shop was only open for a brief time—between mid-September and November 1. But unlike a flower blossom, the Halloween Store was loud, garish, and full of monster-obsessed shoppers.

Tally opened the shop's front door, triggering a wolf howl. She pulled up short, more surprised than scared, before surveying aisles packed with an astonishing assortment of Halloween stuff. There were costumes ranging from Elvis to Elvira, plastic cauldrons, fake cobwebs, pumpkin night-lights, severed fingers, tombstones, enormous spiders, and even Sparky the Skeleton Dog. "Thriller" boomed from scratchy speakers as shoppers rummaged.

Gabe raked a hand through his hair. "We've been here before, T. You know we can't afford most of this stuff."

"I know."

"And the junk we can afford is too cheesy to spook a kindergartner. So . . . ?"

Tally licked her lips. "So maybe we've overlooked something. Something special. I'm not giving in without a fight, are you?"

"No."

"All right, then. One more time." Leading the way down the nearest aisle, Tally fingered skeleton ponchos and felt bats. Nothing jumped out at her saying, *I'm the ultimate scare.* They turned the corner and strolled along the next aisle, and the next.

Gabriel held up a dorky-looking zombie-panda costume. "Yeah, this'll really freak 'em out. I bet Luis didn't get any of his effects here."

"Patience," said Tally. "If we want to find something really special, we've got to put in the time."

A scratchy voice spoke. "You want something special?"

They glanced up. Standing beside a display of zombie makeup was a tall, scrawny high school boy just old enough to grow a sparse goatee.

"Yeah," said Gabe. His tone of voice implied that this guy wouldn't know special if it bit him in the neck and drained all his blood.

"Well, you won't find it here," said the boy.

A snort of amusement burst from Tally. "We're getting that feeling."

On closer inspection, Goatee Boy looked a little ragged around the edges. His sandy hair was matted, and his flannel shirt frayed. Even his smile was yellowish. "Only posers and little kids shop here," he said. "If you want the real deal . . ."

"Yes?" Tally was drawn in despite herself.

"Check out Lucky 8, over on Q Street."

Gabriel scoffed. "That's a crummy part of town. What could they possibly have?"

Goatee Boy's muddy gray eyes glinted. "The genuine article, dude." His lip curled. "You're not afraid, are you?"

"No way," said Gabe. "We just don't like wasting our time."

The teen gave a raspy chuckle in response. "Guaranteed you've never seen anything like it." And with a farewell smirk, he slouched past them and around the corner into another aisle.

"If this store is only for posers and little kids," said Gabriel, "what's *he* doing here?"

"Shopping for his poser little sister?" said Tally. But her gaze was thoughtful. "I wonder . . ."

"You're not actually thinking of going to Q Street?"

"Look, you're right; there's nothing new here." Tally flapped a hand at the shelves packed with tacky Halloween junk. "If they've got the real thing at Lucky 8, why not check it out?"

Gabe shrugged. "I dunno . . ." He rarely refused his sister, but something felt a little . . . off.

"This could give us the edge." She shoved him playfully, mimicking Goatee Boy's voice. "You're not afraid, are you?"

Gabriel shoved her back. "I'm braver than you. And wiser, and older."

"By ten whole minutes. And I'm not so sure about the wise and brave part." But she was glad that her brother had her back. Tally didn't want to mention it, but something about the teen's manner had made her uneasy too.

Still, they'd never beat Luis if they didn't take some chances.

Outside the store, the twins unlocked their bikes, mounted up, and headed for Q Street. As they pedaled, the bright boutiques and restaurants of downtown San Lorenzo faded behind them. In their place, bars, pawnshops, and warehouses sprouted like toadstools after it's rained.

Lucky 8's dusty display window held a headless mannequin, an ancient tortoise shell, and several mummified duck carcasses suspended by their feet. The twins traded a glance before locking their bikes securely to a nearby lamppost. Down the block, a hunched woman wheeled a shopping cart stuffed with bags, chattering merrily to nobody at all.

Tally got a grip on herself. "Okay, let's see what the big deal is." Putting a hand to the cool glass of the front door, she pushed it inward.

A bell jingled, and a musty, earthy smell—like beetroots and dried bat wings—met them as they entered. Unlike the Halloween Store, this shop was a dim cave, full of the oddest assortment of things. On the long counter a row of glass jars displayed pickled animal parts—hooves, snouts, and other, less identifiable bits. Three rows of tall shelving held everything from bamboo steamers to kung-fu shoes, from dog-eared books to eerie masks.

Gabe shot his sister a doubtful look and started down the nearest aisle. His fingers trailed over decks of tarot cards, wind-up Godzilla toys, and boxes of Chinese herbs. "What exactly are we looking for?"

Joining him, Tally narrowed her eyes at the oddities. "We'll know it when we find it."

"That's helpful."

A row of gnarled shrunken heads caught Gabriel's attention, and he stopped to examine them while his sister continued down the aisle. They couldn't be real. Could they?

Sensing a presence, Gabe turned. A caramel-skinned woman with curly hair was studying him. "Need some help?" she asked.

"Um, yeah," he said. Up close, she looked maybe college-aged, with a heart-shaped face and huge green eyes. A pearly half-moon barrette held back her hair on one side.

"What are you looking for?" the woman asked with the ghost of a Southern accent.

"My sister and I have a haunted house," said Gabriel. "We want something that'll give our visitors the biggest scare ever."

"Your house is really haunted?" Her gaze sharpened, seeming almost eager.

He shrugged in apology. "Not *really* really. It's something we do for the neighbor kids. Kind of like a mini–theme park."

"Ah." Half-Moon Woman leaned closer, and Gabe got a whiff of her sandalwood perfume. "You want to spook the little ones?"

"Yeah," he said. For some reason she was easy to talk to. "See, we keep getting beat by this other guy's haunted house 'cause he has better special effects."

"Your competition," she said.

"Right. But if we're going to crush him this time, we need something special, not the same old, same old." He plucked a mummified hand off the shelf and examined it curiously.

"Then that's not what you want," said Half-Moon Woman, taking the object back and reshelving it. "Tell me, what are you willing to pay?"

Gabriel's hand strayed to the pocket where his wallet rested. "We don't have much. But we'll give whatever we've got—for the right thing."

"That's the answer I was looking for." The woman crooked a finger. "Right this way."

Gabe followed her into the next aisle. Rounding the corner, he glanced over at the counter, but the old Asian guy behind it didn't look up from his smartphone.

The woman went up on tiptoe, pulling a cigar box from a high shelf. She presented it to Gabriel with a flourish. "Ta-da!"

He blinked. "Cigars?"

"Not quite."

At that moment Tally joined them. "What's that?" she asked.

"She says it's the real deal." Gabe nodded at the woman.

"Sure, if you want real lung cancer," said Tally.

Half-Moon Woman opened the box. Inside, on a bed of black velvet, lay a yellowed scroll of paper and a small bottle made of thick green glass, with a cork stopper. "Pour some of this liquid into a saucer, surround it with candles, and follow the instructions on the scroll."

"And this is supposed to terrify our visitors?" Tally said doubtfully. "No offense, but . . ."

The woman's smile turned a little feline around the edges. "Luis de la Vega bought something very similar. But if you're not interested . . ." She reached for the box.

Gabriel felt a sudden, unreasoning fear of losing it. "No!" He snapped the lid shut and half turned his body. "Uh, I mean, we'll take it."

"Excellent choice," said the woman. Her eyes widened suddenly. "Oh. You'll need one more thing." She pushed past them, making a beeline for the corner, where stuffed animal heads leered down from the wall.

Tally shot Gabriel a questioning look, but he clutched the box to his chest and followed the woman. As the twins caught up, Half-Moon Woman bent and lifted something from the floor. She turned.

They took a step back. In the woman's arms nestled a massive, sinister-looking boar's head. Gray dust coated the black bristles, but the glass eyes glittered, and the tusks curved wickedly.

"Just set this beside the saucer," said Half-Moon Woman. "It'll give your ritual a real kick." The woman thrust the head into Tally's arms. It was surprisingly heavy, and the bristles prickled her bare skin.

"Um, thanks," said Gabe.

"Just pay at the counter." And with a last, feline smile, the woman glided down the aisle into the depths of the store.

Gabriel frowned. "How did she know that Luis was our competition?" he said. "I didn't mention him, did you?"

Tally shook her head. "Not me. Maybe she's a big haunted house fan." Looking down at the boar's head, she added, "This thing gives me the creeps."

"Good," said Gabriel. "That means it'll creep out our customers too." He led the way to the cash register and set the cigar box on the counter.

Glancing up from his phone, the old man narrowed his eyes at the box. "That's not mine."

"Sure it is," said Gabe. "Your assistant found it for us."

"Assistant?" scoffed the shopkeeper. "I don't have an assistant. What does this look like, Walmart?"

"But she said—" Tally began.

33

"You speak English?" said the man. "It's not mine. You are imagining things."

"But she was so helpful," said Gabriel, craning his neck to scope out the back of the store. No sign of the woman.

"You want the boar? Twenty-six bucks."

Gabe dug into his wallet and fished out five lonely dollar bills. He winced. "A little help, T?"

His sister's lips pursed. "This better work."

"It will."

Digging inside her bag, Tally produced eight more singles. "That's everything."

The shopkeeper gave them a deadpan look.

Spreading the thirteen singles on the countertop, Gabriel flashed the man an apologetic smile. "Um, don't suppose you'd let us pay on an installment plan?"

For a long moment the shopkeeper stared at the twins, then at the boar's head. With a disgusted grunt, he flapped the back of his hand at them. "Take it away. It's not like people were fighting over it." He scooped up the cash, rang the sale, and slipped the bills into the cash register.

"Note to self," he muttered. "Never sell to delusional children."

Tally and Gabe thanked him and lugged their finds outside.

"I feel kind of weird that we didn't pay for this box," said Gabriel.

"You'll get over it."

He started to put the cigar box into his bike basket, but his sister stopped him.

"Uh-uh. This was your idea; you're carrying Mr. Tusky."

He swapped the box for the boar. "Fair enough, but show some respect. This boar is about to put our haunted house over the top."

"How, exactly?" she asked.

"I dunno," said Gabe. "I just feel it."

Back home they set Mr. Tusky on the coffee table, sat on the couch, and opened the box. Gabe's eager fingers unrolled the scroll.

"Well?" said Tally. "What's it say?"

Gabriel read aloud, "'Instructions for raising Raw Head and Bloody Bones,'" and a chill danced down his spine.

"Promising," said Tally, leaning forward. "Go on."

In old-timey language the scroll told how to set up the candles and saucer and how much of the potion to pour into it. It instructed them to chant "Raw Head and Bloody Bones" until *"ye beast's face appears in ye saucer's mirror,"* and then to shout *"Get up and dance!"*

Tally raised an eyebrow. "Really? It's a disco monster?"

"Come on, T. Have some faith."

"All right, all right. And then what happens?"

Looking up from the paper, Gabe said, "'And the revenant shall rise.' That's it."

She sent him an exasperated stare. "You conned me out of my last eight bucks for that?"

"I'm sure it'll work." Her brother frowned. "Hey, maybe it's some kind of levitation trick with the boar's head?"

Tally rolled her eyes. "It better be scarier than that if we want to beat Luis. Give me that thing." She scanned the lines for herself and then checked out the flip side of the paper. It was blank. "What's this Raw Head and Bloody Bones supposed to be anyway?"

Gabe lifted a shoulder. "Doesn't say."

"Well, duh. Let's Google it and find out." She pulled a cell phone from her bag, and Gabriel leaned close.

"Huh." She scrolled through the search results. "This looks interesting. . . ."

A third link led to a description of an old folktale where a witch took revenge on the man who had slaughtered her pet hog. Supposedly, she magically animated the hog's head and bones, and this monster killed his murderer in a brutal way.

The twins read through the story, their heads almost touching. Finally, Tally breathed, "Cool."

"Now *that's* spooky," said Gabe.

Tally leaned back against the cushions, a faraway look in her eyes. She twisted a lock of hair around her finger.

"What?" her brother asked.

Tally smiled. "You know, it just might work. Think we could talk Josh Johnson into dressing up as Raw Head and Bloody Bones?"

The next day Tally and Gabriel passed out flyers and spread the word: the Sotos' House of Terror was open for business. Strangely enough, de la Vega's haunted house was still closed, and nobody seemed to know where he'd gone. The twins spared a brief moment wondering about Luis. But really, this news meant just one thing: they were going to beat him, once and for all!

Gabe and Tally rushed home from school to put the finishing touches on their masterpiece, and when four thirty rolled around, the garage looked as spooky as they could possibly make it. The sun hung low. Clouds gathered.

Right on time, the first batch of kids—mostly third- and fourth-graders—showed up. They surveyed the tombstones and cobwebs festooning the front yard.

"This better be scarier than last year," said Madison Lee, a girl from two doors down.

"Yeah," agreed Big Matt, "or I'm gonna want my money back."

Dressed all in black, the twins offered wintry smiles. "Oh, it's scary, all right," said Tally.

"Anyone with a weak heart, now's your last chance to leave." Gabe turned to admire the garage. He had to admit, they'd done a pretty good job. The skeletons on the roof gleamed in the fading light, the electric candles twinkled bone yellow, and the jack-o'-lanterns were particularly gruesome.

Tally collected the admission fees, and Gabe gathered the kids before the blood-smeared side door. In his best spooky voice, he boomed, "Abandon hope, all who enter here, for this is the Sotos' House of Terror!"

He turned the knob and let the door creak open.

Just then, Tally hit the play button on her iPod, and a fiendish cackle erupted from the indoor speakers. Two of the younger kids jumped. The rest just grinned.

Gabe led the group into the garage draped with black curtains, both to hide the usual garage junk and to create a corridor for visitors to follow. The neighborhood kids pushed through cold chains that were hanging from the ceiling and began walking the path. Dry-ice fog drifted everywhere. The lights were dim and as red as a fresh wound.

When the kids plunged their hands into the bucket of eyeballs (actually peeled grapes), Tally cued up the ghostly moans on her iPod. A couple of kids gasped. Most just giggled.

"You did that one last year," said Madison.

Gabe scowled.

The trick with the hose segments was a dud. Not even second-grader Lucas believed they were snakes. Gabriel thought the haunted mirror with the mannequin hand was spooking everyone, until Big Matt reached out and shook the hand.

"De la Vega's haunted mirror last year was better," he sniffed.

Peeling away from the group, Tally slipped into a narrow corridor between the curtain and the wall, and ran ahead. She fit a skeleton mask onto her head, and when the group passed by, she pressed her face and hands into the spandex that was stretched over a wooden frame. At her gurgling death rattle, Tally heard kids shriek and scramble backward.

Not bad, she thought, *but wait till they get a load of our final trick.*

She rejoined the group as Gabe was seating their visitors on the crinkly, red-spattered painter tarp. As Tally lit the candles, her brother poured the dark green potion into a saucer. The flickering flames turned the boar's head demonic.

"Raw Head and Bloody Bones is one of the most fearsome creatures ever," said Gabriel. "To call forth this monster, we chant its name over and over, until its image appears in this saucer."

The neighborhood kids exchanged nervous glances, unsure how the twins would pull off this trick. But soon enough, they joined Gabe and Tally in chanting, "*Raw Head and Bloody Bones! Raw Head and Bloody Bones! Raw Head and Bloody Bones!*"

The chant continued, and a gust made the candles flicker. *Good,* thought Tally. *That means Josh has joined us.*

And suddenly, an image did appear in the liquid—a hideous, tusked boar's head atop a blood-spattered human skeleton. The kids gasped. *Great effects,* thought Gabe. *I can't believe we got this for free.* He shouted, "Raw Head and Bloody Bones, get up and dance!"

At this, a bolt of blue lightning shot from the saucer and out the side door.

Tally gaped. That was a *seriously* cool trick. And to think they'd gotten it from a dusty old store. Who knew?

For what seemed like forever, nothing happened. Gabe's nerves stretched tighter than a trip wire, and Tally wondered if Josh had forgotten his cue. She glanced around. A few of the visitors chuckled uncertainly.

"Nice try," said Madison. "I actually—"

But just then, a creature emerged from behind the curtain. Everyone screamed and scooted away. It looked just like the image in the saucer—a boar's head with wild red eyes atop a bloody skeletal body with hands ending in bear claws.

As the monster loomed over the group, Tally had time to think, *I never realized Josh was so tall.* Then Raw Head and Bloody Bones boomed, "Who has summoned me?"

That did it. With ear-piercing shrieks, the neighbor kids fled down the curtained corridors and out the door into the twilight. Tally and Gabe whooped, leaned over, and gave each other a high-five.

"Ha!" said Tally. "Take *that,* Luis!"

"In your face, de la Vega!" crowed her brother.

They turned to the costumed creature, which still stood, larger than life. "Who has summoned me?" its creepy voice repeated.

"You can drop the act now," said Gabe. "Great job on the costume, dude. Outstanding!"

Her muted cell phone buzzed in Tally's pocket. When she fished it out, a text message from Josh read: *Running late. Sorry! B there in 5!*

Tally's stunned gaze went from the phone to the monster. She tried to swallow, but her throat was as dry as mummy dust.

Once more, Raw Head and Bloody Bones growled, "Who has summoned me?"

"We did, Josh," said Gabriel. "Duh."

Holding the text message up to her twin's unbelieving gaze, Tally said, "That's not Josh." Gabe's jaw dropped.

"You have brought me through," said Raw Head and Bloody Bones. "Have I done your bidding?"

"Y-yes," Tally managed.

"Very well," said the creature. "Now you must pay the price."

"H-how much do you want?" Tally dug a fistful of quarters from her pocket.

"Keep your silver," rumbled the monster. Its piggy eyes glinted red. "Only blood will pay for blood." With a snarl, it lifted its clawed hands high.

And once more, screams pierced the suburban night.

BRICKS AND BONES

BY EMMY LAYBOURNE

"CREEEEE!" THE FRONT TRUCK OF my skateboard shrieks as I slide crooked down the railing in front of the old bottle factory.

"Sick landing, dude," my friend Ben calls. He comes down right after me, his board flying over the cement stairs.

We've been coming to the McCrary Bottle Works for years; it's the best place to street skate in all of Fredericksburg. It's got huge, wide front steps made of stone, with perfect metal pipe handrails. The ground out front is flat cement, and inside it's completely empty—just huge rooms with nothing but dead leaves and scattered trash from teenagers hanging out. Some of the walls are crumbling apart, but it just makes it more cool when you do a wall plant and bricks come crashing down!

Except a few weeks ago they put up a huge chain-link fence around the whole place, so now the only time we can come is on the weekend, because it's crawling with construction workers during the week. They're going to tear it down tomorrow, so this is our last ride. They're building a Greenway here—like our town needs another stupid superstore.

"Nice!" I tell Ben, even though his landing was a little shaky. But just as I go to high-five him, two beefy hands grab me from behind.

"What are you kids doing here?" growls a mean voice. Ben backs away, his eyes wide. The hands spin me around.

The guy holding me is a real brute—a huge bald construction worker with black hairs sprouting from his eyebrows and ears.

"You kids ain't allowed to be here!" he snarls.

"W-w-we were just going," Ben stammers.

The construction worker lets go, and I stumble forward. I kick my board up and grab it.

Another construction guy walks up. "This place is off-limits," he says. This guy is muscular and blond, with close-set eyes. "What, you kids can't read? It's set to blow tomorrow."

"We know," I say with a shrug. "But we've been coming here for years."

"We didn't think there would be anyone here on a Sunday," Ben says.

The bald one grabs Ben by the shoulder.

"Don't talk back, kid. You shouldn't be here, and you know it! Now beat it and don't come back," he growls. "Or else me and Mandry'll break your skateboards over your heads!"

"All right, all right," Ben mutters.

"Come on," I tell him.

I throw my board down, and we both ride away.

"Don't come back!" the bald one yells.

"You okay, Jamal?" Ben asks as we point our decks for home. I'm rubbing a sore spot on my arm from where the guy named Mandry grabbed me.

"Yeah," I say. "But they ruined our last ride."

"We should go back tonight!" Ben says. "We can skate it in the dark! It'll be awesome."

"I don't know," I say. "Those worker guys kind of freaked me out."

"Why'd they have to be such jerks?" Ben wonders.

"It seemed like they were trying to scare us off," I say.

"Well, they won't be there after dark. We should totally go back," Ben persists. "Come on, Jamal! It'll be epic!"

"Maybe," I say. Ben's always trying to talk me into skating in crazy places, but mostly we just skate the bottle factory.

"I'll come for you at one o'clock," he says.

I shrug and head into my house. Ben talks big, but he rarely follows through on his "epic" ideas. I figure the chances of him coming to get me are pretty slim.

Which is why I'm totally shocked when, just after one a.m., I hear something heavy land on the floor in my room. I'd left the window open like I always do.

I turn on the light, and there's a brick on the floor. It's strangely cold, like it was in a freezer or something.

I'd recognize it anywhere—it's a brick from the factory. Ben must have pried it out from one of the walls at some point.

I wipe the sleep out of my eyes and scrub my hand over my flattop while staring at the brick. I pick it up and turn it over in my hand. I really am going to miss the factory.

Ben's right. We gotta have it to ourselves one last time.

I shrug on my hoodie and grab my board. My heart pounds as I creep out into the hallway and down the stairs. Both my parents snore—don't tell them I told you—so I'm confident they have no idea I'm sneaking out. Besides, this is the first time I've ever done it. I'm nervous. But it's not like anything's going to go wrong. We've ridden the factory hundreds of times.

I don't see Ben in the street. After a few minutes of whispering his name, I head toward the factory. Seems a little weird, but I guess he got impatient and went ahead.

I roll up to the factory, right outside the gap in the fence Ben and I discovered. The factory is completely dark. It looks really different in the nighttime. The ledges look like frowning eyebrows, and the empty windows stare at me like the eyes of a dead man, blank and cold.

"Ben?" I call. "Where are you?"

This is so messed up! Why would he call me out and disappear like this? I'm really mad. I turn around to head home, but then I hear a WAIL. My head whips around. There it is again: a thin, muffled cry. It's coming from inside the factory.

"Ben!" I shout. I wriggle through the gap in the fence, pulling my board last. I race down the hill and then hurtle up the steps. I open the creaky front door. "Where are you?"

I hear the wail again. From inside the building it sounds softer and more hazy. I throw down my deck and skate toward the sound. The cry comes again. I go into the maze of small rooms and hallways at the back of the building. The closer I get, the less it sounds like a kid and the more it sounds like . . . the wind. Oh brother.

I pull into a small room toward the back of the building, and when the wind blows again, I see a broken window. It makes a soft shrieking sound that rises, then dies down. Yup. It was the wind!

Ben isn't here. He must have thrown the brick into my room as some kind of lame joke. But since I'm here, I might as well skate a bit. I skate back into the main room and kickflip up to plant the board squarely on the wall. Perfect!

I land, and then my chest suddenly goes cold! It's like someone threw a bucket of ice water *into* my rib cage. I gasp and splutter, falling onto my back.

That's when I see him.

A ghost. Standing right in front of me near the wall. A ghost kid! He's standing there, hands up, pleading. He's transparent, all gray and white, and wearing old-fashioned clothes. I must have ridden right through him!

I scramble backward. My heart is in my throat! I'm so scared I feel like my chest is going to explode.

I back even farther away, shocked into silence. I have to get out of here!

I jump to my feet and grab my board. The ghost tries to stop me. He's screaming something, but there's no sound.

I ride as fast as I can toward the exit. I dodge in and out of the halls and doorways. I know the factory like the back of my hand, but every time I come around a turn, there's the ghost, coming right through the wall. Cold sweat pours over my body. I'm so scared my feet feel numb.

Then I hit a few loose bricks, and I fly through the air, tumbling. I hit the floor hard. The breath is knocked out of me. I'm gasping, backing away from the ghost boy, who is coming toward me on his hands and knees. His face looks desperate, hungry almost.

I close my eyes and wait for him to attack.

Nothing happens.

When I open my eyes to peek, I see that the ghost is kneeling in front of me. His hands are clasped together, like he's begging.

I draw a breath.

The ghost boy stays there, begging me for something.

"Wh-wh-who are you?" I stammer. He looks up. "What do you want?"

The ghost, um, smiles at me. My heart calms down enough for me to take another breath. He seems to be just my age. He's a white kid with big eyes, and he seems kind of shy, somehow. He's wearing a tank top and tweedy, baggy shorts held up with suspenders. He's got on leather shoes that are a little too big for him.

It's weird; he looks like he just stopped doing some kind of job. His face and hands are smudged and dirty, and his dark hair is plastered to his head by sweat.

He pops up and beckons for me to follow him. He keeps looking back at me and smiling, urging me on.

I grab my board and let him lead the way. He leaves all the small rooms behind, and heads for the back corner of the building. I know just where he's leading me—to the basement!

"No way!" I protest. "I am not going down there!"

Ben dared me to go down there once. I didn't do it then, and I'm not going to now. At night. With a ghost at my side!

"Basements aren't my thing," I tell the ghost kid as he leads me toward the staircase. "Like, really, really not my thing!"

He clasps his hands together again, like he's begging.

"Sorry, kid," I say.

Just then I hear a sound from the front room. The familiar *creak* as the front door opens.

"I'm telling you, Mandry, there's no secret vault! This is a waste of time," says a voice.

No! It's the mean construction workers! Panic rises in my throat. If they catch me here alone, I'm in serious trouble.

"You got a better thing to do?" says Mandry. "There's a bag of cash here somewhere, and we're gonna find it if we have to stay up all night!"

The ghost sees how freaked out I am. Now, more urgent than before, he motions for me to follow him down the stairs.

I gulp. I grit my teeth. I follow.

We hurtle down the stairs and into the darkness of the basement.

Down here, all sound is muffled by the dirt floors and the thick brick walls. I can barely see in the dim moonlight filtering through a small window near the ceiling. Pipes and machine parts are strewn throughout the space. A thick layer of dust covers everything.

The ghost boy darts ahead of me, cutting through the machinery. I set my skateboard against the wall near the staircase and follow, ducking and dodging my way after him. I'm getting really dirty from all the cobwebs and dust.

The ghost heads for the back corner of the factory. He's super impatient, and keeps waving at me to hurry up.

"Okay, okay," I huff. "Chill, man."

He puts his hand on my wrist to drag me along, and I nearly shriek. It's like my wrist is plunged into ice water! Ugh!

"Don't do that!" I say. "Every time you touch me I get an ice bath!"

He shrugs, *Sorry.* And motions for me to hurry up.

Finally, we reach the very far corner of the basement. Cobwebs are draped over the walls, but the only thing they've been catching all these years is a serious amount of dust. The ghost points to the floor.

"What?" I say to the ghost. "What am I looking at?"

He points again. There's nothing there—just bare earth, pressed down hard.

"Nice floor, but look, I gotta get home," I say. "If those construction guys catch me here, I'm dead meat."

The ghost shakes his head. He paces for a moment, wild with frustration. Then he gets to his knees and mimes digging in the dirt.

"There's something buried?"

He nods. Then he mimes picking something up. Like a suitcase. Then he pretends to dig again.

"Look, I don't have, like, a shovel, man! I gotta go . . ."

Suddenly I get it: the bag of money! There's money buried under the floor, and for whatever reason, this ghost kid wants me to have it.

"The bag of money. You don't want those construction guys to find it, do you?"

The ghost kid lets me know that's exactly right.

"Okay," I say. "All right. Time to get digging!"

Could we use the money? Yeah—who *can't* use some free money? My mom got laid off from her job teaching art at the elementary school last fall. She and Dad say everything's going to be fine, but I can see my folks have been cutting a lot of corners. Last week we had macaroni and cheese for dinner. Twice. And my dad's been looking really tight around the mouth lately. Stressed. A bag of money would help a lot.

The ground is way too hard for me to use my hands, so I start feeling around in the dark to find some kind of tool. I'm crawling around on my hands and knees, reaching out in the dim basement. Ugh! I just pray there's no rats down here. . . .

I finally find a length of hollow pipe. If I bang it on the ground, it makes a dent in the pressed dirt. I start whaling on the floor. It works! Bigger and bigger chunks break apart.

I feel a freezing touch on my shoulder. "Don't touch me!" I hiss at the ghost. He puts his hands up, like he's saying sorry. Then he points to himself and then points upstairs.

"You're going to go keep an eye on the construction guys?" I ask.

The ghost nods his head off. I gotta say, he's pretty useful, for a ghost. He swooshes away.

Thunk! Thunk! Thunk! I keep working on breaking up the floor. It takes a while. I start to sweat as I get the hang of it. Suddenly there's a *clang*, and the pipe kicks back a little. It hit some kind of metal. The ghost kid is at my side in a flash.

"They coming?" I ask. He shakes his head. He points down at the floor, grinning. I guess he just wanted to see me find the money!

After a couple more hits with the pipe, I see there's a small, iron trapdoor in the floor. Really small. Just a little bigger than an AC vent. Just big enough for a kid to get into. A kid like me. Did I mention I'm a bit on the skinny side?

The ghost kid rubs his hands together with glee.

"I have to go down there to get the bag, don't I?" I ask. He nods. I sigh.

I stick my fingers into the holes of the grate and pull hard. It doesn't budge. It's too stuck. I grab the pipe and bang off some more dirt from the corners. The ghost kid is urging me on, all the time.

I stick my fingers through again and pull as hard as I can, sitting back all the way. "Aaargh!" I say. Just then it gives way, and I fall back.

"Yes!" I shout. Then two sets of big hands clamp down on my arms. *No!*

"Look who it is, Finn! The skateboarding kid," Mandry says, like he's so happy to see me.

"Good job, kid!" the other guy, Finn, snarls. "You made our job a lot easier!"

I glance around for my ghost friend, but he's gone!

"I knew you kids were after the money!" Finn hisses. He shakes me. "Who told you about the bag?"

"It was a—!" I start to protest, but then I shut my mouth. They'd never believe me about the ghost. What do I do?

Mandry hauls me up. He holds on to my arm with a tight grip. I'm, like, shaking from fear. He doesn't even notice. He drags me over to the empty grate.

He and Finn look down into the hole.

"Huh," Mandry says. "Pretty small hole." He kicks a clump of pressed earth into the gap, and it falls for a moment before we hear it hit the ground. It's a ways to the bottom.

"Let me go!" I manage to say. "My friend will be looking for me."

"I don't think so," Finn says. "If your friend was here, he'd have helped you. No, I think you got greedy and came back to find the bag all by your little, puny self."

"That's not true!" I argue.

Mandry shakes me hard. "Shut it!"

Finn looks me over. "I got an idea," he says. "We'll lower you into the hole. You hand up the money. We'll haul you out, and we won't tell no one you was ever here. Deal?"

I don't trust these guys one bit. I glance around desperately. Where's the ghost?! He got me into this, the least he could do is help me get out!

"No!" I say. "Just let me go, and I won't tell anyone anything. You can get the bag yourself."

"Don't be scared," Finn says. "You just do us this favor. Get the bag, and we won't tell the cops."

Mandry shakes his head. "Your folks'll be pretty sad to get called down to the station at two a.m."

I think of my mom and dad. They'd be so disappointed.

"Okay," I say. "But I want some of the money."

"Deal," Finn says, clapping his hands. "Mandry, where's our rope?"

A few minutes later they've tied the rope under my arms. I sit on the hole's edge, my feet dangling into the dark who-knows-what. At least they're letting me use their flashlight.

I am so mad at that ghost kid! If I ever see him again, I'm going to punch him in the face, even if it freezes my hand off.

"Get on with it," Mandry says. "We don't want to be here when they come to blow the place up!"

I scoot forward. The rope tightens under my arms. I edge off into the small hole.

The two men start lowering me hand over hand. I'm jerked down, down, down. . . .

I shine the flashlight all around. It's a room. A tall room. Perfectly square, with brick walls. There's a bundle of something below me. Fabric? It doesn't look like a bag. . . .

I SCREAM! It's a skeleton! It's a skeleton wearing clothes and clutching a bag!

"What is it?" one of the guys shouts. They let the rope drop, and I plummet right on top of the pile of bones!

I roll off the skeleton and huddle away, panting.

"What's down there?" Mandry yells.

"Bones!" I say, and gasp for air. "A skeleton!"

I can hear the two guys laughing up above me.

And then I see my friend, the ghost. He's sitting next to the skeleton, with his head down.

It's him, I realize. The skeleton is the ghost boy's body. I clench my fists. I really want to be mad at him for getting me into all this, but I can't. He looks so sad sitting there. My hands relax.

"That's you, isn't it?" I ask softly. He looks up at me, silvery tears shining in his eyes. He nods. "I'm sorry."

"Do you see a bag?" Finn calls down.

"Yeah," I say. "It's here."

The two men hoot and congratulate themselves from up above. They're such jerks.

I cross to the skeleton and shine the light on it. Though the clothes are just rags now, I see the same kind of tweedy shorts material as the ghost is wearing. The same shoes.

I carefully lift the skeleton's arms from around the bag. The bag is made of carpet. It's curly and a little moldy, but inside the open zipper I see it's full of stacks of bills.

There are a couple of wooden crates in the room. As I sit down on one, I hear bottles clanking inside. I take out a bundle. It's American money, but so weird-looking. "They're not really bills. They say 'Five Silver Dollars,'" I call up.

"We're rich!" Mandry shouts. "Those are better than real money. They're worth a ton. All rare and stuff!"

"Hand up the money!" Finn snarls. "Tie the bag to the rope."

"Pull me up first!" I shout. "I'll bring the money with me."

"You won't fit through the hole, kid," Mandry says. "Don't worry, we're not monsters. Once we have the money, we'll pull you up."

I look at my ghost friend. He's shaking his head!

"No way," I insist. "You guys gotta bring me up first. I'll, like, tie the bag to my leg or something."

"Tie the bag to your leg? Come on, kid. Quit messing around. We wouldn't leave you down there!" Finn says. "In fact, I think we should split the money with you. It's only fair. We'll give you a quarter of it."

"A quarter?" Mandry shouts at his partner. "No, Finn! Ten percent, tops!"

They begin to bicker. I sigh. I decide they must be honest about pulling me up if they're going to yell at each other about how much of a share to give me. I tie the rope around the handle of the bag.

"Okay, guys," I yell. "Pull the money up."

"Way to go, kid," Mandry calls down. I catch sight of his face in the hole, way up in the ceiling. He gives me a thumbs-up. Then, once the bag is close, he reaches his big, beefy arm in and grabs the bag.

"Okay!" I yell. "Throw down the rope."

I hear fragments of their discussion as I wait for them to throw the rope down.

"Must be over a million dollars' worth. . . ."

"Can't tell anybody or they'll take it away. . . ."

"The kid might tell. . . ."

"Hey!" I shout. "I won't tell anyone. Now throw down the rope."

They act like they don't hear me.

"Can't trust kids. . . ."

"No one knows where he is. . . ."

And then lower, whispered: "And then we can keep it all for ourselves."

"Let me out! This isn't right!" I scream. "Let me out of here!"

But I see the grate slipping back into place.

"No!" I cry. Then I hear them moving heavy machinery over the grate, to seal me down here and shut out the noise.

"No!" I scream. Only the ghost can hear me. He's shaking his head, his hands pressed over his ears.

My heart is pounding in my rib cage. They can't do this! I grab the three crates and stack them up. But since there are only three crates, even in a tower, they don't reach halfway up to the ceiling! Then the crates sway, and the stack crashes to the ground. I jump and land on my feet.

I rant for a while, pacing around the tiny room, cursing the construction workers and their parents. Then I curse the ghost and his parents, and everyone who ever knew him and anyone who ever worked at the bottle factory.

I slump down on a crate in the corner. I'm not giving up. No way. I cross my arms and think. I look around the odd, tall room. Why was it built?

I peer down through the slats of the crate at the bottles inside. They're cloudy with age, but brown liquid sloshes inside.

"What is this, liquor?" I ask.

Ghost boy nods again. I think about the room. From the clothes the ghost is wearing, I'd say he died around 1930. That date and the crates of liquor come together in my head—Prohibition!

I remember it from history class. Liquor was outlawed, and bootleggers had all sorts of hideouts to store their booze and money.

"Were you working for bootleggers?"

The ghost nods again. He's looking at his skeleton, staring at something. I shine my flashlight on the bones and see a glint of silver metal.

Moving closer, I poke at the skeleton with my index finger. The boy perks up as I slide an object out of the pocket of the tweed shorts. It's an old-fashioned pocket watch.

The ghost is so excited now he's jumping up and down behind me.

"Was this yours?" I ask. "Seems too big to belong to a kid."

The ghost points and points to the watch. Mimes opening it.

I press the little knobby thing on the top, and the watch pops open. Inside, the face is totally clean. It's cream colored, with fancy Roman numerals. Then I see the photo sealed into the inside of the cover.

It's a boy, smiling, his arm thrown around the shoulders of a little girl. They're standing in front of Goolrick's Pharmacy, right here in town! That place has been there forever.

"Is that your sister?" I ask. He nods, beaming at me. I have a thought, and I carefully pry the photo out of the setting. On the back, in an elegant scrawl, it reads *Billy Jr. and Wilhelmina, 1931.*

"That your name?" He smiles. He points to his sister in the photo. "Yeah, she's cute."

I close the case and notice it's inscribed with a name: *William H. Gust.*

"This is your daddy's watch," I say. "William Gust. And you're Billy. Well, if I ever get out of here, I'll look up your sister, Billy. I'll get this watch to her."

Billy nods again, solemnly. He puts his hand over his heart, saying thank you.

I sigh, settling down on the ground to sit with my back pressed against the dusty brick wall. It's cold against my skin. I shudder in my T-shirt, shorts, and hoodie. "My dad's going to kill me. If I ever get out of here alive."

Billy smiles. I can tell he feels bad about the mess he got me into. He sighs, silently.

I close my eyes, just to rest them for a moment.

When I wake up, I find I've curled up onto my side and Billy's skull is staring right at me! Let me tell you, it's not a nice surprise to wake up face-to-face with an old, desiccated skull grinning at you. I stretch, and that's when I see the light.

About halfway up the wall, there's a little light coming in; a square of light blue. I shine the flashlight at it and realize what it is—it's daylight! Outside the factory a new day has dawned, and sunlight is coming through a hole in the wall.

"What time is it?" I cry. Billy shrugs. He's pacing the floor.

I yell "Move, move!" 'cause he's blocking my way. I stack the three crates up again. This time, I set them against the wall, for stability. If I stand on my toes, I can reach the hole. It's a small rectangular space, covered with ivy. I yank at the ivy, pulling it out of the way.

"It's a vent!" I shout down to the ghost boy. I can see out, and the little vent is set right above ground level. There are brown weeds growing right in front of it. I never thought I'd be so happy to see dead grass!

The vent is small—too small for me to get through. But the bricks are old and crumbly—at least they are in other parts of the building. Maybe I can dig my way out!

Then I hear something that nearly makes me tumble to the ground—it's the voices of construction workers. "Hey!" I shout. "Help me! Let me out!"

My cries for help get a little more frantic as I remember they're demolishing the building today. TODAY! It could come crashing down on top of me at any moment!

"HELP!" I yell. "Help me!"

It's no good. I've got to help myself.

"I gotta knock some of the bricks out!" I shout to Billy. "Quick, what can I use?"

I climb down my stack of boxes. I look around . . . Maybe I could hack at the wall with my flashlight? Or maybe one of the bottles from the crates. My eyes fall on the long, hard leg bone from the ghost boy's skeleton, but he taps me on the shoulder. ICY!

"Don't touch me!" I shout again.

Billy rolls his eyes and points to a brick lying on the floor. It's come out of the wall, down near the floor, along with a couple others. I peer in the hole, expecting to see dirt behind it, but instead, there's another layer of bricks. Weird.

"You think I should use a brick to hit other bricks?"

He nods really fast. He kind of looks like he's hiding a grin, actually.

I don't know what's so funny—the building could get blown up at any second! I lift the brick, and it's heavy. Like, really heavy.

Good, I think. *Maybe it'll work.*

I heave it up onto the top of my stack, and then I shimmy up there.

WHACK! WHACK! WHACK! I lift the heavy brick and drive it into the crumbling wall.

There's a glint from the brick in my hands. It's . . . There's paint chipping off it. I stop just long enough to flick a chip of rust-colored paint off the brick.

Gold.

It's gold under there.

I'm holding a gold brick in my hands.

And suddenly, I look at the wall in a whole new way. The bricks, I see, aren't shaped quite right. They're more smooth and are a little smaller than normal bricks. And each has a slight pyramidal shape to it.

"Is that a wall of GOLD BRICKS?" I ask the ghost.

He throws his arms out, like *Ta-da!*

Outside I hear the supervisor blowing a whistle.

"STOP!" I shout. And *SMASH! SMASH! SMASH!* I drive the brick into the wall. The space I've made is tiny, but I can just about get my head through.

The whistle blows again.

Oh God! I hack at the wall even harder. There! A brick falls out and I think I can just . . .

I get my head through. Then my shoulder. I'm straining, straining, trying to get out when I feel a COLD, ICY push on my backside. I jump through that hole!

The whistle blows a third time.

"Come on, Billy!" I shout. I poke my head back into the hole. "Come on!"

He shakes his head and turns back to his skeleton. He lays down on top of the bones, and I see him fade away. I tear myself away from the sight.

I hear a fourth whistle!

"Stop!" I shout. I stumble to my feet and take off running around the building.

"Don't blow it!" I scream. I'm waving my hands like a crazy person. *"STOP!"*

The workers are all gathered way outside the fence. One of them looks up and sees me. He points.

"Holy smokes!" he yells. "Cut it! Frank! There's a kid in there! Stop!"

I sink to my knees, falling, hands to the cement. "There's gold down there . . . ," I say, though they're too far away to hear. "There's gold, and the body of a kid . . ." I collapse.

The Elm Grove Senior Center is really cruddy. It smells like bleach and old people, which I guess makes sense because the place is full of them. Elderly people are lined up in wheelchairs out in the corridor, gazing off into nowhere, and wandering around in stained bathrobes. This place is the pits.

There was a huge scene when we first arrived.

The manager's a jerk. He's a short man with a belly busting the buttons of his shirt.

"I don't understand, what relation are you to Ms. Gust?" he kept asking.

"We're friends," my father said. "We want to help her out."

"Ms. Gust has a yearly contract," he protested. "She has to pay the whole year, even if she wants to move out."

"We'll pay it," my dad said.

"It's more than twenty thousand dollars!" the manager said. He crossed his arms, like he knew that would be a huge deal breaker.

"We can pay," my dad repeated. I kind of wanted him to, like, snap out a big roll of bills or something, but my dad's cool. He's patient with everyone, even blowhards like the manager.

"We'll release her when and if your check clears," the manager said. Just then a secretary hustled out. She was gaping at me and had the newspaper in her hand.

"Ronald! Don't you know who this is?" she asked the manager. "That kid's the Skateboard Millionaire!"

That's the dumb name the reporters gave me when the story broke.

The manager's eyes nearly popped out of his head. He stared down at the newspaper and then back up to me. On the front page was a photo of me holding up one of the gold bricks, shaking hands with the school superintendent.

The headline read: "Skateboard Millionaire to Donate Three Million to Local School System."

The manager grabbed the paper and read aloud, "'Local hero Jamal Parker, the twelve-year-old who recently discovered more than two hundred million dollars in gold bullion in the basement of the abandoned McCrary bottle factory, has announced he and his family will donate three million dollars to the Fredericksburg school system. His only condition? The school must build skateboarding facilities at each of its institutions and offer skateboarding as a physical education class. . . .'"

Ronald then did a total about-face. He shook my dad's hand, congratulating him and thanking him and just making a fool out of himself.

"We can accommodate any of your wishes, Mr. Parker. But you know, there's no need to withdraw Ms. Gust from our care. She's one of our favorite guests. Instead, you could upgrade her care. We offer a platinum premium care package—"

As my dad started to protest, I snuck away to meet Ms. Gust.

And now I'm sitting in her tiny room, eating sticky butterscotch candies from a green glass dish.

Wilhelmina Gust is eighty-nine years old. She wears her white hair in two braids that crisscross on top of her head. She pushes the candy dish at me. "Take another," she says. "You're a nice boy, coming to visit with an old bird like me!"

The room is overheated and crammed with porcelain knickknacks. There are three framed photographs on the wall, and if I had any doubt about who she was before, it vanished when I saw the biggest photo. It's her and Billy; looks like they're dressed up for the first day of school or maybe for church. It's him, all right.

"I can't remember the last time I had a visitor," she says, and pats my hand. "When you get to be a certain age, everyone you know is gone long, long ago."

She looks up at the photo of her brother.

"Now, tell me, are you here visiting from a school? Did they send you to cheer us up?"

"Not exactly," I say.

An orderly passes in the hallway outside her room and grumbles at a weak old man snoozing in a wheelchair.

"Can I ask you a question?" I ask in a low voice. I lean in, and she does the same. "Do you like it here?"

"This old rattrap? No. I don't like it one bit." Now she straightens up. She looks kind of indignant. "They're rude to us, and they make the most horrible food. All of it comes out of a can; did you know that? Even the meat! I guess they think because we've lost some teeth we've forgotten what food tastes like!"

I smile.

"Good," I say. "They've got an opening at this other place, and I bet we could get you in." I take a brochure out of my pocket. It's for the best senior center in all of Virginia: the Residences at Darien Park. "It's got a gourmet restaurant, and activities you can do. They have classes in, like, photography and ballroom dancing and, like, learning Facebook—"

"Oh," she cuts me off, laughing. "You're funny. I like you! You remind me of my brother, Billy. You really do."

This is as good a time as any, I guess. I take the watch I got from Billy out of my pocket.

"I . . . I found this," I tell her as I hand it to her.

She takes the watch with a look of wonder on her face.

"Where?" she asks.

"In the basement of a factory," I tell her. As she examines the watch, I really wish I could tell her the whole story, but I'm not allowed to tell her the truth.

After I staggered out of the factory, the supervisor of the crew called my folks and the police. They wrapped me in a silver space blanket, made me sit in an ambulance, and gave me some hot cocoa. My folks rushed there, and I got to talk to them in private, in the back of the ambulance.

I told my parents the story—the whole crazy story—from the brick sailing through my window to my last glimpse of the ghost of Billy Gust. Then I sat there, just waiting for them to scold me for telling tales.

But my parents believed me.

"You've never made up a story like that before," my mom said. "Can't think why you'd start now."

Soon, news vans and reporters were everywhere. The wall to the secret room was broken down, and Billy's skeleton and all the gold were found. My parents made me promise never to mention the ghost boy. Not to anyone. I think they didn't want me getting sent to a nuthouse.

I told the police everything else. Especially about the two thugs who shut me down in the cellar and left me to die. The police picked up Mandry and Finn at a local bar, where they were drinking and showing all their friends the bag of old money. Now they're in jail and awaiting trial. Hope they like how it feels to be locked up, 'cause they're gonna stay that way for a long time.

Anyway, it all means that I'm not supposed to tell Wilhelmina Gust anything about the ghost of her brother. And it's hard. I cross my arms and sigh while she turns the watch over in her frail hands.

"What an amazing gift!" she says. "My father's watch! And you tracked me down? Thank you, son!"

With trembling fingers she opens it. For a long moment she just sits, looking at the photo of her and her brother on the inside cover.

"Our father died when we were little, and Mother took in boarders to pay the bills. Times were lean. Then Billy got mixed up in a rough crowd. He never told me what he did, but I knew he was working for those dirty bootleggers. He always told me we were going to live in style."

She fumbles for a tissue from a box next to her and dabs it on her eyes.

"Then there was a raid, down near the bottle factory, and the bootleggers were taken to jail. Our Billy. . . . He just never came back."

Everything makes sense to me now. Billy must have been trapped down there during the raid, and no one ever found him.

The old woman pats my hand and laughs softly.

"I'm really sorry about that," I say. "I bet. . . . I bet your brother was really sad about it too."

"Well, you're talking about him like you know him," Wilhelmina tuts, a twinkle in her eye.

"I do know him," I blurt out.

"How's that?" she asks.

Just then I hear my dad clear his throat behind me. He's standing in the doorway. He gives me a look meant to remind me of my promise not to tell anyone about Billy's ghost.

"I guess it's just the picture in the watch," I say. "He looks nice. Like a kid who would take care of his sister, no matter what."

Ms. Gust smiles at me. "Oh, you're a dear one. And you're right, that's just the kind of boy he was. A good boy, like you."

My father steps into the room. After he introduces himself to Ms. Gust, he tells her about the skeleton of her brother and the gold that I found. He explains we've decided to pay for her care at the Residences at Darien Park, if she likes the idea.

"I don't like it, I love it!" she says. She has tears in her eyes. "And to think Billy's body will finally be laid to rest. Oh what a day! And what a brave son you have. And generous!" she tells my dad. "You and your wife must be very proud."

"We sure are," Dad says. Now *he's* got tears in his eyes! I feel really awkward, and my neck gets all hot. I look down at my feet, wishing I could disappear into the gold- and brown-flecked carpeting.

All of a sudden my shoulders go freezing cold. I gasp and try to pull away.

It's Billy! He's hugging me, grinning like a fool.

I struggle out of his icy hug, and knock a lamp off a side table. "I told you not to do that!" I shout.

My dad and Ms. Gust both turn to look at me, shocked at my outburst.

I give a lame little chuckle. "Sorry?"

"Jamal's had a rough couple of days," Dad says apologizing. "I should take him home to rest." My dad lifts the lamp and puts it back on the table.

Ms. Gust says she understands, and my dad takes hold of my shoulders and steers me out of the room. But before I go I steal a look over my shoulder. Billy's ghost is standing behind his sister, looking at the watch in her hands. He waves good-bye to me, still grinning.

I raise my hand and wave back.

Then my dad hauls me off down the hall and out into the sunshine.

In the parking lot, Dad opens the doors of our brand-new Mercedes. He didn't want to be too showy with our new money, but my mom pointed out they were having a sale down at the dealership, so. . . .

"Let's go home," he says.

I grab my skateboard from the back seat.

"If it's okay with you," I say, "I'll ride."

RING AND RUN

BY STEVE HOCKENSMITH

IT WAS A DARK AND stormy night.

Cooper didn't like dark and stormy nights. He especially didn't like dark and stormy nights in his new neighborhood. He liked quiet, calm nights back in Indianapolis, before everything changed.

It was Halloween, though, so some rain wasn't going to keep his brother, Dan, from going out. But their older sister, Abby, *was*. Which was why it was dark and stormy inside too.

"Y O O O O O O O O O O O O O O U U U U U U SUUUUUUUUUUUUUUUUCK!" Dan screamed.

Abby sprawled on the couch, cell phone held up before her face. She cupped her left hand to her ear while texting with her right. "Did you say something, young man? You'll have to speak up."

Dan leaned over her. "YOOOOOOOOOOOOOOUUUUUUU SUUUUUUUUUUUUUUUUCK! YOU SUCK SUCK SUCK SUCK!"

"Sorry," Abby said. "Still can't hear you."

Dan whirled around and started stomping around the living room. "Dad said you have to take us trick-or-treating if the rain stops before he's back from his thing!"

"His date," Cooper said. He was looking out the window at the gloomy, wet, empty street. Nobody heard him.

"And it did stop raining so you have to get off your butt and *go*!" Dan went on.

"I still hear rain," Abby said, thumbs stabbing at her phone.

"That's just drops falling off the trees!"

"It's water from the sky. Rain."

"YOU SUCK!"

"And by the way, Dad didn't say I *have* to take you trick-or-treating. He said I *could*. It's a choice."

Dan marched over and started kicking the couch. "You SUCK! You SUCK! You SUCK!"

Abby finally lowered her phone. "All right, stop it, geez! We'll put it to a vote!"

Dan stepped back.

"A vote?" he said warily.

Abby nodded. "On whether I should take you trick-or-treating. Majority rules." She raised her hand. "I vote nay."

Dan shot up his hand. "And I vote yes!"

Then he saw the trap.

It was up to Cooper.

Cooper who didn't like dark and stormy nights. Cooper who didn't like dark *or* stormy nights. Cooper who didn't like *nights*, especially in their new house out in the middle of nowhere.

Dan turned to his little brother. "Come on, Cooper. Say yes," he said. "Don't be a little wuss."

Cooper almost said no, just because of the "little wuss" part. Dan was always calling him a little wuss. It hurt because it felt true. Then he noticed what Abby was doing.

She wasn't even looking at him. She'd gone back to texting. That's how sure she was that he'd be too scared to leave the house.

"Yes," he said.

"Yeah! Majority rules!" Dan whooped. "In your face, Abby! We are gonna get us some tuh-REATS!" He ran off to look for his shoes.

Abby lowered her phone again and stared at Cooper. He thought she was going to be mad at him. Maybe try to scare him into staying in or tell him trick-or-treating was for babies.

Instead she just said, "You sure?"

Cooper wasn't. But he nodded anyway.

Abby rolled off the couch. "All right," she said. "Let's see what kind of candy they give out around here."

Cooper, who was ten, was Batman.

Dan, who was twelve, was a Jedi.

Abby, who was fifteen, was the meaningless void at the center of existence. And burnt toast. And a Tootsie Roll.

She was wearing the black jeans and black T-shirt and black hoodie she always wore, and every few houses she announced that it was a different costume.

"I am a black crayon," she said.

Then later: "I am a goth mime."

And later: "I am a Hoosier ninja."

And a little later: "I am the president's dark, twisted soul."

"Don't get political," Dan told her.

"Why? Because we live in the boondocks now, and I might offend somebody?"

"Yes," Dan said. "And then they might not give us any candy. So shut up."

Abby thought it over as Dan led them to their next stop. It was a house like most of the others in their new neighborhood. Big yard. Lots of trees. Long driveway with a pickup truck (or two). Quiet. Rural. Boring.

"I am a charcoal briquette," she announced. She looked over at Cooper, who'd been sticking close to her since they'd left their house. "How you doing?"

"Good," Cooper said, even though walking along the sidewalk-free country road made him nervous; and the black, starless sky overhead made him nervous; and the occasional rumble of distant thunder made him really, *really* nervous.

Dan hopped up onto the porch and rang the doorbell. Slowly, cautiously, Cooper walked up to stand beside him. Talking to strangers made him nervous, too.

"Trick or treat!" Dan said when the door swung open.

"Trick or treat," said Cooper.

Abby didn't say anything. She'd gone back to texting.

They'd been to a half dozen houses before Cooper saw any other trick-or-treaters: a princess and a Spider-Man, both barely old enough to walk, toddled along on the opposite side of the road. A fully grown witch walked between them, holding each by the hand.

"Remember that time . . . ," Cooper started but trailed off.

"That time what?" said Dan.

"Never mind."

Abby glanced up from her phone and saw what Cooper had been

looking at: the woman with the two little kids.

"The time Mom was a witch for Halloween," she said.

Cooper nodded. "And her fake nose fell into Ruby Wiltrout's trick-or-treat bag and totally freaked her out?"

"I remember," Abby said.

"Oh yeah," Dan said, grinning. "That was hilarious."

"It seems like yesterday," said Cooper. "Sometimes it actually seems like right now when I think about Mom. Like she's not gone. I can almost feel her about to—"

The darkness around them suddenly disappeared, replaced by a flash of harsh, white light that flared across the trees and mailboxes and houses. A moment later the thunder came. As it faded, it was replaced by a new sound: hysterical crying.

The woman across the road had turned and was now dragging her children in the opposite direction.

They were going home. Cooper and Dan and Abby were about to be the only trick-or-treaters again.

"Good," Dan said grimly, his grin gone. "More for us."

He started walking faster. For a while Cooper just concentrated on keeping up.

They had to skip a lot of houses. Most didn't have their lights on, so minutes would go by when Cooper, Abby, and Dan were just walking, looking for the next place that seemed like a good candidate for a stop. Each step, hopefully, brought them closer to something sweet. And each step, Cooper knew, took them farther from home.

Abby noticed him glancing back at the long stretch of dark road behind them. "You know what Halloween is?"

"The best day of the year besides Christmas?" Dan said through a mouthful of half-chewed M&M's.

They'd turned toward a house with Styrofoam gravestones out front and plastic skeleton hands sprouting from the lawn and a life-size scarecrow propped stiffly on a chair by the porch.

Abby pointed at the phony tombstones. *IVANA B. BREATHIN': 1905–1975* was written on one. Another read: *SURFIN' SAM: CAUGHT GREAT WAVES TILL THE GREAT WHITE CAUGHT HIM: REST IN PIECES.*

"Halloween's when we laugh at death," Abby said. "Turn it into something silly so we realize we don't have to be afraid of it. We can be, like, 'You don't bother me, bro. I'm dressed like Batman and I've got a buttload of free candy. I am *alive*, and life is good.'"

Dan swallowed his M&M's and rolled his eyes. "Very deep."

"Sounds like something Adam would say," said Cooper.

Abby smiled at him, then looked back down at her phone.

"That was all me, actually," she said, typing with her thumbs again. "But I'll tell Adam you said hi."

They were only a few steps from the house now, but Cooper was more interested in his sister's texting.

"Ask him what the weather's like in Indy," he said, leaning close to try to look at her phone. "I bet it's not raining. I bet everyone we know has been out for hours and has a zillion pieces of candy. I bet it's just like the last time we went trick-or-treating with—"

"GOT YA!" roared the scarecrow on the porch, springing from its seat and lunging at them.

Cooper screamed, tossed his trick-or-treat bag twenty feet into the air, and fell over backward.

Dan whirled around shrieking and ran straight into a tree.

Abby looked up from her phone and spat out a startled "Geez!" When she realized what she was looking at—a man in a scarecrow costume looming over her prone, petrified little brother—she sighed.

"Not cool, man," she said. "Not cool."

The scarecrow felt so badly he knelt down to help Cooper collect the candy he spilled when the screaming started.

"I'm sorry," the man said, dropping a Blow Pop and a fun-size Butterfinger into Cooper's bag. "We usually don't get many trick-or-treaters, and tonight there've been hardly any. So I haven't had many chances to scare anybody, and . . . well, I guess I overdid it a little bit."

"Gee, ya think?" said Abby.

She'd crouched down beside Cooper and was staring at his face in a way he hated—because he knew she was looking to see if he was crying.

"It's okay," Cooper said, voice trembling, eyes down. He swept his hands over a dark patch of grass near the porch. "I just want my candy. The last house we went to they were giving out Snickers bars. *Full-size.* And now I can't find mine."

"I think I have bark in my teeth," said Dan. He stood beside the tree he'd run into, cautiously probing his mouth with his fingertips.

The scarecrow hopped to his feet and snatched a large metal bowl off the porch.

"Here. Take as much as you want," he said. He began pulling out fistfuls of candy and tossing them into Cooper's bag. "Take all of it."

He walked over to Dan and dumped the rest of the candy into his bag.

"You should call it a night anyway," he said. "It's getting late, and another storm's supposed to blow in any minute. It's not gonna be safe out here."

"Yeah. You're probably right," said Abby. She looked into Cooper's face again. "What do you think? Had enough?"

"No way!" said Dan. "My bag's not even half full!"

Abby kept looking at Cooper.

"I don't know," he muttered.

"One more street! One more street!" Dan chanted.

The front yard went from gloomy gray to nearly pitch-black. The scarecrow had stepped inside and flicked off his porch light.

"Well . . . happy Halloween," he said as he closed the front door.

What little light had been left was gone.

"What is this stuff, anyway?" Dan asked as he and Cooper and Abby walked back to the road. He reached into his bag and pulled out a handful of the candy the scarecrow had just given him. Some of it was in plain orange wrappers. The rest was wrapped in solid black.

Abby laughed. "Oh man—I didn't even know they made that anymore," she said. "It's this weird peanut butter taffy. Dollar-store garbage. Supernasty. It's worse than getting an apple and a tooth-brush."

"Well, then we've *got* to keep trick-or-treating," Dan said. "I don't want a bag full of this junk."

He threw one of the black-wrapped candies across the road. It was too dark to see exactly where it went, but it *plink*ed against something hard in the distance.

"There's a whole bowl of Whoppers at the house," Abby pointed out. "You can have as many as you want."

"Those are for trick-or-treaters," Cooper said.

Abby shrugged. "*You're* trick-or-treaters. The only ones still out, too. All the sane kids are home stuffing their faces in front of the TV."

Dan drop-kicked one of the generic taffies into the void. "I hate Whoppers," he grumbled. "We all do."

Cooper acknowledged his brother's point with a resigned nod. "That's why Dad buys 'em. So we won't eat 'em all ourselves."

They reached a dark, deserted road. They could turn left and forge on deeper into their new neighborhood. Or they could turn right and head for home.

Cooper and Abby stopped. Dan didn't. He just turned left and kept going.

"Dan," Abby said.

"What?" he said without slowing down or looking back.

"*Dan,*" Abby said again.

Thunder rumbled.

Dan turned around. "*What?*"

Abby pointed up at the sky. There wasn't a star in sight—just clouds so black they even blocked out the light of the moon. "It's gonna start pouring again any second."

"One more street," said Dan.

"It's already after nine," said Abby.

"One more street," said Dan.

"If we're not home before Dad gets back, he's gonna be mad," said Abby.

"One more street," said Dan.

"WHY ARE YOU SO STUBBORN?" said Abby.

"One more street," said Dan.

Abby growled and pretended to claw her own eyes out. Then she turned to Cooper.

"We'll put it to a vote again," she said. "What do *you* think?"

Dan looked at Cooper too.

"Come on, dude—one more street. Ya gotta replace that Snickers bar, right?"

Cooper thought it over.

Abby leaned toward him and lowered her voice.

"Whatever you decide is fine," she said, her soft tone clearly adding *Don't worry if Dan calls you a little wuss.*

"Don't be a little wuss," said Dan.

Thunder rumbled again. Louder now. Closer.

"Let's go home," said Cooper.

"Aww!" said Dan.

"After we do one more street," said Cooper.

"Yay!" said Dan.

"But Abby gets to pick it," said Cooper.

"Aww!" said Dan.

Abby flashed Cooper a smile, then faced Dan again.

"Majority rules," she said. "Come on. We passed the perfect street back this way."

Cooper was by her side as she turned right and headed down the road.

Dan just watched them for a moment, muttering about cruddy candy and the worst Halloween ever. Then a flicker of lightning threw a blinding-white light over everything, followed almost instantly by another peal of thunder, and he said, "Hey, wait for me!"

Not long after he caught up to his sister and brother, they reached the side street Abby had picked out. There was a sign where it started.

"Dead End," it read.

Abby explained that it was a cul-de-sac: a short street that ended in a circle of homes.

"Cul-de-*suck*, more like," Dan groused.

The lights were off in every house but one.

"A deal's a deal," said Abby. "This is our last street . . . which makes *that* our last stop."

She started toward the house that wasn't totally dark. It was lit dimly, with nothing but a dull orange glow behind the curtains in the front window.

"Do you think all these people really aren't home?" Cooper asked, eyeing the darkened houses they were passing. "Or are they just hiding with the lights off till they're sure all the trick-or-treaters are gone?"

"Maybe they think Halloween is satanic," Dan suggested.

When he saw Cooper's eyes widen, he continued cheerfully, mood improved by his brother's fear. "Some people do say Halloween's evil, you know. Really evil, not feel-good, fake-o pretend evil, like Abby was talking about. Especially out here, away from the city; there are people who believe the whole thing's demonic."

"Really?" Cooper said.

"Totally! They say tonight's the night when the spirit world and our world, like, overlap or whatever, and if you're in the wrong place at the wrong time, you'll get caught in between 'em. People like Abby wanna pretend Halloween's just a big costume party, but it really is the most haunted night of the year."

As if on cue, lightning flashed, thunder rumbled.

Cooper jumped. Orange-and-black candies flew out of his bag and rained down onto the street like hail. Nobody bothered stopping to pick them up.

"*Dan,*" said Abby, shaking her head.

"I'm just kidding," Dan said.

He let a few steps go by in silence, then elbowed Cooper. "But it's all true," he whispered.

They reached the winding walk up to the one house with light. It, and the houses around it, seemed to be from the neighborhood's oldest days, when homes were built smaller, their yards crowded with ancient oaks and sycamores. The paint on the siding was faded, the cement in the driveway cracked. Overhead, the trees' long, grasping branches swayed and creaked in the building wind.

Abby stopped before the porch and waved Cooper and Dan ahead.

Dan started up the steps—then noticed he was going alone.

Cooper had stopped beside Abby.

"They don't have any decorations up," Cooper said. "And the porch light isn't on."

"So?" said Dan.

"I don't think they want trick-or-treaters."

"Well, there's one way to find out," said Dan.

He grabbed Cooper by the arm and pulled him up the stairs.

"You know what? We can skip this place," Cooper said, dragging his feet. "Whoppers aren't that bad."

Abby put a hand on Cooper's back and boosted him up the last steps to the porch.

"It's okay," she said. "You don't have to be scared."

"Yeah," Dan said, and then added under his breath. "Little wuss."

He let go of Cooper and reached for the doorbell.

Cooper felt the sudden urge to spin around and dart past Abby and run for home yelling, *I am a little wuss and I don't care!* But it was too late for that.

The doorbell rang. Its two-note chime sounded muted, muffled, fuzzy.

Nothing happened.

Maybe they can't hear it, Cooper thought. *Maybe we should just leave.*

He was about to say that when his brother horrified him by ringing the bell again. Twice.

Ding-dong . . . ding-dong.

"*Dan,*" Abby snapped. "Don't be rude."

"It's rude to keep kids waiting on a night like this," Dan snapped back.

"Maybe we should just . . . ," Cooper began. His words faded away.

He could hear footsteps from inside the house. They grew louder, closer, until it sounded like someone was walking right up to the front door. Then they stopped.

Dan held up his bag, thinking the door was about to open.

It didn't.

The kids just stood there, waiting. And waiting.

"Maybe we should just . . . ," Cooper began again, the words coming out so hushed he could barely hear them himself.

Dan didn't hear them at all. "Gimme a break," he groused loudly. "We know you're right there!"

He rang the doorbell two more times.

"Dan!" said Abby. "Stop being a—!"

The door began to open. It swung back slowly, gradually revealing a tall woman with wavy, graying hair and a blank look on her long, pale face. She opened the door only wide enough to peer out at the porch.

"Trick or treat," Dan said to her.

Cooper just stood there.

The woman stared at them, her eyes wide, watery, unblinking. It looked like she was wearing a fuzzy pink bathrobe.

"Trick or treat!" Dan repeated, lifting his bag higher and giving it a shake.

The woman looked away, staring off into space for a moment, as if listening to something no one else could hear.

"Wait here," she said, her voice hoarse, phlegmy.

She stepped away from the door. Her slow, shuffling footsteps echoed beyond the door.

"Dan—be nice," Abby whispered.

"I am being nice. It's not like I said, 'Get off your butt and get me my candy, lady.'"

"Daniel!"

Cooper felt a sudden gust push against his back. His Batman cape swirled and flapped, and a gray glob of cobwebs in the corner over the door undulated, like it was breathing.

The door creaked open a bit wider in the wind, and an unpleasant scent, sour and rotten, seemed to swirl out of the house.

Cooper gasped.

He could see the woman in the bathrobe coming back—and she wasn't alone. A dark, shadowy shape loomed in the gloomy hallway behind her. A tall figure in a tattered black robe, a hood over its head.

Lightning flashed, blasting light over everything for a fraction of a second.

Cooper saw the face in the hood. It was chalky white, with empty eye sockets and a mere hole for a nose, and big, exposed teeth. A skeleton face.

Cooper couldn't say anything, couldn't move, couldn't even think real, formed thoughts. His paralyzing fear was everything.

The thunder came then, so loud Cooper could feel it.

As the woman walked slowly toward the door, the shrouded figure disappeared, merging into the surrounding darkness of the house.

"Here," the woman said.

She dropped something into Dan's bag, something into Cooper's bag, then stepped back and pushed the door shut.

Cooper looked over at his brother, expecting him to say something like *Let's get out of here!* or simply *Run!*

Instead, Dan said, "That was *not* a Snickers."

"Too bad," said Abby. "Time to go home."

She headed quickly away from the house, throwing a worried look up at the sky. The wind was getting stronger by the second, and fat drops of rain were beginning to smack down here and there.

Dan turned and started down the porch steps, rooting in his candy bag distractedly as he went. Cooper went with him, wishing he'd pick up his pace.

"Did you see that?" Cooper said.

"I know. It's nuts," Dan said. He fished a can out of his bag. "Baked beans. She gave us *baked beans!*"

Abby was hurrying out of the cul-de-sac as the rain began to come down harder and faster. She glanced back over her shoulder without slowing.

"Is that what that was? Hilarious!" she said. "I guess Cooper was right: she really *didn't* want trick-or-treaters."

"Yeah, right. Hilarious," Dan grumbled. "We should go back and do a trick on her. Ring and run or something."

"No way," said Abby. "We need to get inside before—"

The rain finally turned into an outright downpour.

"Ahhh!" Abby shrieked. "Run for it!"

She broke into a sprint. Dan bolted after her yelling, "I can't believe this is my Halloweeeeeeeeen!"

"Wait!" Cooper said. "Didn't you see? In the house? *Wait!*"

But between their own yelling and the roar of the pouring rain, his sister and brother didn't hear him. They were faster than him, too, and within seconds they were several yards ahead, swerving out of the cul-de-sac and dashing up the road toward home.

Cooper stopped running. Getting out of the rain didn't matter anyway. His costume was already soaked.

He looked back at the house they'd just come from. The little orange light still glowed dimly in one window.

What had he seen there? Was it a prank, like the guy in the scarecrow suit? Or was it . . . something else?

The woman had been acting strangely from the start. Maybe she was in trouble. Maybe she was being robbed or threatened. Or maybe he'd simply been seeing things because he really was the wuss Dan always said he was.

Or maybe, just maybe . . .

That last "maybe" Cooper didn't even want to think about.

He looked at the other houses around the cul-de-sac. They were all still utterly dark. When he turned back toward the road, Abby and Dan were gone.

There was no one who could help. No one who could do anything.

Except him.

His soggy cape fluttered limply in the wind, reminding him what he was wearing. Who he was supposed to be.

He headed back toward the house.

He started slowly but picked up speed as he went. Not because he was looking forward to getting where he was going. He was just cold and wet, and there was an awning over the porch.

Once he'd gone up the front steps and was out of the rain, he froze. Despite the murky darkness of the night, he could clearly see the doorbell: a small white circle set into the brick, by the door. But he made no move toward it.

He glanced back again. The rain was coming down in heavy sheets, and lightning strobed across the horizon. There was no Abby, no Dan. They were probably a quarter mile away by now. They wouldn't even notice he wasn't with them till they got home, and they'd have no idea where they'd lost him.

He was going to have to do this alone. Or *not* do it alone. He could just stand there till the rain stopped . . . and whatever was happening inside was over. Isn't that what a little wuss would do?

He stabbed a hand out and pushed the doorbell, moving fast so he couldn't change his mind.

Ding-dong.

Before the dong was even done, he *did* almost change his mind. It was too late to keep himself from ringing the bell, but it wasn't too late to run.

Yet he didn't. He stayed. And when ten seconds went by without a response, he rang the bell again.

This time he heard footsteps. Just one set, he was certain. One person.

He took a step back so that he was barely on the porch. One spin, one leap, and he could be racing across the sodden lawn. If he moved fast.

The door opened. Not all the way—only about a foot. Enough for the woman to peep out and blink at him.

"Man-Bat . . . ," she muttered. She looked sleepy and disoriented, as if Cooper had just awakened her from a particularly powerful dream.

"Excuse me?" Cooper said, trying to see past her. But the house beyond the woman's slack face was a wall of solid black.

"Man-Bat. You're back," the woman said, her words slurred. "Or are you a diff'ren' one? Always a lotta Man-Bats on Howaween."

As the woman spoke, her gaze drifted right, left, up, down, never quite zeroing in on anything or staying still. Cooper assumed for a second that she'd been drugged, maybe by the freak in the mask. But then a much simpler explanation occurred to him.

She's drunk, he thought. *And I'm an idiot.*

He must have sensed something was wrong with the woman from the very beginning. It had thrown him off, put him on edge. The sinister figure he'd seen lurking behind her was just an easily frightened kid's imagination run wild.

Oh, well. It could have been worse. At least he hadn't told Dan about it.

And then the smell reached him again—the sour stink he'd noticed when they'd come to the woman's door before. It was the odor of rotten eggs, decomposition, decay. And it was definitely coming out of the house.

"You wanna treat, right?" the woman said. "Lemme get you somethin'."

As she turned and tottered away, the wind blew the door wide open like it had before. And there it was again, lurking halfway down the dark hallway.

A tall black-draped figure.

It was real. Only Cooper could see it, for some reason, but it was truly there, in the house. Though this time there was no flash of lightning to illuminate the fleshless white face inside its cowled shroud, Cooper knew now what he was looking at . . . and what was looking back at *him*.

And looking at the woman. She was heading right toward it, utterly oblivious.

"Why doncha come inside?" she mumbled. "Get outta the rain."

The black form seemed to grow as the woman spoke. It was expanding, stretching out. Opening its arms.

Cooper knew what to do: turn and run away. But there was something he had to do first.

He had to run *toward* it.

"Come on, come on, come on!" he shouted, darting into the house and grabbing the woman by the wrist. "Please, please, please! Let's go!"

"Wha'?" the woman said, startled in her drowsy, droopy-eyed way.

She didn't have much momentum, and Cooper was able to swing her around and tug her toward the door.

"Whacha doin'?" she said.

She tried to set her feet, plant herself, stop. Beyond her, Cooper could see the shape still reaching for them, trying to embrace them, engulf them. The hallway around it went a shade blacker than black as it came closer.

Cooper pulled even harder on the woman's wrist.

"Just *come on*! We've got to get away!"

The woman was already wobbly, off-balance, and she stumbled with him through the doorway and out onto the porch.

Behind her, Cooper could see the whole hall was now a void. A lightless, lifeless black pit. The doorway didn't just lead into the house. It led to Death.

Cooper kept backing away . . . until the world suddenly seemed to disappear from beneath him, and he found himself falling. He lost his grip on the woman's wrist as he went.

He'd forgotten about the stairs up to the porch. Now he was frantically stumble-stepping down them backward, arms pinwheeling. He managed to stay upright as he staggered in reverse down one, two, three, four, five steps. But then he tripped on his own cape, and down he went.

"Cooper!" someone screamed just before he hit the walk up to the house, flat on his rear. His head snapped back and smacked against the wet cement with a splashing *crack* that brought tears to his eyes.

"Cooper!" the voice cried again. Then he heard pounding footsteps growing louder and louder until Abby and Dan were gazing down at him.

Abby dropped to her knees in a puddle by his side.

"Cooper! Are you okay?"

"Man-Bat's lost his marbles," the woman said before he could answer. "Tried to drag me out inna rain."

Cooper sat up straight to look at her. She was standing where he'd left her, still underneath the awning on the porch. Behind her he could see the front door and the dimly lit hallway beyond it. And nothing else.

"Musta eaten too many Smuckers or somethin'," the woman said. "That's a candy, innit? Smuckers? Snuckers?"

Dan and Abby gaped at her.

"Uhh . . . Snickers?" Dan said.

"Thazzit," the woman said. "Anywho, how's . . . how's . . . ?"

The hem of her bathrobe began to quiver wildly, and she held shaky hands out to her sides. Her knees were going wobbly just steps from the concrete stairs to the porch. If she fell . . .

Abby leaped up and bounded to her side.

"Whoa. You look like you need to sit down," Abby said as she wrapped an arm around the woman's waist. "Let's get you inside."

She helped the woman turn and start toward the door.

"No!" Cooper called out. "Don't go in! There's something in there!"

Abby glanced back but didn't stop. "What are you . . . ?" she started to say. Her voice faded as a look of bewilderment spread over her face.

She faced the doorway again. "What's that smell?"

"You smell it too?" Cooper said, pushing himself to his feet. "Get away from there, Abby! Get away!"

Dan put a firm hand on his shoulder. "Geez, dude," he said. "Stop freaking out."

"No. He *should* freak out," said Abby.

She turned and started to lead the woman off the porch.

"What're you doin'?" the woman protested weakly. "I'm gonna get all wet."

"Better than being dead," Abby told her. "We need to get away from the door."

The woman cringed as she stepped out from under the awning and felt the cold, hard rain coming down on her.

"What're you talkin' about?"

Abby jerked her head back at the house.

"Your place is full of gas. There must be a leak, or a pilot light went out or something."

"Pilot light?" said Dan.

Abby nodded.

"In old houses with gas, there's this little flame that . . . um . . . well . . . has to be lit, I guess. I don't know much about it, actually. I *do* know that the gas is really dangerous. If it leaks and you don't notice it, you get all disoriented and fall asleep and die."

"I ain't disorientated," the woman murmured.

Abby looked over at Cooper as she guided the woman off the last step.

"Is that why you came back and pulled her out of the house? You noticed the smell?"

Cooper thought the question over a moment and then simply nodded.

It was *kind of* true. And he didn't feel like explaining. He didn't know if he ever could explain it, even to himself.

"Come here and hold her up," Abby told Dan. "I'll call 911."

"I'm okay," the woman said. "I just wanna go back to bed."

Her eyes rolled up into her head, and her knees started to buckle.

Both Dan and Cooper rushed over to help keep her from falling. When she seemed more-or-less stable again, Abby took her arm away and pulled out her phone.

"Nice work, Batman," she said to Cooper with a smile. Then she turned away and hunched over to try to keep her phone dry as she dialed.

"Wow . . . and we thought you went looking for someplace to hide because you were scared of the storm," Dan told Cooper as the woman swayed unsteadily between them. "You're, like, a hero."

Cooper didn't reply. He didn't feel like a hero. He just felt wet and cold and tired. And, despite what Dan had said, scared.

But it was a different kind of scared he realized as he looked back at the house and its open door. Not the kind he was used to. Not a child's fear. Not dread, not terror. It was more of a wary respect for death—coupled with the knowledge that he could face it if he had to.

He was dressed like Batman, and he had a buttload of free candy. He was alive, and life was good.

Yes, it was still a dark and stormy night—far darker and stormier than when he'd left home, actually—but that was okay by him now.

THE UNKNOWN PATRIOT

BY CHRIS GRABENSTEIN

E WWWWWWWW!" SCREAMED THE PRETTIEST GIRL on the bus when Parker P. Poindexter tried to sit down *right next to her.* "You cannot sit there!"

"I'm sorry," said Parker, pushing his ginormous glasses up the bridge of his nose. "But Mrs. Lipinski told me to take 'the next available seat.'"

"Well, this seat is *not* available, metal mouth," snapped the girl, whose name was Grace. She was extremely popular at Libertyville Middle School. Parker P. Poindexter was not.

"It looked available," said Parker, giving her the thinnest smile because he didn't want his braces to blind everybody on the bus.

"Well, it isn't!" Grace gave Parker a disgusted huff *and* an eye roll.

"Parker?" called Mrs. Lipinski from the front of the bus. "Find the next available seat, please!"

"I'm trying to, Mrs. Lipinski, but—"

"Go all the way to the back."

"Yes, ma'am, Mrs. Lipinski."

Parker did as he was told because that's what Parker P. Poindexter always did. He tugged on the straps of his backpack, which was heavier than usual because, in addition to his usual school projects, he had packed every single item mentioned on Mrs. Lipinski's Colonial Williamsburg Field Trip Checklist.

"You can't sit back here, either, tinsel teeth," snarled Bobby Younger. He'd already claimed the entire rear row of seats so he'd have more room to stretch out and crack his knuckles.

That meant Parker had to sit in the second-to-the-last row. Right in front of Bobby Younger, who flicked Parker's ears all the way to Williamsburg.

A three-hour drive.

Parker couldn't really blame Bobby Younger. Parker's ears were nearly two sizes too big for his head and made excellent finger-flicking targets.

Of course, the ear flicks made it harder for Parker to play his Doctor Who Time Travel game on his iPhone. Bobby flicked his earlobe every time Parker entered Doctor Who's Tardis—a piece of advanced time-machine technology created by the Time Lords, the extraterrestrial civilization Doctor Who belonged to.

With all the ear whacks, Parker's pixelated time traveler ended up being eaten by dinosaurs. Twice.

When the bus finally arrived in Colonial Williamsburg, the driver from the tour company stood up and pulled on a three-sided, tricorn hat.

"A good morning to you all, and welcome to the Revolutionary City," she said into her microphone. "I heartily implore you to remember what that great Virginian Thomas Jefferson once said: 'I prefer dangerous freedom over personal slavery!' Huzzah!"

"Huzzah!" shouted Parker, and nobody else.

Grace, the pretty blonde, raised her hand. "Are there, like, bathrooms?"

"All right, boys and girls," chirped Mrs. Lipinski. "Five minutes for bathrooms. Then we're heading over to the Governor's Palace."

The horde of seventh-graders pushed and shoved and crowded into the aisle. Except Parker. He waited until Bobby Younger was three rows down before he even stood up.

When Parker finally made it to the front of the bus, the driver said, "Thank you, good sir, for your kind attention. I wish you a splendid and adventurous day."

"Thanks."

Parker descended the bus steps and looked around.

He couldn't believe he was actually here.

Colonial Williamsburg! An extremely awesome living-history museum where reenactors in authentic costumes made the 1700s come to life on the streets of a totally restored Colonial city! He was in history-nerd heaven.

"It appears you will have a most long wait for the restroom," said the driver, who'd exited the bus after Parker.

"I don't mind," said Parker.

"Poppycock. I shall let you use the staff facilities, for I know the combination."

"Oh, I don't want any special treatment. . . ."

"And I, good sir, do not want you peeing in your pantaloons!"

"Well, it *was* a long ride. . . ."

The bus driver tapped a numeric code on the "Staff Only" door's keypad: 1-7-8-1.

"Be quick about it, lad. Everyone awaits your swift return."

"Right. Thanks."

Parker went into the staff restroom, but before doing what he needed to do, he studied the map in the Colonial Williamsburg app he'd downloaded the night before.

Funny. He saw the public restrooms, but no separate Staff Only facilities. He figured they didn't bother putting those on the map since tourists weren't supposed to use them anyway.

After washing his hands and checking in the mirror to make sure he didn't have anything stuck in his braces, Parker trotted to the door.

He yanked on the handle, but the door wouldn't budge.

He noticed there was another keypad lock on the back of the door. *Weird.*

Whoever heard of a combination lock on the *inside* of a bathroom door? Fortunately, Parker had seen the numbers the bus driver keyed in. He tapped the same sequence on this second lock: 1-7-8-1.

There was an electric whoosh—way too loud for the tiny lock's little latch.

And, weirdest of all, the door creaked open all by itself.

When Parker stepped out, the visitor center was gone!

"Good day, sir," said a man sitting in the driver's seat of a carriage. It had big wooden wheels and two harnessed horses up front. The driver tipped his three-sided hat to Parker. "We have been expecting your arrival."

"I know," said Parker. "I'm here on a field trip."

"We must make haste. The milliner awaits!"

"Excuse me?"

"Your hat, sir."

"I don't have a hat."

"Indeed. And that is why we must visit the milliner."

"But we're supposed to go to the Governor's Palace first."

"New orders." The carriage driver handed Parker a rolled-up tube of parchment. Parker unscrolled the sheet and read what was written in blotchy black ink: *Make haste to the milliner's shop!*

"Oh," said Parker, "Mrs. Lipinski must've changed her mind. Do you work with the bus driver lady? She has the same hat as you."

"Aye. She is our transportation coordinator."

Parker heard something go *plop*. Something stinky.

"Um, I think your horse, the one on the left, just pooped. You should probably scoop it up."

"We haven't the time. Benedict Arnold rides this way. He aims to reclaim Williamsburg for King and Crown."

"Oh, right," said Parker, tossing his backpack into the carriage and then climbing into the back seat. "I read where he comes to Williamsburg and raises the British flag and junk. I didn't see it on the schedule today."

"Neither did any of us," said the driver. He clicked his tongue and flicked his reins. The wagon rumbled forward.

Parker dug into the pocket of his jeans and pulled out his iPhone.

"I think I should text Mrs. Lipinski. Let her know we're on our way. Hmmm. No bars."

"I beg your pardon?" said the driver, his eyes focused on the road ahead.

"Is there a stronger cell area around here?"

"Aye," said the driver. "The cells are most prodigiously strong at the public jail."

"Oh," said Parker with a nervous chuckle. "I get it. The jail has strong *cells* and probably lots of *bars*, too, huh?"

"Indeed so. Quiet now, lad. We approach the Governor's Palace Green."

Parker looked around. All he saw were reenactors dressed in costumes and wigs from the late 1700s. There weren't any tourists or students on class trips.

"I don't see any schoolkids."

"Aye. And they cannot see you."

"Well, I'll see them at the milliner's shop."

"Nay. The transportation coordinator did not deem your traveling companions worthy."

"Worthy of what?"

"Our noble cause. Alas, so much has gone awry since that spectacularly magnificent fourth day of July five years past."

"So," Parker said nervously, because he was afraid he already knew the answer, "what'd you guys do back then that was so, you know, magnificent?"

"Why, we boldly declared our independence from the English Crown! For we hold these truths to be self evident, that all men are created equal!"

Parker just nodded. Then he nodded some more. He tasted metal in his mouth. And it wasn't from his braces. It was from pure fear.

Parker did some math he really didn't want to do.

Hmm, 1776 plus 5, carry the one . . .

"So, uh, is this 1781?"

"Aye. And the future of our newborn nation has never seemed darker or less secure."

Parker nodded some more.

Because he was remembering the combination to the Staff Only toilets that had, somehow, turned into his own time traveling Tardis: 1-7-8-1.

Oh—1781!

"I, uh, need to get back to m-my school group!" he stammered. "You guys take this reenactment stuff way too seriously for me."

"We need you at the milliner's shop."

"But all school groups are really supposed to stick together. It's against the rules for me to go off on my own."

"It was against the rules for us to declare our independence from England," said the driver, "but declare it we did."

"Well, that was different," said Parker. "I need to go back. . . ."

"When you are ready to return, the transportation coordinator will arrange your departure."

"I'm ready to return now! So where is she?"

"Be still. We approach Duke of Gloucester Street. Not all of Williamsburg remains sympathetic to our cause."

Parker could hear grumbling from citizens milling about in the market square.

"Benedict Arnold is on his way!"

"Where is General Washington?"

"Fie upon it, where is Governor Jefferson?"

"Where is my son?" cried a woman. "I grow so weary of war."

A tough-looking boy, who reminded Parker of an old-fashioned version of Bobby Younger wearing knickers and a straw hat, went up to the old woman and finger-flicked her ears.

"You and your idiot son should've thought about the consequences of this foolish war before you both committed treason against the Crown, madam!"

"That's young Mordecai Morris," whispered the carriage driver. "He is a Tory and a loyalist!"

Parker hugged his backpack close to his chest as the carriage rolled down the street. Soon, they were outside Margaret Hunter's Millinery Shop.

"Hurry inside," said the carriage driver.

Parker hopped down and went into the quaint shop, which was filled with frilly dresses, fancy shirts, and all sorts of hats.

"Good day to you, young sir," said the woman behind the counter. She was wearing a bonnet. The only other lady Parker had ever seen in a bonnet was his grandmother, but hers was made out of crinkly plastic, and she only wore it when she had curlers in her hair.

"Are you ready to take up the task decreed by the hat?"

"A hat's going to tell me what I'm supposed to do? Is this like in *Harry Potter*?"

"I know not this potter named Harold, but our mutual friend has secreted your instructions in its seams."

"And whatever it says might help you guys win the Revolutionary War?"

"Indeed so, brave sir."

"That kid, Mordecai Morris up the street—he's for the British, right?"

"Aye. For five years, he and his family have been taking names of 'traitors and spies,' hoping for a chance to turn us all over to someone as villainous and merciless as that turncoat General Benedict Arnold."

She went to the windows, closed the shutters. "We must get you out of those clothes."

She handed Parker a bundle wrapped in brown paper. "Put these on. Quickly now!"

Parker went into a changing room, slipped off his T-shirt, cargo shorts, and Nike LeBrons, and put on his official Colonial kid outfit: a waistcoat, linen shirt, breeches, and stockings, which looked kind of funny, especially since his breeches ended just below his knees. Black leather shoes with brass buckles completed the disguise.

Parker tucked his iPhone into his backpack and came out of the dressing room looking like he belonged in 1781. Except for the braces. And his glasses. And the backpack. But other than that, he was good to go.

"Now then," said Mrs. Hunter. "'Tis time to see what you have been brought here to do!"

She lifted a velvety blue tricorn trimmed with white fluff off a hat stand. "It arrived only yesterday from Philadelphia. Mr. Franklin's associates have stitched your special instructions into the lining."

"Um, are you talking about *Benjamin* Franklin?"

"Aye. For he is the one who brought the time transportation system here to Williamsburg."

"Is it another one of his inventions?"

"'Twas not Mr. Franklin alone who did invent the time portal. You see, in his early experiments with electricity, Mr. Franklin found himself oddly transported into a time he did not recognize when three bolts of lightning did simultaneously strike the key attached to his kite. Taken to that time yet to be—an epoch beyond that which even you call home—Mr. Franklin met a fellow inventor who gave him knowledge unknown to those of us residing in the eighteenth century. Thus began the work of the Franklin Transportation Authority. When one time period needs assistance from the future, our associates in far-flung eras can transport those who can most help history follow its true course."

"So, uh, why'd they send me?"

"Only time will tell," said Mrs. Hunter.

She picked up her seam ripper and carefully cut the looped stitching on the back flap of the hat. Prying open the fabric, she removed a folded square of parchment and handed it to Parker.

He opened the note and read what was written on it:

> *Keep the occupier occupied.*
> *The fate of our nation depends upon it.*
> *If you fail, the future will be altered.*
> *That, unfortunately, means I might not exist.*
> *If that happens, Benjamin Franklin will never meet me.*
> *The trans-time portal will disappear.*
> *You may never return home.*
> *Good luck.*
> *A Friend from the Far, Far Distant Future*

Parker figured it was a good thing Bobby Younger had stolen his one packet of powdered sugar doughnuts on the bus ride to Williamsburg. His stomach was totally empty. There was nothing in it to upchuck.

"Give me a minute," he said.

"Have you taken ill, good sir?" asked the milliner.

"Little bit," said Parker.

She handed Parker his hat, which she had already resewn.

Parker stared at it for a second.

If you fail, the future will be altered.
You may never return home.

There was a commotion out on the street.

"Benedict Arnold has come!" someone shouted. "He sacked Richmond; we are to be next!"

Keep the occupier occupied.

He had to do what the hat said or he'd be stuck in 1781 forever.

Parker placed the tricorn hat on his head and tugged it down tight. Then he picked up his backpack.

"What is in that satchel you carry?" asked the milliner.

"Everything I thought I'd need for my trip to Colonial Williamsburg. Boy, was I wrong."

Parker dashed out the door and followed the mob racing down Duke of Gloucester Street toward the Capitol, where he saw a soldier in a bright red uniform astride a snowy white horse.

"People of Williamsburg," the soldier declared, "subjects of His Majesty King George the Third, gather round. Pay heed. Peace is at hand. The lawless insurrection in Virginia has, at long last, ended. Now pay your respects to General Benedict Arnold, the liberator of Richmond!"

Some in the crowd dared to boo.

"Traitor!" shouted others. "Turncoat!"

A man with dark and weathered brown skin standing very close to Parker leaned in and whispered, "Benedict Arnold isn't just a traitor.

He's also the most dangerous general in the whole British army. He could win this war for them, if we allow it."

"Um, do I know you, sir?" asked Parker.

"My name is James Armistead," said the man, keeping his voice low. "Once a slave, now a spy."

"For the good guys?"

"I certainly hope so. I pretend to work for General Arnold so I can keep an eye on him for the Marquis de Lafayette and General Washington."

"So you're like a double agent!"

"Indeed." Armistead furrowed his deeply lined brow. "Your job, good fellow, is to somehow remove General Arnold from Virginia before our good friend Lafayette arrives with his French reinforcements."

"Okay. How?"

"Use your wits, lad. Break a few rules. That's what rebellion and revolutions are all about!"

Armistead drifted away, disappearing into the crowd.

General Benedict Arnold, who used to fight for the Continental Army before becoming America's most notorious traitor, rode a mammoth white horse into the dusty square at the front of the Capitol. Arnold looked like a king in his bright red coat with gold tassels on the shoulders. He wore a red sash around his waist, a ruffled white shirt, white gloves, and white breeches. His hat, however, was as black as his wig and his heart.

"Fellow countrymen," he said with a sneer as his horse pranced in front of the citizens of Williamsburg. "Countrymen of British Virginia. Peace is at hand. Your Continental Army is a shambles. On the verge of mutiny!"

A whole battalion of redcoats shouldering muskets marched into the square to set up a protective perimeter.

Parker knelt down. Opened his backpack.

"America may be our home," cried Benedict Arnold. "But our safety and security come from England. If you want peace and comfort, pledge your allegiance, once more, to King George and take down that flag!"

Parker looked up and saw a banner with thirteen red-and-white stripes flapping in the breeze.

Two redcoats quickly lowered it.

"Long live the King!" shouted Benedict Arnold.

"Long live the King!" shouted Mordecai Morris.

Parker dug through all the stuff he'd crammed into his L.L. Bean Deluxe Book Pack when he'd thought he'd just be going to Williamsburg for a class field trip. He even had the ping-pong catapult project he was doing for Mr. Goldblatt's Advanced STEM class, because Parker figured he might have some time to tinker with it during lunch since nobody would want to sit or talk with him anyway.

"*BOO!*" jeered the crowd.

Parker looked up.

The Union Jack, the flag of England, had just been raised above the Capitol.

The town had officially been occupied!

"Time to keep the occupier occupied," mumbled Parker, pulling back the launching arm of his wooden catapult. He was about to load it with a ping-pong ball when, nearby, another horse pooped.

Horses seemed to do that a lot in Colonial Williamsburg.

Parker shook his peanut-butter-honey-and-banana sandwich out of its plastic baggie and used the bag as a mitten to pick up the horse poop and mold it into a ball.

He placed his poop projectile into the catapult's launcher scoop and did some quick trigonometry to determine the best trajectory for his ballistic attack. Mr. Goldblatt once said that to make a projectile cover the most horizontal distance possible, it should be launched from a forty-five-degree angle. Satisfied with his tangents, Parker pulled the trigger.

The wad of horse manure flew through the air.

And smacked Benedict Arnold in the nose.

The crowd roared with laughter.

"Who dares to insult me so?" the furious general hollered as his horse reared up on its hind legs.

The men with muskets started elbowing their way into the crowd.

"Who would dare to insult General Arnold?" the soldiers demanded.

Parker didn't stick around.

He grabbed his backpack and, crouching low, scurried away as fast as he could.

A firm hand clasped his shoulder hard.

"Don't run."

It was the former slave and current double agent, James Armistead.

"You are but a child. No one ever suspects slaves or children unless you act in a way that arouses suspicion. And young patriot?"

"Yes, sir?"

"Keep up the good work!"

"Thank you, sir."

Whistling nonchalantly, Parker strolled up the street while redcoats searched the crowd for a horse-poop-flinging perpetrator.

As he walked, he noticed a pretty tall brick wall between Benedict Arnold and the Capitol.

He also noticed another pile of horse poop. This one was sort of old, crusty, and filled with chunks of straw.

Since Parker still had his hand in the plastic baggie, he decided to scoop the poop, sneak behind the wall, and launch round two.

His aim was even better the second time.

The poop bomb landed inside Benedict Arnold's tricorn hat, where it nested between the upturned flaps. Birds swooped down to perch on the black hat's crown and peck at the strands of undigested hay. While they ate, they pooped, too—streaking the general's big black hat with slimy strands of white. Some of it dribbled down to give his black wig white highlights.

"Find the insurrectionist responsible for these vile attacks upon my person and bring him to me!" shrieked Benedict Arnold. "I will put him in the stocks! I will tar and feather him. I will not leave Williamsburg until whosoever would thusly insult me has been dealt with most severely!"

Parker smashed his catapult under his foot and sprinkled its splintered pieces into a pile of twigs beneath a nearby tree. He pushed his glasses up the bridge of his sweaty nose and headed down Duke of Gloucester Street to the wigmaker's shop. He figured that's where Benedict Arnold would be heading next.

The shop was deserted. Everyone was on the street, listening to Benedict Arnold declare martial law.

Parker saw a black wig propped on a wooden head. It looked exactly like the one Arnold was wearing. Thinking fast and moving faster, he took the wig off its stand and slipped both slimy sides of his peanut-butter-honey-and-banana sandwich inside the wig—sticky side down.

And then he had a brainstorm.

He saw a tea service sitting on a silver tray.

He lifted the teapot lid and squirted in some of the sunscreen he'd packed for the field trip. For good measure he gave the tea a spritz of bug spray, too.

Just as he expected, Benedict Arnold came charging up the street on horseback. Remembering James Armistead's advice, Parker picked up a broom, ducked his head, and started sweeping—becoming the wigmaker's invisible servant.

"Where is the wigmaker?" Arnold bellowed out on the street.

"Here, sir. Edward Charlton at your disposal."

"I need a new wig!"

"Black streaked with white, sir?"

"Just black!"

"Of course sir, of course. Won't you step inside?"

Arnold practically burst through the doors.

"Ah," said Mr. Charlton, when he saw Parker sweeping up. His glasses were thicker than Parker's. "That's a good lad, Benjamin. Kindly fetch the general a cup of tea."

"Aye, sir."

Parker poured the tea while Benedict Arnold removed his soiled hat and wig. He had some kind of cheesecloth beanie on his stubbly head.

"The wig, sir!" Arnold demanded. "The wig!"

"Of course."

While Mr. Charlton raised the wig off it's wooden stand, Parker placed the teacup in front of Benedict Arnold.

And then a miracle happened.

Arnold sipped his tea at the very instant Mr. Charlton lowered the gloppy wig on his head.

"Pffffft!"

Arnold spat out the tea as smooshed banana mixed with gooey peanut butter dribbled down around his ears.

"Are you tying to poison me?" he screamed, his face nearly as red as his coat. "And what is this wig glue? It smells of peanuts and tropical fruit!"

Parker slipped out the door, undetected and unnoticed.

"Clean me up!" he heard Arnold demand. "And who brewed this vile tea? I will not leave Williamsburg until I have his neck in a noose!"

Parker wasn't exactly sure what he would do next, until he saw the Raleigh Tavern Bakery across the street.

"Pies," he said aloud.

He burst into the bakery, which, by the way, smelled delicious.

A baker was pulling a half dozen cherry pies out of an oven on a long wooden paddle.

An even bigger catapult!

"Sir," said Parker, "I'd like to buy all of those pies."

The man smiled. "Oh you would, would you? Have you any coin?"

Parker reached into his backpack and found the coin purse he carried just in case he ever had to make an emergency phone call after his iPhone battery died and he had, somehow, actually found a pay phone.

He squeezed it open and plunked out a shiny quarter.

"I have this coin," he said.

The baker squinted dubiously.

But then he saw the head on the coin.

"George Washington?" he whispered.

"Aye," said Parker. It was a big risk. For all he knew, the baker could've been Mordecai Morris's father.

"Keep your coin, lad. The pies are free. Do with them what you will."

Parker grabbed the long wooden handle. "Thank you, sir."

Carefully balancing the heavy load at the far end of the paddle, Parker made his way to the door, which the baker held open for him.

When he reached the street, he saw the wigmaker and General Arnold coming out of the wigmaker's shop on the opposite side. The wigmaker was busily brushing the shoulders of General Arnold's coat.

"I think I have removed most of the mess, General."

"Leave me be!" snarled Benedict Arnold.

Parker made his boldest move yet. He stepped into the street and hollered, "Hey, Benedict Arnold? You want some cherry pies courtesy of General George Washington, even though he never really chopped down a cherry tree? That's just a myth."

"What?" fumed Arnold. "Who is this impudent child who dares address me so?"

The crowd on the street shrugged. None of them had any idea.

"I, sir, am a patriot!"

And with that, Parker flipped the baker's paddle and sent six cherry pies flying across the street. Two missed, but four smacked Arnold in his face, chest, and belly. His white shirt was dripping with so much red goop it soon matched his coat.

"Seize him!"

Six British soldiers advanced on Parker, their bayonet tips pointing straight at him.

Parker dropped the baker's paddle and backed up.

He didn't know what to do next.

He was terrified. He was also out of ideas! He was so nervous all he could think to do was wave and smile at the advancing troops.

"Uh, hi, guys!"

That's when something meteorologically amazing happened.

Parker wasn't sure if the transportation coordinator was also a weather consultant or if she had arranged for the clouds to part at that precise moment, but a brilliant beam of sunshine suddenly hit his braces like a spotlight. Dazzling light bounced off his silvery smile and blinded the six redcoats.

Bayonets drooped. Soldiers' knees trembled. Mouths flew open in horror.

"Lo!" cried one. "Behold the demon mouth! See how it does sparkle with silvery fire!"

"He is a witch!" shouted another. "A witch!"

The soldiers turned tail and ran away.

Parker started breathing again.

Until someone knocked the wind out of him with a blindside tackle.

Mordecai Morris!

Parker fell to the ground.

"I've got him, General Arnold!" said Mordecai. "I've got the rebel!"

"Leave him to me, boy!" Benedict Arnold whipped off his hat, which was, apparently, stuck to his wig because it was whipped off too.

Arnold didn't care. He stomped across the street in his skullcap.

"Try to make a fool of me, will you, boy?"

The general kicked at Parker.

Parker rolled right and, somehow, found his backpack. He reached into the pocket where he'd stored his iPhone and, before Benedict Arnold could kick him again, Parker pushed the play button.

"Happy" by Pharrell Williams started playing because "Happy" was Parker's favorite tune of all time.

The sound of someone singing inside a sack stunned Benedict Arnold.

It terrified everyone in the street.

It also gave Parker time to unpack his disposable plastic poncho (Mrs. Lipinski's list suggested rain gear, just in case) and heaved it over General Arnold like a see-through net.

"Why you . . ."

Arnold was thrashing and flailing under the plastic sheet when another British soldier in an even grander uniform came prancing up the street on *his* white steed.

Parker dropped to his knees in the mud so he could switch off the music before Pharrell Williams told everybody how happy he was again. Parker also dabbed his finger in a mucky puddle and swiped it across his teeth.

"General Arnold!" shouted the new British commander. "Pray, sir, what is the meaning of this nonsense?"

Arnold was so furious all he could do was sputter. "This—this— this . . . hooligan attacked me most egregiously!"

The man on the horse studied Parker.

"Indeed? A lowly shop boy bested one of the king's commanders?"

"No, Lord Cornwallis," insisted Arnold, throwing off the plastic poncho. "He did not best me. He is a witch boy with teeth like sparkling fireworks."

"Is that so? Show me your teeth, lad."

Parker smiled. His teeth were brown.

"The only thing I can see from this lad's teeth is that he eats too many sweets," said Lord Cornwallis.

"He is a witch, sir!" insisted Arnold.

"Poppycock."

"He made that rucksack sing!"

"Enough, Benedict. I have always feared that you, not being a proper English gentleman, were unfit for command in the king's army."

"But you need me and my sharp military mind. You should take your troops to Richmond. If you encamp at Yorktown, your back will be to the sea, and should the French—"

Lord Cornwallis shook his head and laughed. "Do you really think I will take strategic advice from an untrustworthy commoner who wrestles in the gutter with defenseless children?"

Cornwallis reached into his saddlebag and produced a sealed envelope.

"Here are your new orders, General Arnold. You are to report to New York. We have no further need of your services here in Virginia."

"But, Lord Cornwallis—"

"Good day, sir."

"I am your best—"

"I said 'good day, sir'!"

After the disgraced Benedict Arnold and his troops left Williamsburg, the baker invited Parker to enjoy a steaming bowl of crayfish-and-shrimp stew at the Raleigh Tavern. He'd, of course, brushed his teeth because (a) he had packed his toothpaste and toothbrush, even though they weren't on Mrs. Lipinski's list, and (b) mud might rust his braces.

He was about to start on his second bowl of stew when the tour bus driver—the transportation coordinator—walked into the dining room. She was wearing a long dress and bonnet, but Parker definitely recognized her.

"Good evening to you, friend," she said.

"You're here! Does that mean I can go back?"

"Aye. For you have more than done your duty. Without Benedict Arnold to advise him otherwise, General Cornwallis will, indeed, make camp at the coast, in Yorktown, instead of Richmond. He will have his back to the sea when America's French friends arrive."

"Yorktown was where the British surrendered," said Parker.

"Aye. Thanks in no small part to you."

"So, uh, now what do I do? Go to the bathroom again?"

"No need," said the tour bus driver. "Simply walk into the gift shop."

"There's a gift shop?"

"Aye. Straight through that door."

"I'll kind of miss it here."

"Who knows? Your country might need you again."

"In Williamsburg?"

"Or elsewhere."

"Cool."

Parker went back to his bowl to spoon down a few last bites of the awesome stew.

When he looked up again, the transportation coordinator was gone.

"Guess I better leave too."

He walked to the door.

Pushed it open.

And he was in the gift shop.

The one in modern-day Colonial Williamsburg.

All of his classmates were milling around, checking out the souvenirs.

"People?" said Mrs. Lipinski. "You can shop later. Our first stop is the Governor's Palace. Let's go."

Most of the kids followed Mrs. Lipinski out the door.

But not the pretty blonde, Grace.

She was staring in horror at a whole row of bobblehead dolls under a placard reading: "The Unknown Patriot: Youngest Hero of Williamsburg."

Parker picked up one of the bouncy headed figurines. It was a young boy, maybe twelve years old, dressed in Colonial-era clothes. His ears were two sizes too big for his head. He wore ginormous glasses. And, of course, his mouth was full of sparkling silver braces.

He looked exactly like Parker P. Poindexter.

Parker grinned.

Grace screamed.

"Nooooooo!"

SUMMER OF SHARKS

BY LISA MORTON

I SCREAMED WHEN I FIRST SAW the coyote during my sister's *quinceañera*.

Okay, that might be a little misleading. I certainly didn't scream at the church in San Fernando, where the first part of the day took place. It was after, when we all went up to this fancy restaurant in the hills above Burbank. Vanessa had fallen in love with the place when we'd been there for her birthday last year, and my parents had paid a fortune to rent it out for her big fifteenth-birthday celebration.

As part of her Court of Honor, I had to pose with our cousins and her friends for all the official pictures—the whole group of us, fifteen all together, vogueing on the restaurant's deck, the San Fernando Valley spread out behind us underneath its permanent smog layer. I couldn't wait until the photos were done so I could take off the stupid shoes I had to wear.

Vanessa, of course, looked radiant in a shimmering blue-and-purple gown, her long black hair trailing down her back in big fat curls, a glittery tiara perched on top of her head. In fact, she looked *perfect*, but then again, pretty much everything my sister did was perfect. She was beautiful and smart and hardworking and popular. She was an amazing student; she already had her whole life charted out (she wanted to work in the State Department), and no one who knew her doubted that she would succeed.

I hated her a little, in case you didn't guess. I was three years younger, but she made me feel like a toddler. I was a tomboy with short hair, a geek who was more comfortable with a tablet than a group of friends, and most scoffed at my desire to be a game designer. I had one BFF—Raphael, who I'd known since we were both in diapers—I struggled in school, and I thought a *quinceañera* was just about the dumbest thing *ever*.

Everybody had gathered inside the restaurant's side hall to dance. Papa and Vanessa were doing this traditional waltz thing while Mom sat at the side with my *tía* Lydia, who passed her Kleenex as she cried. I got my backpack, swapped the tight blue satin shoes I'd been forced to endure for my usual boots, then decided to hike off somewhere to play my *Brainshot* game in peace. I was in a mood to kill some zombies.

There was an empty, quiet park just a short distance below the restaurant, nestled into a crook of the hills; a small swath of landscaped green against all the brown. It would only take a few minutes to hike down to it. Papa would text me when it was time to go.

As I walked down to the park, I pulled out my tablet and brought up the main screen for *Brainshot*, hoping Raphael might be online and we could team up. The truth was, I was little mad at him for not coming to Vanessa's *quinceañera*; I was surrounded by my sister's friends, and it made me wish there was just one person there for me. Raphael had a big family, though—four sisters, two brothers, and an eighty-year-old grandmother who lived in a trailer beside the house—and as the oldest, he got stuck with a lot of babysitting duties. I knew not to expect him to show up for anything, but it still hurt a little.

He wasn't online for *Brainshot*, either. I'd have to go zombie killing on my own.

The road to the park was bordered by a steep hill going up on one side, and a large, overgrown flat shoulder on the other. I was walking on the shoulder, focusing on my tablet, when I heard a skitter of rocks hitting the asphalt. I looked up, squinting against the sun, and saw a flash of movement. Something was moving along the top of the embankment.

I walked faster, trying not to be too obvious when I looked up. More rubble fell. Something up there was keeping pace with me.

I almost turned around and walked back to the restaurant. The surrounding area was overgrown—sage and cactus and lots of rock— and I was out here alone, in a frilly blue dress and boots. I'd heard stories of mountain lions still inhabiting these hills, even attacking hikers. Or maybe it was a human up there, running along the top of a cliff, waiting to strike. . . .

I stopped and looked up, waiting. . . .

Nothing. Nothing charged down the hill at me. Nothing made a sound up there. No more rocks fell to the street.

After a few seconds I decided it had been something random—a stray dog or even a jackrabbit—and I continued on to the park.

The park was empty and pleasant. Picnic tables and trash cans were nestled among magnolia trees and agave, on a green lawn that probably used up too much water. I almost settled down on the ground, beneath the shade of spreading leaves, but I remembered the dress I still had on and how Mom would probably kill me if I came back covered in grass stains, so I opted for a bench instead.

I was bent over my tablet and had just popped off my first few rounds when I heard the sound again. I looked up—and that's when I screamed.

Maybe fifteen feet up, the cliff was split by a small canyon. Wedged into the mouth of the ravine was a huge tawny dog. It took me a few more seconds to realize it wasn't a dog—it was a coyote, its golden eyes fixed on me, ears alert, mouth partly open so I could see its really big teeth.

I stopped screaming, but my heart still pounded as I stared at it. I'd seen reports on the news about coyotes showing up in foothill neighborhoods, preying on cats and the occasional small child . . . like *me*. Should I back away slowly? I doubted I could run in my stupid dress. Yell something threatening at it? Pick up a branch and take a swing?

I was pondering all these possibilities when the coyote did a strange thing: it bobbed its head up and down, like . . . a *nod*. It looked like someone offering an enthusiastic yes. It stopped nodding, and I looked into its wide, intelligent eyes, and I felt as if I'd somehow known this coyote *forever*, as if we were old and dear friends. My heart stopped hammering, my terror replaced by wonder.

My phone rang, the opening blast of the *Star Wars* theme crushing the moment. I dropped my eyes for just a second, my hand shot down for my phone—and the coyote vanished. I cursed myself for not putting the phone on vibrate or at least giving it a different ring tone. I wanted to answer it and yell at whoever had chased off the coyote, but then I saw it was Papa calling. He couldn't text me like other people— No, he had to call. But I pushed down my anger as I answered.

He wanted me to come back. We'd be leaving in fifteen minutes.

I said okay, hung up, got ready to head up the hill . . . but not before tiptoeing up to the mouth of the ravine where I'd seen the coyote, just in case. Of course it wasn't there. I didn't see it again on the walk back, either.

But somehow I had the feeling that the coyote and I *would* meet again.

"You shouldn't have left the party. It wasn't safe."

That was Papa, after we were home and I'd gotten out of that dress and back into my cut-off jeans and T-shirt. Vanessa was out with friends, and I was about to head into my room and see if Raphael was online yet. Papa, Mom, and *mi abuela* (whose English was only slightly better than my Spanish) were in the living room watching some news report on the television.

"I didn't go that far. . . ."

Mom nodded at the screen. "He's right, Miki. Look at that."

I stopped and glanced at what looked like a local report. It was a helicopter shot, over a beach, probably somewhere near Malibu. Police and photographers surrounded a crew of paramedics who were loading somebody onto a stretcher. A reporter's voice was saying something about how this was "the fourth shark attack on a teenage girl in this area within the last four months."

"They think this one was thirteen or fourteen," said Papa.

"But these girls were all attacked by sharks," I pointed out. "I'm safe as long as I don't go swimming in the ocean, right?"

There was no way I could ever tell them about the coyote.

Papa said, "Miguelita Chavez . . ."

I loved Papa, but sometimes he was crazy when it came to safety.

He saw threats to Vanessa and me *everywhere*. I thought for sure he was fretting about me right now only because he'd let Vanessa go out with her friends. "I'll be careful," I said as I left the room.

The *Star Wars* theme sounded as I entered my bedroom. I shut the door, saw it was Raphael, picked it up. He didn't even say hi, just asked, "Did you hear?"

"Hear what?"

"Dani Martinez is in the hospital recovering from a shark attack. It bit her in the leg."

"Dani Martinez?" I flopped down onto my bed, stunned. I'd known her since the third grade, when her family had come up from Mexico. We'd never been besties or anything—for one thing she was a year ahead of me—but *everybody* at Revere Elementary knew her. She was pretty and popular, one of those girlie-girls who wanted to be a fashion designer.

"Will she be okay?"

Raphael answered, "From what I heard."

We talked some more after that, first about Dani Martinez, then about swimming in the ocean and how awful it would be to get bitten by a shark, then about my sister's *quinceañera*. "I wish you'd been there," I told him. "I got so bored at one point I wandered off."

"Oh, yeah? Where'd you go?"

"Just to a park near the restaurant. Oh, this weird thing happened there: I saw a coyote. Not like from a distance or something, but close-up, like maybe twenty feet away. It looked at me, and it just seemed like . . . like a *person*, not like a wild animal. It was really awesome."

There was a pause before Raphael asked a strange question: "Do you like coyotes?"

I was so surprised I laughed before answering. "Yeah, I guess. I mean, I never thought about it. I know they're kind of all around LA, up in the hills and stuff . . . why?"

"I just always thought they were cool, that's all."

After that we played a few rounds of *Scorched Metal 3*, until I heard my sister come home. She wasn't alone; I heard a male voice with her. When I groaned I missed a shot and was promptly eaten by aliens. Raphael typed into the game's chat, *Epic fail. Waddup?*

I typed back, *Sis just got home. I hear Parker.*

Raphael wrote, *Watch out for that guy, k?*

I knew he didn't like Parker Madigan, whereas my parents worshipped him. He wasn't exactly Vanessa's boyfriend—Papa had told her she couldn't have a boyfriend until she reached sixteen, and she'd actually agreed to that—but they'd been hanging out a lot lately.

They'd met when Vanessa got to intern for a week in Parker's dad's office; Davis Madigan was a deputy district attorney for LA, and it'd been a big deal for a fourteen-year-old from a public school to score the internship, even if it was only a short one.

Parker, of course, didn't go to our school; his daddy paid for an expensive private school. Parker even *looked* rich, with his perfect blond hair and his perfect teeth and his easy grin. He was cute and smart and friendly, but something about him just rubbed me the wrong way. When I'd mentioned that to my mom once, she'd brushed it off. "Don't be jealous of your sister."

"I am *so* not jealous," I'd assured her. If anyone had a crush on Parker, it was Mom, with the way she giggled and fluttered whenever he came around.

Gotta go, I typed before closing out the game. I'd call Raphael later.

I walked out to the living room to see Parker and Vanessa sitting on the couch, near each other but not *too* near. My mom was just passing them both tall glasses of iced tea, fussing as always. Dad wasn't around, but I knew he liked Parker too.

Parker saw me and smiled, toasting me with the glass. "Hey there, Miki. How'd you like the *quinceañera* today? I didn't see you around for most of it."

"I was there."

Vanessa glowered at me. I made a face at her. Parker saw and laughed.

I turned around and left. I just didn't like the guy.

I saw the coyote again four days later.

It was night, almost ten. The day had been hot—triple digits in SoCal's valleys—and the evening air felt good after a day of enduring sputtering AC.

Everyone else was in the house, watching television (the parents) or talking on the phone (the sister). I was in the backyard with my tablet, testing out a new game I'd heard about in a forum. *Starmind* was still in beta, but it was pretty cool.

I'd just piloted my interstellar ship through an asteroid belt when I heard a sound nearby. Our backyard wasn't huge, but it had a few nice trees and Abuela's rosebushes. The rustling came from those.

I lowered the tablet and squinted into the dark. The bushes rustled again. Something was moving in there.

We get an amazing amount of wildlife in the San Fernando Valley—squirrels, possums, raccoons, even sometimes skunks—so I wasn't really scared . . . until I saw a flash of golden eyes. This was too big even for a raccoon. My breath caught; I started to inch up out of my plastic deck chair—

It stepped out of the rosebushes into the light from the kitchen window, and I saw the tan fur and long snout.

The coyote.

I *should* have been scared, but somehow I wasn't. I settled back down into my chair, waiting.

It stepped forward, and I saw it had something in its mouth. It took another step toward me; it was holding a piece of printer paper. It set the paper down and backed away, waiting.

Moving slowly, I rose and leaned forward to pick up the white sheet. I never took my eyes off the coyote; it held my gaze steadily, with confidence and something else . . . amusement? Affection?

I picked up the paper and turned it to the light. There, in Times New Roman, were these words:

DANI MARTINEZ WAS VISITING PARKER MADIGAN'S BOAT WHEN SHE WAS ATTACKED.

Shocked, I looked up from the words to the coyote. We stared at each other for a last second before it turned and ran off.

I carried the paper into my room and hid it under my mattress. I didn't want to deal with explaining it if somebody found it. I didn't even know how I *would* explain it.

But somehow I knew it was right.

There was only one person I did show the note to: Raphael, when he came over the next day.

He read it and then handed it back to me. "So where'd you say you got this?"

"I . . . ," I hesitated, debating telling Raphael, as I had all night. He was my best friend; I'd told him some pretty crazy things in the past, and he'd told me crazy things, and I thought I could trust him with anything, so I dove right in. "Remember that coyote I saw in the canyon, during the *quinceañera*?"

"Yeah, I remember. He brought this to you?"

I blinked in surprise, mainly because Raphael didn't sound like he was kidding. "Well, as a matter of fact . . . Wait—do you know something about this?"

"I might. . . ."

Raphael had been sprawled on my bed, reading the note. Now he got up, went to the door, and closed it. Something in my gut flip-flopped; he almost never did that. "I think there's something I need to show you, but it's the biggest secret in the world, and you have to promise me you won't tell *anyone*."

This was all making me very nervous, so I made a bad joke. "That depends. If you've got a tiny head growing from your armpit that sings at night, I might have to turn you in—"

He cut me off, something else he almost never did. "Miguelita, this is serious. I have to know I can trust you."

My smirk vanished. "You know you can. You're my best friend."

"Okay." He stood in front of the closed door and gestured me to sit on the bed. "You should probably sit. And promise me you won't scream."

I sat. I nodded once. "I promise."

I waited.

Raphael looked at me. . . .

His face abruptly twisted, growing long and pointed. His black hair turned tan; his brown eyes, gold. His ears disappeared, then reappeared on top of his head, long and pointed.

It was a coyote head, coming up out of Raphael's T-shirt.

I started to make a sound, remembered what I'd promised, and clamped both hands over my mouth. I simultaneously jumped up and buckled, which left me sliding off the bed to the floor.

Concerned, the coyote thing reached down to help me, and I saw a paw where there'd formerly been fingers. I choked back a fresh scream, and in an eyeblink it was Raphael again, bending over me, looking concerned. "Are you okay?"

I lowered my hands, panting a little, staring at him in disbelief. "Am *I* okay? You—you just changed into a coyote!"

"I'm sorry, but it was the only way I could think of to show you so you'd believe me."

He had a point.

I looked at him again, and saw only my BFF, my Raphael. I pulled myself back up onto the bed. "So that was *you* in the park . . . ?"

"Yeah. And it was me in your backyard the other night."

"How long have you been . . . uh . . . a were-coyote?"

Raphael smiled and sat cross-legged on the floor below me. "It's not exactly like that—I don't change into some monster at the full moon. I've always been able to do it, just by thinking about it. I can transform a little, or all the way, and I'm still me when I'm the coyote."

I thought I knew everything about him, so this hit me like a sucker punch. "You've always done this? Why didn't I know before?"

"Because my mom—who's the only other person who knows—

made me promise when I was a little kid that I would never tell *anyone* I could do this. And I kept that promise . . . until now."

That made me feel a little better. "Okay. Why now, then?"

"Because I think Vanessa is in trouble."

"Vanessa? Why? Can she become a coyote too?"

He laughed. "No. There are other people around who can become animals, but there aren't very many. I don't exactly understand how it works; just that some of us are born being able to do it, and we can recognize other people who can do it."

"You can? How?"

Raphael shrugged. "I've only seen a couple of them, but it's like you look at them, and you can see this outline of an animal, almost like lines under their skin."

"So how does this relate to Vanessa?"

Standing, Raphael pulled his phone out of a pocket. "It's Parker Madigan. He's the reason I didn't come to the *quinceañera*. I've seen him, but I don't think he's seen me, and I want to keep it that way."

"Why?"

"Just watch this . . ." Raphael scrolled through his phone, thumbed something, and held the screen up before my eyes.

I was watching a video of a large docked boat, an elegant sailing vessel at least forty feet long and obviously the property of someone with serious money. It was night, the boat was docked, and voices came from within it. I asked, "What is this?"

"Parker Madigan's dad owns this boat. It's docked in Marina del Rey."

"How did you get this?"

"I followed him there last night."

I gaped, almost more shocked by that than a coyote-boy. "You *followed* him? Like, in coyote form?"

"I got my brother to drive me. Just watch."

I did. Finally, a figure emerged from the boat's cabin—Parker, wrapped in a beach towel. He glanced around and then dropped the towel and stood poised for a second on the edge of the boat. "Is he wearing anything at all?"

"Nope."

I was glad the screen was too small to really make out details. This was, after all, my sister's not-really-boyfriend.

Parker jumped from the boat into the water. But what came back up from his dive was nothing human.

It was a shark fin.

I gasped as I looked up at Raphael, astonished and frightened. "Is Parker . . . ?"

He nodded. "I first saw it two weeks ago, when I was coming to your house, and Parker was just leaving with Vanessa. Your sister's dating a shark."

"She says they're not really dating. . . ."

Raphael rolled his eyes. "Whatever. That's not the deal here. Think about it, Miki: a *shark*. . . ."

I didn't have to think very long before it hit me like a gut punch. "The news reports . . ."

Raphael nodded excitedly. "I mean, we don't know for sure, but we got a guy here who's a shark, who's rich and has a boat, and who Dani Martinez was visiting just before she was attacked."

I'd never liked Parker, but I'd never thought of him as somebody who bit people for fun.

"There's something else, too. . . ." Raphael was staring at me hard.

"What?" I asked.

"His dad's a hot deputy DA. Who better to cover up for a shark-kid?"

The bottom fell out of my world. For a few seconds my brain just ground to a halt, like an overheated engine that's given up. When I could think again, I reached for my phone.

"Who are you calling?"

I started to punch the picture of my sister. "Vanessa, of course."

Raphael held out a warning hand. "And say what? That her cool, rich friend could star in a remake of *Jaws*? You think she's going to believe that?"

He was right. I lowered the phone. "No. She's going to say something about how I'm jealous."

"Right. We need to get some kind of proof first. And then we need to show it to someone who is *not* Parker's dad."

"Right." That made perfect sense . . . until I realized it sounded impossible.

It wasn't impossible. Well, at least not totally.

Raphael and I are geeks; it's one of the things that bonds us. We both love games and gadgets. Raphael had a camera that could stream live video to his phone and go a week between battery charges. He remembered a light pole where he thought he could place the camera high enough overhead to be unnoticeable and away from the water, but pointed right at the *Lucille*, Davis Madigan's boat. If we got anything, we figured we'd just throw it online for the whole world to see.

The night that Raphael went to the pier to place the camera, Parker came to our house. He was sixteen and had his driver's license already, and he was taking Vanessa to a concert. Classical music, you know; Parker didn't rock.

Although I was glad he was here and not at his boat, I was still nervous to be near him, knowing what I did now. But I thought maybe I could put it to use—throw him off-balance or something.

He sat in our living room while Vanessa finished getting ready; my mom offered him a glass of water or iced tea, then left when he ever so politely declined.

"Hey, Miki," he said as I wandered in, trying to look casual.

"Hi, Parker." I stood there, abruptly realizing I had no idea what to say next.

He saw me looking perplexed. "Is there . . . is there something I can help you with?"

I grabbed at whatever came into my head. "I was just wondering— do you want to be a lawyer like your dad?"

Parker laughed. "Not even my dad wants to be a lawyer; he's just doing this DA stuff until he runs for mayor."

My body chilled about five degrees. "Your . . . dad . . . the mayor?"

"Yeah. I know—crazy, huh? But he can probably do it. Me, I'd rather go into investing. That's where the *real* meat is."

I felt the last heat drain from my face.

"Are you okay?" he asked.

"I'm fine, just . . ." *Go for it, Miki,* my inner devil whispered. "I just read another article about those girls who've all been attacked by a shark."

Was there something slightly fake about Parker's frown? "Oh, I know. Awful stuff."

"Who do you think could be doing it?"

For the first time he actually seemed to stumble. "Why would you ask 'who' and not 'what'? I mean, it's a shark, right?"

I shrugged. "I guess, but . . . four girls in a row bitten, months apart, by the same shark? Doesn't that seem weird?"

Parker looked at me carefully. . . .

His eyes flashed pure black, no whites or blue iris left, all black— *like a shark's.*

Then they were normal again, clear and blue, as he flashed his killer grin. "The world's a weird place, Miki."

Just then Vanessa walked in, looking more adorable than I ever could, in an iridescent blue dress with her hair falling around her shoulders in dark curls. I loved my sister fiercely right then; I wanted to jump up and put my arms around her and scream at her, "Can't you see what he is?"

Instead, I sat there, numb, confused.

Parker got up, they both said good-bye to me, and I hated myself for letting my sister walk away with a shark.

My sister did come home later that night. I was texting Raphael when she walked in; I'd already told him about my encounter with Parker earlier in the evening. Now I heard Vanessa tell Parker she had a great time and loved the music.

Raphael texted, *She didnt kiss him, did she?*

Not sure, I wrote back.

Well, he responded, *sis is prolly safe—hes not gonna attack somebody hes hung out with so much.*

I asked, *You sure? You didnt see his eyes.*

No. Not sure at all. Dani Martinez hung out with him too.

I offered only a final, sarcastic, *Thx* before signing off for the night.

Two nights later I was in my bedroom reading a blog on game design when my phone rang. It was Raphael. I'd barely answered before he started talking, sounded uncharacteristically panicky.

"Miki, we got trouble: the live feed on the camera just showed your sister at the boat with Parker—"

"Slow down, Raphael." I tried to remember where Vanessa had said she was going tonight. "No, she's out with her friends Olivia and Terry—"

"That's what she told you, but I'm telling you—she's at that boat. I'm watching her walk onto it *right now.*"

It was almost nine p.m. My parents would freak if they knew. "Is it just the two of them?"

"Yeah."

Should I tell my parents? No—the first thing they'd wonder is why Raphael and I were spying on my sister. Should I call Vanessa? She'd just lie to me about where she was and what she was doing. No, this was up to me. "Raphael, I have to do something."

"I know. I ordered an Uber on my dad's credit card. It should be here in five. We can get you on the way to the marina."

"Okay."

He hung up, and I started pacing, not knowing what to do. I ended up putting on a jacket and sneaking out through the kitchen so my parents wouldn't see me. If I had to explain tomorrow what I was doing, that was still better than the alternative—visiting Vanessa in the hospital. Or worse.

The car was there in five minutes; it was a beat-up, dusty sedan driven by a college kid named Ty, who had the biggest hair I'd ever seen, listening to reggae on his stereo. Raphael told him we had to get from the Valley to Marina del Rey as fast as possible. Ty grinned and hit the gas.

That was probably the first time in my life I was glad to be driven by a maniac. It was late enough that the freeways had cleared out, and Ty roared down them about as fast as his car would go. Raphael kept his eyes glued to his phone. Every few minutes I asked, "Anything?"

"No, not since they went up onto the boat."

About the time we left the 405 and hit the 90 freeway, Raphael sat up straighter, his eyes wide. "Wait, hold on— They're at the side of the boat now. . . ."

"What are they doing?"

"I don't know—I can't make out the audio, but I think they're just talking."

I turned to Ty. "How far away are we?"

"Maybe five minutes, maybe less."

Four minutes later he pulled up at the docks. Raphael gave him a twenty-dollar bill as a tip. Ty's grin got even bigger, and he took off.

Left alone I realized we had no plan; I only knew I had to reach my sister as soon as possible. "Which way?"

Raphael pointed and started running. "Down here . . ."

The place was empty this time of night; we jogged past sailboats and motorboats bobbing gently in the nighttime tide, the smell of brine filling our heads. We turned at one point, and the boats got noticeably bigger and more expensive. "*Lucille*'s the last one on the left," Raphael said.

I saw it now, and could just make out two figures behind the railing around the edges of the boat. I ran toward them, not caring how crazy I was about to sound.

As I got closer I heard them talking, but they heard my footsteps on the wooden dock and stopped talking, turning to see who was coming. When I ran up to the bottom of the gangplank, I hesitated as Vanessa saw it was me. "Miki? What are you doing here?"

"Vanessa, you have to come with me, right NOW. Trust me—you're not safe."

Parker laughed and stepped between me and Vanessa. Peeking around him, Vanessa frowned. "What's wrong, is everything okay at home?"

"It's not home—it's *him*."

Vanessa realized I was glaring at Parker. She was about to respond when Parker stepped toward me. "Miki, what's going on?"

With his back to Vanessa, she didn't see how he grinned at me, his mouth splitting at the sides, going around the edges of his head to reveal huge, pointed, knifelike teeth. I bit back a reaction but held my ground, as scared as I was. Then I remembered Raphael, and I turned—only to see he wasn't there.

I was alone with a shark-man walking toward me.

Just then a new voice interrupted, an older voice. "Parker . . . ?"

A man emerged from the boat's cabin, a tall, good-looking man in his fifties, whose face I'd seen in news reports: Parker's dad, and one of my city's deputy district attorneys, Davis Madigan.

Parker's face instantly rearranged itself into human form as he turned. "Yeah, Dad. . . ."

Davis stepped up and surveyed the scene casually. "Everything all right here?"

Vanessa was angry now. "I'm sorry, Mr. Madigan, everything's fine—it's just my sister has some crazy ideas about me not being safe. . . ."

"Really? Where would she get that?"

Mr. Madigan stood behind Vanessa . . . and changed. His skin turned gray, eyes big and black as the night sky, his mouth filled with teeth—

He was a shark too.

I choked on a half scream as Davis Madigan loomed behind Vanessa, who was still unaware. "You . . . you're . . ."

When he spoke, Mr. Madigan's voice sounded rough, barely capable of speech. "Did you think it was my son attacking those girls? You got close to the truth . . . but too close. I'm afraid something needs to be done about that."

It had never been Parker. It had been his dad biting people, biting victims provided by Parker. And no one would ever catch him. Now he stood behind my sister, opened his gigantic mouth, and started to bend down.

Before I could do anything (and what could I do?), a tan streak flashed by me and hurled itself at Davis Madigan. Snarling and frothing, the coyote hit the shark-man with enough power to knock him down. The shark head snapped at the coyote, who twisted to avoid the biting jaws. The coyote nimbly jumped to the side, and Madigan leaped up to lunge. Vanessa screamed and ran down the gangplank to join me, rushing past the stunned Parker. I stayed rooted, terrified, sure I was about to see my best friend get chomped by a shark.

Instead, the coyote barked and jitterbugged, and when the shark-man made another grab for it, he miscalculated and went overboard.

We didn't wait to see what happened next: I grabbed Vanessa's hand, and we started running for shore. The coyote shot past us at one point, and I felt tears of relief spring to my eyes. "Raphael!"

Vanessa heard and gasped out, "What? Where?"

I didn't answer, just kept moving.

We'd almost made it to shore when the water beside us erupted and a huge great white shark jumped up beside us, its mouth open, all of its teeth showing.

Vanessa and I both screamed, but we dodged and kept going. I didn't look back, but I heard the huge splash as the shark hit the water again.

And then we made it to shore, where Raphael waited for us. He was just tugging on pants and shirt, his feet still bare. He didn't wait to put on his shoes; he just grabbed them and nodded up to the street. "Keep going!"

I glanced back once and saw we weren't being followed—no crazy were-shark thing was coming after us.

We'd made it.

I almost felt sorry for Parker in the resulting fallout.

The video had gone live, just as Raphael had planned, but it mysteriously disappeared within an hour. However, Davis Madigan was arrested the next day and slapped with dozens of charges. The overall story was that he'd deliberately tried to feed his son's friends to a shark. His career was over. Parker's mom, meanwhile, decided to take him back east and she sold the LA house. The boat was impounded as evidence.

Vanessa bought Raphael's story about having a new dog that was part coyote, and she stayed quiet about any of the rest of it, embarrassed about ever having been friends with Parker at all.

I was briefly a little mad at Raphael for leaving me alone when I first faced Parker, but he explained that he'd been trying to get out of his clothes so he could take coyote form, and I forgave him. Last week, Raphael and I launched a Kickstarter campaign for a new game we're designing called *Animen*. The campaign looks like it's going to fund. It's going to be an awesome game.

After all, we know how to make 'em scream.

RULE SEVEN

BY RAY DANIEL

MY DAD SCREAMS LONG AND loud.

"Ha!" I say to Mikey. "I scared him good. I get a doughnut."

My dad works in Hollywood making creepy scenes in horror movies. Because he scares people for a living, he's almost impossible to scare himself. He bet me a doughnut that I'd never scare him. I got my chance when he turned the old Wagner place into a haunted house to raise money for an animal shelter.

My dad is really good at his job. He has all these rules for making things scary, and the Wagner place meets Rule One: start with a scary setting. It's big and gray, set up on a hill, with scraggly trees all around it. It didn't have a graveyard, so my dad installed one in the front yard.

I say, "He definitely owes me a doughnut."

Mikey tugs my sleeve. "Do you think I could get a doughnut too, Josh?"

I shine my flashlight under my face to make it look scary. "A *doughnut*? Mwahahahaha!"

Mikey slaps my arm. "Stop it! That's weird. Can I get a doughnut

I pull the flashlight down, point it up the path to the house. "Sure. You can get a doughnut."

I head toward the house, but Mikey hangs back.

"What?" I ask him.

"What if we see a real Wagner ghost?"

"What's a real Wagner ghost?"

"If a Wagner dies in there, the body becomes a zombie . . . or something. They call it a Wagner ghost."

"A Wagner ghost."

"Yeah!"

"Who told you that?"

"Everyone knows that."

"That's why my dad picked this place. Because of Rule Two."

"What's Rule Two?"

"Start with a scary backstory."

"What's a backstory?"

"It's a story about what happened in the place before. Usually you have to make it up, but this place had its own backstory."

"You mean the zombie ghosts?"

"Exactly. People will be scared before they go in."

"So it's just a backstory? The zombie ghosts aren't real?"

I smile. "Who knows."

"They might be real?"

I shrug.

"Oh no!" says Mikey, holding back. "I don't want to be a zombie!"

Scaring Mikey is almost as much fun as scaring my dad, but we had to move.

"Oh come on. It's just a story."

"How do you know?"

"Because there's no such thing as ghosts."

"You think?"

"There probably aren't even any Wagners left."

"You sure?"

I lead the way. We climb up the front steps, the little switches my dad installed clicking under our feet. If the house had power, they would have caused holograms to pop up. But I'd killed the power at the main box to get my dad to go inside in the dark.

Mikey stops at the front door. "We shouldn't go in there."

I smile because of Rule Three: make people say "Don't go in there!"

I creak the front door open.

"Dad!"

Nothing.

Mikey calls, "Mr. Hornsby!"

Still nothing.

"Dad?"

We step into the front hallway. I point my flashlight around the room. The haunted house is laid out in a big circle. People follow a path through the different rooms, each one getting scarier.

Mikey takes a step down the path, slips, and falls.

"Eww!"

He's sitting in a puddle of ooze on the floor. That's not supposed to be there. That's supposed to be dripping down an ooze fountain, not leaking on the floor. We needed the ooze fountain for Rule Four: go for the gross out.

I help Mikey stand. Run my flashlight along the floor, looking for the ooze trail back to the fountain. There isn't one. Just this puddle. Flies buzz around the edge of the puddle, landing at the edge and sipping.

"Is this that ecto stuff?" asks Mikey.

"You've been watching too much *Ghostbusters*. That's just glue and water."

"Really?"

"And borax."

"Flies sure like borax."

I've made a lot of borax slime, and this slime is different. More like pure boogers. Also, flies don't like borax.

"Yuck," I say.

"It's just glue, right?"

"Yeah." I look around the room. "Just glue."

I call out, "Dad! The ooze is leaking!"

The house creaks.

"Where is he?" asks Mikey.

"Must be checking out my prank. He likes to study a good prank."

I point my flashlight through the dining room. We walk. Plastic ghouls, cloth ghosts, and rubber zombies all sit in their coffins, nooks, and armoires. They're quiet because there's no power to activate them. When the power is on, they'll pop up and scare people. Well, mostly scare little kids. But little kids are people too, I guess.

The house creaks again. And again. Footsteps?

"Mr. Hornsby, c'mon!" yells Mikey.

The footsteps stop.

"I'm leaving," says Mikey.

"We're almost there," I say. "Besides, we have to clean up the ecto so nobody falls."

"Ecto?"

"I mean the glue."

"Why did you call it 'ecto'?"

"Dad!"

The key to scaring Dad was to make a joke that didn't use electricity. That way he wouldn't see it coming. He had told me never to go down the basement in this house, but I had snuck down there to set up the gag and turn off the power. Then I ran and got him. Told him that we must have blown a fuse. That's why he came in. My gag is right next to the power box, deep in the basement.

We push through some spiderwebbing. Flies buzz, trapped in the sticky mess.

"Yuck," says Mikey. "This place is gross. Someone should clean it."

"I just dusted this morning," I say. "I put in fake webs."

Mikey watches a spider suck on a wrapped fly. "These aren't fake webs."

There shouldn't be any spiders in these webs. "Dad?"

We enter the dining room, and I look up. If we had power, there would be holographic ghosts flying around the chandelier. It's part of Rule Five: misdirection. We get people to look up at the ghost, and then a stuffed werewolf runs at them, or actually glides at them on a track. But now the room is quiet and empty except for the creaking.

We push through into the kitchen, where the door to the cellar stands open, a black rectangle in the wall. It's pitch-black in the cellar because of Rule Six: keep them in the dark.

"Is he down there?" asks Mikey.

"Should be. That's where I put the gag," I said. I shine my flashlight down the cellar stairs. "Dad?"

No sound.

"Did he have a heart attack?" asks Mikey.

"That's not funny."

"It sounded like you really scared him."

We start down the steps, heading for the fuse box. Cellar air blows on our faces. It smells like dirt. I shine the flashlight around. Nothing. We keep going.

"Mr. Hornsby!" call Mikey. "Come out!"

We listen. Silence.

"Let's turn on the lights," I say.

"What? Down there?"

"Yeah."

Mikey sits on the step. "I'm not going."

"Okay. Sit up here in the dark."

"I don't want to sit in the dark."

"I've got the only flashlight, and I'm going down."

"You suck."

"I need to find my dad."

We reach the bottom step, our sneakers touching the bare dirt floor.

"Didn't your dad say never come down here?"

"Yeah, because of the rats."

"Then why are we down here?"

I hear a sound, and point the flashlight at it. Beady eyes look back at me from a corner of the room. A big gray body scurries away. I move the flashlight to the wall. A metal box hangs there, the big switch on the side pulled down to kill the electricity. "We need to turn on the lights."

"Finally!" says Mikey, and he pushes the big switch up.

The lights blast on in the cellar, just as a screeching sound hits us. We turn, and a zombie—a man with a torn, bloody face—rushes at us, mouth open, teeth snapping. Mikey screams and runs toward the stairs.

He yells, *"Run! Run!"*

I stand my ground as the zombie zooms at me, its jaw popping, its arms outstretched. They reach for me, encircling me, pulling me close as the teeth snap. And then it stops. Just like it was supposed to.

That was my gag. The zombie was supposed to scare my dad, but he had never seen it. My hands twitch as fear rushes in.

Why did he scream?

Mikey stands on the staircase, hands to his mouth, eyes wide.

I duck out from under my zombie on a string. "Don't be a baby."

The lights go out.

I aim my flashlight at the fuse box and see one of the fuses has melted through.

"Replace it! Replace it!" says Mikey.

"We can't," I say, remembering what my dad taught me about tech. "It'll just burn out again. We need to find the short circuit."

"Let your dad find it."

"Why did he scream?"

"What?"

"My dad screamed. But he never sprung the trap. Why did he scream?"

"Let's get out of here."

We stand in the pitch-black cellar, with only my flashlight on Mikey's face. "We have to find him."

I start up the cellar stairs. "C'mon."

"There really are zombie ghosts."

"No, there aren't. There isn't a rule for real zombie ghosts."

"Yes there is," says Mikey. "Sherlock Holmes's rule. If you eliminate everything else, all that's left is the zombie ghosts."

"There are no zombie ghosts."

"They made your dad scream."

I lead Mikey up the stairs, through the kitchen, past the dining room, and back to the front door.

"Watch out for the ecto," I say, playing the flashlight beam over the puddle. It's gotten bigger. More flies crowd around it.

"You said it was just glue."

"Yeah, it should just be glue."

Mikey looks from the puddle to me to the front door. We had left it standing open.

"I want to go home."

"We need to find my dad."

"We should call the police."

"We need to look for him."

Another scream like the first one echoes through the house. Mikey bolts out the front door. "I'll get help!" he yells over his shoulder, and he's gone.

I'm alone.

Another scream? Is it even my dad? Was it ever my dad?

"Dad?"

I know he is in here.

Mikey was right about one thing. Once you've eliminated all the possibilities, the only thing left has got to be true. I'd looked for my dad on the first floor and in the basement. He wasn't in either. He must be upstairs.

I shine my light on the big curving staircase that leads to the second floor. He'd told me never to go up there, either, but that's where he has to be.

This whole idea of scaring him was stupid. For what. A doughnut? I could have just bought my own doughnut. I shine the light on the staircase. It looks safe enough.

Step on the first stair, hear a switch click. My dad would have used that to have a holographic ghost tell people not to climb the stairs. But there's no electricity, so no ghost.

I start climbing the stairs, stopping on each creaky step to listen.

"C'mon, Dad, this is ridiculous!"

A low moan drifts through the house.

"Jossshhh. . . ."

"Dad?"

The moan turns into a rumble, then stops.

I reach the top of the steps, and the smell hits me. The stink of rot, like hamburger left in a cooler for a week with no ice.

"Dad?"

I walk along the hallway, shining my flashlight at the doors, then over the railing down to the entryway. The smell gets stronger with each step.

Another moan. *"Jossshhh!"*

I walk past a door. The smell recedes. I stop. Turn. Sniff. Use my nose to find the source. The second-bedroom door. I put my ear to the door. I hear buzzing. Like a distant lawn mower, or bees.

I push the door open, point the flashlight inside. The buzzing blasts me.

Flies fill the room like smoke. A living cloud. They see my flashlight, fly at me, surround me. Surprised, I gasp; inhale three flies. I spit them out, drop to the floor, let the cloud swirl overhead, shine my light again into the room.

Flies wriggle over a body in the center of the room.

"Dad?"

I cover my mouth, step farther into the fly room. They land on me, crawl on my ears, tickle my neck. I walk up to the body on the floor. I aim my flashlight on its face. A gross mess looks back at me, skin peeled back, eyes gone, maggots boiling out of the nose.

Glowing blue smoke slips from the lipless mouth. I back up and watch as the smoke forms itself into a blue glowing man with black eyes and a scruffy beard. He opens his mouth.

I whirl to run out the door, but stop. My dad is standing behind me, blocking the door.

I point at the hologram. "Dad, that's not funny. That's gross!"

My dad shakes his head. "Jossshhh," he moans. He takes a step toward me, still blocking the door.

The glowing man says, "You thought I was one of your pathetic pranks."

I gasp, inhaling another fly.

"I AM NOT!" the glowing man yells.

I point at the man. "Dad, who is he?"

The ghost points to the pile of meat on the floor below him. The body boiling with flies. "I was that," he says. "Monroe Wagner."

Now I remembered. Monroe Wagner had been a homeless guy in town.

He continues, "Now I am the Zombie Lord."

I run toward my dad. Grab his hand, try to spin him toward the door. "C'mon, Dad, let's go!"

My dad takes my hand, then grabs my wrist.

"Yes," says the glowing man floating above Monroe Wagner's body. "Bring him to me."

"*What?*" I yank on my arm, trying to pull free.

"Bring him to me," says the ghost.

Pulling me by my arm, Dad shuffles toward the fly-ridden corpse with the glowing ghost rooted to its mouth.

"No, Dad, no!"

My dad looks at me, his eyes sad. He says, "Josh, I can't . . ."

"You have to fight it!"

Another step. Wagner's ghost reaches out a hand, smoke fingers reaching for my face. He says, "Soon I will have two in my army."

My dad keeps dragging me. I yank and tug. "No! Dad, no!"

He takes another step, his hand clamped over my wrist. I drop to the ground, swing in his grip, lose my flashlight. It rolls out of reach. My dad takes another step. The flies buzz in my ears.

I shift in my dad's clutches, get my feet under me. Reach out with a foot. Remember that there was one rule we hadn't used yet: Rule Seven. It's a rule my dad would use in movies, but never in real life. "Don't want to cause a heart attack," he would say.

I kick the flashlight toward my hand. Grab it.

It's time for Rule Seven: make them jump!

I flip the flashlight under my chin, shine it up so that my face looks like a scary death mask, and scream as loud as I can. My dad's eyes go wide, startled. He screams. We scream together.

My dad's eyes change. He looks from me to Wagner's ghost, says, "Let's get out of here!"

Before we can run, one of the smoky fingers grazes me, touching my face. I stop, turn, realize that I want to stay here with Monroe Wagner.

My dad drags me out of the room. I kick and struggle to stay. It's not until I'm halfway down the staircase that the spell breaks. Then I start running with my dad down the stairs, past the ecto puddle, and out the front door. We don't stop running until we're standing in the street, far away from the Wagner place and its zombie ghost.

My dad leans down, his hands resting on his knees as he catches his breath.

He says, "Josh, that thing took over my mind. I'm sorry I scared you."

"I'm sorry I scared *you*. Using the flashlight was all I could think to do."

"It was smart. You're a smart kid. Come here." My dad hugs me. "Boy," he says. "You really *did* scare me."

"Yeah, I'm sorry."

"I guess I owe you a doughnut."

CAT GOT YOUR TONGUE

BY WENDY CORSI STAUB

 SCREAM," JAX STILLMAN WHISPERS.

"A scream?" Tacey Bennett shivers in the summer sun.

"Was it a word?"

"What do you mean?"

"You know, like 'Owww!' or 'Nooo!' or . . . ?"

Jax shakes his head. "Just a scream. It was the last sound she ever made."

Tacey looks again at the girl, Felicia Roberts, sitting on the rope swing in the yard next door. She looks just like every other seventh-going-into-eighth-grader Tacey knows. Well, not *just* like them. But close enough.

Felicia is medium-size—not tall and not short, not heavy and not thin. Her tawny hair hangs past her shoulders. No braces or glasses.

Tacey had both until a few weeks ago. The orthodontist removed her braces before she left California, and she lost her glasses somewhere along the three-thousand-mile cross-country road trip. She can see pretty well without them, but Dad said they'll have to replace them now that they've arrived in Maine.

She used to be a little larger than medium-size, but she lost her appetite when her mom got sick. She started growing taller then, too, which probably has nothing to do with losing her mother or with the move, although if she thinks long enough, she can trace all the bad things in her life back to those events. Now she stands a head above all the girls and a few boys, Jax included.

Her hair is the color of macaroni and cheese—not the good, rich homemade kind Mom used to make, but the fake kind with the powdery sauce that lumps no matter how much you stir.

She spent all last year trying to grow her hair long. Instead, it grew up and out in a wiry mess. She had it cut before they moved in June. It was supposed to look swingy and carefree like the model in the salon's magazine. Unfortunately, it looks more like . . .

Well, like Jax's hair.

That makes sense, since they're cousins.

Tacey would prefer to look like Felicia and the other girls her age. That might make it easier to fit in here.

Not that Felicia does. According to Jax she used to be a regular person, until she suddenly stopped speaking.

"Don't stare at her," Jax says in a low voice. "She's going to notice."

"I doubt it."

Felicia isn't facing in their direction. Nor is she swinging. She isn't even moving. She's just sitting there, looking up into the wooded hillside above a neighborhood that looks nothing like the flat-roofed stucco condos back home. Here, houses are huge and old, topped by gables and turrets and iron grillwork. They look like haunted manors on cartoons—the kind where bats fly out of attics, and creepy caretakers sneak around in tunnels behind bookcases.

"So why did she scream?" Tacey asks Jax, dipping her paintbrush into the open can on the ground between them.

"Nobody knows. It was in the middle of the night."

"Did you hear it?"

"Yeah."

"Were you scared?" she asks, trying not to drip the bright blue paint on her sandals or red-painted toenails as she brushes the rough wooden wall of the garden shed.

"Nope. I thought it was a bobcat, so I went back to sleep."

"She sounded like a cat?"

"Bobcats sound like a girl screaming in the night. Don't you have them in California?"

"Not in the last place we lived. We had real girls screaming in the night."

"For real?"

"It was a rough neighborhood. Sometimes people screamed and yelled in the street, sometimes you'd hear tires screeching, and there were a lot of sirens."

"Then why are you so homesick?"

"Because it was home," she says simply.

It's been two weeks since Tacey and her dad arrived in Cranberry Cove, Maine. They're staying with Jax and his parents, her uncle Doug and aunt Milly, who was Mom's sister.

They look alike, but Aunt Milly wears skirts and blouses and hosiery, and her gingery hair is always pulled back in a tight bun. Mom's hair was long and loose, and she lived in blue jeans, with bare feet.

Tacey never even met her aunt until she came to California for Mom's funeral. That's when she talked Dad into moving East.

He didn't really want to, but Aunt Milly has a bossy way of taking charge. Plus, Dad had lost his job after taking so much time off to care for Mom, and the landlord was about to kick them out for not paying rent. So here they are, staying in a big old shabby house next door to the even bigger, shabbier, older house where Felicia lives with her grandmother.

This is the first time Tacey has seen Felicia. Spotting her, Tacey told Jax they should go over and say hello, thinking it would be nice to have a friend around here other than her cousin.

"So she screamed in the night, and then she just stopped talking?" she asks Jax. "Did she hurt her vocal cords or something?"

"Nope." Jax dunks his brush into the paint and slaps it on the wall, spattering the grass and his sneakers. He doesn't seem to notice. "Her grandmother took her to a bunch of doctors, and the doctors said there's nothing wrong with her throat. They said she'll snap out of it sooner or later."

"How do you know all this if she can't talk?"

"Her grandmother told my mom. She thought Felicia had laryngitis, and she gave her tea with honey and lemon. But Felicia wouldn't drink it, and she wouldn't write anything down to answer questions. She just stares off into space." Jax rubs a small blue blob on his sneaker. It smears into a big blue blob.

"Why don't we go over and see if she'll tell us what happened?"

"Because we're painting."

Aunt Milly decided the old shed on the back of the property urgently needed painting this morning, after Tacey and Jax baked brownies. It turned out they'd used some kind of fancy imported French dark chocolate she was saving for a special occasion, and they kind of made a mess, and the brownies burned and set off all the smoke alarms. The last straw, Aunt Milly said. She was still upset they hadn't asked her permission to hang out at the fire pit in the park last night with a couple of high school kids.

"I was worried sick!" she shouted. "And don't you know fires are against the law until the drought passes?"

"We didn't start the fire," Tacey said reasonably. "We just toasted marshmallows."

Aunt Milly, who considers fruit a dessert, made a face.

This morning, after the brownie incident, she found some old paint in the garage and told them to paint the shed.

"That will keep you guys busy while I'm working," she said. She's a sales rep and spends most days on the phone in her home office.

Tacey grumbled to Dad that she can keep plenty busy on her own, reading books and playing video games with Jax. Dad reminded her that they're guests here until he can find a job.

He doesn't seem to be trying very hard. He still mopes around missing Mom, sometimes staring off into space like Felicia. Only, he *can* talk. He just doesn't feel like it. She misses the old Dad, who smiled and joked around, and she misses her kindhearted mother. She misses everything, even their dumpy apartment.

"Anyway," Jax says, "this isn't the first time it's happened."

"What do you mean? The first time *what's* happened?"

"A few months ago this kid down the street, Leo Katz, screamed really loud in the middle of the night and lost his voice too."

Tacey stops moving the paintbrush over the shed wall. "What happened to him?"

"I heard he's in a hospital in Boston."

"Is something wrong with his throat?"

"No, something's wrong with his brain." Jax waves at a mosquito buzzing around his sweaty face. "It's a psychiatric hospital. Some people think Felicia is trying to copy him."

"Why would she do that?"

"Maybe she wants attention. She's still upset that her mom took off and left her with her grandmother."

"For good?"

"I guess."

"It's hard to lose your mom."

He nods as if he knows, and Tacey finds herself resenting the fact that he doesn't. Sometimes she feels as if she's the sole member of a lonely little club with mandatory membership.

"What about Felicia's dad?" she asks Jax, who's still trying to shoo away the mosquito.

"She doesn't have one."

"Wow. Poor Felicia."

"Yeah. My mom says that when stuff happens to kids, they act out with bad behavior."

She narrows her eyes. "What stuff?"

"You know—bad stuff. Got it!" Jax smashes the mosquito against his glasses, leaving a rather patriotic if gory smudge of red mosquito blood and blue paint.

"You need to go wash that off."

"Yeah. Be right back." He tosses his paintbrush onto the ground and heads for the house.

She looks next door again. The motherless and fatherless girl is still sitting, still staring, still alone.

After a moment's thought Tacey balances her brush on a tree stump with the bristles hanging off the edge and walks toward the straggly hedgerow.

Up close, Tacey can see that Felicia's hands are gripping the swing's rope handles so tightly her knuckles are white. She doesn't glance in Tacey's direction as she stops beside the swing.

She's still fixated on the hillside.

Tacey turns in that direction. From the yard next door, she could see only trees. But from here, through the branches, she can see something about halfway up the incline. A house?

"What's up there?" she asks Felicia.

No reply. She wasn't really expecting one.

"I'm Tacey, by the way. I'm staying next door for the summer. Maybe longer."

Still nothing.

"My cousin Jax said your mom left. Mine did too."

It isn't the truth, exactly. Her own mother couldn't help leaving. But when she glances at Felicia, she swears she sees something flicker in her green eyes.

"I had to leave my home and my school and all my friends to come here to live with our relatives. I miss my mom," she says, "and the way things used to be. Know what I mean?"

One of Felicia's hands has let go of the rope swing. It's still fisted, but not quite so tightly.

"Sometimes I get so mad that my mom is gone that I want to scream. And sometimes at night I have a hard time falling asleep, and when I do, I dream that she's still here. But then I wake up, and she's not. Do you ever have that dream?"

No response.

"How about nightmares? Is that why you screamed that night? Were you having a nightmare? Or . . . did something happen to you?"

The green eyes close in a slow, deliberate blink.

Next door, the screen door creaks open and bangs shut.

"What happened to you?" Tacey asks gently.

"Tacey?" Jax's voice calls from the other side of the hedge.

The girl flinches.

"Coming!" Tacey calls back to Jax.

She waits a little longer, hoping Felicia might respond.

"Tacey! Where are you?"

She sighs. As she turns to walk away, she notices that Felicia's hand is open, slack against her knee. Her palm is raw and bloody from her fingernails digging into her flesh, and the nails . . .

Her nails are sallow, curved, and pointy, sharpened into claws.

Tacey finds Jax by the shed, picking specks of dirt and strands of grass out of his paintbrush.

"Hey, where were you?" There's still a faint blue smudge on his glasses.

She doesn't mean to lie, but when she opens her mouth, one drops out. "In the house."

"No, you weren't. I was in the house."

"It's a big house," she says with a shrug. Her hand shakes as she picks up her paintbrush again.

Jax watches her as she dips it into the paint and spreads the paint over the wall.

Then he dips his own brush and gets back to work.

After a few silent minutes Tacey clears her throat. "Hey, Jax?"

"Yeah?"

"What's up there?"

"Up where?"

"In the woods. On the hill. That house." She points at the trees beyond Felicia's house.

He squints. "How can you see it?"

"My eyes are a lot better than yours. I told you, I don't even need my glasses anymore."

"Oh. Well, it's the witch's house."

"The *witch*'s house?"

"She's probably not a real witch. I mean, she's *not*. She's just an old lady. But everyone calls her 'the witch' because she looks and acts like one."

"You mean . . . does she ride around on a broomstick and wear a pointy hat and cast spells?"

"I've never seen her. I've just heard about her."

"From who?"

He shrugs. "Everyone in town."

"Let's go check out her house."

"No way!"

"You said she's just an old lady."

"She is. But I, um . . . I don't like to hike in the woods. There's poison ivy and bugs and, uh, you know. Wild animals."

"I think you're scared."

"I think you're crazy."

They stare at each other for a long time.

"Anyway," he says, "we have to finish painting."

Tacey sighs.

She bends to dip her brush again, glancing into the yard next door as she straightens.

Felicia is gone.

She must have walked away when they weren't looking, but . . .

Tacey can't help wondering if she simply vanished.

After a late dinner and watermelon for dessert—her aunt's idea of a special treat—Tacey collapses into bed in her small third-floor guest room.

She's so exhausted that she's positive she'll go right to sleep for a change. Instead, she finds herself wide-awake.

The night is warm and humid. The windows are open. Crickets' steady chatter floats in through the screens, along with the occasional barking dog and the hum of a fishing boat in the cove a few blocks away. Every so often, a slight breeze moves the tree branches to create weird shadows across the slanted ceiling. They look like arms reaching through the windows, reaching for her.

Remembering Felicia's peculiar claw-fingernails, she tries to convince herself that it was just . . . just . . . a new style of manicure or something. *Maybe the girls here in Maine polish their nails a sickly yellow shade and file them into points, or. . . .*

Something.

She gets out of bed and looks out the window that overlooks the backyard and, beyond, the wooded hillside where Jax said the witch lives.

From here, she sees only trees.

Wondering about the view from Felicia's house next door, she glances over.

In the windowed cupola above the mansard roof, she sees the

silhouette of a girl motionlessly watching the woods.

Shuddering, Tacey pulls down the shades and climbs back into bed.

Just go to sleep. You'll forget all about this in the morning.

But the more she thinks about the woods, and the witch, the more she wonders about Felicia. Tomorrow, she'll convince Jax to go up the hillside with her. If he refuses, she'll go alone. What could happen in broad daylight? She'll bring her cell phone with her, just in case—

A scream, loud and shrill, shatters the night.

Heart pounding, Tacey jumps out of bed, throws open the door, and races down the narrow hall to her father's room. His bed is empty.

She flies down the stairs to the second floor, rounds the corner— and crashes into a filmy figure in a long white dress with ghastly pale skin and flowing hair.

It's her turn to scream, until she realizes that it's not her mother's ghost. It's just Aunt Milly in her nightgown, with a layer of cold cream on her face.

"Shhh! Tacey, you'll wake up Jax. And probably the whole neighborhood! What's wrong?"

She opens her mouth. Nothing comes out.

For a terrible, terrifying moment she thinks that she too has lost her voice in the wake of a scream.

Then she manages to ask, "Where's my father? He isn't in his bed."

"He's downstairs talking to Uncle Doug. He'll be up soon. Go back to—"

"I heard a scream."

"That was just a bobcat in the woods."

"It sounded like a person."

Aunt Milly nods. "Yes, they do, don't they?"

"How do you know it wasn't?"

"Wasn't what?"

"A person."

She smiles. "We hear them all the time around here. You'll get used to it, I promise."

She doesn't want to get used to it. She wants to go back home. Hot tears sting her eyes.

"Oh, sweetie." Aunt Millie puts an arm around her and pulls her close. Her hair, finally out of its bun, tickles Tacey's bare arms. She smells like spearmint toothpaste and lotion. Mom used to smell just like that at night. For a moment, Tacey closes her eyes and pretends that she *is* Mom, hugging her.

Then Aunt Millie's voice says, "You need to go back up to bed. I need you and Jax to wash my minivan early tomorrow morning before I leave for my sales meeting."

"But I need to talk to my dad."

Aunt Milly hesitates. "He's having a hard night, Tacey. He's missing your mom. Let's let him be, okay? Come on, I'll come back up and sit with you if you're frightened."

"I'm not *frightened*. I just thought someone was screaming. I mean, I'm not a baby. I don't need someone to tuck me in."

But even as she says it, her voice catches. Mom still used to tuck her in sometimes, before she got sick. After she did, Tacey would tuck her in, making sure the blankets were snug around her mother's frail body. She'd sit on the bed and watch her sleep, listening to her breathe.

Wordlessly, Aunt Milly steers her back to the stairway, up to the third floor, and back to bed.

Her aunt kisses her forehead, then settles in the wooden rocking chair across the room, watching, listening.

Tacey forces herself to breathe slowly, through her nose, and makes a little snoring sound as if she's dozing off. If she pretends she's fallen asleep, her aunt will leave. Then she'll sneak downstairs, find her father, and tell him that they have to go home. Home to California, where no one makes her paint sheds or wash minivans, and there are no bobcats screaming in the night, no silent, staring girls next door or witches in the woods.

The rocking chair rocks and creaks, back and forth, back and forth. . . .

Tacey breathes in and out, in and out. . . .

Tacey opens her eyes.

Aunt Milly is gone. The room is dark and still. She fell asleep after all.

She gets out of bed and walks over to the window. Lifting the shade, she looks at the cupola next door. No sign of the person she saw standing there earlier.

Unless she imagined it or maybe dreamed it? The whole thing, including the scream?

Maybe, she realizes, the whole experience was a bad dream—yesterday spent in the hot sun painting, Jax's strange account of neighborhood kids who scream and then go inexplicably mute, the witch's house. . . .

But this is exactly how she felt when Mom was sick. Every morning she'd wake thinking none of it was real. Then she'd see the hospital bed in the living room, and Mom's wan face, and another dread-filled day would begin.

Beyond the window, the eastern sky is fringed with a glow of sherbet-colored sunrise.

Aunt Milly's going to keep me and Jax busy again today. We probably won't get a chance to investigate the house in the woods until later tonight.

Tacey doesn't want to wait. And she doesn't want to go at night—especially alone. Something tells her Jax isn't going to accompany her. He might even tell on her.

She dresses swiftly, putting on long pants, sneakers, and a long-sleeved T-shirt to protect herself from poison ivy and yes, bugs. What about wild animals?

She grabs her cell phone from the nightstand and practices dialing 911 before tucking it into her pocket. She tries not to wonder how quickly she'd be able to dial if she were being mauled by a bobcat or a bear.

Slipping out into the hall, she sees that her father's bedroom door is closed. She turns the knob slowly so that it won't click, and pushes the door open a crack. Her father is sound asleep, curled on his side, hugging his pillow as if it were a person.

He's missing your mom, Aunt Milly had said.

Tacey closes the door quietly and tries to swallow an aching lump. If she had to speak now, she wouldn't be able to, and it has nothing to do with a scream.

Maybe that's the problem with Felicia. Maybe sorrow is clogging her throat, paralyzing her vocal cords.

I have to find out what's going on with her. Maybe I can help.

She creeps down the stairs. In the kitchen, the stove clock tells her it's past five a.m. She doesn't have much time.

Her gaze falls on the supper dishes, left in the drying rack beside the sink. Something glints among the plates and forks—the blade of the big knife Aunt Milly used to cut up the watermelon for dessert. Tacey looks at it for a long time. Then she gingerly grabs the handle and puts the knife into her back pocket. When she takes a step, the blade pokes into her skin. She removes it from her pocket and holds it in her hand, fist around the handle, blade pointed down. There.

She's ready for wild animals or anything else that might cross her path.

Tacey's footsteps are accompanied by a cricket chorus as she heads toward the wooded incline. The air is warm and damp, the grass wet with dew.

Feeling as though she's being watched, she looks back at the house, half expecting to see her aunt on the back steps or Jax in his bedroom window. No one is there.

She cuts through the yard next door, searching the windows and cupola for Felicia or her grandmother. They aren't visible, but that doesn't mean they aren't there.

She hurries toward the trees, eager to leave behind the open space and envelop herself in protective foliage. A gap in the underbrush reveals a sloping trail, slippery with a carpet of rotting leaves and tangled with vines and rocks. She uses the glow from her phone to illuminate the terrain and picks her way up, wondering why she still feels as though she's under surveillance. No one is stirring in this remote place at this hour, not even forest creatures.

High overhead, an owl hoots as if to disprove that theory.

As the trail twists and climbs, she decides this might be a bad idea. Especially when she checks her phone for the time and sees that she's lost the signal. What if the wild animals awaken and attack? What if she trips and falls and breaks an ankle? No one would hear her cries for help. She should have at least told Jax where she was going, or left a note.

Turn around. Go home.

For some reason she can't seem to make her body obey her brain's command. It's as if she's being propelled by some unseen force. As she rounds a bend, she sees a clearing.

The witch's house.

It's a small shuttered cottage with a gingerbread porch and gabled roof. Bright lamplight spills from its windows. Even in the dark she can see that it's painted the same bright blue as Aunt Milly's shed, which should probably reassure her. Instead, it feels like a warning.

Go home. You need to go home right now!

Yet her feet propel her toward the house. If she goes back, she won't know why Felicia keeps staring up here. And if she doesn't know why, she won't be able to stop wondering, and worrying, and wanting to go home.

About to set foot on the bottom step of the porch, she freezes, hearing voices.

"It's your turn, Felicia."

At the familiar name, Tacey lowers her foot to the ground and takes a step backward, away from the porch.

"I don't want to play anymore." A girl's voice floats out into the night through the open window. "I just want to go home."

"You *are* home."

"No, she isn't," a male voice pipes up.

"Shush, Leo." The first voice is female and authoritative, with a bit of old-lady warble.

"No! I want to go home too."

"You've already tried that, haven't you? And what happened when you went back? Did your family welcome you with open arms?"

"I don't want to talk about it."

"A wise decision, as it isn't your turn to speak, nor to make a move in the game. Now, then, Felicia."

"I'm tired of playing. Can't I go to sleep?"

"You've been catnapping all day and most of the night. Now it's playtime. Play!"

Tacey creeps along the porch toward the nearest window, the knife trembling in her hand, thoughts racing along with her heart. Clearly, Felicia and Leo haven't lost their voices after all. But why are they here, at the cottage in the woods? And who is the woman? She doesn't sound like a witch, yet there's an ominous edge in her voice when she says "play."

Tacey takes another step toward the window, and then another. One more will do it.

But when she puts her foot down beneath the sill, a twig snaps beneath the rubber sole of her sneaker.

"What was that?" Leo asks.

"Be still! Someone is out there!" the woman hisses.

Tacey turns and runs, careening over the rutted clearing to the trail. As she descends she hears a distant rustling behind her. Someone has come after her. She picks up speed, clinging to the knife, frantically trying to outrun whoever—whatever—is chasing her out of the woods.

At last she sees the gap in the undergrowth. She sprints out of the woods—and spots the last thing she ever expected to see in the yard next door.

Felicia, sitting in the rope swing, staring at this very spot, as if she was expecting Tacey.

"How . . . ?" Panting, she looks back over her shoulder, hearing a thrashing in the trees as her pursuer closes in. "How did you get here?"

Felicia doesn't respond.

Dazed, Tacey races on toward her aunt's house. Only when she climbs the back steps does she dare to look over her shoulder . . . just in time to see a furry creature barrel from the woods. It's small, with spotted fur, and . . .

"That's a bobcat," says a voice behind her.

Gasping, she turns to see Aunt Milly. She's still wearing her nightgown, along with a disapproving expression.

"It chased me." Breathless, bewildered, Tacey sees the bobcat come to a stop several yards away.

"What were you doing in the woods at this hour? And why do you have my carving knife?" Aunt Milly plucks it from her hand.

"I— For protection. I was hiking and—"

"Let's go. Inside." Her aunt steers her into the house, closing and locking the door after them.

Tacey takes one last look at the bobcat through the window. It seems to stare back at her for a long moment before turning and disappearing into the shadowy forest, under the watchful green gaze of Felicia.

"You just need to follow the rules while you're living in someone else's house," Dad tells Tacey.

"I didn't know there was a rule against going for a hike."

"Armed with Aunt Milly's good cutlery? In the middle of the night?"

"It's morning."

"The sun is barely up." He rakes a hand through his dark hair, making it stand up even higher than when he first got out of bed to address what Aunt Milly referred to as a "situation." His eyes are bloodshot, underscored by dark circles.

"Twelve-year-old girls shouldn't roam around the woods alone in the dark. You know better. Things can happen."

Yes. She shivers, thinking of the strange little house, and the voices. . . .

Felicia? Leo?

She'd been certain they were inside, held captive by a woman—the witch? But Felicia was here, sitting calmly in the yard, and there's no way she could have gotten there ahead of Tacey.

"—just a little longer, okay?"

She blinks. Her father is talking, but she's lost track of the conversation.

"I'm sorry, what, Dad?"

"I just need you to hang in there a little longer. I have a job interview today."

"Here?"

"Cranberry Cove is home now, Tace." He reaches out and gives her hand a squeeze. "Aunt Milly and Uncle Doug and Jax are the only family we have. You said you liked it here."

She did say that.

But now . . .

"We need to try to make this work, because . . . I don't know what else we can do. Can you try?" Dad asks. "Please? For me?"

She nods. "Okay."

* * *

"I don't get it," Jax says, sponging drippy suds from a bucket over the minivan. "How can there be another Felicia? It's an unusual name around here."

"I know. And why does this Felicia keep staring up at that very spot in the woods? And what about Leo?"

"He's in the hospital. How can he be in the woods—playing games, you said?"

"That's what it sounded like," she agrees, uncoiling the garden hose, waiting to rinse off the car. "But they both wanted to go home, and they couldn't."

"You must have heard wrong."

"Maybe I did. That's why we have to go back up there."

"Why?"

"To see what's going on and make sure it's nothing bad." If it is, she can't stay here.

Jax shakes his head, eyes wide behind his glasses. "The woods are dangerous."

"I know, poison ivy, bugs, wild animals. . . ."

"I'm not making it up. You said a bobcat chased you home."

"It did," she says, "but it wasn't vicious."

"But my mom—"

"She'll never even miss us. She said she's leaving for a meeting at noon. That's in five minutes. We'll know when she leaves."

"But—"

"Man up, Jax."

"I'm not a man. Neither are you."

"I know, but . . . we have to. Come on. It'll be fine."

If only she felt half as confident as she sounds.

* * *

"Shh." Tacey holds a finger to her lips as she and Jax stealthily cover the last bit of ground to the cottage.

He nods solemnly. He's clutching a butter knife, as is she. Better than nothing. Aunt Milly's good carving knife had disappeared from the kitchen, along with the knife block that usually sits on the counter—too dangerous and too expensive, she said earlier, for kids to lose outside.

Again, voices drift out the open window.

"No, not like that. You creep up and *then* pounce." The woman's voice sends chills down Tacey's spine.

"I *am* pouncing," the girl protests.

"Show her how it's done, Leo."

Tacey inches closer to the window. The sill is at eye level. She rests her hands on it and stands on her tiptoes to peer over the edge.

For a moment she's certain the room is empty, other than a pair of cats playing with a rolled-up sock. Both are wearing bright blue collars.

Then she hears the woman's voice again, and follows it to a shadowy corner of the room. "There now, see? Leo has the hang of it. Soon you will too, Felicia. Give it a try."

An ancient woman is sitting in a rocking chair, watching the cats. She's dressed all in black. Her face is withered, her hair stringy, and her nose long and pointy. She looks like . . .

Jax, pulling himself up to look into the room, whispers, "The witch."

In that moment Tacey realizes that the cats aren't just cats. *They're bobcats.*

And they're . . . talking.

"You have to use a little more force," the larger one says—a male, with a spotted coat, the same cat that chased Tacey from the woods this morning.

"Like this?" The other, a tawny shade, with wide green eyes, leaps upon the sock.

"Felicia!" Jax screams in horror. "That's her voice!"

The cats turn to look at the window.

"Run!" Tacey shouts, and she and Jax take off toward home.

"Go!" The old woman is shouting somewhere behind them. "Catch them before they tell!"

Tacey hears a violent rustling behind her, just like before.

This time they don't make it out of the woods. Jax trips over a vine, and falls. Hearing him cry out, she turns to see the male bobcat pounce on him.

But he doesn't attack. His paws grab the collar of Jax's T-shirt.

"Help me!" he begs. "Jax, please. It's me, Leo. She cast a spell on me."

"Me too!" The female cat is there, looking from Jax, on the ground, to Tacey. "It's Felicia."

Jax just lies on his back, eyes wide in horror.

Tacey finds her voice. "How can we help you?"

"The collar," she says. "Take off the collar. Hurry!"

"Mine too," the other bobcat begs Jax. "Please."

Tacey reaches out, her hands shaking so hard she can hardly grasp the blue collar. She fumbles for the clasp, tries to unhook it; tries again.

On the third try it comes loose in her hands.

With a bloodcurdling scream, the bobcat wrenches itself away, leaving her holding just the blue collar as it races back up the hillside, trailed by its companion.

Jax gets up slowly, holding the other blue collar.

"Are you okay?" Tacey asks.

He nods.

"Say something, Jax. You're scaring me. Can you talk?"

"Yeah. What are we going to do with these?" He gestures at the collars.

"We're going to make a fire in the fire pit and burn them."

"Fires are—"

"I don't care," Tacey says. "Let's go."

Together, they run down the hillside.

Felicia is waiting for them at the bottom. For the first time her green eyes meet Tacey's. She opens her mouth . . . and speaks two heartfelt words:

"Thank you."

That night, Tacey's father comes into her room to find her staring out the window.

"The police were just here," he says.

"What did they say?"

"They combed the woods. No sign of an old woman or of a blue cottage."

"They don't believe us?"

"They're . . ." He hesitates. "They think you might be confused."

"All of us? Me, Jax, Felicia, and Leo?"

That afternoon, not long after they burned the collars, Jax learned that Leo had suddenly started speaking again in the hospital, telling the same story Felicia told the police—that an old witch had cast a spell in the night that caused him to switch bodies with a bobcat.

"You've always had an active imagination, Tace," her father says. "And you've been through a lot. But I have great news."

Maybe they're moving back to California.

"I got the job," her father says.

"That's . . . great." Swallowing a sigh, Tacey turns away from the window. "Congratulations."

"Thanks. Now get some sleep."

As she climbs into bed, an anguished female scream echoes outside in the night.

"Just a bobcat," her father assures her.

"I know," Tacey says as if she believes it—but really, just to hear the sound of her own voice. "Will you stay until I fall asleep?"

"Of course," he says, and she lies awake for a long time, listening to the rocking chair creak.

THE I SCREAM TRUCK
BY BETH FANTASKEY

N OOOOOO!"

My little brother Ripper's shriek is shrill, high-pitched—
and quickly erupts into laughter as my best friend, Will, and
I start tickling him after tackling him. We're supposed to be
playing touch football, but at some point, when the sun went down, the
game got rougher, and everybody started tackling.

"Knock it off, Maxine!" Ripper complains, although it's hard to
make out his words. He's squirming and breathing hard. But Will and I
listen and back off—first sharing a grin that says Ripper's being a baby.
As usual.

Brushing grass off my knees, I stand up, and Will rises too.

"Who's got the ball?" Will asks, both of us looking around at a
half dozen other kids who are laughing as Ripper scrambles to his feet.
We're all in a vacant, weedy lot in the weird town my family just moved
to. I don't even know some of the kids' names, and in the dark, it's
hard to see their faces let alone a brown football. I'm glad Will came to
visit for a week. Sometimes Nightingale Corners gives me the creeps,
although Mom and Dad swear I'll get used to the place once I start
middle school in the fall.

"Anybody seen the ball . . . ?" Will's voice trails off because he's heard something. I hear it too.

A happy tune, playing in the distance.

"I scream, you scream . . . I scream, you scream . . . I scream, you scream . . ."

It sounds like little kids are singing, their voices soft, because the ice cream truck is still pretty far away. At least I assume the noise is coming from an ice cream truck. I can just barely hear the sound of grinding gears disturbing the still, hot, humid night.

Will looks at me and grins again. I can see his white teeth. "Max, you got any money?"

"Yeah, Maxine," Ripper adds hopefully. He's caught his breath. "I want a popsicle!"

"I dunno," I tell them. But I'd like something cold too, and I dig into the pockets of my old cutoffs. Then, just as I do find a couple wadded-up bills, I look uncertainly at the other kids. None of them seems excited about the prospect of ice cream, which is forbidden in my house because my parents are vegans. Ugh. I have to sneak it when I can.

"Don't you guys want anything?" I ask my mostly nameless neighbors, who've grown very quiet. They shuffle and stare at the ground. "Won't the truck come by here?"

Nobody answers my questions. The little crowd is dispersing, on some cue I don't understand. I hear a couple kids say stuff like "I gotta go" and "It's getting late."

Only one boy—I think he's about eleven, like me—doesn't shuffle off right away. He's a nervous, frail kid, and I actually know his name. Dwight. He steps closer to me, Will, and Ripper, and moonlight glints off his eyeglasses. "Hey, I'm not supposed to say anything," he

BETH FANTASKEY

whispers. Then he looks quickly from side to side, like he's afraid somebody will overhear, before adding, in an even softer voice, "But you guys don't want—"

"Dwight!"

A girl calls his name sharply, and he jolts, like he's in big trouble.

Will and I share confused looks over Ripper's head while in the distance, the song continues to play. I'm not sure why it's cut off in the middle. Maybe the recording is broken.

"*I scream, you scream . . . I scream, you scream . . . I scream, you scream . . .*"

"Dwight!" the girl calls again. I think her name is Dot, and I'm pretty sure she's Dwight's sister. "Come on!" she snaps. "We're gonna break curfew!"

Dwight looks over his shoulder, obviously trying to decide if he has to heed that summons. Then he glances back at me, Will, and my brother. "I'm sorry," he says, like he just did something wrong. "I'm *really* sorry!"

Then he runs off on pale, wobbly legs. It's just me, Will, and Ripper in the lot, and the truck sounds closer. Or maybe the night is just quieter without a bunch of kids around.

"What's up with that guy?" Will finally asks after Dwight and his sister disappear behind one of the mostly dark houses that line the street. He looks at me, frowning. "Is everybody in this town vegan or something? Is that why your parents moved here?"

"I have no idea," I admit, still watching the inky black spot that swallowed up Dwight. "I don't know why nobody wants ice cream."

"Maybe we should go home too," Ripper suggests, tugging on my T-shirt.

He's eight and worries about getting in trouble.

Me and Will . . . not so much. In fact, Will kind of prides himself on being rebellious. He once boasted that he can start a car without a key—like a car thief—but I think he's lying about that.

"*I scream, you scream . . .*"

The sound is coming from a few blocks over. Maybe getting a little closer. Maybe not.

"How much money do you have?" Will asks, nodding at my pockets. "I'm really hot—and hungry."

"Guys . . ." Ripper sounds very uncertain.

To be honest I'm kind of ready to head home too, even if that means we get stuck eating the frozen tofu my mom calls "nice cream," because the stuff doesn't hurt any animals. In truth it's not so "nice." And don't cows need to be milked? How is that hurting them?

The more I think about the tofu, the more I want real ice cream. And I don't want to look like a chicken, either, although Dwight kind of freaked me out. I dig into my pockets again but then narrow my eyes at Will, who's really cheap. "Don't you have any money?"

"I'll pay you back," he says, not exactly answering my question.

I can tell by the way his teeth are gleaming again that he's got cash hidden somewhere in his baggy cargo shorts, but I pull my hand out of my pocket and count out a whopping seven dollars, which I got for babysitting turtles back in my old neighborhood.

"Come on," I say, starting to forget about Dwight's strange behavior. He's probably just a strange kid, and besides, my mouth is watering. I hope the truck has more than just chocolate and vanilla. I also hope we can catch it. I grab Ripper's shoulder and give him a shove because he's not moving, and the song seems to be getting softer now. "Let's go!"

Will is always up for an adventure. "We'll follow the song," he says. "The truck can't be that far away."

Ripper looks like he's going to protest one more time. Then he shuts his mouth, and we all stand quietly for a second, trying to figure out the direction the song is coming from.

"I scream, you scream . . ."

"This way!" Will cries, pointing toward what I believe is west. I think he's more excited about hunting down the truck than actually eating ice cream. "Follow me!"

We all run down the street, our footsteps loud against the pavement even though we're all wearing sneakers.

Nightingale Corners shuts down after dark, and we don't see anybody else as we head through the streets. We make a few turns, and the houses start to get farther apart. I can't imagine that the ice cream man makes many sales in such a lonely place, but the song is still playing, getting louder.

"I scream, you scream . . ."

"I see it!" Will finally calls—just as the song stops. He's gotten ahead of me and Ripper, who are both winded. As we catch up, I see Will standing on a small rise at the very edge of town. There are no more houses around, and lots of trees and shrubs, one of which half conceals a big wooden sign that says "Welcome to Nightingale Corners! Home of America's Only—" Overgrown leaves and branches cover whatever makes the town unique.

Will waves at us. "Come on! I think he's quitting for the night, and we came so far!"

Ripper looks up at me, clearly nervous. "We're pretty far from home. . . ."

I'm thinking the same thing. That we had a sort of fun time during the chase, but that we should turn around. Especially if the truck is parked for the night. But I don't want to be a baby like Ripper, and Will still sounds excited. And impatient.

"Hurry," he urges, waving again. "What are you waiting for?"

I look down at my brother and shrug. Then I lead us up the rise, past the wooden sign, to meet Will. And when I look down into a small clearing at the edge of the woods . . .

What the . . . ?

The ice cream truck sits right by the trees, the beat-up, blue vehicle silent and dark now. The song no longer plays. But as Ripper and I step closer, following Will, I can see a big poster affixed to the truck's side, advertising everything that's usually for sale, from popsicles shaped like rockets to ice cream sandwiches rolled in chocolate chips.

The treats look good. What I don't like is the truck's name, spelled out in white letters across the side of the van.

I SCREAM TRUCK!

Those letters look cheerful enough, but I still have the willies. Plus, the truck is obviously shut down for the night.

Ripper and I catch up to Will, and I grab his arm. "Hey, maybe we should . . ."

But before he can even turn to look at me, the truck's front door opens, nearly causing me to yelp. I'd thought the owner was gone for the night, but as we all watch, a little man in a white apron and a white paper hat climbs down off a seat that seems way too high for him. I can't help wondering how he reached the pedals to drive.

Ripper and I both start to back away, and Will finally seems uneasy too. He also takes a step backward. My hand is still on his arm, and I clutch him tighter. Not that I'm *really* scared.

"Hey, kids," the man greets us, wiping his hands on his apron, which is covered in dark stains. I guess he served a lot of chocolate that night. His voice is squeaky and raspy at the same time, and as he comes closer I can see that his face is deeply lined. His eyes glitter in the moonlight, and I can't see his teeth when he smiles. It's like they've all fallen out.

"I'm closed for the night," he tells us, taking a few more steps toward us. This time we all stand still, although Ripper grabs hold of me. Normally, I'd shake him off, but I don't. "Sorry, but—"

"It's okay," I say quickly. Beside me, Ripper nods vigorously in agreement. "We're not really hungry."

"Yeah," Will adds, with a nervous glance at me. There's just something creepy about the ice cream . . . er, I Scream . . . man. "We'll catch you next time."

The wizened little man hesitates, then shrugs. "Aw, what the heck." He gestures to the truck. "Help yourselves. It'll all be melted by morning, anyhow."

I don't know much about running a business, but it seems to me that the old man should store the leftover stuff in a working freezer. Will and even Ripper must've thought the same thing because we all share confused looks.

"Go ahead, kids," the man urges, gesturing to the truck. "I'm going home."

We probably should've thanked him, but we just stand there, watching the old guy disappear into the woods.

"Who lives in an empty forest?" I finally ask when I can't see his white apron moving through the trees. I turn to Will and Ripper, frowning. "And why is he giving away ice cream?"

Now that the strange man is gone, Will has regained his bravado. He smiles and shakes free of my hand, already heading toward the truck. "Who cares?" he asks over his shoulder. "It's free ice cream!"

He has a point, and I am also feeling more brave. I look down at Ripper. "What do you think?"

"I *would* like a popsicle," he admits, "now that we're here. And it's free."

I think about how I had to feed turtles for two weeks to get seven dollars, and about the tofu waiting at home, and I call to Will, "Wait up!"

A few moments later we are climbing into the truck, which smells way better than it looks. Like sugar cones, chocolate, and vanilla. Will is the first to step into the back, which is surprisingly roomy, but dark, until he reaches up overhead and finds a light like the kind most regular cars have.

"That's better," he says after clicking the switch and bathing the truck in a dim glow.

"We shouldn't leave that on too long," I remind him, edging my way into the back of the truck too, with Ripper on my heels. "My dad says those little lights drain your battery. . . ."

Then I stop talking because, as my eyes adjust to the light, I see that the walls of the truck are lined with photographs. Pictures of kids. Kids who look like they've eaten a lot of ice cream, if you get my meaning. Not to be rude, but it's true. And none of them look too happy. Their eyes are all wide, like they've been surprised by the camera's flash.

"Holy cow!" Will says, drawing my attention away from the pictures. He's opening a big silver bin and leaning over it. I quickly realize that he's opened a freezer. When the cool air hits the hot, humid summer night, a fog forms. Will tries to wave it away, but it starts to fill the truck. He doesn't seem to care. "Look at all this ice cream!"

"Lemme see!" Ripper shoves past me. He's warming to the adventure, now that sugar is involved. He leans over the freezer. "Wow!"

I get pretty curious too, and push Ripper out of the way. The freezer is filled with popsicles and cartons of ice cream, the flavors stamped on the tops. I squint and start to read out loud. "'Chocolate,' 'Rocky Road,' 'Neapolitan' . . ."

"Stop reading and start eating," Will urges, beginning to pull the lids off the cartons.

There is a lot of ice cream for us to sample. It's like the truck didn't sell anything that evening. Each tub is full to the top, the smooth surfaces, in pretty colors, just waiting to be ruined. Kind of like a fresh, snowy field that you want to mess up with footprints.

"Here," Ripper says. For once, he's been resourceful and located a bunch of plastic spoons. He hands them out.

Will accepts one. I do too. "Thanks."

Then we all take a moment to stare at one another, spoons held aloft.

"Are you sure we should do this?" I finally ask.

We seem doubtful. Then Will reminds us, "The old man says all this will go to waste. You're not supposed to waste food, right?"

That's true. And we are all hot and hungry after chasing down the truck. A moment later we are digging in, cramming our faces full of ice cream. Ripper seems to have forgotten that he wanted a simple popsicle. He's sitting cross-legged on the floor, a big tub of cookies and cream in his lap and a blissful expression on his face. His arm moves robotically, and he makes little *mmm* sounds now and then.

Will and I just keep making the rounds, sampling every flavor, again and again. Except for banana. I hate banana. But I make up for that by taking extra bites of rocky road.

A half hour later, the three of us are half sick. But so happy.

And feeling a little guilty.

"We should at least offer to pay something for all this," I say—although I don't reach for my seven dollars. I'm not sure how much the old man would charge for ice cream that was going to be ruined, anyhow. Then I look around the truck, which is kind of a mess. "We ate *a lot*. Maybe we should leave a dollar or two."

"Or . . ." Will looks mischievous. "We could come back tomorrow night. Thank the old guy and offer to pay. Maybe he won't take any money."

Ripper stands up, groaning. I swear, his belly looks bigger than it did an hour ago. But he understands that Will is angling to get more ice cream tomorrow. "Yeah," Ripper agrees. "We should come back!"

And that's how it starts.

Five nights that begin with us playing with the other kids in the vacant lot.

The song we hear in the distance.

"I scream, you scream . . . I scream, you scream . . ."

Dwight's worried expression as he heads home with his sister, Dot.

And the ice cream, which we never have to pay for because the old man always tells us, *"Help yourselves. It'll all be melted by morning, anyhow."*

By the sixth evening—the night before Will is supposed to go home—we're all fat and sluggish. I don't even really want ice cream anymore. But I know that Ripper and I will never be brave enough to go to the truck without Will. This is our last chance to eat as much ice cream as we want. When we hear the song, we rest our hands against our swollen stomachs and groan—but we trudge off together. Toward the west, around the corners, past the partially obscured sign. "Welcome to Nightingale Corners! Home of America's Only—"

The old man welcomes us, and we don't even offer to pay, like we did the last few nights. We just thank him and watch him walk into the forest in his stained apron. I don't know how or why it gets stained. He never seems to sell any ice cream.

As usual the tubs are all full, and we grab our plastic spoons and take our now-familiar places. Ripper sits down heavily to gorge on cookies and cream while Will and I dig into container after container after container.

Soon my stomach feels huge. It *is* huge. Just like the bellies of the alarmed-looking kids whose pictures hang inside the truck.

"Weird," I whisper through a mouthful of chocolate marshmallow.

Will has also put on a few pounds, and we bump against each other as he tries to reach the strawberry. "Sorry," he mumbles—just as we hear a loud rustling sound, and murmuring, outside the truck.

Will, Ripper, and I all stop eating, our spoons frozen in midair, halfway to our mouths.

"You should see what's outside," Will suggests, addressing me.

"Why me?" I complain as the rustling and murmuring grow louder. My heart's pounding a little. "Why not you?"

"You're closer to the door."

He's talking about the door in the back of the truck that the ice cream man would use to hand out treats and collect money. And I am the closest to it. It's also pretty obvious that we need to see what's going on. It sounds like the truck is surrounded by . . . something.

"I'm scared," Ripper admits in a whisper. He's still sitting on the floor and holds the lid of his ice cream carton like a flimsy shield. "Maybe we should stay still, and see if it . . . they . . . go away."

Only whoever's outside doesn't leave. Something bumps into the truck. The whole thing rocks.

I'm really scared, but I feel like we have to find out what's happening.

Will nods, silently letting me know that he agrees, and I reach for a latch I'd never really noticed before with fingers that shake like crazy. Then, taking a deep breath, I fling open the door, only to wince as a bright light assaults my eyes.

"You guys really scared me," I say, resting one hand against my chest.

The truck is surrounded by a whole bunch of people, including kids I recognize from the vacant lot. We've played together all week, and I've started to learn their names. It's hard for me to see because somebody took an obnoxious flash photo of me just as I opened the door, but I try to greet a few of my new friends. "Hey, Alec. Mike. Lucie . . ."

Then I turn to give Will and Ripper a reassuring, if shaky, smile, in case they don't realize we're not really in danger. They are hanging back from the door. So much for Will being a big, tough guy.

I face the crowd again and cock my head. "Why are you all here?" I'm struck by an idea, and I grow concerned. Especially since, as my eyes readjust to the darkness, I realize that everyone seems to be holding shiny, silver utensils.

"Did you all hear about the free ice cream?" I ask. "Because I don't really know if it's for everybody."

"It's not for everybody," somebody says.

I recognize the voice, and I look down to see that Dwight has pushed his way to the front of the crowd. He seems more apologetic than ever before. And, for some reason, he's holding not a spoon, for ice cream, but a fork. And a knife.

I get a funny, tickly feeling in the pit of my stomach and look around to discover that no one seems prepared to eat ice cream. Everyone carries a fork. And a knife.

Except for the old man in the stained apron. He has a camera slung around his neck. And a *cleaver* in his hand.

"Maxine?" Ripper's voice is high and nervous.

"Max?" Will sounds anxious too.

They've finally stepped up behind me and are peering over my shoulder.

I meet the old man's gaze for just a moment, and he shrugs—a halfhearted gesture of apology—before snapping Will's and Ripper's photos too.

"You fattened 'em up nicely this year, ice cream man . . . or should I say, butcher!" someone calls out, laughing. A cruel, harsh sound. "And with three of 'em, we'll remember this feast for years to come!"

I can't believe what I *think* is happening. And I can't seem to form any words, either.

I just look down at skinny, pale Dwight, our only hope for an ally. He'd tried to warn us that our gluttony would have consequences. But tonight, the moonlight glints off his glasses—and his utensils. And he sounds only partly apologetic—and mainly hungry—as he licks his lips and tells me, Ripper, and Will, "I'm sorry. But you *do* look tasty."

There is this strange moment of silence, and I feel like I've been stuck in the ice cream freezer for two days. I'm frozen solid and can't move a muscle. Not even to look at Will or Ripper. I just keep staring at Dwight's knife and fork.

Then Ripper, who might not really understand what's happening, whimpers, and that seems to launch Will into action. I'm still stuck in place, but he pushes past me, nearly knocking me out the door. I teeter, about to fall, while Will jumps into the driver's seat. I hear him moving around, making a lot of noise, but I have no idea what he's doing.

Maybe he's searching frantically for some way to call for help? If so, he's too late. The townspeople stumble forward like zombies, glassy-eyed and practically drooling. They're led by the butcher, whose cleaver glitters in the moonlight. And those stains on his apron . . . I guess I know what those are now.

"Will?" I cry, finding my voice. He's still rummaging around in the front seat. The old man reaches for my arm. I haven't quite regained my balance, and my knees are wobbly, but I try to pull back. I dare to glance at Ripper, who crouches, wide-eyed, by the freezers. "Don't move!" I warn him. I have to protect my little brother for as long as possible. Then I call again, "Will, help me!"

He doesn't answer. Or, if he does, I don't hear him over the roar of the engine, which rumbles to life. The song begins to play. "*I scream . . . you scream . . .*"

And I do. I scream at the top of my lungs when the old man grasps my wrist with his free hand, tugging on me—just as Will, who has never driven anything in his life, as far as I know—presses down on the gas pedal. The truck lurches a few feet forward, and I lurch too, then try to pull back. But the little man has a strong grip. I'm not going to escape. Will and Ripper can, though.

"Just drive!" I yell at Will. "Go!"

I look away from the butcher long enough to see Will twist around in the seat, trying to figure out what to do. Some of the townspeople head to the front of the truck, like they're ready to block us. I can hear them muttering, and through the windshield, I see their shadowy figures moving to surround us.

"Go!" I urge Will again, even as I try one last time to twist free of the old man's grasp. I use every ounce of my strength to pull backward, and manage to drag him halfway into the truck.

I can't hold him for long, and he opens his mouth to laugh at me—then his eyes grow wide with surprise, his lips form an O, and *he* screams. In pain. Because Ripper has sprung up like an angry dog and sunk his teeth into the butcher's wrist. In a split second—probably *for* just a split second—I'm free.

"Drive!" I holler at Will. I grab Ripper and pull him back with me. We both fall against the freezers. "DRIVE!"

My parents never believed what I told them about that night. Not even when they saw the I Scream truck, banged up and parked on our front lawn. My family is only moving out of town now because my mom and dad are ashamed that Ripper and I had been accessories to a vehicle theft.

Will hadn't been lying when he'd boasted about being able to steal a car. Like I'd suspected, he didn't know much about driving, though. We'd had a few minor accidents on the way to my house, where we'd tumbled out of the still-running truck and run inside to tell my parents the whole tale. They'd called the cops—not to save us from killer townsfolk, but to turn us in and teach us a lesson. But by the time the police arrived, the I Scream truck had vanished.

"Ripper, you okay?" I quietly ask my little brother, who sits in the back seat of our packed-up station wagon, staring out the window as we drive out of town. Forever, I hope. He can't corroborate my story, because he hasn't talked since that night. Maybe that's okay. As more days pass, I find it harder and harder to believe that our neighbors actually planned to eat us. I've almost convinced myself that the whole thing was a big prank.

Smiling, I shake Ripper's arm, trying to coax him back to normal. "Are you ever gonna say a word again?"

Ripper doesn't even look at me. He just keeps staring out the window. Then, just as we pass the awful spot where the I Scream truck used to be parked, leaving Nightingale Corners behind us, my little brother raises his hand, points his finger—and screams bloody murder.

"AAAAAAHHH!"

I spin around in my seat, expecting to see the truck parked in the clearing.

But it's not there.

All I see is the wooden sign, which is rattling in the breeze caused by our passing car. The gust of wind also sweeps aside the bushes, so for just a split second I can read every word.

"Welcome to Nightingale Corners! Home of America's Only Cannibal Feast!"

THE WITCH OF BYRON'S BAYOU

BY HEATHER GRAHAM

A **BLOODCURDLING SCREAM CAUSED LIAM MCCARTHY** to jump—even though he knew it was just his sister, Emmy, who was doing the screaming.

And Emmy screamed over anything—absolutely anything—and everything. She'd probably seen a spider; there were a few of them out here in the old house.

Liam told himself he should try to be patient with her. Emmy wasn't doing so well with the move. While their mom said it was the best thing in the world for them, Emmy obviously didn't agree. She was being such a . . .

Well, he knew what he was thinking was something he wasn't supposed to be thinking. It just wasn't "politically correct" and all, but honestly!

She was being such a *girl*.

Emmy screamed again

Liam left his perch on his bed in the garret room up in the attic he had claimed for himself and ran down the stairs.

There was Emmy, just standing in the middle of the parlor—screaming.

"What?" he demanded. *"What?"* He didn't see a darned thing.

She turned to him, pointing at the fireplace, shaking. "I saw . . . I saw her! She was right there. Right there! Like, clear as day. The witch. The old witch of the bayou they talk about! She was there, right there."

Liam inhaled and exhaled, still staring at his sister with surprise.

No, she hadn't wanted to make the move, but. . . .

Money. Money was tough for their little family right now. Their dad had just been deployed and talking to him was hard; he was in the Middle East somewhere, and even he didn't know where he was going to be day to day. Only one thing was for sure: he was off fighting and wouldn't be home for a very long time. The store where their mom had been working in the city had closed down, but when they'd been out to the bayou for Auntie Kate's funeral, Missy Dandridge at the Pink Partridge had told their mom, Carrie McCarthy, that she could have a job there anytime, and it might be a really good thing if she came home, anyway. Auntie Kate was gone; the old plantation house on the hill belonged to Carrie and her family now—it would be a great place for the McCarthys to live until Brendan came home from his military service for good. And they might just like it out in the tiny town of Byron.

"This place is freaky and scary and terrifying! And I won't stay here!" Emmy insisted.

"You're not going to freak me out," Liam told his sister. "I think the stories about the witch of the bayou are pretty cool. She just tried to help people. Some creepy old dude killed her because she didn't want anything to do with him."

Liam hadn't had the least problem with the move. They weren't more than twenty miles from New Orleans, and everything he knew about

Byron's Bayou was darned cool. The pirates had used the waterways and lived and counted treasure on some of the high ground here. Civil War soldiers had fought and died on the battlefields by the Mississippi River, and the graveyards were full of cool, old vaults and mausoleums and such. The old trees were so tall and strong they broke through gravestones; and at night, and especially when fog rolled around, the decaying old church and burial ground were eerie and supercreepy.

He'd had good times there already with his friends Jennie Oliver and Hank Leewood; they loved to go there at night; find a little patch of land just outside the church and graveyard, with its little stone wall; start a fire; and roast s'mores while they made up stories to creep one another out. They'd freaked themselves out and run home only once!

Liam figured he knew why Emmy was getting scared; this was the first time they were going to be alone in the house at night. There wasn't anything all that close to them, though the old Dandridge house had never been a big plantation. Liam had learned in school what most people thought of as a plantation was something huge and white, with great big columns, where only rich people lived.

It really just meant "farm"—but once, this place had been a nice enough farmhouse. It was two stories tall, built around 1820, and it still had a supercool curved stairway, giant marble mantels, cool little garrets, and a dumbwaiter for when people used to send food straight up a tiny elevator from the kitchen to those waiting for it upstairs.

And Liam had also loved Auntie Kate—she'd been the coolest. She always told the best stories, and she even had wild black-and-white hair herself and could have scared any kid in a horror movie.

"I saw a witch!" Emmy insisted, shaking. "I saw her. It was as if she were jumping out of the fireplace at me!"

"She was jumping at you. And then?"

"And then I screamed!"

Liam shook his head, and he saw the flash of anger sweep through Emmy's eyes. She was older than him—by a year. And—or so she liked to tell him—a thirteen-year-old girl was way more mature than a twelve-year-old boy.

"You're acting like a baby," Liam said. "Mom only works part-time so she can be with us as much as possible with Dad away. Act too much like a jerk, and she'll be scared to leave us alone to go to work!"

"I'm not acting like a baby!" Emmy protested, but the doorbell rang, and she screamed again.

"It's just Hank and Jennie," Liam told Emmy. "They're coming over; we're going to play video games or watch a movie or something. You can watch with us, if you want. I mean, if you can keep from screaming. Jennie doesn't scream through everything."

"Her brother is older, more mature—and protective!" Emmy announced in a huff. Well, of course. Liam was pretty sure Emmy had a crush on Jennie's brother, Jake. Jake was pretty cool most of the time. But then, Liam knew Jake wasn't *his* brother—he was Jennie's—and that made all the difference in the world.

Jake was already tall, and he'd grown some major muscle. Liam had to admit that he didn't have that kind of muscle, though he was a darned good baseball player. He could whip around the bases like nothing.

Girls tend to prefer football guys, he thought. Like Jake. Except for Jennie. But she was just cool with her light brown ponytail and sizzling hazel eyes. She could laugh, she could play in the dirt—and she *never* screamed. She was just the best girl ever.

The doorbell rang again. Liam hurried to the entry and threw open the door, expecting his friends.

It wasn't Jennie, but it was Hank. "Come in, come in. We've got some cool movies to watch."

"Just Emmy here?" Hank asked. "I mean you and Emmy? Where's your mom?"

"Working."

"Oh yeah. That's right; Saturday night. So what do you want to watch? I brought a new haunted house movie; it's cool. My mom says it's our age group," Hank said. "I think you'll like this, Emmy—it has the actor you think is so cool in it. What's-his-name? Jack Black!"

"She can watch—as long as she doesn't scream every second!" Liam said. "Jennie's coming over too."

"Yeah, I just saw her—her and her big bro, Jake. They're walking through the cemetery. Jake was stopping to read some headstone; they have a history thing on it next week in school—you know, on the battles that were fought here. I figure they'll be here soon."

"We can go out and find them if you want," Liam offered.

"Juvenile! Playing in a graveyard!" Emmy said.

"Yeah, whatever," Liam said. "We're going to go to meet them." He started out the door, Hank tailing behind him.

Emmy came running after them.

"Hey! You just said this was juvenile."

"And I told Mom I'd watch you!"

"And you're chicken! *Bawk, bawk, bawk.* Emmy thinks the witch is in the house. You know, the old witch who supposedly died about a thousand years ago," Liam told Hank.

"Cool! You really saw a witch?" Hank asked Emmy.

"No! She's a freak who screams at everything!" Liam said. "Don't feed into it!"

Emmy rapped him on the back of his head. "And you're a freak who likes to play in old cemeteries!"

"Hey, well, you know, you're both right!" Hank said cheerfully.

Hank led the way. There was a patch of scraggly forest and brush right next to Liam's new home, and where the brush ended, the first of the old tombstones could be found. The cemetery had aboveground vaults and belowground vaults—they were up on a hill here, so graves could be dug pretty deep.

Many of the old graves were falling apart; they were so old that the writing was worn clean off them. Some were really cool, with old death's heads and skeletal cherublike things. Liam thought the vaults and mausoleums were the neatest. Some were just kind of sealed and not so big. Some had iron gates and could be opened, just like miniatures of the big mausoleums that could be found at some cemeteries.

This one was all overgrown with vines and weeds. And now, with the sun going down, it was exceptionally cool and creepy. A little bit of mist was rising around them.

"Okay," Emmy said. "This is it. We've come far enough!"

"What do you mean 'far enough'?" Liam asked. "You know, Lover boy's out here somewhere. Lover boy isn't afraid of cemeteries."

"You little creep!" Emmy said.

"You like Jake?" Hank asked her.

"Liam is being a little cockroach!" Emmy said.

"I was just asking," Hank said, "because Jennie thinks he likes you."

"Oh . . . Oh, well, cool, then," Emmy said.

"Hey!"

They heard a shout, and looked across a bunch of old stones, and through a trail of the mausoleums, they could see Jake and Jennie.

Liam started running toward them.

Then he heard it again.

A scream; a bloodcurdling scream.

He swung around, nearly tripping over one of the evil-looking little gargoyle things that stuck out of the ground.

It was Emmy.

Naturally, it was Emmy.

And she's being such a jerk, such a big jerk! Now she's probably screaming because Jake is there. And she wants him to run to her rescue and hold the silly screaming ninny she is.

But he was Emmy's brother.

Just a year younger.

And so he began to trot back to Emmy.

Jake and Jennie had come running toward the sound of Emmy's scream, of course. And, being a good friend, Hank too came running across the broken stones and through the old vaults.

Jake was a pretty manly man for a teenage kid; he was already by Emmy's side.

He had an arm around her.

But Emmy was still shaking. She didn't look like a girl who had just been screaming to get a boy to put his arm around her.

"She was there, I'm telling you; she was there! She wears all black, and her hair is black but has some wild, like, white in it. . . . She's a witch; you can see she's a witch. She was there, waving her arms at me all crazy like!" Emmy was telling Jake.

Jake was frowning. Frowning himself, Liam looked at Jennie's older brother. "Come on, Jake, it's not like she doesn't have a wicked imagination."

And Jake stared at him. "There was something . . . something in the bushes before," he said. "I was already getting the creeps, telling Jennie we needed to get to your place, when you all came and Emmy started screaming."

Liam just stared at Jake. It was dumb. Just dumb.

"You believe Emmy saw a long-dead witch who supposedly lived around here?" Liam asked.

"I'm not feeling really good out here," Jennie murmured.

Liam had to look around Jake's body to see Jennie. She was serious too. She offered Liam a weak smile. "My mom was okay with us walking over to your house, but she called a minute ago to say she's going to come and pick Jake and me up in a few hours—she doesn't want us walking back."

"Your mom thinks there a witch in the cemetery?" Hank asked, disbelieving.

"No!" Jennie said. "No, she's just . . . I don't know. Maybe it's just that kind of night."

Liam sighed. "There's not even a full moon. And hey, I read. You guys do a lot of freaking out—I do a lot of reading. The so-called 'witch' was never evil. She was killed by an evil general because she wanted nothing to do with him. She was good and helped people and cured them. So—"

"There's something out here," Jennie said, ignoring Liam and turning to look at her brother. "I'm scared."

"Emmy, look what you've done!" Liam said.

"No, no, Emmy didn't do it!" Jennie protested. "It just seemed creepy out already. We were, like, kind of hearing things."

"Like the breeze moving through the trees. Come on, guys! I'm the one who just moved here from the city," Liam reminded them. "You're all from the country!" he said, looking from Jake to Jennie and on to Hank.

They all just stared back at him.

Then suddenly, a flock of birds shot straight up into the sky. It was like a movie, there were so many of them, and the way they moved. . . .

It was like they formed a dark shadow monster in the sky.

Emmy screamed again.

Good grief, could that girl scream.

"The church!" Jake said. "The church! It's holy, or whatever! Demons can't go in a church, right?"

Liam just couldn't believe it.

Birds.

And they were all running.

And they'd left him!

"Hey!" he shouted.

It was growing dark; he didn't really want to be standing there alone in the old graveyard.

"Hey!" he shouted again. And he ran after them. "You guys have all gone nuts!"

"Locked!" Jennie said, pushing at the door.

"No, no, the Reverend Hopkins never locks the church. He says that's one of the great things about being here—you don't have to lock the church! He likes it open— He likes people to come and go when they want," Jake said.

He proved his point. Jennie just hadn't pushed down hard enough on the handle.

Jake opened the door.

They all tumbled in.

Jennie let out a mild expletive. "It's dark!" she said.

"Don't swear in church!" Hank warned.

"There are long matches there for the votive candles . . . and it's not pitch-dark—look, those little floor lights are on up by the altar," Liam said.

Jennie lit several of the votive candles. "I'll bring money later, I promise!" she whispered, looking toward the altar and the cross.

"Should we lock the door now?" Hank asked.

"I thought evil entities couldn't come into the church," Liam said.

"Maybe we should to be safe," Jennie said.

"Honestly? I really don't think evil entities can enter a church!" Emmy said, looking around nervously. "I mean, I don't think so."

"Maybe it's a *rougarou*," Hank said thoughtfully. The *rougarou* was a famous monster, particular to their area. It came from their distant French heritage and was a monster like a werewolf.

"There's no *rougarou*," Liam said.

They jumped as they heard a sudden, strident sound.

It was only Jennie's phone. She gasped and then laughed as she answered it. She looked around at them as she said, "Hi, Mom."

She went very still and silent, listening to what her mother had to say. "Yes, Mom, of course. Um . . ." She paused, looking around at all of them. "We're actually at the church right now, Mom. It's all good. Well, you know Jake and his research. . . ."

She listened again.

And then she said, "Love you, Mom," and hung up.

"What? What? What was that all about?" Jake asked.

"Yes, please, what's going on?" Emmy demanded.

"Jennie?" Liam asked.

"She's worried—my mom is worried," she said.

"Why?" Jake asked.

Jennie looked around at all of them again. "Some guy escaped from Angola State Prison," she said in a rush. "I guess he was a really bad guy. He was supposed to be maximum security . . . um, on death row. I don't know what happened—you know Mom, Jake, she gets a little crazy when she's worried. Anyway, he's out. Hey, the prison is almost two hours from here, but. . . ."

"Lock the doors!" Emmy said.

"What?" Jake asked, looking confused.

"Lock the doors! Maybe bad entities can't enter churches, but I'm pretty darned sure that a crazy killer could break in. Oh my Lord! There's a killer on the loose!" Emmy said. "Jennie, um, is your mom coming to get you? Can she get us all home? Or to a police station? This is scary—really scary."

"She's coming, but she had to go to Baton Rouge today. It's going to take some time for her to get here," Jennie said. "She said to make sure that it's all locked up here, and that we should sit tight. She said maybe Hank's mom or, Emmy, maybe your mom could come get us?"

Liam looked over at his sister. He nodded. "This is real, right? Some guy—*some guy who committed a crime bad enough to be on death row*—is out there?"

"And a witch!" Emmy murmured.

Liam swung around, looking out of the church. The little nightlights up by the altar were really dim.

The votive candles that they'd lit weren't bright either.

The moon had risen; it bathed the graveyard in a soft glow.

Liam found himself staring at one of the old vaults. It had the name Windsor sculpted into the stone over the door. The thing was big—had to house nine or ten people. The gates to it opened—meaning that people could go in to leave flowers or tokens, as if it was a regular big, shared mausoleum.

He didn't know any Windsors. Never had. And he'd never heard of anyone visiting a deceased loved one named Windsor.

Now, as he stared out through the old cut-glass windows of the church, Liam saw something. The moonlight allowed him just a glimpse of *something*.

Something that seemed like a shadow—growing in the Windsor vault, getting bigger and bigger, darker and darker.

He was scared, of course. They were all scared. They didn't need to scare themselves or give one another the heebie-jeebies talking about local ghosts and legends.

There was a killer on the loose.

But . . .

He suddenly felt Emmy grip his hand.

She was staring at the tomb as well.

His sister could see what he was seeing.

And for once, she didn't scream. Maybe, for once, she was actually just a little too scared to scream.

"What is it?" Jake asked.

A gust of wind suddenly seemed to stir through the church.

The candles went out.

Then there was a sizzling sound—and the little night-lights by the altar went out as well.

HEATHER GRAHAM

"What the heck?" Jake murmured.

"A ghost . . . a witch . . . ," Emmy said, barely forming the words and causing sound to come from her mouth.

"More likely a flesh-and-blood killer," Liam said. But, he realized, his voice was shaky. He was terrified. He didn't know what he believed himself.

Something struck one of the windows. Glass shattered.

Emmy screamed.

They all screamed.

And the loudest, worst scream, Liam realized, was coming from himself.

Then, just as they had all screamed, they all fell silent.

The night seemed to be excruciatingly still as they stood in darkness—eased only by the moonlight outside that fell upon tombstones and cherubs and death's-heads and angels and made them all glow with a weird and translucent light.

They listened.

Hank began to whimper when they heard a banging sound that came from the back of the church.

Then he screamed again—and bolted out the front door.

"Hank!" Jennie shouted.

Then they heard the chuckle from the back of the church. It was deep and rich, the kind of chuckle that made the hair seem to stand up all over Liam's body. For a moment he was so cold he was afraid he'd crack if he moved, just like an ice sculpture hit by a hammer.

"Children, children, children— Oh, little children, come to me!" came the voice.

He was at the back of the church. Liam was pretty sure that he wasn't an evil entity from the graveyard; he sounded like a man.

A bad one. A very bad one.

Liam could feel his sister next to him, feel her fear—and he knew she was going to scream. He reached over and clamped his hand on her mouth and drew her down to the floor.

They couldn't see the man at the back of the church.

He couldn't see them.

"Don't scream, don't scream—please, don't scream!" Liam whispered. "Emmy, you and Jennie go—you get out, you get down to the parsonage, you make a call, you get the cops up here now!"

"He'll see us open the door," Jennie protested

"I won't leave you," Emmy told Liam. "I'm supposed to be looking after you!"

"I'll go!" Jake volunteered quickly. "Jennie and I will get help back to you."

Liam saw the way Emmy looked at Jake. He wasn't so sure she was going to have a crush on him when morning came. But that didn't much matter. Hoping morning did come at all right now seemed to be the right thing!

"Sure, Jake, you go—Emmy and I will run to the back where the vaults and mausoleums are all at weird angles. He can't run everywhere," Liam said.

"We're gone! Good luck, everyone!" Jake said.

He grabbed Jennie's hand, and they bolted out the door.

"We have to get out too now, down low—down real low!" Liam said.

Emmy nodded, catching his hand. She was shaking so badly he was afraid he wasn't going to be able to run with her.

But she did just as he said; Jennie and Jake were obviously

disappearing. If the convict at the back of the church had been watching them and counting, he'd know that there were two more kids.

Hopefully, he'd believe that they were still in the church.

Jake and Jennie burst out of the graveyard, running to the left. They'd reach a main street eventually, but they'd have to go through the woods first.

Liam wasn't sure why they'd gone that way; straight would have led to the road. Heading to the right would have led them through the trees and brush between the graveyard and the house on the hill where Liam and Emmy had so recently come to live. . . .

Liam had Emmy's hand. He chose to run toward the right.

He bounded over a sarcophagus-like tomb with a memorial to Jonathan Drake, CSA, Civil War, Bradford's Company B. He nearly tripped on the broken knee of a praying cherub.

"Liam!"

Emmy jerked at his hand and brought him closer to her, behind the giant wings of an angel that looked over a tomb for the veterans of foreign wars.

"What?" he asked in a hushed whisper.

"Behind us—he's right behind us!" Emmy said.

And she was right. He could hear the footsteps, heard the furtive sound of the man coming after them. Liam barely dared to breathe. He held tight to Emmy's hand. Neither of them moved; Liam knew Emmy was trying just as hard as him to stay perfectly still.

They saw him then.

He was still in his prison uniform. He was holding something that he tapped silently against his leg. It wasn't a gun; it was some kind of a stick or a pole.

It was a tire iron, Liam realized.

He was walking, walking on by them. He stopped now and then, and swung around, as if trying to catch them somewhere, catch them off guard.

"Come out, come out, come out and play, children. I know you're here!" he said.

Liam heard Emmy swallow.

"Shh," he warned her.

The man kept walking. He was going deeper and deeper into the graveyard—heading in the wrong direction. Any second now, Liam and Emmy could turn . . . and run into the brush and trees and back to their house. By now, even chicken-poop Jake would have figured out that he needed to dial 911, not that Emmy and Liam were keeping the convict busy!

It was time; it was time to move. He squeezed his sister's hand.

They left the angel. They started to tiptoe down the ragged trail through the graves that led away from the convict.

Quiet, quiet, quiet. . . .

And then, to Liam's horror, he sneezed.

He and Emmy both froze.

"Aha! There you are, my little darlings, my precious little people! Old Ollie doesn't want to hurt you now; Old Ollie just wants to play."

"Run!" Liam told Emmy.

"I'm running!" she promised.

And she was running. Emmy could run. She was really just as good at running as she was at screaming.

But then she tripped. She tripped over the in-ground grave and broken stone of Abraham Moriarty, "born June 5, 1899, departed his earthly coil, May 14, 1978."

"Emmy!" Liam shouted.

He stopped himself, reaching for her hand. He knew that the convict—Old Ollie, as he'd called himself—was now coming for them at a lope.

Old Ollie could run too, or so it seemed!

"Liam, go, just run!" Emmy said.

"No! Come on, come on, get up!"

"I can't! My ankle!"

Liam could feel the earth itself pounding as the convict Old Ollie came after them. He'd be on them in just seconds.

But . . .

No matter what, he couldn't leave Emmy.

"Go!"

"No, you're my sister."

"Liam—"

"Don't get all gushy! Mom and Dad would kill me," he said.

But Emmy could barely move. It was everything Liam could do just to stagger on, trying to support her weight.

And then Emmy screamed.

It was one of her real-true-most bloodcurdling, horrible screams ever.

Liam stopped and looked ahead.

They'd come to the massive Windsor mausoleum. And the black shadow that had seemed to sit upon it earlier had grown immense.

But as Liam stared ahead—his heart thundering—the shadow seemed to twist and form, grow darker, and then . . .

The shadow descended down to Earth, right in front of them. And the shadow was a woman; she was dressed in black. She had wild black-and-white hair that seemed to flow and move and sweep around her head, as if it were some strange kind of a crown.

She looked at the two of them, beckoning them forward.

"Ohhhh . . . not on your life!" Liam whispered.

Emmy was still; dead still. It almost seemed as if she pressed Liam behind her, and then . . .

Emmy smiled.

"It's all right," she said. "It's all right."

The woman nodded an acknowledgment to her and went on past them.

The wind picked up; dust and leaves and little branches started to swirl and sweep around on the ground.

The mist became a fog, all wrapped up in that whirl of nature.

Then . . .

Lightning zigzagged across the sky.

Thunder clapped.

Liam groaned. "Of course!" he murmured as he and Emmy turned as one.

The convict—Old Ollie—was no longer coming for them. He stood at a halt, mesmerized, staring at the woman in the long black gown.

She lifted her arm, pointing toward Old Ollie.

He was suddenly lifted off the ground. About ten feet up, he was spun around and around and around.

Liam watched, blinking, amazed.

He heard the sound of sirens. He knew that Jake, Jennie, or Hank had gotten out a call.

Old Ollie spun and spun.

And Old Ollie crashed back to the ground.

As suddenly as it had come, the whirl of the wind was gone. The mist seemed to dissipate.

Liam stood with his sister, beneath the giant wing of a praying angel and before the great iron gates that led to the tomb that read *Windsor.*

Police were hurrying along the path toward the convict, Old Ollie—and Liam and Emmy.

"Down on your knees, hands behind your back!" one of the policemen shouted.

"Yes, yes!" Old Ollie said, staring at Liam and Emmy, as if they were demons themselves. "Yes, yes! Take me back, take me back, I want my cage!" he shouted.

A tall, attractive policewoman made her way past her partner—who was putting cuffs on Old Ollie—and hurried up to Emmy and Liam.

"Are you two all right?"

"Fine, just fine," Emmy said.

"You two led him on a merry chase; you survived him," the policewoman said. "Excellent work!"

Liam and Emmy looked at each other. He knew they were both tempted to explain that the legendary witch of Byron's Bayou had really saved the day. No matter how Old Ollie might scream and rant and rave, no one was really going to believe him.

A week later Liam walked through the woods on his way to the graveyard. He had a handful of flowers he intended to set around the Windsor mausoleum.

There was no one about, and the graveyard was a little misty, but Liam figured graveyards tended to be creepy just because people didn't really keep up with them.

They forgot.

They'd forgotten about Elizabeth Windsor.

He'd gotten the real story from his mother; he and Emmy had tried to tell her the truth of what had happened. Of course, between them, their words got more and more garbled as they went.

But their mom had just listened and nodded and hugged them and kissed them and tucked them into bed.

And the next day she'd told them about Elizabeth.

She'd been a healer. She'd grown all kinds of wonderful herbs, and she could help people when their stomachs hurt, and she could put poultices on bites and wounds and scratches. She was beloved—until a general who had come in during the Spanish rule had wanted her to come and live with him. He'd been a cruel man, and the people hated him—just as Elizabeth Windsor had hated him.

In the middle of the night, she'd been dragged out of her house, taken before the church, hanged, and then burned to a crisp.

However, the family had always known where to find her remains; sixty years later, when a Windsor had become sheriff of the parish—an American holding by then!—he'd dug up what remained of his great-great-aunt and had her remains placed in the tomb.

People had been seeing her now and then for ages. . . .

Most often, they were afraid!

Liam placed his flowers—violets and roses—around the tomb. He paused in front of it, at the massive iron gates. "Thank you!" he said.

He was just about to head home when he froze, fear slipping into him.

He heard a scream.

A loud, horrible, bloodcurdling scream.

He gasped for breath; it was Emmy. He'd recognize that scream anywhere. . . .

He found energy; found a way to move. He bounded around the Windsor tomb and came to the little area by the giant winged angel.

There was an old concrete bench there, almost as worn as some of the tombstones.

Emmy was on the bench.

The *witch*—or whatever ghostly remnant it was that remained of Elizabeth Windsor—sat on the bench with her.

Emmy smiled brilliantly at her brother. "Liam! Elizabeth is helping me out here. I'm going to try out for the school video project—I want to play the heroine. She has a lot of screaming to do. Elizabeth thinks I'm really good! See?"

Emmy began to scream again. That horrible icy scream . . .

Liam smiled at Emmy, waved to the witch . . .

And ran.

BLOODSTONE

BY PHIL MATHEWS

CAN'T TAKE ANY MORE OF this torture! NO MORE!" I screamed.

"Yikes. Are you okay?" an unfamiliar voice said.

"Who said that?" I said, looking around what I thought was my empty bedroom.

"That isn't *torture*, that's *homework*. You're fine."

I looked all over my bedroom but couldn't see where the voice was coming from. "Where are you?"

"Behind you, but you can't see me or touch me. It's against the rules," an older man's voice said.

The voice came from over my left shoulder, but I turned and saw nothing. "If you're really here, prove—"

I heard an exhale from behind me and turned back to see the paper I was supposed to be writing fly off my desk and float to the floor like a feather. I sat in my chair, motionless, staring at the empty sheet with my mouth hanging open. "My homework!"

"Looks like a blank paper with your name on it, Greg. By the way, I'm Larry. Sorry to rush you, but we have to stop the ghost of Dillard Blake from killing someone in this house tonight. You know Dillard Blake, the seaman, don't you?"

"Dillard Blake? The one they made the rhyme about? 'Dillard Blake, Dillard Blake, if he sees you, your life he'll take. Never caught, free to roam, finally stopped by a bleeding stone.' That guy? I didn't think he was real."

"He was real, and he *was* finally caught after leaving a blood trail, so now he's cursed to leave one just before he kills."

"He's got quite a curse. How can I help?" Larry had my full attention, which isn't always an easy thing to do. Maybe it was because he hadn't told me who Blake was going to kill.

"If you follow my instructions, we can stop Blake from killing your tutor in this house tonight."

"Laura? Why would Blake want to kill her? She's only in high school." Of course, I was only twelve, so who was I to talk?

"Blake never needed a reason to kill before and still doesn't. Tonight it's your tutor, Laura, unless we stop him."

"What are you, a guardian angel?" Laura was nice enough to have a guardian angel.

"Not much of one. As I said, it's against the rules for me to even touch anyone. How about if I be the angel and you be the guardian? We'll be a guardian angel together."

"What can *I* do? I'm in sixth grade, and I already need tutoring on my English over the summer."

"Don't worry about Blake, he's just a bloodthirsty, murderous ghost. Focus on saving Laura, and you can stop him."

My head felt hot. If Larry didn't want me to worry about Blake, he wasn't very good with words. "I think I'd have a better chance at an A in English than stopping a bloodthirsty ghost. Can't *you* do something?"

"The rules stop me. There are lots of rules here. But Blake has rules too. Once you save Laura, he'll be gone."

"But I don't know how."

"There will be a moment when something terrible can happen. It'll only last for a few seconds, and then it'll be over. Watch out for her at that moment, and you'll both be fine."

"How will I know when that is?"

"Once Blake arrives. You can't miss it. First, you'll hear him humming 'Blow the Man Down,' which is kind of a dum, dum, dum-da-dum, dum. And then you'll see a blood trail you can follow. It'll look like the red specks on that bloodstone you're wearing around your neck. Follow the signs and protect Laura."

"I don't—I don't think I can handle this."

"Of course you can—with my help, anyway."

"Really? Why is that?" I waited, but there was no reply. Larry left me talking to an empty room. It would've been embarrassing if there were anyone there to hear me.

I took my English homework to the dining room table and watched Laura cook up mac and cheese with bacon while I pretended to work. It was hard to believe *anyone* would want to hurt her. She had straight blond hair pulled back and tied behind her head; was a little over five feet tall, maybe just an inch taller than me; and usually wore bright colors—a pink shirt and white pants today. She was also kind and had dimples when she smiled. I would see the dimples when she was especially pleased with my schoolwork—which means I rarely saw them. Maybe Larry was mistaken and Blake was after someone else.

"Are you sure you're working?"

"I'm trying. I guess I must be hungry. And it isn't as if this elephant I'm reading about is as interesting as Harry Potter or Sherlock Holmes."

"Dinner is almost ready. Soon you'll have eaten, and you can go back to your *required* reading. When you finish the required reading, you can read whatever you want."

"So my reward for reading would be more reading? You're going to make a great teacher someday," I said sarcastically.

Laura ignored me and continued, "Let's stick to a schedule. After you eat you'll have an additional twenty minutes to work while I clean the kitchen, and then we can review what you've done before your mother gets home. When's it due again?"

"In two weeks, when school starts."

"Correct. That time will be gone before you know it."

"Yeah. Be careful around that stove, it looks hot."

"I'm always careful. Pasta's done . . . just need the strainer."

Laura got a stepstool out and put it under the cupboard above the stove. Once she stepped on the top step of the stool, the humming started. "Dum, dum, dum-da-dum, dum."

Blake was here! I couldn't see him, just like Larry said, but I knew where he was going. And then drops of red started appearing on the white kitchen tile. The trail was moving toward Laura! I gasped and then sprang out of my chair, taking three quick steps toward her before I stumbled.

"Whoa—" Laura's feet shuffled as the chair beneath her tipped and then fell away. I slammed into the counter, but regained my balance in time to see Laura's head falling backward and her feet swinging upward, with the hard stone tile floor waiting beneath her.

I took one more step and started my best into-second-base slide when I heard her scream. It was loud and unnerving. I never saw anyone that frightened before. My hands shook as I stretched toward Laura. My slide continued, and she fell right into my arms. I caught and braced her head and shoulders, gently holding them in my hands and lap.

Laura's feet slammed onto the floor, and I slid into another cupboard, which made a cracking noise, but at least she didn't land on her head. The humming had stopped and was replaced by the echoes of Laura's scream, and then silence.

I could see Laura's teary eyes looking up at me as her head remained in my hands and lap.

"Are you okay?"

Laura nodded before speaking. "Ow."

She sat up, and I placed my hands on her back for support.

"If you're hurt, I can get on the phone and call for help."

"I'm fine, but I think I broke your bloodstone." She pointed at the floor next to me. Lying there was the birthstone I wore around my neck, and the now-broken chain that went with it. The blood trail was gone. "Did I do that?"

"I don't know. I was a little busy sliding under you. You sure you're okay?" I didn't want to tell her what I was really thinking: her arms seemed to be far from my neck the entire time.

Laura rubbed her back. "I'm fine. I can't believe I fell off that stool. I'm usually sure-footed. Sorry about your necklace."

I picked up the bloodstone and chain. "Don't worry about it. We aren't even sure you did it."

"It must've been me. You were busy catching me, and we're the only two here."

Either that, or Blake didn't like my bloodstone for some reason.

"*Pssst.*"

The next day I heard the hiss in my room. I was alone with the door closed, so I just started talking.

"I didn't think I'd hear from you again, but here you are when I'm working on my homework. Again."

"The easiest time to contact you is when your concentration is weakest."

I ignored his comment and changed the subject. "Did you see that I stopped Blake yesterday? I did it!"

"I did, and you were heroic. We're halfway home now."

"What do you mean? I stopped him."

"You certainly did, but he's going to make another attempt today."

"Wait a minute. It was just going to be that one time. I thought you said there were rules. He's cheating!"

"It bothers me as much as it does you, but it isn't as if I can accuse the ghost of a murderous seaman of cheating before he tries to kill someone. Just hang in there, you're doing great."

"That's it? Can't you get me a better deal?"

"You're right, but I can't stop him—only you can. Do you still want to help her or not?"

I bit my lower lip before speaking. "I'll help her. But I still don't know what I'm doing! Wait a minute . . . could Blake have been *afraid* of my bloodstone? I think he broke its chain."

"That makes sense. The bleeding stone is what finally caught him. You could be right. Since he's after Laura, why don't you give the bloodstone to her? She lost hers not that long ago. If you save her one more time and then give her the bloodstone, I'm sure Blake will never bother her again."

"Hey, you *were* right about Laura. She used to wear a bloodstone, too. How do you keep track of things like that?"

"It's what I do. Good luck, Greg. And be patient. He's coming tonight, but I can't say when."

"Okay, I'm going. So will he be angry with me after what happened last time? Is there a chance he might try to hurt *me*?"

I waited, but there was no reply. Larry left me talking to myself again. I wondered if I would need a guardian angel while I worked with Laura's guardian angel as I went out into the dining room and took my usual seat at the table.

"Finished already?"

"Um, no. I can't work in all that quiet. Besides, you might need me to catch you again." I grinned weakly.

"I'm sure I'll be fine; last time was just a freak accident. Besides, my mom and I are moving tomorrow, so I'm going to have to learn to get along without you soon anyway. And you're going to have to get along without me, so get back to work while I'm still here to review it with you."

I kept waiting for Blake to show up, humming his goofy tune, but nothing. Laura prepared dinner, we ate, we reviewed my homework, which didn't go as well as I hoped, especially considering that I saved her life yesterday, and then Mom came home.

"So how are we doing?" Mom asked as she checked emails on her phone.

"You mean me and my protector?" Laura said.

"'Protector'?" I said.

"Today you stood beside me in the kitchen every time I handled a knife or stood near something hot. Yesterday's event might have turned you into a bit of a worrier."

A worrier? Me? Someone who doesn't worry about doing

homework, taking out the garbage, cleaning my room. No one worries less than me—until Blake came along.

Mom took some money out of her purse and handed it to Laura. "Thanks, Laura. We're really going to miss you around here. Right, Greg?"

"Right." I kept looking all over the room as I listened for the humming. Still nothing.

"Greg, will you give me a hug before I go?" Laura extended her arms to me.

"No, I, uh—I can't say good-bye yet." I listened for the humming that still wasn't there. Then I remembered Larry saying the attack could happen anytime today. "Can I walk you home?"

"Oh, that's sweet," Laura said. "But it's just a couple of blocks."

"Then I should be back soon," I said as I looked at my mom.

"Is your homework done?" Mom said.

"Of course. We can go over it together when I get back if you like."

Mom looked me over carefully, the way moms do when they aren't sure they believe you. I couldn't help but be disappointed in her lack of trust, even if she was right about my homework not being done. "Okay, that's a good idea."

Great. If Blake didn't get me, my mother would.

Then Mom's phone rang. "Okay, I have to be on this call. Greg, I want you back in your room, reviewing your homework when I get off the phone." Mom was already walking to her room with the phone to her ear before I could answer.

"You will," I said as she disappeared behind her bedroom door.

As Laura and I left my house and we walked toward hers, I glanced in every direction for trouble and still didn't hear the humming. We lived on a quiet street, and it wasn't dark outside yet. It was a clear, cloudless summer day, so I expected to spot trouble right away and was determined to not miss anything.

"Greg?"

I looked back to Laura. "Yes?"

"It's so nice of you to walk me home. You've turned into such a nice young gentleman."

"Thanks. You probably guessed that I wanted to speak to you alone." The street remained quiet, and so did the sidewalk. I kept looking around while trying to talk to Laura at the same time—it wasn't easy.

"You had plenty of time to do that before your mother got home."

"I just—wanted to make sure nothing happened to you."

"Oh, I'll be fine, but now I'm worried about you. Won't you be in trouble when your mother sees your homework isn't done? You remember the changes I told you about, right?"

"It'll be done soon. I just have to make up some nice things to say about that book I'm reading."

"Why don't you write about what you didn't like?"

I stopped walking. "You can do that?"

"Of course."

"No problem. I can write a whole book about why I didn't like that book."

I looked around again and saw nothing dangerous. Then I looked into Laura's eyes and felt a little nervous, so I put my hands in my pockets. And I felt my birthstone. I held it out to Laura. "I'd like to give you this."

"That's so nice, but I can't take it. It's yours."

"Sure you can. The chain's already broken, so I can't wear it anyway.

You could put it on one of your chains, couldn't you?"

"Probably, but—"

"Please. I need you to take it. It's really important."

"Why's that?"

"I'm not sure. Please—just take it."

She took the bloodstone from my hand, and I breathed a sigh of relief. Maybe it would protect her from Blake.

I immediately knew it wouldn't as we approached the Johnson and Elm intersection. I could hear the humming. "Dum, dum, dum-da-dum, dum."

I didn't see a threat in front of us, so I turned quickly to face any danger behind us, but there was nothing! *Where is he?* I hoped the bloodstone would keep her safe, but Blake was still nearby, humming his deadly tune.

I glanced back at Laura, who kept walking when I had stopped. And then I saw the blood trail start following her—drops of red on the light-colored sidewalk—as she reached the crosswalk and turned to look at me. I could feel my heart in my throat.

Laura was maybe five steps ahead of me. Five precious steps! I could still hear the humming—"dum, dum, dum-da-dum, dum"—over the sound of my feet pounding the sidewalk as I desperately closed the distance between Laura and me.

One, two—the sound of a racing motor.

Three, four—the sight of Laura turning into the street to see what was behind her.

And there it was: the car I'd heard, zooming right at us, going the wrong way on a one-way street!

With my momentum still taking me forward, I reached out and

grabbed Laura's left wrist, threw my weight backward, and pulled as hard as I could.

The two of us fell backward. I fell flat on my back, onto a sidewalk that was harder than I ever realized. Laura had better luck and landed on something softer: me!

The car raced past us and took out a mailbox in front of the first house down Elm Street, before stopping at the second house down the street.

"Ow." I looked at the side of Laura's face as I sat up. She was watching the car and then turned and looked at me. When I saw her smile and dimples, I knew we were okay and smiled back.

Laura then got up and hurried over to the stopped car, with me following her. Mrs. Dunston, one of our neighbors, was behind the wheel of her green four-door car, with a cracked windshield and a mailbox sitting on its hood. She was sweating and had gray hair hanging in her face. There wasn't a mark on her.

"That mailbox is in the wrong place . . . ," Mrs. Dunston said.

Yeah, Laura and I almost were too.

Laura called the police, and we waited for them to see to Mrs. Dunston before we continued our slow limp to Laura's home. And nothing else happened on the way there that would interest anyone— well, with maybe one angelic exception.

"Pssst."

I looked around my bedroom to make sure Mom hadn't wandered in to see how I was doing with my homework.

"Larry?"

"Yeah. So everyone's fine, and she kept the bloodstone."

"Yes, and she thanked me for saving her life again. She even hugged me and gave me a kiss on the cheek. And she said that whenever she looks at it she'll think of me and her father. Her father gave her *her* bloodstone before he died. The one she lost. You should've seen the shocked look on her face when I asked her if her father's name was *Larry*. I never saw anything like it, *Larry*."

"That's because you couldn't see *your* face when she kissed you," Larry said. "You looked just as shocked."

"Of course. You were there too. Were you the one humming?"

For the first time Larry didn't answer right away. Finally: "Yes. How did you know?"

"Because Blake didn't try to push us in front of the car or even hold us in front of the car. As far as I could tell, he just hummed and left the blood trail. Kind of helpful for the ghost of a murderous seaman."

"Smart kid. Okay it was only me, not Blake. I was just trying to protect my daughter. Laura was fated to die, and because I wasn't sure where the dangers would come from until the last minute, it was easier to use an imaginary Blake to get you moving in the right direction."

"After she hugged me tonight, I felt kind of sad. It's . . . hard to explain."

"You don't need to, I understand. It was a good-bye hug. She's hugged me before, too. I can still remember that last hug. So no one would understand better than me."

I waited for Larry to say something else, but about thirty seconds went by without any noise at all, so I spoke up. "You're sure Laura will be okay? Will the bloodstone help?"

"She'll be okay. As for the bloodstone, I just wanted her to have something to remember me after she lost the last one. And she said she'll remember you, too. As it should be. It was your bloodstone, and you did decide to give it to her."

"Hey, wait a minute. If *you* wanted her to have my bloodstone, and Laura didn't break its chain, was *that* you? It wasn't me or Laura or Blake. Isn't *that* against the rules?"

Only silence answered me.

"What about the chain, Larry? What was that?! *Larry?!*"

When he didn't reply, I gritted my teeth and looked back at my English book, but I couldn't stop thinking about Laura and Larry.

If I were Larry, I'd have broken that chain too.

AREA CODE 666

BY CARTER WILSON

ER MOTHER'S TERROR-FILLED SCREAM CONSUMED Julia's mind yet again.

Every night, as she tried to sleep, the visions always ended the same: with her mother's bone-piercing shriek of horror. All Julia could do was pray for sleep. She couldn't help her mother. No one could, not anymore.

Sleep came, but only after she had tossed and turned for more than an hour. When Julia woke the next morning, it took her a half second to remember today was a special day. Today was her birthday.

Her dad gushed over her at breakfast and promised a surprise at night. Julia had to go to school, but that was okay, because all her friends were there, and her best friend, Syree, had even covered her locker door in birthday wrapping paper. Birthday cards and folded notes spilled out when she opened her locker, making Julia thankful for all the friends she had. Making things even better, by the end of the school day, Julia had almost no homework assigned, which was as common as a lunar eclipse.

That evening at home, Julia's father handed her a small box.

"Happy twelfth birthday, sweetie."

The box was just the size and shape to contain what she hoped it did. Julia tore into the small box and pulled out the beautiful work of art.

A *phone.*

Finally, after two years of begging, her very own phone. It felt slick and dense in her hands, like a perfectly smooth chunk of white obsidian.

This wasn't her *best* birthday ever—that one was her ninth birthday, when her mother was still alive, and they had gone to Six Flags, where Julia had wedged herself between her parents on her first-ever roller-coaster ride.

But this was still a great birthday. After gifts, Julia's dad took her to Camparelli's for dinner, where he teasingly pouted about her getting older as they shared an obscenely large sundae for dessert. At home they curled up on the couch and watched *Psycho*, a movie he was concerned would be too scary (though she'd already seen way worse on Netflix without him knowing).

Finally, as bedtime neared, Julia disappeared into her room and started setting up her phone. The very first thing she wanted to do was text Syree, but her dad came in and reminded her to take the trash out before bed.

"Sure, gimme a minute."

His voice deepened into his lecturing tone. "No, Julia, that's the deal, remember? Your phone doesn't start ruling things. It's just a tool, nothing more. So please put it down and take the trash out, and just a couple minutes more with the phone, and then put it away for the night, okay?"

Julia felt the pull of the phone, and already had a sense of its power of attraction. It felt comfortably warm as she placed it gently down on the nightstand.

"Okay, Dad."

Minutes later she picked it back up and swiped her finger along the screen, unlocking it. Julia was surprised to see a message notification.

Huh, Julia thought. *No one even has my number yet.*

She didn't recognize the sender's number, and then realized it was probably Verizon welcoming her into the family. But then she saw the attachment, the slightly blurred, grainy photo, and knew immediately the message wasn't from her phone company.

There was only a one-word message that accompanied the photo.

Julia.

Just her name in the message field, nothing else.

Julia held the phone closer to her face and squinted. She could make out the *what* of the image. What she couldn't understand was the *why* of it.

It was a doll. Specifically, the face of a doll, zoomed in so it only showed from the bottom of the nose up to the midforehead. It was an old-fashioned kind of doll, the creepy kind you'd find in a dark corner of your grandmother's attic, dust-covered and alone. The doll in the photo had smooth, round cheeks, the skin glazed white as mountain snow. The nose was disproportionately tiny, with two darkened, functionless nostrils through which air never passed. And then there were the eyes.

The eyes were the blurriest part of the photo, as if the doll had snapped awake midpicture. There was almost no color to them, just the faintest, lightest hint of blue—the color of a desert sky on a blistering hot day.

No, Julia thought. *The color of a ghost.*

A chill rolled inside her guts, lasting only a second but leaving icy discomfort in its wake.

She looked again at the sender's phone number, not even recognizing the area code: 666.

What kind of area code is that? She'd have to Google it later.

"So?"

Julia jolted and saw her dad in the doorway.

"How is it?" he asked.

She looked up at him and immediately felt guilty, though she didn't know why.

"How's what?"

"The phone, what else?"

"Oh, it's great." She pressed the home button on her screen, and the message disappeared. The last person she wanted seeing it was her father, who held out as long as he could in getting her a phone because of all his rants about privacy concerns. Some creep sending her a weird doll picture within minutes of setting up her phone was just the ammunition her dad needed to take her gift back.

"Thank you again," she added, smiling to hide her discomfort. "I *really* love it."

He came in and wrapped her arms around her, hugging her the extra-tight way that had been his habit ever since the accident. She wondered if he held her like this out of love or a need to protect her, but guessed it probably was a little of both.

They were all each other had.

"I can't believe next year you'll be a teenager."

"And I can't believe you'll be a fossil," Julia said. "Where does the time go?"

"Very funny." He released her from his hug. "Let's give the phone a rest and get ready for bed. School day tomorrow. Saturday you can sleep in all you want."

She didn't want to put it away, but this wasn't the time to protest. "Okay," she said, then plugged the phone in next to her dresser. As she set it down, it felt hot to her. Hotter than just a minute ago.

Julia went through her nightly routine: wash face, check for signs of impending pimples. Brush teeth, Waterpik braces. Change into her nightly sweatpants, the blue ones with the frayed ankles, the cotton so soft and perfect she dreaded the day she would inevitably outgrow them.

Her nightly routine was always accompanied by music, streamed from her iPod to a small Bluetooth speaker on a shelf in the corner of her room. Upbeat music, fast tempo, happy lyrics. She needed this because at night, when she finally had to turn the music off and burrow under her covers, Julia was left with a smothering silence, a ripped heart, and a head full of black thoughts.

It was always the same, no matter if she kept her bedroom light on or turned it off, whether she pulled the covers over her head or slept on top of them. She'd even tried sleeping with her head at the foot of the bed, but nothing made a difference.

Nighttime was when she always saw her mother.

Every night, the moment Julia closed her eyes, she saw her mother's face. It always started as a memory of the actual last time she saw her, three years ago in the funeral home. Julia had never seen a dead body before, and her very first one was her own mother. Of course, at nine she was old enough to understand that "dead" meant "never coming back," but seeing her mother in the coffin, Julia couldn't get the concept to stick in her brain. It was, literally, incomprehensible.

In Julia's nightly vision her mother always reanimated. She'd flash her eyes open, move her fingers around a bit, and then slowly, stiffly lumber out of the casket. Then she'd always spy Julia in that stuffy little viewing room and start asking questions.

"What are we doing here?"

"Why was I in that box?"

"Why am I wearing my favorite red dress?"

Julia would have to explain through her tears and a trembling voice how there had been a terrible accident. How a college student had been speeding and texting on his way to work and blew through a red light, the one on the corner near the Walgreens, less than a mile from their home. How he hit her mother's car right on the driver's side going fifty miles an hour.

Every night, when Julia closed her eyes, she'd tell this vision of her mom how she had died in that accident, and the man who hit her had walked away with just a few scrapes and bruises.

In her vision her mom never believed Julia. That is, until her mother started patting down her own body, feeling her skin and bones through the thin, silky fabric of her favorite red dress, only to discover parts of her were simply missing.

Only then did her mom look back to Julia and begin to scream.

This is how Julia fell asleep each night. Her mother, screaming for help, and Julia just standing there in that awful little, suffocating room, unable to do anything but stare at her in horror.

Tonight, as Julia closed her eyes and steeled herself against the inevitable images that would pull her into the nightly void, she heard a sound. A small ding.

It was the notification sound on her phone, which was faceup on the floor next to her bed. The little green notification light pulsed in the dark, a tiny little emergency beacon, summoning her.

Julia leaned over and grabbed it, vaguely aware she was embarking on a new relationship with this device, one in which she would reach for it every time it called out to her, knowing it would control her, just as her friends' phones all controlled them.

She reached down and swiped the screen. Another text.

Same 666 area code.

Another photo.

It was the doll's face again, though this time the camera had pulled back a bit farther, revealing the doll's long, ink-black hair, thick and wavy, a few strands resting haphazardly across the forehead. And it *was* a little girl—that was clear now. Little puffy lips, pursed and baby-like, red with a trace of painted lipstick that seemed just wrong for such a young thing. And the eyes. The ghost-blue eyes were now noticeably pointed just a bit off-center, as if looking at something just over Julia's shoulder.

Again, the message contained just one word. This time, it was:

don't

Don't what? Julia wondered.

She held the phone at arm's length, staring at this frozen girl, the one who seemed to have some kind of warning to give.

Julia stared until the screen autodimmed and then faded to black, leaving her once again in the dark of her quiet room, vastly alone with only memories and questions, none of which would make sleep come fast or peacefully.

* * *

Friday. The weekend couldn't come soon enough.

Julia showed off her new phone to her friends, who all seemed to approve. She and Syree traded numbers, marking Julia's first contact in a list that would soon blossom with dozens of names, most of which would appear in daily messages and group chats, things which Julia would soon learn were just pointless half conversations and emoji art shows, all used as a means to distract from homework.

She didn't tell Syree about the two messages from 666.

In study hall, however, Julia did sneak her phone out and check for new messages. None. Then, with the phone strategically placed beneath her desk at an angle where she could still read the screen, she Googled *666 area code.*

The first page of results told her more than she expected to learn.

That number was no longer an area code, and hadn't been in use for over ten years. It had once been the area code for the town of Reeves, Louisiana, but the folks there had it changed, since the number 666 was otherwise known as the "number of the beast."

Julia had never heard that term. New search.

666 number of the beast

Millions of results, the first of which was heavily biblical and confusing. Things about the Book of Revelation. Then she found a site that explained it in simple, stark detail.

The beast is the Antichrist. The devil. He is known by his number, and that number is 666.

Back to the search results. Most sites were all about the devil, but she did find one site about angels. Something about angel numbers and numerology, whatever that was. She tapped on the link.

If you encounter the number 666, it is a good sign, despite the common lore. It means the Universe is reaching out to you, asking you to believe and trust in It. That magic is happening in your life RIGHT NOW.

That definition of 666 is much better, Julia thought. She started reading more when an unpleasant voice jarred her.

"Well, Julia, did you finally get a phone?"

She looked up. Oh God. *Mr. Hendrie.*

It was no use trying to hide the phone. She'd been busted.

"Sorry, I'll put it away."

He towered over her, and his enormous belly—barely contained inside an ugly, plaid, button-down shirt—rested way too close to her face. His meaty face was covered in black, wiry hairs that looked like thousands of spider legs, and currently this face held a dark scowl. Mr. Hendrie thrust his hand at her.

"You'll give it to *me.*"

She slowly lifted the phone up to him and cringed as his chubby, sweat-glazed fingers snatched it from her. She hated the idea of his gross hands on it.

"After class," he said. And as he waddled back to the front of the room, Julia felt the judging gazes of twenty-five pairs of eyes, and her face flushed with heat. Knowing she was visibly turning red made it worse.

A painfully slow forty-three more minutes passed until the bell rang, and Julia went to Mr. Hendrie to get her possession back. He gave her a brief lecture about the entire school system falling apart and then handed it back to her. She promised once again not to use it in class.

When Julia was finally out of the classroom and in the crowded hallway, she turned the phone over and saw the blinking light. Julia swiped the screen, and there were two messages waiting for her.

The first was from Syree: *heard fat monster busted you*

She was going to write back when she saw the other message.

It was from 666. Another photo.

Julia walked over to a group of lockers and held the phone close to her face as she tapped on the photo. For a moment she was aware of the chaos around her, the swarm of middle schoolers racing to their next class, bodies bumping and jostling, lockers creaking open and slamming shut, shouts, laughter, shrieks, names shouted from one end to the other, and the rising heat from all those kids crammed into a narrow passage.

But then everything slipped away when the photo opened. The only thing that existed in the world was on the four-inch screen in the palm of her hand.

There was more of the doll this time. Some of the body. A little blue dress, the color of a robin's egg, with a white lace collar. The doll's hands were crossed neatly across her belly, her fingers clasped together, prim and proper. Julia could see just a bit of a dark, textured background behind the doll's head.

Again, just one word in the body of the message.

forget

Despite the heat from all the bodies in the crowded hallway, Julia felt cold. Cold as the ice she saw in the little girl's distant gaze, that eternal stare that looked not so much like the doll had just woken, but rather that she was dead.

Someone's messing with me, Julia thought, *and it's not even the tiniest bit funny.* But that didn't answer the one question she couldn't figure out.

How do they have my phone number?

* * *

That night in bed, that same question rolled around in Julia's head, and the moment she started to drift to sleep, her mind moved away from that question and back to where it always went at that hour.

To the stifling little room at the funeral home.

To the open casket with glossy wood paneling and gleaming brass side railings.

To her mother's face, so perfect and smooth, skin as unblemished as the doll's.

But tonight, for the first time, something was different. As her mother climbed from the casket, reaching out with long arms and bony fingers, demanding and pleading to know what had happened to her, there was something different.

Her mother's dress was not red this time. It was blue, the color of a robin's egg, with a white lace collar.

Saturday morning. Julia woke and looked down at her phone, which was plugged in and facedown on her bedroom carpet. She didn't even want to check it, but she knew she would. She thought about the relief she would feel if there were no messages from 666, and she murmured a small wish for that very thing before looking.

She turned it over. The light was blinking.

"No."

She could choose not to swipe the screen and see what was waiting for her. She could just leave it on the floor and get on with her Saturday, happy in her ignorance. This is what she *could* do, but knew it wasn't what she *would* do.

As she feared, it was another message from 666.

Another picture of the doll, same blue dress. Another view, slightly more zoomed out than the last one. This time the whole body of the doll was visible—at least it would be had there actually been a whole body. But this doll extended only to the tops of her legs. A few inches below the doll's waist, there was nothing. No legs, no feet, not even the fabric of the dress. Everything just stopped on a fine edge, as if sliced off by the most precise and sharpest of surgical blades.

Julia could also now see more of the background, which was clearly the base of a tree. The half doll was propped against the trunk, just where cracked and rough tree bark met a bed of fallen leaves on the ground. A final resting place.

Again, one word in the message.

me

Four messages, four words. And now, strung together, the words created a command.

Julia don't forget me

Julia had the sickening, sudden sense of being watched. She looked around frantically, but saw nothing. Her breath came in rapid bursts, and her chest flushed with panicky heat.

She looked at the photo again. There was something else, wasn't there? Something a little off, aside from the fact *all of this* was very much off. Something different about the doll in this latest photo.

She scrolled though the previous photos in the series of messages. The first photo only captured the eyes and the nose, but the next three photos showed all of the doll's face. And there was . . .

There.

The mouth.

In the second and third photos, the girl's mouth was closed. Tight, puffy, little lips, pursed shut.

But in the fourth photo, the mouth was open. Just a little, just enough to see a crack of dark between the lips. As if the doll was trying to talk.

Julia don't forget me

This wasn't a joke. Julia knew it as much as she had ever known anything. These messages weren't coming from someone trying to have a little fun with her. They were coming from someone else, or *something* else, entirely.

Her thumbs hovered over the glowing screen, her palms moist with sweat. Then she did something she hadn't done with the previous three messages. She replied.

Who are you?

There was no answer for at least a minute as Julia stared deeply into the screen, her heartbeat racing. When the message finally did come and the phone buzzed in her hand, she jumped.

By the barn on the rail tracks. Red balloon.

Oh my God oh my God oh my God . . .

What does that mean? she typed.

This time, there was no response.

After a few minutes she turned her attention away from her phone and closed her eyes, taking deep, long, meditative breaths, counting every exhale. When she got to forty-three, she felt her heartbeat finally slow back down, close to normal. Then she went downstairs.

She found her father sipping coffee, reading a book. This was what her parents always did together on Saturday mornings. Now, her father continued the ritual on his own, but Julia knew the true pleasure of Saturday mornings was gone for him, having fallen away, as all things eventually do.

She felt an overwhelming pull to tell him about the messages, but she knew where that would lead. He would take her phone away, telling her *this exact thing* was the reason he didn't want her having a phone in the first place. He'd rant about all the predators in the world, and Julia would be phoneless again.

He looked up from his book.

"Morning, sweetheart."

"Hi, Dad."

"Sleep okay?"

I never sleep okay, Julia thought.

"Sure."

"You have a lot of homework this weekend?"

She shrugged. "Not bad, I guess."

She dangled her phone in her hand, and it felt warm again, hot even, as if the secrets contained on it were slowly smoldering. Secrecy was becoming a part of who she was, and she hated it. Hated that she was too young to be an adult to her father, and too old to be his little girl anymore. And she longed for something—anything—different than the script of usual four- or five-word sentences they exchanged.

How was your day?

All right.

You have much homework?

Manageable.

What do you want for dinner?

Whatever.

She craved anything other than the small talk that grew smaller the older she became. She wanted to tell him how a boy in her science class had spread a rumor that she and him were dating, and for all of last month she dreaded 8:40 a.m. to 9:25 a.m., when she had to see him. She wanted to tell her dad about the vision of her mother in the stuffy little room at the funeral home and ask him if he had visions too. She wanted to ask him if he thought he'd ever date again, or if he planned to go on forever, reading a book by himself on Saturday mornings, a permanently empty chair by his side.

But she wouldn't because her dad was her dad, and Julia was Julia, and together, this is how they were.

"Do we have plans today?" she asked him. This was another question from their script.

"I have to do some work," he said. "You have something in mind?"

"Syree wanted to hang out," she said. Which wasn't exactly true, since she hadn't yet asked Syree this.

"That's fine," he said. "Just be home by four, okay?"

Julia looked at the screen on her phone. That gave her a little more than six hours.

"Okay." Julia started to walk away as her father nosed back into his book, but she turned and said, "Thanks again for my phone, Dad."

"Mmmmm-hmmmm. You're welcome."

"I love you, Dad."

His gaze never rose from the pages. "Love you too, hon."

She made herself breakfast and messaged Syree while she was eating.

Need to show you something. Can you hang out?
Sure, where?
I'll come over, Julia wrote back. **30 min.**

She got dressed and grabbed her bike and rode the two miles to Syree's house. The outside air swept over her cheeks, and there was the slightest touch of coolness to it, the first hint that the sweltering summer was finally dying and would soon be replaced by the crispness of fall. She pedaled hard and fast, and her tires gave off a rhythmic, satisfying hum as she whisked along the pavement.

It wasn't long before she coasted into the driveway of Syree's house, where she found her friend waiting on the front porch, both hands wrapped around her own phone, thumbs tapping the screen with the speed of a woodpecker's beak jackhammering a tree. She barely noticed Julia approaching.

"Anything interesting?" Julia asked.

"No," Syree said. "I got added to this group chat with, like, fifteen people, and it's all stupid stuff. I mean, they are *literally* saying nothing."

"So why are you replying?"

Syree looked up at her with an expression suggesting Julia surely must have lost her mind.

"Because, I told you, I'm *on* the group chat."

"Put that down," Julia said. "There's something I need to show you."

"Hang on," Syree said.

Julia took the phone from Syree's clutch, feeling, for a moment, like a parent.

"Hey!"

"Listen to me," Julia said. "This is serious. I haven't told anyone about this."

"God, what is it?"

Julia unlocked her own phone, brought up the string of messages from 666, and then handed it to Syree.

"Start from the beginning," Julia said.

* * *

An hour later, after they had time to agree on a plan and find the courage to execute it, the girls rode together, their pace slowing as they edged their bikes along the outskirts of their small town toward the section of County Road 17 where it turned from hard asphalt to packed dirt. Right at the seam in the road, Syree stopped altogether, and Julia did the same.

They were on a small rise a few miles from Julia's house, and in this quiet section of expansive scrubby fields that had so far escaped the development of new, cookie-cutter neighborhoods, the breeze cuffed them slightly about their necks. A hawk wafted in looping circles overhead, like dandelion fluff drifting on a child's breath.

"There it is," Syree said.

The barn was in the distance, perhaps a quarter mile away, a solitary structure that had been there ever since Julia started holding memories. It stood abandoned and alone, its red paint flecked and sunbaked, the color of old, dried blood. A section of the roof had caved in by weather and time; upheaved planks of rotten wood, splintering to the sky like matchsticks. Weed-covered railroad tracks passed just in front of the barn, though Julia had never seen a train use them. She thought of this part of town as a time capsule, holding remnants of what once was for those who ever cared to go back and reminisce. Most people, though, were too busy looking at whatever was right in front of them.

"I see it," Julia said. She'd told Syree everything after showing her all the messages. Syree had dismissed it as a gag, but was excited for an adventure. But here, now, on this quiet dirt road in a section of the town from an abandoned time, Syree looked anything but adventurous.

Julia pushed the bike forward using her feet. "Let's go."

"I don't know," Syree replied. "This doesn't feel right."

"We've come this far."

"You know this is crazy, right? Some freak wanted to lure you out here, and now here we are. Julia, I can't even get a signal out here."

Julia reached for her own phone and confirmed this. No service.

"It's okay," she said.

"Let's go back."

"No. Let's go closer."

"*Julia*, come on."

"It's okay, Syree. You can leave. I'm going on."

"It's not like I'm going to leave you here."

"Then *come on*," Julia said, and with that she began pedaling again, her pace slow.

Syree called after her, "God, you can be so stubborn."

Small pebbles crackled under her tires, some kicking up from the road, pinging against the metal spokes. Julia led and Syree followed at a distance, and as Julia rounded a slight bend in the road, she saw it.

A red balloon, helium-filled, tied around a lower branch of a thick and ancient oak tree. Its string was just long enough to keep it from hitting the branch above, and the balloon danced back and forth in the wind, straining against its tether.

The branch was at least ten feet off the ground. *Someone needed a ladder to tie it there,* Julia thought. And it was a regular rubber balloon, not one of those Mylar kinds. The regular ones didn't hold helium long, Julia knew, and this one looked plump and taut, as if it had just been filled.

She stopped short of the tree, her tires shimmying along the loose dirt. Syree pulled up next to her, breathing hard. Julia felt it too, a pounding inside her chest, a shortness of breath. Tingling in the fingertips. All the telltale signs of nerves.

"Julia, this is too much, let's get out of here."

"Not yet."

Julia dismounted her bike, lowered the kickstand, and leaned it into the dirt. Then she began walking the last several feet to the tree. To her left the low afternoon sun stretched long and deep in the sky, creeping the shadow of the nearby barn closer to Julia's feet with each passing moment.

Syree called out desperately from behind. "Julia, you're freaking me out. Come back here!"

Julia just held up a hand and kept on walking. She was close to the tree now, could smell its musty bark. Could hear the rustling of its leaves, a few of which fell in the breeze, scattering near her feet. As she reached the base, she looked up again, saw the balloon, which bobbed in the wind faster than before, as if excited to see her.

Then Julia walked around the base of the massive tree, and that's when she looked down and saw the doll.

Julia stopped breathing.

It was the one from the photos, though the mouth was open even a little wider than before, and the ghost eyes weren't staring dead in the distance, but instead looked directly at Julia. And the bottom half of the doll wasn't missing at all, as it had appeared in the final photo. Rather, the bottom half was buried in dirt at the base of the tree.

"Julia, what is it?"

Julia didn't reply. Instead, she leaned over, wrapped her shaking hands around the chest of the doll, and gently pulled. The doll resisted at first, then slowly emerged from its little grave, revealing intact legs and lower dress, all stained by the earth. There was a small paper tag on the doll's left ankle, secured with a faded red ribbon. Julia brought the doll up to her face and read the tag.

Happy birthday, Julia. I love you.

And then she remembered. It was such a clear memory it seemed impossible that Julia had ever forgotten, and the suddenness with which it came back nearly buckled her knees.

She knew this doll. This was *her* doll, a gift given to her by her mother on Julia's fourth birthday. But the doll had disappeared a day later, and by the time anyone realized it, it was too late. Her parents had likely thrown it out by mistake with all the wrapping paper and boxes of Julia's gifts, and the garbage had already been collected. The doll was forever gone, wallowing in a landfill somewhere, and Julia had cried hard and long when her parents told her the news.

That was the same birthday her mother filled the living room with red balloons, all of which lived for a day or two before falling one by one back down to Earth.

Now, as Julia clutched the doll, she instinctively looked to her left— to the barn, to the small, cracked window by the open barn doors.

Movement.

Someone was there, watching.

It was almost imperceptible, with the sun in her eyes and the amount of dirt streaked on the window, but it was definitely a person. A woman. Long hair, kinked and brown, just like her mother's. Julia could just make out a smile on the woman's face.

Julia felt herself pulled toward the specter and took a step closer to the barn.

"Mom?"

And then whatever was there suddenly vanished into the

otherworldly darkness from which it'd come. Or perhaps it had never been there at all.

As much as Julia wanted it to be her mom—her actual living and breathing mom—she knew it was something else. A phantom, an imagination, a ghost, an angel. Right then, Julia decided she would not go into the barn. Chasing ghosts wouldn't help her any more than reliving the same vision every night. And she suspected whatever any of this meant, whatever any of it was, it came from a world that didn't overlap with her own.

The universe is sending me a message, Julia thought. *And I have an answer.*

"I won't ever forget you," she said.

She squeezed the doll in her hand just as she felt the first few tears roll down her cheek.

She walked back to Syree, who seemed poised to ask a question but didn't. Like a true best friend, she seemed to know when not to say anything at all.

They rode home back along the dirt road in silence, the sun brilliant and red like the color of the faded ribbon around her doll's ankle.

That night Julia propped the doll up on a shelf in her room. She hadn't cleaned the dirt from its lower half, thinking the doll had been on some kind of journey and deserved to proudly wear the marks from it.

She didn't know what she was going to tell her father about the doll when he eventually saw it, but maybe she would simply tell him the truth. Maybe they would have a real conversation, full of long questions and deep, searching answers, about all sorts of things, big and little, happy and sad. Things not in the script.

Her phone buzzed, announcing a message. Julia flinched, just a little, and swiped open her screen. The message was from Syree.

U ok?

Julia answered as honestly as she could.

I think so.

She didn't wait for Syree's next message. Julia turned the phone completely off and put it on the shelf next to the doll. As she looked at the doll, and the doll looked at her, Julia knew she would never hear from 666 again. No more communication was necessary.

She turned off her bedroom light, got into bed, and pulled the heavy covers up over her. Julia closed her eyes and waited for the vision to come. Waited to be back in the small and stuffy funeral home, waited to see a version of her mother who was scared and alone. And screaming.

For the first time in three years, Julia didn't see that vision. She no longer needed to, she realized. She had her closure, and even if she didn't quite understand it, what happened today was beautiful, strange, and necessary.

As she gradually fell asleep, Julia only saw her mother's face, looking at her through the dirt-streaked barn window. Smiling, happy, and, more than anything else, not forgotten.

THE TROUBLE WITH SQUIRRELS

BY DOUG LEVIN

AHHGGH!" THAT WAS ME SCREAMING, but I quickly lowered the volume to "Ewww."

There, right in the crosswalk, was a squashed, pulpy squirrel. I had been looking at my phone and nearly stepped on it. Except for the bushy tail, the creature was stretched out flat, nearly a squirrel pancake. Even its head was squished into the asphalt. The crows had already eaten the eyes, and they'd been tugging at the innards, too. I felt a little queasy as I hurried the rest of the way across the street.

I'm big for my age (twelve)—and tough when I want to be—but I have a secretly gentle heart. It's embarrassing, but sometimes in a dark movie theater during the sappy part, I can feel my eyes sting, like I might cry. But I don't look away. *You're tough, too, Duncan,* I'd tell myself. *Remember it!*

But worst of all, I can't stand to see animals hurt. Two years ago my mom went vegetarian, and for a month, we only ate tofu, beans, and spaghetti *without* meat sauce. She said she wanted to be "healthier, happier, and more humane," but I really think it was because my steak-

THE TROUBLE WITH SQUIRRELS

When my mom gave up her vegetarian diet, she and my sister, Katie, celebrated by going for burgers, but I decided to stick with it. Weird, I know, but I just didn't want to be eating a slab of Elsie the cow or Wilbur the pig.

So that squished squirrel . . . it was gross but sad, too. It wasn't the first dead one I'd seen—not by a long shot—but it was the first one I'd almost stepped on. In fact, this spring I'd seen more squirrels than ever. The cute little critters skittered across roads, tightrope walked power lines, played in trees, and scampered across roofs. One morning, three of the little guys nearly ran over my feet—all gleefully carrying peanuts, strangely enough.

Unfortunately, the squirrels were making trouble, too. Down the street, a pair had nested in the attic of my friend Nathan Benton's house. He said his parents had to pay two thousand dollars to have the squirrels removed and the eaves repaired. But that wasn't the worst of it.

"The squirrels ran Sissy off," Nathan had said. Sissy was the Bentons' fat orange tabby cat. "My mom is really mopey."

"I don't think squirrels can run off a cat," I said.

"Well, they did." Nathan looked at me harder to see if I could handle another piece of information. "You know what else?"

"What?"

"My dad told the critter catcher he could just drown the squirrels."

I felt a little sick at the thought. Those squirrels were just trying to get by. "What did the critter catcher say?"

"He said they were more human about it."

"Humane," I corrected.

"Whatever. Anyway, the critter catcher says the gray squirrels are invaders, so they've got to go."

"I wonder why they're invading."

Nathan shrugged. "The critter guy says he's been doing a lot of work in our neighborhood. They must be nesting here or something."

"Maybe," I said doubtfully. I had never seen a baby squirrel. They must stay hidden until they're full-grown.

"I bet they ate Sissy," said Nathan, a little too eagerly for my taste.

I shook my head. "Squirrels don't eat cats."

"How do you know?" he'd shot back.

Nathan and I are friends, but I don't think we're ever going to be best friends.

After I nearly stepped on the squished squirrel in the crosswalk, I decided that I had to do something. The little guys were dying—and making trouble, even though they didn't mean to. But what could I do? I couldn't go into the squirrel-catching-and-relocating business. But I did know how to use the phone.

"I'd like to speak to a wildlife control officer," I said when a woman answered my call to the county animal control department.

"I might be able to help you," the woman said in a casual, friendly tone, not at all like what I'd expected from a government official. "What's the trouble?"

"Squirrels," I said firmly. "Lots of them."

"Don't I know it," said the woman. "They're like mosquitoes this year." She laughed with a snort.

"Exactly," I said.

"Well, what's the trouble, then?" said the woman, now sounding more official. "They in your attic or crawl space? You seen any acting strangely or any that looked sick? How old are you, anyway?"

I ignored that last question. "I haven't seen any sick ones, but a pair did get into my friend's attic."

"Yeah?" She didn't sound impressed.

"Well, they're everywhere over here in the Holly Oaks neighborhood. They're cute, but they're getting hit by cars. I hate to see them dead and rotting and getting eaten by the crows." I caught my breath, then added, "We're feeling pretty overrun."

"You are, huh?"

"I thought you could do a big roundup and move them back across the river and into Forest Park."

The woman was silent for a moment, then said in her most annoying adult voice, "Honey, unfortunately, at this point, overrun isn't good enough. I need a sick squirrel, an aggressive squirrel, or a freshly dead squirrel before I can send someone out."

"They were carrying peanuts," I said desperately.

"Well, I can tell you for certain that peanuts do not grow in this climate. Walnuts and hazelnuts, yes, but not peanuts. Cutting off the source of those peanuts might help."

"So you can't do anything?"

The woman sighed. "They'll thin out soon enough."

So much for help. I said good-bye and hung up.

The squirrels, of course, didn't thin out. They multiplied. They were still in the trees and on the roofs, and running to and fro in the streets. They darted slyly around, bright-eyed but mangy, playful yet also a little menacing.

A week later Nathan Benton's dad picked me up in his big black Cadillac. Mrs. Benton was traveling for work, so Mr. Benton was taking Nathan and me out for an early dinner. He'd gotten chummy with me since my dad moved out, which sounds nice, but I was still suspicious.

"Boys," he said after I got into the back seat, "I'm taking you for a big, juicy steak."

I didn't say anything.

"Can I get french fries, too?" Nathan asked.

His dad craned his neck and eyed us in the rearview mirror. "You can get baked, mashed, or"—he paused for emphasis—"*steak* fries."

"Okay," Nathan said obediently.

At the steak restaurant—called, no kidding, *Sir Loin's*—I looked the menu over for a vegetarian option. The pickings were thin.

Nathan ordered a London broil, and Mr. Benton ordered a T-bone.

The waiter turned to me, and I said, "I'd just like an order of mac and cheese. And could you hold the bacon bits? I'd also like a side of spinach."

I looked at Mr. Benton out of the corner of my eye. I wasn't sure if he was mad or not. His face sure looked strange.

"Don't you want a steak?" he asked. "You should have a steak."

I shook my head. "No thank you. I'm not hungry for a big steak."

"You could get a smaller one. The eight-ounce filet."

I shook my head.

Throughout the meal Mr. Benton kept glancing at me like I was an exotic—and maybe dangerous—animal. After this, I thought he wasn't going to try to be my buddy anymore. Just as well.

The car was silent as we drove back to our neighborhood. It was nearly dusk, and the falling sun made the sky a blurry mix of orange and black. A block from my house, a squirrel darted out into the road, and Mr. Benton slowed down. The creature stopped midstride and reversed course, and then Mr. Benton hit the gas and turned the wheel.

I felt a very soft thump and heard a sickening pop. I turned and looked out the rear window. The dead animal was still twitching a bit, stuck to the road. The blood in my body ran a horrified lap.

"Score," muttered Mr. Benton, looking back through his rearview mirror.

"Did you mean to hit him?" I blurted out.

"Why not?" said Mr. Benton, shrugging. "Those little jerks cost me more than two thousand bucks. I'm running them down whenever I get a chance."

I was nearly shaking when I got out of the car. I wondered now if Mr. Benton had hit the squirrel that I'd nearly stepped on. Running down squirrels had to be a crime. It also left behind a mess.

The next morning I called the county animal control department again. The same woman answered, "Animal control."

"I have a dead squirrel to report," I announced. "Hit in the road, a block from my house."

"Yep. We're getting a lot of that this time of year." She sounded bored. "What's your address?"

I gave it to her.

"We'll have it picked up within seventy-two hours," explained the woman.

"Seventy-two hours?!" That seemed like a long time.

"Within seventy-two hours," the woman repeated. "We've only got so many hands, and a lot of dead little bodies."

"I guess," I said, thinking out loud, "I guess I could pick it up myself and bury it."

"That's up to you. I recommend you use gloves and then seal the body in a plastic bag. It can just go in your trash. You bury it, some other animal will dig it up."

I had hardly been able to look at the dead squirrel I'd nearly stepped on. I realized I would never be able to scrape up a squirrel and bag it. "Okay, but if I don't get to it, you'll still pick it up?"

"We'll be there," promised the woman.

I thanked her and hung up.

I wondered if Mr. Benton was actually chasing squirrels around in his car. I had seen a lot of dead squirrels in the road, but then, there were still a lot of squirrels running around. They must've bred, well, like rabbits, and thrived on a good supply of food. Or at least a lot of peanuts.

I went back outside, down my driveway, and up the block toward Mr. Benton's latest kill. Flies were circling the squashed squirrel. I looked farther up the street. It seemed like the squirrels were always coming from that direction. I saw one across the street now, loping through a flower bed.

I looked both ways and crossed. The squirrel saw me coming and skittered under a fence. The street was perfectly quiet, and I looked in all four directions since I was standing at an intersection. A movement caught my eye, half a block up. A squirrel was crossing.

As I walked up the sidewalk, I saw another squirrel with a mangy gray coat, and still another, more brown, across the street. I kept my eye, though, on the one that had crossed up ahead. It seemed to be moving with real purpose.

The squirrel scampered north and then beelined across the next street. I picked up my pace and turned the corner. I stopped abruptly, staring in astonishment. Several squirrels scurried in the street on this block. And in the yards and along the fences and on the telephone wires,

I saw even more. I walked down the block, parting small gatherings of squirrels here and there. The animals paid little attention to me, other than to clear out of my way.

They were thickest in the middle of the block, on the north side of the street. I crossed and walked cautiously down the sidewalk. The squirrels were scampering happily—and in great numbers—beside a property that held a washed-out yellow house. I had never paid this house much attention because it squatted for the most part behind a row of large, bushy rhododendrons. They weren't flowering now, and their leaves and branches formed a hedge in front of a concrete path that presumably led to the front door. The squirrels ran up and along a fence that concealed the backyard.

And now I saw exactly what I was looking for—even though I hadn't known it.

Two cabin-shaped feeders—sort of like bird feeders—were nailed to a gnarled walnut tree on the other side of the fence. The squirrels came and went, up and down the tree. They swarmed around the feeders, standing on small platforms and coming away with peanuts in the shell. At the foot of the fence, empty peanut shells covered the ground.

I took a long slow breath. Who put out squirrel feeders? I had never heard of such a thing. I wondered what Mr. Benton would do. He did have a gun case with a shotgun in his den. The residents of this house were probably serious environmentalists. That was okay by me, except now we had too many squirrels in the area. It might even be against the law to feed wild animals—even though squirrels weren't that wild. Maybe these people didn't realize all the trouble they were causing.

I ducked behind the wall of rhododendrons and walked up the concrete path to the front door. There was no doorbell, so I opened the screen door and knocked three hard whacks with my fist. I stepped back and let the screen door snap back into place.

The windows to my left were dirty with dust and abandoned spiderwebs in the upper corners. Heavy vinyl blinds covered the windows.

I stepped forward to knock again when I heard the deadbolt snick open. The door opened about a foot, revealing the face of a small old man, whose eyes were big and round behind thick glasses. Behind him stood a woman of about the same height, who must've been the old man's wife. She clutched her hands against her chest, but her eyes were eager and curious.

"Yes?" said the old man. I thought maybe he had a faint accent. He peered past me, apparently to see if anyone else was on the walkway. "What can I do for you, young man?"

I realized I hadn't exactly prepared anything to say. I wasn't expecting to find a frail old couple.

"I'm here," I began, "from the neighborhood. I live just a few blocks away." I flipped a hand over my shoulder, back toward my home. "It's about—" I hesitated, then said, "It's about the squirrels. All the squirrels you're feeding."

The woman's eyes brightened spontaneously. "Aren't they wonderful?" she blurted out.

The old man shot her a look, and her enthusiasm dulled a bit. "You say you're from the neighborhood?" said the old man, smiling. "You mean you're here as a representative?"

I hadn't expected a cross-examination. "Well, not exactly. I live in the neighborhood. I'm just here on my own." I caught my breath, then added hastily, "But my friend Nathan Benton, his family's had a lot of trouble with squirrels too."

"Well, why didn't they come too?" asked the old man. He glanced over my shoulder again, as if Nathan and Mr. Benton might be hanging back.

"I don't think they know you're feeding squirrels. In fact, I know they don't, or they would've said something. You would've heard from Mr. Benton already. He's very angry about all the squirrels."

The woman leaned forward and whispered in the old man's ear. "Of course, of course," he muttered to her. He turned his attention back to me. "I'm sorry, Hortense is right." He stepped back and held his hand out, palm up, and waved me toward him. "Why don't you come in?"

I hesitated a moment. I know I'm not supposed to go into strangers' homes, but this old couple seemed harmless—except for all the trouble they were causing with the squirrels. "Okay. I promise not to take up much of your time." I planned to tell them what the county animal control woman said: no more peanuts for the squirrels.

As I stepped inside, the old man said, "Oh, we have time to spare. We have very few visitors, and Hortense and I know each other so well that we hardly need to speak a word to one another."

The entryway turned to the left and opened into a low-ceilinged living room with old-fashioned furniture. The woman—Hortense *was* a weird name—pointed to a fancy armchair with a carved wood frame. I sat down in it.

"Tea?" she asked.

"Oh, no thank you," I said, though I was pleased they were treating me like an adult. "You don't have to bother."

"No bother," said the old man, sitting on the sofa. He nodded, and

Hortense disappeared toward the rear of the house. "Now what brings you here, Mr. . . . ?"

"Duncan Ringbone," I said.

The old man smiled and held out his hand. "Rudolph Severin."

We shook, and he sat on a big red sofa across from me. "I don't think I've ever seen you in the neighborhood," I said.

"No, I expect not," said Mr. Severin, shaking his head and smiling, without offering further explanation. "But I saw you once, out the window," he went on. "Walking with a girl younger than yourself."

"That was probably my sister, Katie. She's seven."

"You should've brought her, too," said Mr. Severin. "Hortense loves little girls."

The old man fell silent now, waiting, it seemed, for the matter at hand. I wondered where to begin. It suddenly seemed awkward to complain to this nice elderly couple about feeding the squirrels. Maybe where they came from, people fed squirrels all the time.

"You wanted to talk about our squirrels," Mr. Severin prompted before I could begin.

I looked past him to see if the old woman was coming back from the kitchen yet. She wasn't. I leaned forward and said in a calm, polite voice, "I think you're attracting too many squirrels to the neighborhood. They're everywhere, and they're getting in people's houses, and they're getting hit by cars."

"Oh yes," Mr. Severin said, ignoring nearly everything I had said. "We like to be on friendly terms with them."

I hesitated. How could I explain that he wasn't really helping the squirrels at all? He was turning people like Mr. Benton into squirrel-killing psychos. "They are cute and lively . . . ," I began.

"And delicious," added Mr. Severin, smiling.

I wasn't sure I'd heard him correctly. *Delicious?*

"I hope that Lapsang souchong tea is agreeable to you," said the old woman, carrying a tray into the room. "It's also known as Russian Caravan tea." She set a glossy wooden tray on the coffee table and poured steaming tea into china cups. She handed me a cup on a saucer. It had a strong, smoky aroma.

"Thank you," I said. I blew on the surface and took a sip. It had a powerful wood-and-smoke flavor, a little strange.

"Have a cookie, too." She pointed to a plate that held a handful of cream-colored cookies with peanuts on them.

The old woman sat on the couch as well and sipped from her own steaming cup. "This is our favorite tea. It goes well with every meal, especially game."

"My sister is a three-star chef with squirrel," said Mr. Severin.

That caught me by surprise, and before I could stop myself, I said, "Your sister?"

The old man smiled broadly. "Surely we look too much alike to be nothing but brother and sister?"

I looked more closely from one face to the next. If you looked beyond the wrinkles, the differences in hairstyle, and the old man's thick glasses, and just observed the inner parts of their faces—narrow-set dark eyes, wide mouths with small teeth, and pixie-like button noses—the two actually did look a lot alike.

"I guess that's true," I finally said. "I hadn't noticed at first."

Ms. Severin—I guess that was her proper name—reached for a cookie, so I followed her example. They had a rich, nutty flavor. "Delicious," I said between bites.

"It's the rendered squirrel fat," said Ms. Severin. "It adds extra flavor, better than lard or butter."

I slowed my chewing, but now I had mashed-up squirrel cookie in my mouth. I managed to swallow, but set the rest of the cookie on the saucer beside my cup of tea. "So you're really—" I began. I stopped and looked more closely at them to see if they might be joking. "You're really eating squirrels?"

"Well, of course," said Ms. Severin. "And why not? God brings them right to our doorstep."

"With a little help from the feeders," added Mr. Severin.

I must've looked disbelieving because Mr. Severin asked, "Would you like to see the operation?"

It all seemed a little shocking—no, really shocking—but maybe it was a gag. I simply nodded. Mr. Severin stood and said, "This way."

I followed him to the back of the house, with Ms. Severin on my heels. A narrow hallway led to a corner with two closed doors at the bend. Mr. Severin turned a deadbolt and opened the door in front of him, which led down two steps to the enclosed backyard. We stepped onto a cement patio that bordered a small square of grass.

I saw squirrels chasing one another around the little plot of lawn and through flower beds. Others scampered up the walnut tree or along the lip of the high fence. A pair darted mischievously back and forth around a garden gnome. Occasionally, a squirrel ran up to a feeder—there were several in the yard in addition to the two in the tree—and took a peanut. I thought many of them looked quite fat and satisfied.

"This is a lot of squirrels," I said.

"It has been a very prolific year," said Mr. Severin, with pride in his voice. "A mild winter, a damp spring, and, voilà, a bumper crop of the little devils."

I saw no traps or cages. "So how do you get them?" I asked. "Slingshot?"

Mr. Severin laughed with a high pitch. "Nothing so inefficient and primitive. Here, let me show you."

He led me across the yard to a shed, which was padlocked shut. He pulled a large ring of keys from his pocket, snapped open the lock, and slid the metal door back.

Inside the dark shed, I saw a stack of wire and wood boxes. They were traps, I realized, with feeders on the inside and little doors at one end, presumably that opened in only one direction.

"Once we have a group that is really quite comfortable here, feeding happily with no worries, Hortense and I close up the open feeders and put out the new feeders—the ones inside the traps. They fill up over a few hours, just like lobster traps."

"And then comes the fun part," said Ms. Severin, who had edged up behind me.

"What happens?" I asked, though I had an idea.

Mr. Severin grasped my arm and turned me around. "Now you have to see the basement."

We walked back across the patio, Mr. Severin still speaking. "We have that old cellar door there." He pointed to a horizontal door that jutted out from the cement patio along the edge of the house. "But we'll just go in through the house."

We crowded back into the hallway. Mr. Severin closed and locked the back door, then removed his keys again, and turned a deadbolt in the other door. He swung it open. A dank and musky odor wafted into the hallway. He snapped a light switch, and a single naked bulb on a wire illuminated a wooden staircase.

Mr. Severin headed down the stairs. I followed cautiously, with Ms. Severin bringing up the rear. I didn't know if I wanted to see what happened in the basement, but I had already come this far. Before I even reached the cellar, I heard the sound of small feet and bodies shaking wire cages. I followed Mr. Severin into the dim space.

I had never been in a tannery or visited a furrier, but this area of the basement appeared to have been converted into a place for processing and shipping animal hides. Stacks of pelts lay on a wide table, along with unassembled shipping boxes and a postal scale. Some of the animal skins were small—about the size of pressed squirrels—but I also saw larger furs, raccoons, and what looked like—I wasn't quite sure—a coyote, or maybe even a dog.

Ms. Severin rushed past me toward an open door on the far end of the basement. I caught a glimpse of a metal table and a large steel pot. She pulled the door shut and turned to smile at me.

"After the pelts are dried, we ship them home," said Mr. Severin. "They fetch a reasonable price."

I turned toward Mr. Severin to ask where exactly home was, but then I stopped. Behind him, in the shadows at the other end of the basement, I saw the cages. They were stacked nearly to the ceiling. I stepped around the old couple and approached the rows of cages. They held mostly squirrels, dozens of them, running back and forth in the tight space. The animals pushed against the doors, which rattled but were held tight by spring fasteners.

"This is where we fatten up the thin ones," said Mr. Severin. "The peanuts run down from the trough above." A long wooden tub, presumably filled with peanuts, was fastened along the top row of cages. Small chutes fed peanuts into the cages.

Near the far corner of the room, I saw cages in other sizes, too, holding other animals. A large mangy dog slept in the corner of one. Others held raccoons, rabbits, and even a fat, bucktoothed nutria. Another section of wire compartments was filled with a half dozen cats. I stepped closer. One orange tabby looked a lot like the Bentons' missing cat, Sissy.

I kept moving down the row of cages, shocked to see all these trapped animals. Below two stacks of cat cages sat a larger, empty cage, strewn with wood shavings. I put my head up against the mesh and saw that in the far corner of the cage, instead of a water bowl, there was a can of soda, a box of orange juice, and a bag of potato chips. A few comic books and a worn paperback—I think it was a *Harry Potter* book—were stacked alongside the snacks. My heart skipped a beat when I realized that this cage wasn't for an animal.

I turned quickly, and saw that Mr. and Ms. Severin were carefully sneaking up on me. He held a long pole with a loop on its end. It was the type of contraption that I'd seen an alligator hunter use to catch a big bull gator on an Animal Planet show.

"Just relax, Duncan," said Mr. Severin softly, in the tone a dogcatcher might use with a cornered stray.

I took a step back, and then another. In a few feet I'd be pinned against the far wall, with no way out. I continued to backpedal, when I stepped on a water bottle that must've fallen off a cage. My ankle rolled, and I fell into a bank of cages, grabbing them for support. The cages— the whole stack all the way to the ceiling—swayed precariously. They weren't bolted to the wall.

I stood straighter, meeting the eyes of Mr. and Ms. Severin, who had frozen in place. They looked worried, as if I had just figured something out.

I bent my knees, stretched my arms wide, and grabbed the wire mesh of two cages. With all my might—and I'm big and strong for my age—I leaned back and rocked the stack of cages forward. Metal shrieked. The whole bank of cages tumbled all around me and over the Severins. The trough of peanuts ripped loose, and peanuts poured everywhere.

The basement was hazy with dust, and broken cages covered the floor. Escaped animals—mostly squirrels—ran loose throughout the basement. I still had to get out of this place.

Two groans rose from beneath the mass of upended and broken cages. I wove my way through the jumble and headed toward the cellar door. I could barely see Mr. and Ms. Severin through the pile of debris pinning them down.

I climbed a few concrete steps into the darkness beneath the cellar door. I could barely see the door's slide bolt, but I got ahold of it and slid it back. I pushed with all my strength, and the metal door screeched open. Daylight poured into the basement.

While I shielded my eyes against the brightness, a warm, furry body threaded its way between my legs. An orange tabby—Sissy—nuzzled her face against my leg.

"You!" Mr. Severin yelled from back in the basement. "Stop!"

I picked up Sissy and scrambled up the cellar steps and out into the backyard. Down in the basement, Mr. Severin's angry face peered up from the bottom of the stairs. I slammed the cellar door closed on him. Without even looking for a gate, I set Sissy on the thick top rail of the fence and climbed over. I landed in a strip of grass along the sidewalk.

I got to my feet and grabbed Sissy. I ran for two blocks, the cat clutched in my arms, before stopping to catch my breath.

The street was perfectly quiet, but a moment later, Nathan Benton rounded the corner on his mountain bike. He slowed down as he approached, and his eyes narrowed warily.

"What are you doing, Duncan?" Nathan asked as he got closer. His eyes widened. "Is that Sissy?" He stopped a few feet from me. "What're you doing?" he repeated. "And why do you have my cat?"

I took a deep breath and raised a triumphant finger. "I believe I have just solved the mystery of the neighborhood's squirrel problem."

THE NECKLACE AND THE MONSTER

BY JEFF SOLOWAY

IMMY SCREAMED. I DON'T KNOW why; I was the one about to get pulverized.

Oscar Edelman grabbed me by the shirt with two hands.

His lunkhead friends crowded in behind him.

My third day at the new school was not going well.

"Gimme my phone." His breath was like the bottom of a Dumpster.

"I told you," I said. "I didn't steal it."

Who'd be crazy enough to steal a phone from Ox Edelman? He was only one grade ahead of me, but he's built like a refrigerator. Kids warned me about him my first day. Then they all stopped talking to me—except to ask about my dad.

His fingernails dug into my chest as he grabbed bigger handfuls of my shirt. Why does everyone say bullies are cowards? All the bullies I know love to fight, and they'll take on anyone—big or puny, tough or wimpy—because fighting is what they're good at. Kids say Ox practices on a punching bag at his dad's gym. I think he gets enough practice on sixth-graders after school. Like me.

"Does that hurt?" Ox asked.

"Yeah." If I said no, he'd only rake my skin harder.

"Then why don't you hit me?"

"Because I don't want to hurt you."

Everybody laughed, both the lunkheads and the regular kids who had gathered to watch the action. I was lying, but not the way they thought. I wanted to throw a punch, just one, just to show him that beating me up wouldn't be a total breeze. But I'd just moved in with my aunt a week ago, and if she found out I was fighting . . .

"Your dad's a thief," Ox said. "Just like you."

"He is not!"

"Then why's he in jail?"

It got so quiet you could hear the leaves flitting around the playground behind us. Everyone wanted to hear my answer. Ox had just insulted my dad. But it wasn't an insult. It was true, and everyone knew it. My dad had even been on TV.

Ox laughed. His teeth were big and yellow like slabs of cheese. He drew back one dirty fist. I could hear Timmy smack his hands over his face. He can't even handle the scary parts in a *Toy Story* movie.

"Aide!" somebody yelled.

Ox's fist froze in midair. His lunky friends turned and shoved through the crowd of kids behind them.

One of the school aides was marching toward us. Everyone scattered except Ox.

"What's going on?" The aide was only barely taller than Ox.

"Someone stole my phone," Ox said.

The aide squinted at me and looked me over from head to toe, like the phone might be bulging out from my clothes. She must have seen my dad on the news too.

Ox leaned closer to me. "See you tomorrow," he whispered. "Bring my phone—or face the consequences."

Probably the biggest word he knew.

Timmy and I walked home. His elementary school is next door to my middle school, so Aunt Mina has me pick him up. It's the least I can do after all she's done for me.

"Did he hurt you?" Timmy asked. He's only six.

"No way." I wished I was back at my old neighborhood, where I had friends. But I didn't have a home there anymore. When my dad got arrested, I had to move in with my aunt Mina and Timmy.

It can't get any worse than this, I told myself, but I knew Ox would make it worse. Tomorrow he'd have a plan to keep the aide distracted while he tried to batter my brains through my ears.

If only Dad were around. He always knew what to do. It had only been a week since his arrest, but it felt like years.

That night, when Aunt Mina came into our bedroom, Timmy started jumping up and down on the bed in his Curious George pajamas. He looked like a whole roomful of monkeys at the zoo. He made me stay and listen to his bedtime story.

"Tell me a story like the one last night!" He loved his mom's stories. "About the cell phone that turns into a frog! Or another one about how Uncle Dave got rich?" Uncle Dave is my dad. "That one was classic!"

Aunt Mina has dark brown hair that she poufs up on her head like a serving of soft-serve ice cream. She frowned and tilted her head sideways until it looked like the ice cream was going to slide off the cone. Her stress relief necklace dangled over her shoulder.

"Not that one." She didn't want to talk about my dad in front of me.

Timmy plopped himself down on the bed. He could tell right away that he'd said the wrong thing.

Aunt Mina's got a temper. That's why she bought the necklace. Just after I moved in last week, she stepped on one of Timmy's Legos while she was clearing space for my bed. Her face got red and her forehead wrinkly. She screamed: "This mess *makes me sick!*"

That's why I'm so terrified of getting in trouble at school.

"Any story is fine." Timmy put on a big fake smile. "But not a scary one. Tell me one about how me and Peter karate-chop the bad kids before school!"

Aunt Mina frowned. "Are you two having trouble?"

"No way," I said. "Nobody messes with Timmy. He's the toughest kid around."

"I give them the monkey chop. Hiya!" Timmy wiggled his butt.

"What are you doing?" I asked.

"Monkeys karate-chop with their tails."

Aunt Mina laughed. I've always loved her laugh—it sounds like three or four sneezes in a row.

She sat on Timmy's bed and started the same way she does every story, with a "Once upon a time . . ." Then she told a story about a kid named Timmy, also known as "Monkey Man," who could jump higher than an elephant and had karate-master moves he learned from a wise old chimpanzee in the Congo. While she told it, she kept fingering the crystal on her necklace. She told me it replaces her anger with creative energy. She bought it a few weeks ago, when some old woman in a New Age shop saw her yelling at Timmy on the street.

Timmy loved the story. There wasn't a scary moment in it. As soon as it was over, he lay down and shut his eyes, but I knew he wasn't ready to sleep. He wanted to imagine the story again.

Aunt Mina and I left him. Out in the living room she said to me, "I don't want you fighting. No matter how much those kids are bugging you."

Bugging. As if Ox Edelman was an ant you could flick off with your finger and not some kind of human rhinoceros.

"What if someone attacks me?"

"Back away and find an adult."

Adults were never around when you needed them.

"Fighting almost killed your father," Aunt Mina said. "He was always coming home with bloody knuckles or a black eye or worse. I always had to bandage him up afterward. Once, somebody smashed a beer bottle over his head. I thought he was going to bleed to death before I got him to the emergency room. Some nights when he was out, I couldn't sleep. I was afraid he'd get himself killed or kill somebody else. When he moved out of our parents' house it got even worse. You know what saved him? You. After you were born, he got a job. He stopped going out late. He never fought again. The idea of you or Timmy fighting . . ."

"I know. It makes you sick."

Her face turned bright pink. She was about to get angry. I wished I hadn't said it.

But she rubbed the necklace between her fingers and calmed down. "Yes," she said. "It makes me sick to my stomach. Peter, your life is like a story that you're telling everyone. People think they already know how your story will end up, because they think it's the same as your dad's. But it's not. It's *your* story. You control it, just like I control the stories I tell Timmy. You can make your own ending. I'm already proud of you. You had to change schools. You had to move in with us. I know your dad is proud too."

If only I could control my dad's story.

"When do you think he'll be able to come home?" I asked.

She sighed. "I just know we love him no matter what he did."

The cops found a whole mountain of cash in my dad's car. He swears he didn't steal it. I believe him, but no one else does—not even Aunt Mina.

I went to bed. It was early, but I needed time to think. My mattress is next to Timmy's bed. He was still awake. Some toy was glowing under his blanket.

"Good story, Timmy?" I whispered.

The glow disappeared. The room was pitch dark.

"My mom's stories are the best," he said. "They come true."

Next morning I hustled out the door early with Timmy. I was hoping I could drop him off and scoot inside my school before Ox was ready for me.

No luck. Ox and the lunkheads were waiting for me by the basketball court a block away from the elementary school. They were all grinning like they were excited for Christmas. No adults were anywhere near. Someone was jackhammering down the block on Second Avenue. The crossing guard would never hear us.

Other kids came running up, filling up the spaces between the lunkheads. They knew what Ox was planning to do to me. I looked over their faces. Some were excited. Some were laughing. A few looked sorry for me.

"Timmy," I said. "Go on to school."

Ox swaggered up to me. "Got the phone? Or should I smash your face and then ask?"

"None of the above," I said.

Ox had to think for a minute. Multiple-choice tests weren't exactly his thing. He gave up. "Hand it over or I start pounding!"

"Make him cry!" one of his friends shouted.

Aunt Mina would never forgive me if I got into a fight. But I couldn't just stand there again and get clobbered.

Timmy giggled. He had a weird grin on his face. I figured he was so scared he was losing his mind. "Timmy, get to school *now.*"

The lunkheads had formed a circle around me. I couldn't run. No one was going to help me. I was afraid of Ox, but I was also feeling like Aunt Mina when she flips out—sick of all this. Sick of these kids, sick of being afraid, sick of hearing people whisper about my dad behind my back. I wanted to throw a punch, even if Ox destroyed me afterward.

But Aunt Mina had laid down the rule. How could I break it? She was the only parent I had left.

"Say cheese!" Timmy pulled something out of his pocket: a yellow cell phone. He held it up and mashed his finger into the screen to take a picture.

Ox squinted at the flash. "Is that—my phone?"

Timmy giggled. "Mine now, dork brain!"

A few kids snorted. A few gasped. Timmy and I were now both going to die.

"Where did you get that?" I asked him. Then I remembered the glow under his blankets last night. He'd had the phone all along.

Ox was finally done being confused. "*You* stole it!"

He thrust his big paw at Timmy's face. I tried to lunge forward to block him, but I wasn't going to make it. One of the lunkheads behind Ox shut his eyes, as if even he couldn't watch what was about to happen.

But what happened was weirder than anyone expected. Weirder and more amazing.

Timmy screamed. Not a scared scream, not a "Help me!" scream, but a kind of savage screech. Ox stopped short. Then he looked down, as if to make sure that Timmy was still a tiny first-grader and not some rampaging ape.

That's when Timmy jumped.

I've never seen a kid jump like that. I've never seen a pro basketball player jump like that.

Timmy jumped higher than Ox. He hung in the air, shot out his foot, and twirled like an Olympic skater. He must have spun six times in the air, gaining speed every time. His foot cracked Ox right in the nose. Ox yelped and flopped down to the sidewalk.

Timmy hit the ground and jumped again. This time, when he spun, his foot thumped one of Ox's pals in the gut and then another one in the side of the knee. They both toppled over.

Timmy landed on his toes.

"Hiya!" he yelled, waving his hands around like a maniac. "Hiya! Hiya! Who wants a piece of Monkey Man!"

By now, most of the lunkheads had dashed away, even the ones who got kicked, but Ox was still sitting on the sidewalk. He was holding his nose. Blood oozed between his fingers.

"That little kid kicked me." It was hard to understand him with his hand over his nose.

The crossing guard finally came running. "Who did this?"

"Those two!" Ox pointed at us with his blood-wet hand. "And they stole my phone!"

"I don't have a phone," Timmy said. "Just my frog. See?" He stuck his hand into his pocket and showed us a live frog. Its little green head was poking out between Timmy's fingers.

We had to wait outside Timmy's principal's office while she called first my principal and then Aunt Mina.

"How did you do that?" I asked.

"I told you about my mom's stories," Timmy said. "Remember the one she told two days ago about the phone that turns into a frog?"

"Sure. But it was just a story."

"No! In the story the meanest kid at school has a phone, but because he's so mean, the phone turns into a frog and hops into my backpack. Remember? That's how she told it. And that's what happened!"

He took out his frog again. He pointed at it with his other hand and snapped his fingers—and it was a yellow cell phone. Ox's phone.

I made him change it from a phone to frog and back again three times before I believed it.

"Have her stories always come true?" I asked.

"Last couple of weeks. What should we ask for tonight? How about a story where we fly on a magic subway train to Florida! And the alligators let us ride on their tails. But only the nice alligators. I don't want a scary story."

It was about two weeks ago when she bought the necklace, the one that was supposed to convert her anger into creative energy. Apparently, it was working better than anyone could have imagined. Or maybe Aunt Mina has a lot of anger.

"Timmy, last night you said your mom told a story about how Uncle Dave got rich. Was that after she bought the necklace?"

"Yeah. But I guess it didn't come true."

"It did. Remember when they found that pile of cash in his car? It all came from a bank in our neighborhood. That's why he's in jail now."

"But it wasn't his fault. It was the story's! You can tell the police."

"They won't listen."

"That's not fair."

"It's okay, Timmy. Here's what we do. The next story we ask for—"

"Yeah?"

"Is about how Uncle Dave gets out of jail."

"Yeah!" Timmy liked my dad.

I wasn't sure how the necklace worked, but I had just seen its magic in action. Aunt Mina could make any story she told come true. She had made a phone turn into a frog. She had made Timmy turn into Karate Figure Skater Monkey Man. She could save my dad. And she didn't even know it.

And good thing she didn't. She might be too scared to tell another story. So far, they hadn't worked out too well. We'd have to trick her into telling a story for my dad. Or maybe I could borrow the necklace from her and try telling a story myself. I'd do whatever it took.

When Aunt Mina showed up, she looked like she wanted to hurl us through the principal's window. Especially when she heard that we were not only fighting, but fighting over a stolen cell phone. She barely moved her lips as she apologized to the principal. Her fingers had tightened into claws. The crystal on her necklace was glowing bright pink.

I knew Timmy was scared, but he still stood up for me. "I got in the fight," he said. "Not Peter."

"And what about that boy's phone?" asked the principal.

"I didn't steal it! It just hopped into my backpack."

That didn't help.

I tried to look serious and guilty and sorry, even though I hadn't actually done anything. I knew no adult would believe that Timmy had beaten up all those seventh-graders. I promised Aunt Mina and the principal I'd never fight again.

And I knew I could keep my promise—as long as my dad came back. If he was safe, I could handle anything.

Back home Aunt Mina stormed into her bedroom and slammed the door. She refused to come out. I had to make pizza bagels for dinner. While they were in the toaster oven, I tiptoed to her door.

"Aunt Mina? Do you want a pizza bagel?"

She didn't answer. I tried again.

"Aunt Mina? Do you think I could borrow your necklace for a minute?"

"Forget it!"

I left her alone. I could wait. I kept thinking about my dad. Aunt Mina tells better stories, but he tells better jokes. When he's in the middle of a joke, his head starts bobbing and his cheeks start jiggling, as if he can barely hold in his laughter. He gets everybody laughing with him before he's even done. He has thick arms and shoulders from playing basketball when he was a kid. When I was little he used to hug me every night before I went to bed. I could hear his heart thumping against my face. I felt like nothing could ever touch me. I'm too old for that now. But at least I had a plan to get him home.

When we were done with dinner, I had Timmy get into his pj's and brush his teeth. I said I'd tell him his bedtime story tonight.

"But then it won't be real."

"We'll have the real one tomorrow, when your mom's feeling better."

I could handle one more day without my dad.

"What if she won't tell it right? What if she doesn't believe us?"

"If we have to, we'll sneak into her room at night and grab her necklace. That's what gives her—"

Aunt Mina stuck her head in the doorway. "Steal my necklace?" Her voice was sharp and cold. "Is that your next little scheme? After all I've done for you. And for your father."

How could I explain? "Aunt Mina—"

Timmy stood up on his bed. "Mommy, we have a great idea for a story!"

"Not now, Timmy," I whispered.

"But I want to tell her! We need a story to help Uncle Dave."

Aunt Mina stepped inside Timmy's bedroom. Her hair had come undone and was now falling all over her face, like someone had dumped a pile of anger on her. "You want a story?"

"Yeah!" said Timmy. "You know why? Because your stories come true!"

"Timmy, not now!" I said.

But Aunt Mina wasn't listening. She was shaking with anger. "How about this story? Once upon a time two ungrateful boys were living in a small apartment with one rule. One rule! No fighting. But they broke the rule anyway!"

"Is this a scary story?" asked Timmy.

"It's a true story!" she said. "But I can make it scary. So what happened next? I've got it! The mother got so angry that they broke her *one single rule* that she locked them in their room and turned into a fire-breathing monster and ate them alive. Because that's what they deserved! The end. How about that? You like that story?"

She stared at us. I thought I saw little jets of steam coming from her nostrils. The crystal on her necklace was as bright as a flame.

"I don't think I like that story," said Timmy.

"Aunt Mina, wait!" I said.

But she stomped out and slammed the door behind her.

I jumped up and grabbed for the doorknob. It was locked.

Timmy's door doesn't have a lock.

I didn't know what to think. Something that crazy couldn't come true, could it? But I had already seen Timmy jumping and twirling like some kind of turbo-powered ballerina-kickboxer. And I knew my father had been arrested because of a gigantic mound of stolen money that had appeared in the back seat of his car.

"That doesn't count," said Timmy. "That's not coming true. Right?"

Did it count? Aunt Mina had said "Once upon a time" and "The end." Did that make it a story? And the necklace had been glowing. "I don't know."

"What if I don't want Mommy to eat me?" Timmy asked.

"She won't." No, she'd never hurt us. She loved me. She loved Timmy even more. Sure, she had a temper, but there was no way her own story could transform her into a monster.

I heard a ribbit. The frog had jumped out from under Timmy's blanket. Timmy snapped his fingers, and it turned into a cell phone again. The magic was still working.

My heart started to pound.

"She's so funny," Timmy said. "She cracks me up. Right?"

I'd heard about moms who went insane and attacked their kids with a frying pan or something, but Aunt Mina never would. She laughed at every goofy thing Timmy did. She hugged him every time he was scared and kissed him every single night. Her freak-outs always blew over after a few minutes. Maybe she'd scream a little louder, or a little longer, or with a little more spit than usual.

I hoped.

"What's that sound?" Timmy asked.

At first it was low and rumbling, like a dog growling. But then it got louder, like a whole pack of dogs. Wild dogs. Wolves. Howling.

"Does your frog phone make calls?" I had to yell to be heard. Maybe we could call the fire department. Or animal control.

"No. But it can take pictures. And it has Subway Surfers!"

Great.

The howling got louder.

"I hate this story!" Timmy ran back to the bed and dove under the covers.

I tried the doorknob again. Still locked. I jumped up and kicked as hard as I could at the door. It rattled in its frame, but stayed shut.

The roaring suddenly stopped. As if the wolves had all run away, maybe because they were afraid of something even bigger and more ferocious.

I kicked again at the doorknob. Then I backed up and took a run at it with my shoulder. It flew open, and I tumbled outside.

I stood up. I was alone in the living room.

Timmy tiptoed up behind me. "Where's Mommy?"

"RIGHT HERE!" The door from Aunt Mina's bedroom swung open, and there she was.

But she wasn't Aunt Mina anymore. She had the same gray eyes and thin eyebrows, but besides that, she didn't look like anything I'd ever seen, even in the zoo. She had grown so tall she had to hunch under the doorframe. Her brown hair, now long and stiff, stood up on her head like a big dead bush. More hair, shorter and bristly, like a porcupine's, covered her shoulders and arms. Her fingers had stretched out and hardened into claws. Her eyes were red. Thick yellow goo, like grease, leaked from their corners and made streaks over her face. Her necklace hadn't grown, but now it was glowing a deep red, not pink. She grinned at us. You could see her long, needly teeth.

"You smell funny, Mommy," said Timmy. "Maybe you should take a bath. And also stop being a monster."

The monster roared. The noise slammed into us like a tractor trailer on the highway. "You broke *my rule!*"

Timmy snapped his fingers. He must have been hoping he could zap the monster back to normal like he had zapped the frog back into a phone. Nothing happened.

The monster stepped forward. The claws of her feet dug so deep into the floor that little wood chunks flew up and skipped across it.

There was only one place to run. I darted for the bathroom, pulling Timmy behind me. I pushed the doorknob button to lock the door behind us.

There was a window next to the toilet, and outside the window, a metal fire escape. If we could get out there, maybe we could get away. But Aunt Mina was always careful to keep the window latched so Timmy couldn't accidentally open it. The latch was on the top of the window frame. I jumped up onto the toilet seat to reach it.

"Open up!" The monster was outside the door, but she was so loud it sounded like she was screaming in our faces.

The latch was old and rusty. I couldn't move it. I jumped to the floor.

The door whipped open and slammed against the other side of the wall. The monster had to duck her enormous bush of hair under the doorframe just to fit through. Flames flickered from her nostrils. Spit sizzled around her mouth. A drop of it fell onto the sink. I could smell the monster's thick, swampy breath.

We were trapped.

The monster saw my footprints on the toilet seat. "You disgusting kids!"

A few of the old tiles in the bathroom cracked from the force of her voice.

"Aunt Mina, look at Timmy. He's your son. Remember?"

"You." Her voice was now a raspy whisper. "You want to steal my necklace."

She made her claws into two huge spiky fists and spread them wide to crush us between them. I jumped on Timmy and tackled him to the floor. She missed us, but one of her fists smashed into the mirror over the sink and deep into the wall behind it. She bellowed in fury. I pushed Timmy forward between her legs, and we scampered out into the living room.

We heard a tremendous crash. The monster came stomping through the ruined wall.

I looked at the front door. To get to it we'd have to sprint right under her claws. There was no place to run and no place to hide in this little apartment.

Then I had an idea. We had to take control of the story.

"Bedroom, Timmy."

We raced back into his room.

Through the open doorway we saw the monster lift her head and let out a noise that sounded a little like a chuckle, a little like a growl, and a little like a chicken being crunched up by an alligator.

"Get in the bed," I told Timmy. "You're going to ask your mom for a new story. A nicer story. It's the only way to change her back."

I hoped he understood.

The monster folded her arms and squeezed through the doorway after us. She stopped and made a disgusting burbling sound deep in her throat. "I'm getting hungry!"

"How about a new story, Mommy?" Timmy suggested.

The monster stopped burbling. "A new story?"

"Yeah! One where Mommy loses her weird hair and sharp teeth and smells better and starts being nice again. How about that one?"

The monster stretched out her arms. Her nail were like iron spikes.

"Keep going, Timmy!" I said.

"And she says sorry and everything is okay and nobody gets eaten," Timmy finished. "The end."

"The end," the monster growled. "The end *for you*."

"No!" said Timmy. "That's the *old* story. We want a new one."

"Start with 'Once upon a time,'" I said.

The monster stuck out her long yellow tongue and ran it over her fat lips. "Once upon a time . . ."

Was that enough to start the story? Now I just had to get her to tell the rest.

"Good!" I said. "Now say 'The monster disappeared!'"

The monster roared again. "NO! The monster punished the children. Because they broke her rule!" Now fire was pouring out between her needly teeth as well as her nostrils. I could feel the heat on my forehead, like a sunburn. Timmy screamed.

"Aunt Mina," I said. "This is your son! You love him. You don't have to be a monster. Tell a new story. Say 'Once upon a time.'"

She snarled. A fleck of spit flew from her lips and landed on my skin. It burned.

"Once upon a time," the monster said.

"Yes! 'The monster remembered that she loved her son.' Say it, Aunt Mina!"

Timmy was curled up on the bed, his knees held tight to his head. But he opened one eye.

"The monster remembered," she growled.

"Good!" I said. "Remembered what?"

"That . . ."

"Yes?"

"That . . ."

"Say it!"

"That the children deserve to die!"

She jumped up and down on her clawed feet. I could feel the floor shake. Her fat, scaly stomach jiggled. Timmy moaned.

What could I do? My dad yelled at me sometimes. His face got just as red as Aunt Mina's. He lost control, but then he calmed down. This monster would never calm down. Sometimes adults go crazy. This one had gone worse than crazy.

But I remembered that the story wasn't over. "What's wrong with breaking a rule?" I asked.

The monster swung her head toward me.

"What's wrong with stealing a cell phone?" I asked. "Or a necklace?"

The monster tossed her head back. Flames spurted from her throat again. She suddenly stopped. Maybe she was afraid the ceiling would catch fire and collapse all over us.

What else could I do but keep going?

"What's wrong with leaving a few toys on the floor?" I said.

"What's wrong?" she roared.

"Yeah! What wrong? Kids do that. We're kids."

"What's wrong?!"

"Yeah! Tell me!"

I hoped there was still some Aunt Mina left in that hairy disaster.

"Leaving toys on the floor," she said, *"MAKES ME SICK!"*

Just what I hoped she'd say. But was that now part of the story?

She pointed her claws at me. The nails were flecked with white paint from when she had smashed the wall. Soon they'd be covered with my blood.

But as she was stepping toward me, I knocked a box of Timmy's Legos onto the floor.

She stepped on them. She hopped on one foot. She let out not a roar but a huge, angry yelp.

And then she stopped.

She frowned.

Her bulging eyes rolled.

"I feel," she grumbled, "funny."

She clutched at her stomach. Her claws poked into her scaly body. From deep within, we heard a kind of squishy gurgling sound.

Had it worked? She said the toys on the floor would make her sick. Did that count as a story? Had the story made her sick?

"Maybe you should sit down," I said.

The monster opened her mouth. All the fire in her throat had gone out. I pulled Timmy off the bed. The monster lurched forward. A jet of green goo shot from her mouth and splashed all over Timmy's bed. It oozed off his blankets to the floor.

It sure smelled like she was sick.

"I feel terrible," the monster mumbled. She rocked backward and slammed down on her enormous rear end.

"I still want to— Ohhhh!" She couldn't even roar anymore.

Timmy was crouching in a corner. "What's wrong with the monster?"

"We made her sick," I explained.

"Do something!" she yelped. She couldn't even roar now.

"Poor Mommy Monster," said Timmy. "But you're still gross."

"I can help you," I said, "but you have to do exactly as I say."

Her huge bushy head started wobbling. "I'm gonna throw up again."

"Not on me!" yelled Timmy.

"I can help," I said.

"Do it," the monster grumbled. "Or I'll kill you." She tried to push herself off the floor with her claws. She snorted, and sparks fell from her nose. Could she gather strength for one more jet of flame?

I knelt right by her head. Her wet eyes looked yellow now. I could smell her puke-breath.

"Repeat after me," I said.

"Why?"

"It's the only thing that will make you feel better," I said. "Say 'Once upon a time.'"

"Once upon a time." She moaned. "My stomach!"

"The monster turned back into Aunt Mina," I said.

"The monster turned back into Aunt Mina," she repeated.

"And never bothered anybody again."

"And never bothered anybody again."

"The end," I finished.

"The end."

"And," I added quickly, "my father came back."

"And your father came back. Huh?"

Nothing happened. "Timmy," I said. "You better leave."

He didn't move. I didn't know if he was too scared or too confused. The monster moaned again. What else could I do?

I snapped my fingers.

Things started to change.

Her body shortened and became slimmer. Her claws shrunk back into hands. Her huge bush of twiggy hair flattened out over her head, until it was Aunt Mina's hair again. It needed to be combed, and it smelled like puke, but it was hers. Now she looked like Aunt Mina all over, but much paler.

"What happened?" she mumbled. "What's that smell?"

"You yakked, Mommy," Timmy said. "Big-time."

"I think," Aunt Mina said, "I better go to bed. You boys have a nice sleep or whatever."

She stumbled off, past the ruined door and the smashed bathroom wall. The crystal dangling from her neck swung back and forth. She shut the door.

"I'll clean up in here," I said. "You can sleep in the living room tonight."

I found Timmy a clean blanket from the closet and tucked him in on the couch.

I had changed the story. I had saved him, and me, and Aunt Mina too. I had saved everyone—well, except my dad. And now my reward was I had to clean up the monster puke.

I wrapped the puke up in Timmy's blankets as well as I could. I rolled them up tight and shoved them down into a trash bag. The smell from the bag almost made me gag. I used paper towels to mop up the slime that spattered the floor and walls. I didn't mind the work so much, or even the smell.

What really bothered me was that I waited until after I said "The end" to add the part about saving my father. That was my chance, and I had blown it.

Now I had a decision to make. Should I ask Aunt Mina to tell another story tomorrow night? A story that would save my father? But maybe she'd wouldn't want to tell any more stories. Maybe she'd decide to chuck the necklace in the river. Or maybe she wouldn't remember what happened or wouldn't believe in the necklace's power. She'd tell another story without thinking of the consequences, and we'd have another disaster. Maybe a worse one. Could I take the chance? It wasn't just my own life at risk. It was Aunt Mina's and Timmy's.

There was a knock at the door.

I stood up.

Another knock.

A new monster?

I ran to the door and peered through the peephole.

It was my father. I opened the door.

"They let me go," he said. "I don't know why. But I'm free."

He hugged me. My body was warm all over. I could feel his heartbeat. I could have stayed in that hug forever.

From the living room I could hear Timmy mumbling, already half asleep. "Tell another story, Mommy. But not a scary one."

THE ONLY CHILD

BY JOSEPH S. WALKER

JAKE SCREAMED, GRIPPING THE SHOULDER restraint so hard that his knuckles turned white as his car crested the second big hill and plunged seemingly straight down and impossibly fast.

He'd managed to keep it together on the first hill, but now all thoughts of staying cool and being grown-up vanished as the car shook wildly and the wind roared past his ears. He was sure something had gone wrong and he was going to die, his mangled body pulled from the coaster's wreckage, but then they reached the bottom of the drop and shot back up, twisting into a loop that made him stop worrying about dying and start worrying about throwing up.

That second hot dog at the concession stand had been a big mistake.

He had told his parents that since he was finally old enough and tall enough to ride the Golden Eagle roller coaster, he wanted to do it alone. Dad couldn't go anyway because it would set off his vertigo, making him throw up for sure, and Jake didn't want to be the kid who had to have his mommy with him. All morning and into lunch, as the three of them had walked around the amusement park in the sweltering heat, he had pleaded and begged, promising a hundred times that he could handle it. He was no baby.

282

He was almost a teenager!

"Fine," his mother had finally snapped at him across the picnic table. She wiped her sweaty forehead with a napkin. "It's too hot to put up with your whining anymore. You go right ahead, mister, but I don't want to hear a word of complaint if it makes you sick."

Jake had sprung up from the table before she could change her mind, dashing for the line and waving over his shoulder at her shouts that they would meet him at the ride's exit. He felt a little guilty about how pushy he'd gotten, but how many chances would he get to do this? He decided that the long, boring wait in the winding Golden Eagle line would be punishment enough, which meant he was free to enjoy the ride. And when he finally got to the front and was put into a car with a cute girl about his age, with her parents in the car behind them, it had even seemed like he was being rewarded.

But now the ride was rocketing toward another loop, and it didn't feel much like a reward. He gripped the harness still more tightly. He wanted to look at the girl, to see if she was scared too, but he was afraid she'd be laughing at him, and anyway, trying to turn his head would just make him dizzier. Maybe he had inherited Dad's vertigo, something he had never worried about before.

They hit the loop, and he screamed again as he went upside down and felt his weight lifting from the seat, only the seat belt and the harness keeping him from breaking away on his own path to the hard ground.

There were two more giant hills, a third loop, and a lot of very sharp turns before the cars finally, mercifully, glided back to a stop at the station. Jake still clutched the harness so firmly that his hands ached. Park workers came scuttling down both sides of the rails, popping up the restraints and unlocking the seat belts, directing people to exit to the right.

Jake got to his feet, feeling unsteady and woozy. He didn't look at the girl as she and her parents raced off to another ride, chattering happily like the rest of the riders.

That was fun, Jake told himself firmly. *I want to do it again. Sometime.* He was only half convinced this was true, but he was completely convinced that his parents, and especially Mom, would be unbearably smug if he showed them how scared he'd been. He took a moment to gather himself and began walking slowly down the curving exit path. The rest of the riders were well ahead of him, and he was alone by the time he came to the park's main concourse where Mom had said they would meet.

There was nobody there. It wasn't just that his parents weren't around; through some fluke of the park's ebb and flow, there was nobody in sight in any direction as he came to a confused stop with the toes of his sneakers on the concourse bricks. He could still hear the noise of people, shouts, and laughter and music from every direction, but the sounds might as well have been coming from ghosts. He couldn't even see the people in the gondolas of the aerial tram that went from one side of the park to the other since he was standing directly under the lines.

He seemed completely alone.

The panic he'd felt on the ride started to surface again, but just as he felt it rising, a group of little kids came tearing around a corner, chased by a frantic mother, and the spell was broken. In a few seconds the concourse went from deserted to mobbed as people emerged from every direction, everyone moving fast, chattering, looking at maps of the park and guzzling sodas. But where were Mom and Dad?

There was a small playground across the concourse. Jake hustled across and climbed to the top of the slide, hanging on with one hand as he turned to scan the crowd from his higher vantage point.

There! He saw his dad's distinctive, dorky plaid baseball cap off to his left, bobbing above the crowd and moving away from where he and Mom should be waiting. *Weird.* Jake jumped to the ground, stumbling a bit as he broke into a run, weaving around people and craning his neck. Dad was entering the big central plaza of the park. Jake dodged around one last group of confused tourists pointing in different directions, and now he was only a few feet away. He could see Mom now, walking to Dad's right, and between them—

Between them was Jake.

Jake skidded to a stop. Although he was behind them, he knew these were his parents, clearly and unmistakably, and the kid walking between them was, just as clearly, himself, with the same blue T-shirt, the same khaki shorts, the same white sneakers with his initials in red marker on their backs. The only difference between them was that this other Jake had a balloon. The string was tied to his right wrist, and the balloon itself, way up above even Dad's head, was huge and round and dark reddish purple, the color of a bruise several days old.

Jake's jaw went slack. For a moment the ground seemed unsteady under his feet, and he felt a prickle at the back of his neck. How could he be both here and there?

He couldn't, obviously. This had to be some other kid who happened to be dressed like him, and his parents just weren't paying attention. *As usual.* He ran forward, going past and swinging around to face them.

"Hey!" he shouted. "It's me!"

Without even breaking stride, the three of them walked right past him, his father brushing him aside slightly as they passed. Jake felt cold, rigid with fear. He'd seen the face of the other kid now, but it wasn't some other kid. It was him, the him he saw in the mirror every morning—the same face, eyes, hair, everything—the very essence of Jakeness, grinning stupidly up at Mom and holding his big dumb balloon.

Jake shook himself. He couldn't just stand here and let them walk off. He turned and saw the ugly balloon moving away and ran after it. This time Jake grabbed Dad's arm with both hands, yelling at the same time, but Dad just shook him off, not even seeming to look down or notice that he was doing it, and kept walking forward. Jake ran around them and stood directly in front of his mother, holding up his hands to make her stop. His parents both had dazed, sleepy expressions on their faces, and as they reached him, his mom simply pushed Jake aside without even looking at him, shoving him so hard that he almost fell to the concrete of the plaza.

Jake's heart was thudding, his breath shallow. Mom and Dad hadn't looked at him, but the other Jake had, and not with the smile he'd been giving Jake's parents. His eyes had been cold and rimmed with red, his mouth sneering. In the split second that they'd been looking at each other, the other Jake had parted his lips, and the teeth inside were not like Jake's teeth—there were too many of them, and they were too sharp. Jake froze in terror at the sight, and when Mom had shoved him, he was sure he'd heard the other Jake snort with laughter.

This wasn't just some other kid trying to steal his parents. That thing had done something to Mom and Dad. Drugged them or hypnotized them. What could he do? He wanted to cry—just curl up on the ground and bawl—but that wouldn't do anything. He needed help.

There was a security guard nearby, leaning against a lamppost.

Jake darted up to him and tapped him on the shoulder, and the guard looked down at him lazily.

"Sir, my parents," Jake said. "They've got some other kid with them. He looks like me but he isn't; we've got to stop them."

The guard nodded, yawned, and looked up at the gondolas floating by overhead. He didn't move from the post.

Jake grabbed at his hand. "Sir, please!"

The guard lifted one foot from the ground, planted it on Jake's chest, and shoved. Jake stumbled backward several feet, landing on his butt. There were swarms of people around, but none of them paid any attention, and the guard just kept looking around, seeming to watch everything except Jake.

"Don't bother," said a quiet voice behind him. "They can't really see you."

Jake jumped back to his feet and spun around. A girl a couple of years younger than him stood there, wearing a simple pink dress and big sunglasses with plastic blue frames. She looked odd, out of place. *She looks . . . faded,* Jake thought, as though everyone and everything around her was in a high-def video while she was in an old photo, dug out of a shoebox in the back of a closet. Her hands were folded primly in front of her, and her head was cocked a little to the side. She seemed to be looking right at him, though with the sunglasses it was hard to tell.

"What do you mean?" he asked. "Who can't see me?"

"Him," she said, pointing at the guard. "Or your parents. Or anyone else."

Jake looked at his hand, which seemed perfectly normal. "I'm invisible?"

"No," she said. Her voice was quiet and somehow dry like sheets of paper rustling against one another. "You're just . . . not important enough to notice anymore. You're like a buzzing fly that gets waved away without really thinking about it. You've been replaced."

He stepped closer to her. "It's that other boy," he said. "The one with my folks. What did he do?"

Her lips tightened. "It's not a boy," she said. "We call it the Only Child."

"'We'? Who's 'we'?"

"The rest of us," she said, gesturing around the park. "You're not the first. Look, there goes Paul now. He's been here since before me."

Jake looked to where she was pointing and caught a glimpse of a boy, his back to them, slipping through the crowd, his clothes faded and out of focus like the girl's. Jake knew that if she hadn't pointed, he never would have noticed the boy at all.

When he looked back she was starting to wander away, moving slowly toward the Golden Eagle. "Wait," he cried, grabbing her shoulder. She was solid enough, though touching her immediately made his hand feel like it had gone to sleep, all pins and needles. He pulled her around to face him. "You have to help me. Please!"

She shrugged. "Help you? How? If I knew, would I be here? Any of us?"

"But what is it? What can I do?"

"Nothing," she said. "It's the Only Child. Call it a demon or a monster or a ghost, it doesn't matter. Your family belongs to it now."

"No," Jake moaned. He shook his head. There had to be something. He looked around wildly and saw the balloon, the hideous balloon, way over at the far side of the plaza. He started to trot after it.

To his surprise the girl followed him, keeping pace with him easily as he moved through the crowd. He was almost knocked over a dozen times by people who paid no attention to him, though she glided around them easily.

"It happened to all of us," she said. She sounded like she was patiently trying to make a stupid child understand the alphabet. "The Only Child will leave with your parents, and you'll be stuck here. And then in a few months it will be back and choose someone else."

"I'll stop them from leaving," Jake said. He was breathing hard from trying to talk and follow the balloon at the same time. The girl didn't seem bothered by it.

"You can't," she said.

"I'll follow them. I'll take the bus to our house and call the cops, and they'll come and arrest it."

"The police won't listen to you any more than the guard did," she said. "But anyway, you can't leave. If you try to leave the park, you'll just find yourself back inside. I've tried it hundreds of times."

Jake stopped. Ten feet ahead of him, his parents and the thing were standing at a game tent—a ring toss. His dad and the thing pretending to be Jake were both tossing small rings, trying to drop them over the necks of soda bottles. His mother was looking at the prizes stacked at the front of the booth—stuffed animals, model cars, pocketknives, hats, an assortment of random junk that would have fascinated Jake an hour ago.

"It's toying with them," the girl said. Jake ignored her. He'd just noticed something. The thing was tossing the rings with its left hand. Jake was right-handed. The thing, the Only Child, didn't know that— but Jake's father, of course, did.

He sidled up to his father on the side away from the thing. "Dad," he hissed. The man didn't look at him. "Dad," Jake said louder, and this time he reached out and pinched Dad's arm as hard as he could, twisting the bit of skin. Dad jumped and looked down at him, actually looked at him, and Jake felt a burst of hope and gratitude. He grabbed Dad's arm again. "It's me, Dad," he yelled. "I'm Jake. I'm right-handed, remember? Look, that thing is throwing leftie!"

He had taken too long. By the time he said his name, the flicker of interest and awareness in Dad's eyes had died away, and once again he shook Jake off fiercely, sending him sprawling onto the ground. He wanted to scream, to burst out in hysterical yells, but as he opened his mouth, the Only Child stepped between him and Dad, staring down at him, and Jake's mouth went dry, the yell coming out as barely a squeak. The thing looked at him and shook its head, lifting a finger to its lips, lips that looked just like Jake's.

Shhhh.

Jake swallowed. He was about to start scrambling backward on his butt, desperate to get away from the thing, but then he saw something that pinned him in place and made him feel that the ground was about to swallow him.

The balloon was not tied to the Only Child's wrist—*it was growing out of it.* A tendril of flesh, like a misplaced finger, came out of the back of the thing's right wrist and, as it rose, gradually altered to look more and more like a silver ribbon, the kind you might see tied to any other balloon. Up close, though, it was unmistakable. The Only Child and the balloon were a single thing.

Jake was so transfixed by this that he barely noticed as his dad flipped his last ring toward the bottles, and the three of them turned and walked away, the Only Child giving him one last disdainful smirk.

Jake crawled into the narrow space between the ring toss and the next tent, shaking with fear. He couldn't imagine trying to stop the thing again. He couldn't even imagine going near it again.

He sat against the canvas of the tent, clutching his knees to his chest and rocking slightly.

The girl crawled into the space and knelt to face him. "Now you see," she said. "There's nothing you can do."

"What will it do to them?" Jake asked flatly.

"We don't know," she said. "None of our families ever come back. But the Only Child will."

"What will happen to me?"

"You'll stay in the park," she said. "It's not so bad. You won't grow up. But you'll fade a little more every year. And eventually, you'll just be gone." She settled down onto the ground, cross-legged. "It takes a long time."

He buried his head in his hands. "Why don't you stop it? If there are so many of you, why don't you team up and stop it?"

"You can't fight it."

He looked up. "Why not?"

She frowned. "You . . . you just can't. It's the Only Child."

"Stop saying that like it means something! It's just the stupid thing you call it!"

She shook her head. "Just accept it," she said. "This is your place now. With all of us."

Jake felt himself getting angry. It was better than being scared. "Maybe that's just what you want. Maybe you just want more people stuck here with you in your lousy park."

Leaning over, he pulled the tent flap aside a few inches and scanned the part of the crowd he could see. He saw sweating parents, screaming kids, and bored workers, but no faded children. "Where are all these others, anyway? Why aren't they here with you telling me all this?"

Now it was her turn to look down. "They don't spend time together if they can help it. It's too sad. I try sometimes to get the others to play or just talk, but they just drift around the park, waiting to fade away."

"So you're just . . . alone," he said.

"Yes," she whispered. Then she looked up. With a gloomy half smile she reached up and took off her big blue sunglasses. Jake bit his tongue to keep from crying out.

She had no eyes. The skin of her forehead simply continued, with only her nose and her mouth breaking the flat unbroken plane of her face.

"Alone in the dark," she said.

"But you pointed," Jake said. "You must be able to see."

She smiled more widely, the expression only making the blankness more unsettling. "We can see, in a way," she said. "You'll find out. Your eyes go first. That takes a few years. Then other things. You'll get quieter. Move less." Her voice dropped to a whisper again. "The ones who have been here longest say it's peaceful."

Jake closed his eyes and imagined being unable to ever open them again. Maybe the girl was right. There was nothing to do but accept it, accept that his last real conversation with his parents had been an argument over a roller coaster, accept that he was going to spend long years here alone, or nearly so.

There was a rustle, and then the girl was sitting beside him. "That's it," she said quietly. She put her hand gently on his shoulder, and again he felt numbness begin to spread from the place where she was touching him. "It's okay. It doesn't hurt. I'll show you around."

Jake took a deep breath. She was right. There was nothing he could do.

"It's easy. Just forget."

The numbness was spreading through him. It was easy. It would be easy to lean back against the tent, perhaps sleep, and just wait for whatever it would be like. . . .

"Forget them."

"NO!" he cried out with a feeling like breaking up out of the water after a dive. He shook her hand off and scrambled away from her, stumbling to his feet. "No! You're tricking me! You just want me to give up because you have!"

She stood herself, leaning back against the tent and putting her sunglasses back on. "There's really nothing else you can do," she said. There was no longer anything soothing or restful about her voice. "Night is coming. They may be gone already. And once they're out of the park and you're trapped here, it really is over."

"There must be *something*," Jake said. He rubbed his temples, urging himself to think. The Only Child. Its teeth, its red eyes. The faded children and dazed adults. The ugly, bruised-looking balloon that was part of it. *Anything. A weak point.*

Thinking about the balloon again, and the way it was attached to the Only Child's wrist, made him shudder with revulsion—but it also reminded him of something. A video they'd watched in biology class last year, about some kind of giant snapping turtle, a strong, vicious, but slow hunter. It had a tongue that looked just like a worm, and when a fish would come to investigate what looked like a tasty meal,

293

the deadly jaws would close with a force and speed that the video said could shatter bones.

The child is just the lure.

Jake stepped forward and grabbed the girl by the shoulders, pinning her against the tent. His hands went numb immediately, but he ignored it. "The balloon. It's always got the balloon, right? The Only Child?"

"What?" She squirmed against his grip. "Yes, of course. That's how we know it's back."

He had to get to the exit before his parents left. He turned away from her and sprinted out of the narrow space between the tents, back onto the main concourse, looking up at the sky. The girl was right. Night was coming.

A thought struck him, and he skidded to a stop and then turned to run back to the ring toss tent. He elbowed past three people who were playing the game and grabbed a pocketknife from the stacks of prizes, right under the nose of the man running the game. Nobody paid any attention to him.

He slipped back out of the knot of people. The girl was there, reaching out her hands to him, her mouth open, but if she said anything, he didn't bother to listen. He broke into a run, heading for the main exit of the park. As he went he pulled the knife out its box, tossing the package aside and unfolding the biggest blade. It was only a few inches long, but there was no time to look for anything else.

The crowd was already noticeably thinner than it had been earlier, and he was tortured by the idea that he was too late, that he'd wasted too much time back there feeling sorry for himself, listening to her urge him to surrender. What if they were already gone? What was the thing going to do to his parents once it had them outside? The girl had said that none of the parents ever came back. Had he seen them for the last time?

No—he saw the balloon up ahead, definitely moving toward the exit, but still twenty or thirty yards away from it. Jake put on an extra burst of speed. He knew what he was going to do. He would get only one try to do it right. There were footsteps behind him, keeping pace with him. The girl. She was yelling something, or maybe just sobbing. He had no time to listen.

They were directly in front of him now, with nobody in between. His mom was on the left, rummaging through her purse, no doubt already looking for her keys. His dad on the right, walking as he did when he was very tired and just needed to get home. In between was the Only Child, half turned toward Jake's mother, as if to urge her on, as if eager to leave.

At the last second, as Jake came flying up, it seemed to sense something, and the evil little replica of his own face started to turn, but it was too late.

Jake took a running leap, as high as he could, and caught the ribbon in his left hand. Immediately, the entire left side of his body felt numb to the point of death; cold, like being plunged into a freezing mountain lake.

There was a howl of rage, but he wasn't sure if it came from the false Jake or from above him. His momentum carried him past his father and the Only Child, and although every part of his being recoiled from it, he pulled the ribbon in tight between his left arm and his body.

As he continued forward and down toward the ground, the ribbon was pulled with him, the balloon following it down. His feet and then knees hit the concrete, and he kept the ribbon under him, scrambling forward to pull it down all the way until the balloon was on the ground directly in front of him. It radiated the dull heat of a living thing, heaving in a way that was not like a balloon at all. Jake could sense it fighting him, trying to break free and return to the air. Being this close to it was bringing Jake even closer to throwing up than the roller coaster had.

There was a hand on his back—the girl? His parents? The Only Child? He couldn't tell whose it was or whether it was trying to pull him back or help him forward. There was no time to think about it.

No time to think at all. He raised his right hand and, with all the force he could muster, drove the blade of the pocketknife into the very center of the balloon thing.

There was a scream that seemed to come from everywhere at once. An angry wind lifted Jake and threw him several feet back. He saw his parents staggering backward, the girl on her knees, holding her head as if in agony, and the Only Child, its Jake features melting away to reveal something hairy and writhing for just a second before there was a blinding flash of light that took the entire world away.

"Feeling better, buddy?"

Jake opened his eyes. He was on a bench just inside the park entrance. Dad was sitting next to him, holding a bottled water he'd just taken from Jake's lips. Mom stood over them, her hand on Jake's forehead.

"What—what happened?" he asked.

"You fell down, pal," his father said. "Seemed a little groggy there for a minute."

"Too much sun," Mom said. "I knew it was too hot for this today."

Jake looked around. A few people were glancing at the three of them curiously, but none of them seemed to be faded, and there were no strange balloons around.

He moved his head and arms experimentally, surprised to discover that he felt fine. "I'm okay," he said. He looked back and forth between the two of them. They both looked like they always had, nice if a little distracted, but they could obviously see him clearly. "Are you guys all right?"

His father barked a short laugh. "You're the one who fell down, cowboy." Jake had never understood his father's compulsion to call everyone by anything that wasn't their actual name.

"So . . ." Jake tried to figure out how to ask the dozens of questions he had. He settled for "Where's my balloon?"

They both looked confused. "I don't think you had a balloon today, sport," Dad said. "You sure you're okay?"

So . . . it had all been a dream or something? Jake didn't care. He just knew that he wanted to get away from this place. "Absolutely fine," he said, leaping up. "Come on, let's go!"

His parents exchanged confused looks, and shrugged. They followed Jake, who seemed simultaneously anxious to get out of the park and unwilling to get more than a foot or two away from them. He breathed a sigh of relief as they passed under the iron arch marking the entrance to the park.

They stopped at the edge of the immense parking lot. Mom sighed and looked at Dad, who immediately got the message. "You guys wait here," he said. "I'll go get the car."

"Thank you!" Mom said, handing him the keys. She plopped down on an open bench, arranging her purse and their bag of souvenirs around her. "You should sit down too, Jake. You're probably still a little feverish."

"I'm all right," he said. He was looking back at the park entrance, thinking about the girl. "I never even asked her name."

"Whose name?" his mother asked. She was flipping through her cell phone. "Oh, your aunt Jane has called four times today. I'd better see what this is about." Within a few seconds she was chattering away. Jake heard her say that they'd had a fine day, but that the heat had gotten to all of them.

Jake kicked himself mentally. Stupid to be feeling guilty for never asking an imaginary girl her name. Clearly he had hallucinated the whole thing, some confused half dream brought on by the sun and the dizziness of the roller coaster. He'd tell his parents about it on the drive home, though he already knew they wouldn't really get it. He stuck his hands into his pockets.

"Ow!" Something in his right-hand pocket had cut him. He pulled it out carefully.

It was the pocketknife, still open, the blade covered with something sticky and purple, and the edge now marked with his blood where it had sliced into his knuckle.

Jake stopped breathing. There was a honk behind him, and he turned to see Dad at the curb, Mom already opening the door to get into the car, both of them looking at him expectantly.

And way off at the far edge of the lot, crystal clear, he saw another family getting into another car.

A father, a mother—and a girl with a balloon the color of an angry bruise.

KAMIKAZE IGUANAS
BY ALISON MCMAHAN

FOR CHARLOTTE AND FOR JACK-HENRY

The green iguana, originally from Central and South America, is not native to Florida.

Duh. Green Iguanas. Could this assignment be any more boring?
I pull my hair back into a ponytail and keep reading.

It is regarded as one of the most invasive species since it was introduced into the ecosystem, probably by irresponsible pet owners, in the mid-1990s.

Those irresponsible pet owners! Letting their iguanas run away . . .
I have to make a PowerPoint presentation on non-native species
in Florida. Which should have been an easy cut-and-paste from the
internet, except Mr. Matlo, our science teacher, thinks he's clever, so he
made a rule.

We have to take our own pictures.

I have to go out and find three non-native species, take pictures of them, and write them up. I got some Egyptian geese yesterday. Now I need an iguana. Then after that, who knows?

Who cares?

One of the benefits of Mom *downsizing* our lives is that our new condo complex has a pool. I grab my phone, mutter something to her (I'm still not talking to her), and go out there. Not because I really think I'll find an iguana by the pool, but because I can't think of anywhere else to go.

I work my way around the pool fence, slowly, camera phone at the ready, waiting for an iguana to run out.

A group of kids is huddled around one of the barbecue grills. I'm hoping they're just trying to keep warm. It's, like, freezing, even though this is South Florida.

"Hey."

One of the huddlers has seen me. I recognize him, vaguely, from school. He's one of those guys, the kind who's good-looking and knows it. He goes by Spike. So lame.

His squad, Thing 1 and Thing 2, are with him, of course.

"Hey." I walk over to him.

"You're the new girl, right?"

"Yeah."

"Whatcha doin'?" That's Thing 1.

I hold up my phone. "Lookin' for non-native species. Did you do that assignment yet?"

"Oh, we got one right here."

Like an idiot I go right up to the grill where they are standing.

My stomach clenches. The PB&J from my lunch tickles the back of my throat.

There's an iguana lying on the grate.

It looks dead.

"Did you kill it?"

Thing 1 and Thing 2 bend over laughing, slapping their thighs. What is it with Florida that everyone acts like they're a cartoon character?

"Of course not." Spike taps the iguana on the head. The iguana does not respond. "When they get this cold, they go into hibernation. He'll wake up in a minute."

I'm about to ask how he knows that when I see it: It's a gas grill, and the flames are on, licking up toward the iguana's belly.

"Hey!" I grab the iguana under the arms. Spike has him by the tail. Each of us pulls, like it's a tug-of-war and the iguana is the rope.

"Ouch!" Spike lets go. He holds his hand up.

"See what this jerk-girl did?"

His hand has a long cut through it. Sliced as clean as a razor.

I put the iguana down on the ground, gently but quickly. I don't want my hand to get sliced through. The iguana's tail now has a ninety-degree turn in it. "You broke his tail."

"You broke it. Shoulda left him alone."

"I'm taking him to the vet." I switch off the grill. The flames startle, flicker, and die.

"No point." Spike reaches into the cabinet under the grill. "I'm better than a vet."

Just then the iguana wakes up. Lifts his head and looks at me, his eyes unblinking.

His eyes are like deep, dark, cave entrances. They invite me in. They promise to reveal mysteries that no one else will ever know.

I fall into those eyes so far, so deep, that I don't even see Spike lift the heavy iron spatula until it's too late.

He brings it crashing down and slices off the iguana's tail right at the break.

Thing 1 and Thing 2 cheer.

I scream.

I scoop up the iguana and run.

Heart pounding, I make it back to my room before Mom sees the iguana. He doesn't move much. Just blinks every now and then.

I set up a cardboard box with a towel, put the iguana in there, throw some shredded lettuce in with him.

The iguana seems completely uninterested in the lettuce. I find a couple dead cockroaches on the porch—Mom says they're palmetto bugs, but they look just like the cockroaches in New York—and throw those in for good measure.

Then it occurs to me the cockroaches were probably poisoned, so I take them out again.

The iguana doesn't move.

I look for blood on my shirt, and in the box, but there's hardly any. Maybe iguana tails are like lizard tails. Will it grow back?

I could take the iguana to Mom and ask her to take us to the veterinarian, like she used to do when our cat was sick. Back when we had a cat. Back when we lived at home.

But now I'm looking at the iguana, and I get this really strong feeling that I shouldn't tell Mom. I remember the day Mom took our cat to the ASPCA, even though I screamed and cried.

No way I'm telling her about the iguana.

The iguana's still not moving.

"Are you cold?" I pick him up and lay him on my chest. I make sure not to touch what's left of his tail.

"I'm so sorry he did that to you." I stroke him lightly, hoping my body warmth will help him. "We're going to make him pay. I don't know how, but we will."

The iguana just blinks.

I stare deep into his eyes, the dark pupils surrounded by a band of gold.

The iguana stares back.

Mom calls me to dinner.

Startled, the iguana jumps off my chest and scampers under the bed. Moves as quick as lightning.

"That's what I'll call you. Green Lightning. What do you think?"

The iguana stays under the bed, and Mom yells again. I don't want her to come into my room, so I go out.

"Takeout again?" I sit down at the table and contemplate the fried chicken from the grocery store, the canned green beans.

"I cooked the potatoes."

"I don't like 'em baked. I like mashed. You know that."

Mom sighs but doesn't scold me. This is the longest conversation we've had in days. Since we moved here.

"Look," she says, pulling the skin off the fried chicken, "I can't cook until—"

"—until you get everything in the kitchen set up. I know, I know."

I reach for her chicken skin. "This is the best part. Why do you buy fried chicken if you don't like it?"

"Because you do."

I'm sorry I said anything. She turns everything into a guilt trip.

I eat the skin. I wonder what she has in the fridge that the iguana would eat, since the lettuce didn't work.

"We could unpack the kitchen together." Mom peels off another piece of the skin, but this time she eats it before I can grab it. "Then I could start cooking again."

"I like fried chicken."

Those wavy worry lines appear on my mom's forehead. Her eyes droop. She presses her lips together, as if she's trying not to cry.

Now I feel bad.

Then I remember I'm still angry at her. I'm never going to forgive her for getting divorced and moving us here.

We used to be different. I miss that. I really do.

But there's no way I'm going to admit it.

"Besides, I have to find the third non-native species."

Mom keeps her eyes on her plate. She moves her food around without eating it. "How many do you have?"

"I have Egyptian geese and iguanas. I got some good pictures. But I need a third one."

"Crocodiles."

"Get out of here!" I point to the magnet on the fridge door with a crocodile and its gaping, open mouth showing off its sharp, scary teeth. "Crocodiles are everywhere in Florida! How can they be non-native?"

"Look it up."

I heave a huge sigh. I really don't want to work on this assignment anymore. "Well, even if they are, how am I going to get a picture? The dork teacher says we have to take the picture ourselves; it can't be from the internet."

"Take a picture of the magnet."

"That's cheating. Not allowed."

Mom takes another bite of chicken, skin and all, chews, and thinks. "Remember when we went to the reptile farm? On our drive down here?"

Of course I remember. It was just, like, ten days ago. It was excruciating. Mom trying to turn the complete disaster that our life is now into fun.

"I have that picture of you holding a baby crocodile. The crocodile in the picture is a man-eating Nile crocodile."

"That cuddly baby crocodile was a person-eating crocodile?"

I can't believe Mom said "man-eating." She's the one who always says it should be "person." Because otherwise it's like only men are people.

"Oh yeah. That's the only reason you let me take a picture of you with it. You thought it was cuddly."

She stares at the pile of chicken bones on her plate. "I can take the time to dig it up . . . if you help me unpack the kitchen."

I know this is blackmail, but if I have to research stupid non-native animals, it might as well be a crocodile that eats people. "Okay."

My mom looks up, her mouth open, her hands in the air. "Great." She shoves her plate away. "I'm tired of eating on paper plates."

I hate everything about school. I especially hate my locker, which is a bottom locker. I have to sit on the floor to get my stuff. The people with lockers around me act like I'm not there. I get elbowed and kneed and even hit by a backpack as my locker neighbor slams her locker shut and leaves.

Today I don't mind. At least not much. I'm looking forward to Mr. Matlo's class. I have a nice PowerPoint all ready, with some nice, gory details.

Which is good, because Mr. Matlo calls on me first. He likes to pick on me, just like everybody else does.

I hook my laptop up to the projector. I hear Spike snicker. He and his friends at the back of the class are whispering to the people around them. More snickering.

Just you wait, Spike. Just you wait.

I show the slide of the Egyptian Geese. I don't say too much about them because they're boring.

I show the slide of the iguana. A picture I took of Green Lightning, on the grate, before Spike cut off his tail.

The picture makes me choke up. Look at the beautiful tail he had, before that bully Spike ruined it. I'm so mad I can't speak.

Mr. Matlo nudges me. "Okay. An iguana. What do you have to tell us about iguanas?"

I look at Spike again. Mr. Matlo almost never calls on him. Like he's afraid of Spike or something. Maybe he's afraid of Spike's rich dad.

I used to be that kid. The girl with the rich dad who all the teachers were nice to no matter what.

I say my stuff about iguanas, and the irresponsible pet owners who let them run free and now they're all over, and go to my last slide.

Me holding the person-eating Nile crocodile. I enlarged the picture so only the crocodile would show on the slide. They didn't make us use computers so much at my old school, so I don't know how to crop images, and I wasn't about to ask my mom. At home it looked okay.

But now something goes wrong because when I click it, the full picture comes up, showing off me and that stupid grin on my face, and my braces in all their hideous glory.

"Which one is the invasive critter, the croc or her?" That's Spike. Of course.

The class titters. Thing 1 and Thing 2 laugh.

But I'm ready for him. For this.

"It's true I'm new here." I click for the next slide. "But at least I'm not an iguana torturer like you." I showed my picture of Green Lightning again. "This is what he looked like before. Just yesterday afternoon, in fact."

I switched the slide. "This is what he looks like now."

I showed a close-up picture of Green Lightning's bloody stump of a tail.

Even in the half-light of the flickering screen, I can see Spike's face is all red. I wonder if anyone has ever challenged him before.

He scoffs. "What'd you do to him?"

"And this is how he got that way." I show the next slide, of Spike slamming down the heavy metal spatula on Green Lightning's tail.

A lot of gasps and then quiet in the room.

"That's Photoshopped," says Spike.

"I don't know. Your buddy took it." I point to Thing 2. "Check with him. I got it off his Instagram."

I looked at Mr. Matlo. Here's his chance to stand up to Spike the bully, both the son and the Spike-dad. Will he take it? "Iguanas are a protected species, aren't they, Mr. Matlo?"

Mr. Matlo shakes his head. "No, they aren't."

Spike exhales with a sharp little laugh. He leans back in his chair and crosses his arms behind his head, as if he didn't have a care in the world. "You see. It doesn't matter."

Mr. Matlo continues, "But . . . torturing them like that . . . That's animal cruelty. It's a crime."

Ah, Mr. Matlo. You're my hero after all.

"Angus, I'll have to ask you to stay after school."

Angus. Like the beef? That's Spike's real name?

No wonder he'd rather be called Spike.

"And you—" Mr. Matlo turns to Thing 2, who's pulled his phone out. Probably trying to delete the picture. "Give me that phone. Now."

It's the weekend, but the cold spell hasn't broken. It's thirty-five, thirty-six degrees at the most in the middle of the day.

We've unpacked most of the kitchen, so Mom and I have real plates and real forks and real knives now. But the table is covered with boxes and wrapping and whatnot, so we sit on the sofa and eat while we watch the local news.

Mom probably takes this as another sign that she and I are getting along better. But I'm there because of the iguanas. The newscaster says there are lots of them. Going into hibernation because of the cold. Falling out of trees. Landing on cars. Hitting people in the head. Kamikaze iguanas.

After dinner I do the dishes without Mom asking. That way I can grab some lettuce from the fridge and take it to my room.

I open the closet and pull up the lid to Green Lightning's box.

The box is empty.

I look under the bed. No glittering yellow eyes.

I feel like someone stuck a knife in my heart. He's gone somewhere to die, I'm sure of it. I should have shown him to Mom; we should have taken him to the vet; he'll die all alone, and I'll never have another friend.

I tear my room apart. Blankets, clothes, school bag, candy wrappers.

No sign of Green Lightning anywhere.

My mother calls me. "Come help me unpack the books."

I pretend I haven't heard her. I duck into the bathroom, hoping Green Lightning is there.

No Green Lightning.

Mom yells at me again.

I flush the toilet, to justify not hearing her. I look in the hall closet. I even duck into my mom's room, which is even more of a mess than mine.

I slide into the kitchen, bent low so Mom doesn't see me from the living room.

No Green Lightning.

My mom's phone rings. She answers it. It's Dad.

Dad is the last person I want to talk to, so I edge my way over to the sliding door, crack the door open just a bit, and go outside, pulling the door shut after me.

Green Lightning is not on the porch.

Maybe I should look more in her room. What if he's under her bed? Or in her closet?

But I don't want to go back in now and risk her putting me on the phone with Dad.

Even our porch is filled with bags, boxes, plastic wrap, and things from home, like a huge easy chair that won't fit in this apartment.

Just looking at it makes me more homesick than I already am.

I run out to the lawn. There's a strip of grass that Mom calls "our lawn," as if anything could compare to the huge front and back lawns we had in New York. Beyond that, a golf course, our view of it broken up a little by some big trees.

Maybe Green Lightning doesn't want to live in a box. Maybe he wants to live out here in a tree.

But it's still too cold for him.

"Green Lightning! Green Lightning!" I call for him, but not too loud, so Mom doesn't find me. "Come back in, or you'll die!"

Mom has parked my old red Radio Flyer wagon next to an empty flower bed. Instead of looking for a job like she's supposed to, she must've gone to a nursery because my wagon is packed full with potted flowers, plants, and herbs.

And in the middle of it all, Green Lightning.

Eating all of Mom's plants.

Rather than move him, I take out the pots, until finally Green Lightning is alone in the middle of the wagon.

I crouch down and look deep into his beautiful eyes.

"What should I do, Green Lightning? Where do you want to go?"

Green Lightning tells me.

I pull the wagon all over the condo association. It takes a few hours. I look in hedges and up in trees. I climb a few trees.

It's still only thirty-seven degrees out, so the iguanas-in-hibernation are everywhere. I pick up the ones I find and set them in the wagon next to Green Lightning.

Sometimes I find an iguana that's dead. I know because ants are already crawling into its eyes.

By the time I reach the pool, the wagon is full of hibernating iguanas. Green Lightning sits atop them, his head held high, like a king.

KAMIKAZE IGUANAS

I pull the wagon into a sunny spot and cover them with a space blanket I found on the porch. I'm hoping that will warm them up.

"Whatcha got in your little red wagon, alien?"

It's Spike and his squad. All clustered around the barbecue grill. Do they ever go anywhere else?

"We've got something for you, Ms. Alien." Spike snaps his fingers. Thing 1 and Thing 2 step aside, and I see now what they're cooking.

Green Lightning's tail.

I run at Spike, my fists up, but Thing 1 and Thing 2 grab me before I get anywhere near him.

That was stupid of me.

I kick them, hit them with my elbows. But they're bigger. Stronger.

Spike leans in to my face.

"So, what's in the wagon, little alien? Your doll collection? Do you still play with dolls, little alien?"

I spit into his face.

He straightens up, wipes the spit away, and with it that evil smile.

I kinda wish that smile was back because the look that replaces it is cold. Calculating. Cruel.

Not good for me.

"We have to clog up that spitting mouth, don't we, boys?" Spike turns, grabs the iguana tail off the grill, tossing it from hand to hand like a hot potato. "Ow, ow. Hot. Hot. Hold her steady, boys."

The boys hold me steady.

Spike grabs my hair with one hand and pulls my head back, sharp.

I open my mouth and scream.

He stuffs the burning hot iguana tail down my throat.

He stands back as I twist and turn and try to get away from the hands that hold me trapped.

I scream, but this hot thing burns my lips, my mouth, my tongue, my throat; chokes me, kills my voice.

Tears squeeze out of my eyes. I work my jaw, trying to force it open, to spit out the tail. But Spike has one hand on top of my head, the other under my chin, locking my jaw closed.

I gag and gag and gag.

It tastes like coal. Like grit. Like bacon.

Like death.

I'm breathing through my nose, fast short breaths, but it's no good.

I'm going to choke to death. I'm going to die.

Suddenly, the pressure eases up. Spike has let go.

I hear a splash, but I can't see anything because Thing 1 and Thing 2 have also let go, and now I'm doubled over, pulling Green Lightning's burnt tail out of my mouth, dropping it, heaving up my lunch and my breakfast and my dinner and probably everything I've ever eaten since I moved to this horrible place.

A scream.

I manage to look up, still clutching my stomach, still another heave coming up.

Spike is in the pool.

But he's not alone.

There are, like, twenty iguanas in the pool with him. Swirling around him like quicksand.

Biting him.

Pulling him down.

His cries fade, his head goes underwater.

It's a beautiful sight. Spike, or rather, Angus the bully, getting pulled down by iguanas that just a few minutes ago were nearly dead of cold.

Spike's head emerges from the water. "Help me! Help m—"

His cries are drowned out as he's pulled down again.

Thing 1 and Thing 2 stand at the edge, yelling out words of encouragement, their arms flailing.

They don't get into the pool to help him. Some friends.

I wipe my mouth. I can feel my grin, even though I'm covered with puke.

Where's Green Lightning?

Can he even swim, with no tail?

My heart starts beating fast, like it's running. I'm still taking short, quick breaths. I don't need to puke anymore, but there are butterflies in my stomach.

I try to spot him in the writhing mass of green Angus patty. But all the iguanas I can see have tails.

Then I see him, watching from the pool's edge. As if he senses my fear and worry, he lifts his head and his eyes meet mine.

Spike's head is still under the water. In fact, I can't even see his head anymore because there are so many iguanas swimming on top of him.

"Stop." I hear myself say it. I can't believe I'm saying it, but I know this isn't right. "Please, Green Lightning, stop. He'll be good now. I promise."

Green Lightning tilts his head. He has to think about it.

"I'll get in trouble if you don't stop them now," I say. "They'll blame me."

Green Lightning straightens his head up. He looks over at the iguanas in the pool, now contentedly swimming in circles around the spot where Spike used to be.

Spike is still in the water, somewhere underneath them.

As soon as Green Lightning turns to them, even though he hasn't made a sound, the iguanas swim away. They climb out of the water and cluster in a sunny spot on the other side of the pool. Some disappear into the hedges or climb a tree.

Thing 1 and Thing 2 still stand at the edge of the pool, too scared to go in.

It's up to me.

I dive in, straight down to where Spike is half sitting, half floating at the bottom of the pool.

I grab one of his arms and get his head to break above the water. But he doesn't cough. He doesn't breathe.

We're in the deep end of the pool. The only way I can keep his head above water is if I keep mine under.

Pretty soon I'm out of air.

I let go of Spike. He sinks back to the bottom.

I blast up to the water's surface, suck in air, and yell at his squad.

"Help me!"

I go underwater and hook my hands under Spike's armpits. I half swim, half drag him into the shallower end.

Finally, his so-called friends are in the water next to me, lifting him up.

I slap Spike's face, punch his chest.

"Breathe, numb-nut!" I scream at him. "Breathe, you dumb ox! You miserable excuse for a human being! Breathe, iguana killer!"

As if those were the magic words, Spike gags and coughs up water.

I don't wait around for him to open his eyes. I'm out of there.

I look for Green Lightning, but I don't see him.

I don't see any iguanas at all.

I'm headed to Mr. Matlo's class again. My throat is sore. I have a headache because Mom still can't find the hair dryer, so I had to go to bed with wet hair. But it's warming up, finally, so I'm not too worried.

I don't bother with my locker. I'm too fed up with the elbows and knees, the books falling on my head. I go straight to class.

And there's Spike, flanked by his squad.

Blocking my way to the science classroom.

The normal hustle and bustle of school quiets down. People realize something is happening. They stop to watch.

I know no one will help me.

But I don't stop. I don't try to hide. I walk with my back straight, pretending I'm a runway model, my eyes on Spike's. I don't blink.

I stop three steps away, just out of his reach.

Spike stares back at me. He's got scratches and bite marks all over. Some of them are held shut with butterfly bandages. I wonder if his pretty-boy face will have scars forever. The thought makes me smile, just a little.

No one says anything. A long moment goes by.

Finally, I decide to get this over with. "I didn't have to stop them, you know."

Spike nods. "I know."

"I won't next time." I try to sound sure of this, sure that there will be a next time, though I doubt I'll ever see Green Lightning again.

"I know," Spike says.

I point one hand at Thing 1 and another at Thing 2. "And you should also know that when you were drowning, your so-called 'friends' were too chicken to jump in and save you. Until I did."

His friends go pale and look away, as if they wished they weren't there.

Spike steps away from them, closer to me. I force myself to stay still, to not back up. I will not let him see that he scares me.

"I know that too." He reaches his hand out slowly, as if to touch me, then stops, his hand in midair. "We're cool now, right?"

Oh wow. He's afraid of me.

Me.

I nod. Such a tiny little nod, only he can see it.

Spike tries to pat me on the head.

I duck out from under his arm. I don't like anybody patting me. Especially not on the head.

Then I hear Spike's bloodcurdling scream.

Spike's face is as white as the floor tile, his eyes are bulging, his finger pointing at something behind me.

I turn to look. There's my locker.

And there's a tail-less iguana sitting calmly in front of it.

"Green Lightning!" I run toward him, so happy.

Behind me, Spike screams and screams.

THE NIGHTMARE EXPRESS

BY DANIEL PALMER

FROM OVER A BLOCK AWAY, I heard my mother scream, "Nicodemus Lionel Watson, remember now, whatever you do: DON'T! BE! LATE!"

I'm sure you're thinking a couple of thoughts because I'd be thinking them as well. Why would my mother (who is a very good mom) name her son (who is a very good son) Nicodemus? Sounds like an open invitation to playground bullies, right? But it's not as bad as you might think. Nicodemus is a family name. My grandfather had it—my great-grandfather too—and I'm told the name goes as far back as our family tree has branches. Most of the time I go by Nick, and the Nicodemus name comes out only when my mother is dead serious about something.

Which brings me to the next thought you might have had: why was my mom, on this particular blue-sky fall morning, screaming "Don't be late!" from the open window of our little house on Elm Street in Worcester (that's a city west of Boston)?

Before I answer, you need to know a little something about my mom. She works for the transportation department, driving a big city bus. I guess years of getting from one stop to the next, always at a very specific time, turned her into a crazy stickler for punctuality.

And I do mean *crazy.*

For example, let's say I have to go to a birthday party starting at noon (which I did last week for my pal Max, who turned twelve like me). We'd arrive at eleven thirty sharp, inevitably and embarrassingly always the first ones there. If we have tickets for a movie, you best believe we're eating popcorn in the lobby at least thirty minutes before the first preview flickers on the screen. Doctor's appointment? We arrive with enough time to give me five exams. Swim team practice? I'm in the pool so early, I come out wrinkled like a walnut with red eyes. It doesn't matter where I go or what I do, if I've got someplace I'm supposed to be at a scheduled time, my mom always makes sure I'm never, *ever* late.

"Early is on time and on time is late," my mom always said.

Now, if you're an astute reader (that means "aware") you might be wondering why my mom wasn't bringing me to school on the morning she screamed at me from that open window. Obviously, I have to get to school at a scheduled time.

Here's where things get a bit complicated.

I go to Kirkland Academy, which is a private school just outside of Boston. To get to school I have to take an hour-long ride on a train we call "the Commuter Rail." Every weekday morning I catch the seven a.m. local, and ride it with a bunch of doctors, lawyers, and all sorts of business types who commute into the city for work. It makes for a long day, but I'm lucky to go to such a good school. I happen to like school, so I don't really mind the travel.

Usually, my mom walks me to the train station to make sure I catch the seven because if I miss it, the next train isn't for another twenty minutes, which would make me—you guessed it—late.

But on this particular morning my mom had the flu, as in high fever, bad cough, achy, stuffy head, couldn't think straight, couldn't walk straight flu. Even though I insisted I'd be fine seeing myself to the train station, she still made a bunch of phone calls on my behalf, looking for someone to make sure I got there early as always. It was the same story all around: everyone wanted to help, but for whatever reason nobody could. My dad was traveling for work (he did that a lot), leaving just me and my too-sick mom to figure it out on our own.

"I'll be fine going by myself," I said.

"Don't worry," I told her.

"You can count on me," I assured her.

She sniffled. She coughed. She wheezed. She told me to stay home.

I told her I had a big swim meet after school that I couldn't miss.

Eventually, after a lot of back-and-forth, hemming and hawing (that's sort of like back-and-forth), she agreed to let me go, but not before reminding me ten dozen times to avoid any and all distractions, delays, long cuts, side cuts, and back cuts, no exceptions allowed. I was to get myself to the train station thirty minutes before the seven a.m. local arrived, and if I got there so much as a minute late (she'd be awaiting my call), I'd be grounded for a month. That would mean no swim team practice and missed meets, and there'd go my chance for the coveted league championship.

Swim racing happens to be my favorite thing in the whole wide world, and I happen to be the fastest freestyler on the team, so for me it was all the incentive I needed to obey.

Sort of.

What I didn't realize until that morning was how much there was to do on my way to school. There was never any stopping to smell the roses with my mom. She'd pull me along with haste, eager and anxious to get me to the train station on time, meaning early. Without her to hurry me up, I popped into Mr. Kroger's grocery store to buy myself a pack of chewing gum, figuring a quick stop would add only a few minutes to my trip.

I guess that detour gave me the itch to do all sorts of things my speed-it-up mom never lets me do. Which was why I stopped to pet Mrs. Wertheimer's tabby cat, Bartholomew (get it, Bartholo*mew*), that was sitting at the edge of her yard, as if it were expecting me. Admittedly, I felt a jolt of guilt as I played on the monkey bars at the Ash Street playground. Afterward, I sent my mom a text message to let her know everything was fine and not to worry, which wasn't exactly a lie.

I promised I'd text her just as soon as I was on that train.

But there was so much happening on my walk to the station, so many things I never got the chance to do, that I had a hard time not doing them all. I climbed an apple tree in Dumbarton Circle, ran up and down the ramps at the Skylark Street skate park, got into a game of four square with a bunch of kids waiting for their school bus, stopped to smell the fresh-baked bread inside Carmichael's Bakery, chased a squirrel down Lamont Avenue, and even helped a nice lady carry her groceries across Grant Boulevard. I was having so much fun that I completely lost track of the time.

Well, you can probably guess what happened next. I made it to the train station, all right—just in time to see the red lights of the last car of the seven a.m. local vanish down the dark tunnel, without me inside it.

Naturally, I started to panic, and I do mean the knocking knees, heart-pounding, tight throat, clenched stomach kind of panic. Even my sweat was sweating. I had no choice but to call my mom and confess that

I had missed the local and would have to catch the next train to school. I'd be grounded for a month, probably longer. No more swim team for me, and there'd go my shot at winning the league championship trophy.

So imagine my surprise when just as my train pulled away, I saw the headlights of another coming down the same dark tunnel. I scratched my head and wondered why there'd be a second train so soon after the first one had left.

Now imagine my delight and indescribable relief when I heard the station announcer say: "Arriving on track ten, seven a.m. local, making all local stops, including Kirkland Academy."

In hindsight there were a few strange things about that announcement, starting with the station announcer giving my school's name as a station stop. He usually says "making all local stops." And the announcer's voice sounded kind of ominous. It was deep, and echoed darkly. I thought I heard heavy breathing, too.

I didn't give any of it much thought because I was so overjoyed that for the first time ever, at a time when I desperately needed it, two seven a.m. locals were running back to back.

I would text my mom from the train as planned, and all would be right in the world. *No harm, no foul,* as my dad would say.

The second train came to a shuddering stop with a big whoosh of air and a harsh screech of brakes. The long line of silvery cars with oval windows looked just like my usual train. I glanced around and noticed I was alone on the station platform. I figured everyone had crammed inside the first train, not realizing a second train was so close behind.

I anticipated stepping into a mostly empty train car, but to my surprise it was packed with people, all wearing gray overcoats and gray fedora hats. They had their heads down, reading actual newspapers. I didn't see anybody with a cell phone. The train car was as quiet as a library, too, which was also a bit unusual.

I took the only seat available.

The train doors closed.

The wheels groaned to life.

The car began to move.

And we were off.

It wasn't until we got going that I noticed how badly this particular train car smelled. It was a horrible stench, as if someone had combined swamp gunk, sweaty socks, rotten eggs, spoiled milk, and creamed corn (I happen to hate creamed corn) into a big, boiling, nasty-smelling stew. Nobody else seemed to mind the offensive odor, but I was having a hard time keeping my eyes from watering.

I was just about to ask the guy next to me if he smelled something awful, when he handed me his newspaper and said in a very strange voice, "I think this story is about you."

They way he spoke, low and rumbly like a clap of thunder, creaky like an old door, was something straight out of a nightmare. My body froze with fear, but somehow I managed to take the paper from him. The headline on the front page jumped right out at me.

BOY ARRIVES LATE, SUMMONS GYPSY'S CURSE
by Sari Foru

Nicodemus Lionel Watson the Fourth, who on the
morning of September 23rd, as a result
of being late for the seven a.m. local

train, has officially invoked the curse
of Gypsy Glenda Goodfried, High Priestess
of Darkness.

The curse was established in 1913, after
Dr. Nicodemus Lionel Watson the First, on
account of a broken wagon wheel, arrived
too late to attend to the needs of Glenda
Goodfried's ill son, Walter, who subsequently
died of his sickness. Grief-stricken, Glenda
cursed the entire Watson family by combining
all sorts of potions, powders, and things of
an abominable nature, before uttering
the following words:

"Name all Watson boys Nicodemus,
If you wish them to survive.
And I curse ye more, to settle a score
For a life that's been deprived.
From this day on, for evermore,
Watson children must never be late.
For if they are, then like my son,
They shall suffer a terrible fate.
From the darkness of Hades comes my revenge,
So remember these words that I say.
If they're not on time, the fault isn't mine
When the nightmares take them away."

*As a result of this curse, Nicodemus Lionel
Watson the Fourth (yes, that's you, Nick) is cursed
to ride the Nightmare Express for all of eternity
with no possibility of escape.*

*Glenda was not available for comment, as she
died many years ago, but a spokesperson for the
family laughed maniacally before closing the door
on this reporter's face.*

My hands shook so uncontrollably that I ripped the paper in half. A cold trickle of sweat dripped down my neck as goose bumps prickled my skin. I felt the stare of the man next to me, so I turned my head slowly to meet his gaze, realizing now that the horrible stench was coming from him. In fact, everybody on this train, myself excluded, smelled like something that had crawled out of the graveyard. To my horrified surprise all the overcoats and hats had transformed into something tattered, and smeared with dark stains.

I stood up, sputtering, and the other passengers stood as well. At the exact same time they removed their hats and coats, as if part of a choreographed dance routine. I could see their flesh was gray as clay and scabbed all over. They had hair like dirty spaghetti; eyes red as rubies; and mouths filled with yellow, stained teeth, sharp as daggers. They began marching toward me, taking lumbering, off-kilter steps that made me think of one word:

Zombies!

I screamed.

Yeah, I'm not proud of it, but if a hundred red-eyed zombies with sharp teeth were headed your way, I'm pretty sure you'd scream too. I could feel their cold hands tugging on my shirt and pulling at my hair. Their foul-smelling breath made me gag. Fingernails sharp as claws dug painfully into my flesh. I'd never had a zombie nightmare before, but I pinched myself anyway on the off chance I was dreaming.

I wasn't.

I looked out the window to see where we were, hoping this train might make a stop so I could get off, but it was blacker than a moonless midnight out there. The zombies came at me, groaning and moaning as they closed in. Some had their arms stretched out in front of them; some had no arms at all.

I looked all around, searching frantically for a way out, and noticed a metal handrail bolted to the ceiling about six feet off the ground and running the length of the train car.

Good thing I had practiced on those monkey bars!

I jumped up on my seat. Stretching my body to its limit, I managed to grab the metal bar with both hands. Even though I'd never been able to do a single pull up in gym class, I found the strength to lift myself high enough to wrap my legs around the bar.

I held on for dear life.

Lucky for me, zombies can't jump.

Suspended in the air, hanging upside down with both my heels crossed over the bar, I crawled monkey-like from one end of the train car to the other. Those foul-smelling zombies pawed at me from below. They yanked on my backpack, trying to pull me off, but I held on so vigorously my fingers ached and my legs throbbed.

When I reached the end of the bar, I jumped down onto a huddled mass of zombies awaiting me below. I managed to punch and kick my way out from that cluster of rotted flesh. Zombies can be quite persistent, but their undead bodies have naturally lost a lot of strength.

I pulled open the pass-through door to the next train car and leaped inside. I tried to slam the door shut, but a bunch of zombie arms, legs, and hands got in the way. No matter how hard I pulled, the door wouldn't latch shut. The train cars were all connected, so I couldn't step onto an outside platform and jump off.

I figured this was the end.

The zombies would overrun me for sure.

To my astonishment and great relief, those zombies wouldn't cross from one train car into the next. I wondered if they were too brain-dead to figure out how to walk through an open door, but then it hit me. The zombie car must be their domain: It was where they lived, and they couldn't leave no matter how badly they wanted to eat my brain.

Another thought filled me with dread:

Whose domain had I just entered?

I was relieved to see it was suddenly light outside. I guess we'd come out of a tunnel. I could see the train zooming along a familiar landscape as we barreled through Oakmont Station without slowing. I noticed the time on the station clock read 7:20 a.m., which struck me as odd. The local train always pulled into Oakmont by 7:10.

On top of everything, this train of terrors was running ten minutes behind schedule.

I checked on those zombies, making sure they stayed put, which fortunately, they did. Then I checked out this new train car. It was empty. *Safe*, I thought. So I zipped open my backpack and got out my phone to call my mom.

Suffice to say, cell reception on the Nightmare Express is pretty lame.

I inventoried my other supplies, thinking anything and everything might come in handy. I had my lunch box (peanut-butter-and-fluff sandwich, chips, and an apple), notebook, pencil holder, laptop, my drumsticks (I play in the school band), ruler, math textbook, the pack of chewing gum I bought at Mr. Kroger's store, and my swim goggles.

Basically, nothing helpful whatsoever.

Somehow, some way, I had to get off this train.

There were no emergency exits, so I kicked at a window as hard as I could. It didn't take long to realize that if I continued down this path, the only thing I'd break would be my ankle. The way out, I decided, was to get to the last car on the train, where I hoped to find an exit door.

I headed down the aisle of the empty car, grateful no zombies were chasing after me, when something seized my legs and I fell forward with a cry. Before I knew what was happening, I was upside down, or sideways, or some ways. All I knew for certain was that my feet were up in the air. The rush of blood to my head made me dizzy.

I tried to move my legs, but some ropelike substance had bound my ankles tightly together. I pulled on the rope as hard as I could, but it wouldn't break or budge. All it did was vibrate in my hands with an audible hum. It left a sticky residue on my fingers. I had a sinking feeling that this rope wasn't a rope at all.

I stopped struggling, and that's when I realized something truly terrible. Upon closer examination the train car, which at first had appeared empty, was actually filled with this semitranslucent ropelike stuff going in all sorts of directions—just like a massive spiderweb.

That was when I heard the clicking sounds: a steady *tap-tap-tap* against the floor, like lots of legs moving all at once. I spun around while suspended upside down, trying to see whatever was headed my way, fearing I knew the answer.

I was right.

Coming at me was a massive brown spider so fearsome, so hideous that I stopped breathing. It was as big as a pony, with legs so long it couldn't walk down the aisle without climbing over the seats. The spider's body was covered in coarse hair the length of saplings. Its eight eyes, each the size of a dinner plate, were filled with gloating delight. A pair of hairy fangs longer than walrus tusks covered a gaping mouth that opened and closed hungrily. Gooey saliva dripped from the fangs like a waterfall.

It was breakfast time, and apparently I was the morning feast.

I had to act fast.

I pushed my legs outward, trying to break free, but the web wouldn't budge. Desperate, I swung my body from side to side, pendulum-like, but that only spun me in a circle.

Rearing back on its spindly legs, the spider made a bubbling, hissing sound so dreadful my blood turned to ice.

It sounded very hungry.

And that was when I got my big idea.

I slid off my backpack, careful not to drop it. Holding on to the strap, I unzipped the top and fished out the peanut-butter-and-fluff sandwich from my lunch box, along with the pack of gum. The spider lunged at me as I tossed the sandwich and chewing gum into its ravenous mouth.

As soon as the creature began to chew, the peanut butter, marshmallow fluff, and gum mixed together to make its mouth unbearably sticky.

Naturally, a sticky mouth full of peanut butter, fluff, and gum would make anyone panic, including this horrible brown spider the size of a pony. It spun around wildly, probably wishing it had a big glass of milk to wash everything down. The sharp hairs on the spider's legs and those sharp spikes on its feet came dangerously close to slicing me in two, but I swung my body away just in time.

Instead of cutting me, the spider cut the web that was holding me up, just like a knife passing through butter. I tumbled to the ground with a thud. That loosened the webbing around my ankles enough so I could pry myself free.

The angry spider ignored me as I raced down the aisle, careful to avoid more webbing as I went. Soon I had the door to the next train car open. I went through it, too scared to worry about what might await me on the other side.

Something sharp smacked against my cheek the second I set foot into the next car. Before I knew it, lots of little sharp objects were hitting my arms, legs, and face. An onslaught of something that felt like tiny needles pricked my flesh all over. I tried shielding my face with my arms, but then I couldn't see what was attacking me.

I jumped out of the aisle, thinking to use the seat as a shield. The maneuver worked, but now I was pinned down in that location.

Poking my head up from behind the seat like a prairie dog on patrol, I saw a small army of tin soldiers no more than ten feet away. They stood in proper military formation, three abreast, going back too many rows for me to count them all. They were at least three inches high, with evil grins painted on their tin faces, and tin rifles lanced with sharp bayonets aimed right at my head. All were dressed in colorful military uniforms—red jackets with gold buckles, red hats, and blue pants.

They began to march toward me, stiffly on account of not being able to bend their arms or legs. Their aim was still pretty good. Bullets from their tin guns bounced off my face like metal raindrops.

I couldn't hear myself think over the constant *pfft-pfft-pfft* sound of so many tin rifles firing all at once. Every time I lifted my head to check on their position, I got pelted with more tiny bullets.

I had to think quickly. At some point the soldiers would overrun me like those dreadful zombies. The bullets might not deliver a mortal wound, but those bayonets looked downright lethal.

I searched my backpack for something to get me out of this grim situation. Eventually, my hands brushed against the smooth wood of my drumsticks.

Maybe I could beat the soldiers back with my sticks.

Beat the soldiers. . . .

The word "beat" gave me an even better idea.

I was so scared, I wasn't sure I could get the drumsticks out of my backpack, let alone use them. I took a deep breath and peered up from behind my cushioned seat. The soldiers continued to advance, shooting as they went. In no time those sharp bayonets would slice me to pieces.

Gripping my sticks tightly, I hit them rhythmically against the seat, tapping out a steady *rat-tat-tat* beat. I looked up.

To my delight the soldiers stopped advancing. Their grins had vanished. They looked suddenly quite serious. I drummed a second rhythm, another quick *rat-tat-tat*, again in marching time. Just as I had hoped, these soldiers snapped to attention, with their rifles now resting unthreateningly against their shoulders.

I stood up, careful to keep my marching beat going. The soldiers, being good soldiers, marched in formation back and forth from one end of the train car to the other. They paid no attention to me as I moved down the aisle. They were too focused on marching to the beat I played.

I stopped hitting my drumsticks for a second to see what would happen. Sure enough, the soldiers immediately began regrouping into an attack formation. So I kept on drumming as I walked down the aisle to the pass-through door that would lead me to the next domain.

My joy at defeating the tin soldier army was short-lived.

All the pass-through doors contained a portal window that gave me a view into the adjacent car. Peering through that window, I saw that the next car was filled—and I do mean *filled*—with water. It bubbled and swirled just like a big tank at an aquarium.

Just then something massive and dark swam in front of the window, blocking my view. It turned its body slowly and swam away, then turned again and swam toward me once more.

The enormous sea monster moved in big lazy circles, eyeing me hungrily with its gigantic yellow eyes. The terrible beast had the body of a squid, the tentacles of an octopus, and the mouth of a giant-sized chicken.

Laugh all you want, but if you saw a giant chicken beak, I bet you wouldn't think it was very funny.

Bottom line: I was trapped.

My arms were getting tired playing the marching beat, but if I stopped for even a second, those tin soldiers would gore me with their lances.

I felt utterly defeated.

I would never see my mom or dad again. It appeared I was doomed to spend the rest of my life (short as that might be) riding the Nightmare Express.

As I gazed longingly out the window of the train, pining for freedom, I saw the train pass through Oakmont Station once more. Again the station clock read 7:20 a.m.—ten minutes late, same as before. The train seemed to be making an endless loop on an endless track where it would always arrive late.

Thinking this through, it made perfect sense. My own tardiness had gotten me stuck on this freaky ride.

How long had my mother known about the gypsy's curse? It had to have been passed down from generation to generation. It was certainly why we always arrived everywhere so early, and why Nicodemus was such a popular family name. She probably never told me about it because she worried, rightly, that I'd never leave the house.

I thought of what my mother always said: *Early is on time, and on time is late.*

An idea struck me. What would happen if we pulled into Oakmont Station ahead of schedule? What if we arrived *early*? Would it, could it, break the gypsy's curse? If I could somehow make this train go faster, I might be able to find out.

It seemed my only hope.

There was no way I could get past that sea monster, but I could backtrack to the engine car, which was just beyond the zombies' lair.

I was about to make my move when suddenly, both my drumsticks snapped in two.

This crazy train did not want me to escape!

The tin soldiers turned on a dime and began marching my way. Their rifles lowered and those tiny bullets started flying once more. My eyes went wide with fear at the sight of their approaching bayonets.

I tried to beat a marching rhythm with my hands, but it was no good. The bullets continued to pelt me without letting up. I had so many welts on my face I must've looked like a guy with the world's worst case of acne.

I was trapped between a sea monster with a chicken beak and a tin soldier army with a bad attitude. I returned to my backpack because it had helped me out before. I didn't see anything useful in there until I picked up my swim goggles.

It was a crazy idea.

It was a brainless idea.

But it just might work.

I had to get to the train's engine to speed it up, right?

But first I had to get rid of those tin soldiers.

And what did tin soldiers hate most?

That's right: water.

I slipped on my swim goggles, took a big breath, and held it. Then I pulled open the door to the sea monster's lair, expecting a rush of water to come barreling at me.

But nothing happened.

The water magically stayed in the sea monster's domain, blocked in a gravity-defying way by some invisible force—along with that sea monster.

Evidently, the water played by the same rules as everything else and was stuck in Sea Monsterville.

In a moment of clarity I realized my plan was doomed to fail from the start. I mean, how did I expect to outswim a sea monster?

I was thinking up a plan B when I felt a tin soldier needling my side with his stupid bayonet. I picked him up and angrily tossed him into the water, just to get him out of my way.

He started to sink before my eyes when from out of nowhere the sea monster swam at him with a sudden burst of speed, snapping the soldier in half with a crunch of its massive beak. Suddenly, I heard a deep rumbling, like a dam breaking free.

I got a sinking feeling of impending doom. Tossing the tin soldier into a new domain—the sea monster's lair—must have snapped some sort of spell. Now these creatures could move freely from train car to train car, which meant the sea monster could come after me.

Before I knew it, a wall of water exploded from the monster's lair and hit with enough force to knock me off my feet. It wasn't freezing water, but it wasn't like taking a bath, either. The rushing river sent me spinning end over end, bouncing painfully from seat to seat. I got swept up in the fast-flowing current and did the only thing I could think to do.

I swam for my life.

The raging rapids bowled over the tin soldiers, like they were pins falling after a perfect strike. I managed to catch a cresting wave doing my best freestyle stroke. Behind me the sea monster chomped down hard, luckily snapping up a mouthful of a cushioned seat instead of my fast-kicking legs. I continued riding that wave, aiming my body for the open doorway to the spider's den. I passed from one train car into the next like a speeding torpedo.

Ahead, the spider was still busily chewing on that peanut-butter-fluff-and-gum sandwich. It swiveled to check out the commotion. I swear I saw fear bubbling in its big black eyes. The water swallowed the spider whole and sent it tumbling away.

Before I knew it the water had carried me back into Zombie Land. With no place for the water to go, it quickly began to fill up the zombie car. It was obvious the zombies were terrible swimmers, and all of them would have drowned had they not already been dead.

I managed to keep my head above the fast-rising tide while the sea monster, instead of eating me, munched greedily on floating zombies and sinking tin soldiers. The spider had spun a web and was holding on for dear life.

As the water continued to rise, I took a big gulp of air and dove under. I struggled mightily to open the engine room door, but with all the water pushed up against it, the door wouldn't budge. I waited until the water had almost filled the train car completely and then took a second big breath before diving under once more.

Thanks to science class, I knew I just had to wait for water to fill up the train car so the pressure could equalize. This time, when I pulled on the engine room door, it came open.

Water flooded the engine room compartment and should have short-circuited the electronics, but somehow this train kept on rolling.

I looked for an engineer, but nobody was driving the train. I never thought I'd be glad to say that!

I pushed the lever controlling the speed as far forward as it would go. The train accelerated like a rocket ship. Water sloshed all around me as it continued to fill up the engine room.

The train kept accelerating, going faster and faster.

I waited for something to happen, but nothing did.

The curse had not been broken!

By this point the sea monster had tired of eating zombies and tin soldiers. It stuck its massive head into the engine room, snapping at me with its oversized yellow beak.

I swam to the left.

It missed me by inches.

I swam to the right.

It missed me again.

Water continued to fill the car.

I said my good-byes.

If the sea monster didn't eat me, then soon enough I would drown.

I glanced out the window of the engine car and saw we were passing through Oakmont Station at 7:05 a.m., five minutes *ahead* of schedule. But the train zoomed through the station without stopping. I deflated on the spot. My big plan had failed.

The beast lunged again, but this time I was too tired to move out of the way.

My head vanished inside the monster's open mouth.

I gazed with horror into an impenetrable darkness.

I smelled lots of chewed-up zombies.

The monster's mouth began to close.

I braced myself for the agonizing pain to come.

And . . . and . . .

Instead of being eaten, I found myself standing on my train platform back home. Strangely, inexplicably, I was right back where I had started. It worked! Getting to Oakmont Station early had broken the gypsy's curse!

The platform was crowded with the usual collection of doctors, lawyers, and various business types. A train was approaching. The station announcer spoke: "Now arriving on track ten, seven a.m. local, making all stops."

All local stops. No mention of Kirkland Academy.

The announcer's voice wasn't eerie or ominous.

The train came to a stop with a loud hiss of air. I boarded quickly. I wasn't going to miss this ride for all the gold in the world. The car was packed with people looking at their cell phones. Nobody here wore a grimy gray overcoat or tattered gray fedora.

Soon as the train doors closed, I got my phone out.

This train had good reception.

Strange as it was, instead of thinking about those horrible monsters, I thought about today's swim meet. Swimming had literally saved my life. I could keep on swimming, too, and even race for the league championship—but only if I kept the secret of the Nightmare Express. No way could my mom know that I had arrived late for the train.

But secrets had consequences. They had nearly cost me my life. They were like another curse I had to break.

I called my mom.

"Hope you're on that train," she said, sounding rather anxious.

"Mom," I said, "we need to have a serious talk tonight when I get home after my swim meet, six o'clock sharp. And don't be late."

THE GIRL IN THE WINDOW

BY TONYA HURLEY

'LL NEVER FORGET THE DAY she arrived in our sleepy port town of Thomaston, Maine. Not so much sleepy, actually, as dying. Literally. The windows were papered with going-out-of-business signs, and there were more people in the cemetery than on Main Street, where I lived.

It was three thirty p.m., and I'd just gotten home from school. I watched with bated breath as they loaded her in and positioned her just so. A reporter from the *Thomaston Times*, our local newspaper, was here to document the excitement, interviewing rubberneckers who had nothing better to do than gather to gawk at the spectacle.

There she was, in the window right across the street from our apartment—from my bedroom, to be exact—which meant I could look at her anytime I felt like it. Just like those rich people who live on Central Park West and get to see the Macy's Thanksgiving Day parade balloons float by their condos at eye level. You see, living in a semighost town on the coast of Maine, even a new mannequin was big news.

The Higgin family, proprietors of the last department store left in town, were desperate for customers and had brought her in to model the latest party dresses they were selling. She had a real job to do, and she did it well. Too well. Before long, everyone wanted what "Lydia"—that's what they named her—wore. Especially me.

The store manager put the most expensive dresses on her, a new one every week, so that girls would lose it over the frocks on the regular, and pester their parents, who had no choice but to pay up or risk long tantrums at home or crying jags outside the store. Everyone loved Lydia, but the parents in Thomaston—not so much. One thing's for sure, she was good for business.

Needless to say, she was the talk of our middle school from the second she arrived. Especially on Fridays, when Higgin's staged its changing-of-the-dress ritual. The unveilings always produced massive turnouts, so if I couldn't get close enough, I would run up to my room with binoculars to see what she was wearing. I spent a lot of time looking out my window, wishing I were someone else, somewhere else. At least now, there was something to see.

Lydia looked to be around my age, eleven years old. Black hair tied back neatly with a white silk ribbon. No blank-expressioned, stiffly posed, cookie-cutter department store dummy was she. Her fingers were so lifelike; her eyes deep green, the color of the sea; and on her face she wore a sweet smile. She was happy. Always happy. And why shouldn't she be? Everything about her was cool, even her name. So much better than mine, Mable. Ugh. You couldn't get more boring. Her hair was dark and shiny, and her skin was pale and perfect. Lydia was the envy of every girl in town, a social media darling turning up in post after post in an endless stream of selfies and tweets. Our very own It Girl.

The thing that interested us—interested me—the most about Lydia, though, was the very reason she'd been brought here: her clothes.

The white lace dress she wore when she first arrived was a stunner. She looked like a bride. Oh, how I wanted that dress. I spent hours fantasizing about what I'd do if I owned it—the glamorous parties I'd be invited to, the places I'd go and the people I'd meet. It would literally change my life, I was sure of it.

But I didn't get that dress or any others for that matter. You see, we were poor. My mother worked two jobs, and there was barely enough money for food and rent, let alone extras like fancy clothes. But a girl could dream. And boy, did I.

Each day after school I would make a beeline for the store. The little bell dangling from the front door would jingle, announcing the arrival of a new customer—my arrival. I would walk the perimeter, riffling through the bins, picking items off the shelves, trying to look as interested as possible in purchasing while eventually heading to my real destination—Lydia.

Miss Serling, the persnickety saleslady dressed in fitted tweed suits, would circle me as I stared at the mannequin, like a predatory animal taking measure of its prey. In response, I would clasp my hands behind my back daintily, and squint my eyes, as if I were studying a masterpiece in an art museum.

"Can I help you?" she'd sniff, a certain frustration in her voice.

"No thank you, just looking," I'd reply, same as the day before and the day before that.

It was a little dance we did, she and I. The poor girl and the saleslady. She knew I wanted the dress but couldn't afford it. I knew I wanted the dress and couldn't afford it. But it didn't cost me anything to look, and it didn't cost her anything to be polite and let me. Besides, I don't think she minded very much. She always looked slightly bored. It was slow at that time of the afternoon, and at the very least I gave her something to do. She probably figured she was doing community service by keeping a little urchin off the street.

"You spend an awful lot of time here," she observed . . . snidely. "Shouldn't you be with your friends somewhere, gossiping or shaming one . . . another?"

She was right. I was. I'd become obsessed. Hanging out less and less with my school friends and more and more at Higgin's. The more time I spent in the store, eyeing Lydia and her killer wardrobe, the more comfortable I felt. Like Lydia and me were becoming friends, too.

"I'd rather be here with Lydia," I replied. "Don't worry, I won't steal anything."

Miss Serling just shook her head and walked away in a huff, heading to the storeroom to do some inventory or whatever she did back there.

This was our alone time. Just Lydia and me. When I would talk to her. Tell her about the mean girls in school and how horribly they treated me, just because I didn't have the money and clothes they did. She never answered of course, but I found it therapeutic. To be able to talk things out with someone who I knew wouldn't judge me and who I knew would listen just made me feel better.

But, as often happens in small towns, jealousy started to set in. The other kids wondered why I was spending so much time with her. People started to talk. And not just about me and what I was doing at Higgin's. Curiosity about the bizarre lifelike mannequin turned rapidly to gossip and then suspicion. Some wondered where she came from and why she was so real looking. Others believed she was the Higgin's youngest, who had gone missing many years ago, but was really accidentally killed by one of her siblings. Mr. Higgin had preserved her, they said, to avoid a scandal, and that the family couldn't part with her, like those people who live with mummified dead relatives in their homes for years. There were other stories too, like the ones where people saw her move in the window at night, and others that said they made appeals to Lydia for certain things like money and good grades, and they always came true. I didn't believe most of it, except for the appeals part. That, I got.

Spending so much time with Lydia, even in one-way conversation, she had become a revered figure to me. She was a mystery all right, but not the kind they were thinking of. To me, she was a kind of sacred mystery, a store-window saint, always there, in the Church of Retail to help me with my problems. Saint Lydia of the Lonely and Insecure. The only thing missing was a row of votive candles to light at her feet. But Miss Serling would definitely flag that as a fire hazard.

If there were one to light, I would've lit it to get the outfit she was wearing for my birthday—a kelly green dress with tulle around the bottom and a navy blue silk sash around the waist. It was perfect. How I dreaded showing up the next day wearing an old, secondhand outfit when every other girl in my class showed up in a brand-new expensive ensemble after their birthdays. People would literally wait in the halls to see what you were dressed in—to see your big gift.

"What I wouldn't give to have that dress," I said out loud.

"Careful what you wish for, dear," Miss Serling, who'd overheard me, replied.

"Today is my birthday," I blurted out, thinking maybe she'd take off the dress and hand it to me wrapped in an orange Higgin's bow.

She flashed a sympathetic smile, the first I'd ever seen from her. "We're closing early today. Why don't you run along home now? I'm sure your family is waiting to celebrate with you."

She seemed sincere for a change, not just being nice to get rid of me.

"My mother makes me a red velvet cake every year. Melts in your mouth," I said with a big fake smile.

"You're making me jealous," she said, which for some reason made me feel better.

"I'll save you a slice, if my brother doesn't eat the whole thing."

"I'll look forward to it," Miss Serling replied. "Happy birthday."

We stepped out the front door, and she locked it. "See you tomorrow," I called out.

"And I'm sure I will see you," Miss Serling said.

I stopped outside to wave good-bye to Lydia in the window and get one last good look at that dress, when all of a sudden I heard someone whisper:

"Happy birthday."

I looked to see if there was anyone around, but there wasn't. Not a single soul. Maybe it was just Miss Serling calling out to me again before leaving the shop? I walked a few steps to the curb and waited to cross the street.

"Happy birthday."

I heard it again. But there was still no one there. I shook my head to make sure my mind wasn't playing tricks on me, and then bolted across the street. Just in case.

With my heart racing I ran up the steps, following the smell of dinner all the way to our apartment on the third floor. Mom had made all my favorites—fish sticks, green bean casserole, and mac 'n' cheese with extra cheese bubbling on top. And of course, the pièce de résistance, the decadent pink-frosted red velvet birthday cake.

I scarfed down my dinner and anxiously waited for my brother and mom to finish. Finally, Mom cleared the plates and then reappeared with a gift in hand and matches for the cake. We always did gifts first. It was the law in our house.

"Happy birthday, Mable," my mother said as she handed me a box wrapped in purple paper and dotted with glittery gold stars. Whatever was inside had to be special. I ripped it open excitedly to reveal a gorgeous pair of navy blue sparkly flats.

"OMG, these shoes would be so amazing with the dress in Higgin's window!"

The words fell out of my mouth. I couldn't help myself, and I couldn't take them back. My brother shot me a *how could you be that ungrateful* look, and my mother tried her best not to appear disappointed, but I'd obviously insulted her. She must've spent a week's salary on them. Every year for our birthdays, my brother and I got a new pair of shoes, and every year we hoped for something different. But shoes were the only things my mother refused to buy secondhand, and new ones cost a tiny fortune.

Mom lit the gold candles on my cake, and she and my brother sang "Happy Birthday" to me, completely out of tune.

"Make a wish," she said.

"Already did." *And there was nothing careful about it,* I thought, recalling what Miss Serling said earlier.

I puckered my lips and inhaled all the air I could to blow out the candles, but before I exhaled, they flickered and went out. My mother looked confused and then checked to see if there was an open window somewhere. There wasn't. "This apartment has the craziest drafts," she said, relighting the candles.

It happened again. The candles went completely out, as if someone else was making a wish on my cake. I would have blamed it on my brother, only he looked as perplexed as we did, and he sucked at acting.

We were all baffled and a little spooked.

My brother tried to laugh it off. "Maybe you got the trick candles by mistake, Mom."

"Yeah," I agreed halfheartedly. "That must be it."

I couldn't shake the creepy feeling, but did, for Mom's sake, and because of the cake. It tasted like heaven, and I shoveled down every last sugary crumb.

"So, do you like the shoes?" Mom asked quietly, putting her hand on mine.

"I love them so much," I replied. "Thank you, Mom."

"Go try them on."

I went to my room, slid off my shoes, and sat on my bed, looking at the flats. I couldn't stop thinking about how they would look with Lydia's dress. My eyes moved from the shoebox on the floor toward the window until I caught myself gazing across the street into Higgin's window. Staring at her.

Nothing could have prepared me for what I saw. "What the heck?"

The dress I was fantasizing about, the dress I wanted more than anything in the world, the one Lydia wore earlier, was gone. Replaced by another.

But Miss Serling locked up and left with me?

I spun around to run into the kitchen so I could tell my mom when I caught the sight of something spectacular hanging in my closet.

It was Lydia's dress. *The* dress.

Hanging in *my* closet.

I grabbed it off the hanger and held it up to me in my full-length mirror. I never had a reason to look at myself in it before this. I slipped on the frock and twirled. And twirled. And twirled. I put on my new shoes and stared in awe.

"I'm gonna be late for work, honey. I hope you liked everything," my mom yelled out to me.

I heard the apartment door open and close. I scurried out from my room into the hallway, hoping to catch her.

"Mom! I can't believe you got me the dress!"

But all I heard were footsteps fading down the stairs.

I catwalked back into my room and beelined over to my mirror. We recently learned about the Greek myth of Narcissus in school, the hot boy who saw his reflection in the water and then lost his will to live because he couldn't stop staring at himself. Now, with this dress on, I totally got it. I was starstruck by the sight of me.

"I can't believe I have an actual birthday dress to wear to school tomorrow. The girls are gonna be so jelly they'll need a mold to get through the day."

I spent what felt like hours posing, taking selfies, posting them, and basking in the avalanche of likes and loves.

Soooooooooo pretty!

Queen!

This. Is. Everything!

The comments and emojis burst onto my page like Pop Rocks in my mouth. A digital explosion of approval.

"Boom!" I shouted, and replied "Muah" to some and Snapchatted big phony kisses to others. Until a comment appeared from a girl in my class.

Wow. Somebody robbed a bank.

Troll, I thought.

It was mean, but it got me thinking, Mom could never have afforded this dress. Unless maybe she worked something out with Miss Serling? A layaway plan or something? A secret deal between the two of them? Didn't seem likely, though. But then how did it wind up in my closet? I took it off with care and hung it back up. *Everyone is expecting to see me in it now,* I thought. I wouldn't want to disappoint them. *But what if I stain it and it has to be returned,* I wondered. I looked at my Twitter and Instagram, counted up the likes, and shrugged.

"Who cares," I said to myself. "Happy Birthday to *me.*"

I stood at my bedroom window for a good long while, watching Lydia across the street, trying to figure it out. When out of nowhere I saw her blink. At least I could have sworn she blinked. But you know how if you stare at something long enough, you start to see things? So, I kept my eyes locked on hers to see if it happened again. Until I started to doze off.

"Good night," I whispered as my eyes closed.

The next morning I dressed for school decked out in Lydia's finest. I stepped off the bus and into the hall like a supermodel hitting the runway, actually trying to draw attention to myself for a change. The audience was gathered already, due to my social media publicity campaign. Mouths hung open, backpacks dropped in surprise, hands were placed firmly on hips in disbelief and envy as I passed.

All the girls who usually smirked at me, ignored me, or made fun of me took notice. Some even came over to talk to me. I wasn't the poor girl in the hand-me-down outfit anymore. I was their middle school idol.

At the end of the day, I got off the bus and sauntered up the stairs of my building, as if I walked on air.

"Where'd you get that?" my mother asked as she opened the door.

"What?" I asked.

"You know what," she scolded. "The dress!"

"I thought you got it for me?"

Mom was silent. And when my mom was silent, that only meant one thing—trouble. I'd rather her yell at me all day long than be silent.

"You know we can't afford that."

"But it was hanging in my closet!"

I can tell she didn't believe me. It's the same sort of look I remember her giving me when I was two and walked out of the convenience store on the corner with a handful of candy I hadn't paid for.

"I don't want to hear lies," she said. "Take it back."

"No!" I shouted. "All the girls at school loved it. Loved it on *me*. I felt special. Like Lydia. Don't you understand?"

"It's you that's special, not the dress," Mom said. "Don't *you* understand?"

"You have no idea what it's like. Spending your whole life ashamed. Wanting to be somebody else."

"Either you take it back, or I will."

I ran to my room and slammed the door. I changed clothes and put the dress on a hanger, pitying myself the whole time before hobbling out to the kitchen.

"This dress made me really happy," I said to my mom, who was taking a lasagna out of the oven.

"Be happy in your own skin," she advised. "Go on now, take that back and then wash up for dinner."

"Yeah, right," I complained as I trudged down the stairs and across the street to Higgin's.

Miss Serling barely looked at me as I walked back to her sitting at the register.

"Lydia is over there, or have you forgotten?" she said.

"I'm here to see you."

"Really? What on Earth for?"

"I think this belongs to you," I said, handing over the dress.

It felt like my heart would beat out of my chest. I know Miss Serling could hear it, that's how nervous I was. She looked at the dress and then at me several times in rapid succession. Her face reddened with anger.

"I knew I should've kept a closer eye on you!" Miss Serling grabbed the dress before I could complete my denial and held it up behind the counter checking for damage or stains but found none. "Good thing for you."

"So are you going to ban me from the store or something?"

She mulled it over for what seemed like forever and rendered her verdict.

"Well . . . you did bring it back," she said. "And it's undamaged. I won't ban you, but don't ever let anything like this happen again. If I have to go to Mr. Higgin, he won't be as generous. He prosecutes shoplifters all the time, you know."

She threw me a look of pity, which I hated more than anything. It doesn't matter if she banned me or not. I was too embarrassed to come back. I walked out the door without even stopping to talk to Lydia. I figured she'd probably overheard anything she needed to know.

When I opened the door to leave, the bell at the top rang, but I also thought I heard something else.

Laughter.

"Stop laughing at me!" I yelled to Miss Serling behind the counter, months of pent-up resentment breaking through. Only, when I turned around to see her, she wasn't there. *I must be going mad.*

The week passed, and every day I fought the urge to visit Lydia. Instead, I watched her flaunt a plum silk dress from my bedroom window. She stood there so beautiful, free from all the worries, all the drama that real girls like me had to face each day.

Mom and I didn't discuss the dress, but the girls at school kept asking when was I going to wear it again. I just smiled coyly and laughed. I secretly feared that one of their moms would hear something from Miss Serling and find me out. Humiliate me.

The very next morning I opened my eyes and dragged myself over to my closet to find something to wear. And find something I did. That very dress that Lydia wore all week, the plum silk one, hanging right there in my closet!

I rubbed my eyes to make sure I wasn't dreaming. *How,* I wondered, *did this get here?* Was my mom rewarding me for being honest? Or Miss Serling making a kind of peace offering? Or maybe Mr. Higgin just plain felt sorry for me?

With the school bus nearly here for pick up, I didn't have time to think about it, nor did I want to. I swept my hair up like Lydia's, put the dress on, threw an old dress into my backpack, and left for school. Thankfully, Mom wasn't back home yet from her night shift.

I hopped on the bus and flashed Lydia a thumbs-up. There she was, in a new metallic silver party dress. It was divine, and the pleats at the bottom glistened like new-fallen snow. I wanted it more than anything

I'd ever set my eyes on. It dawned on me that I was still wearing hand-me-downs, only now they were from a dummy.

Everyone had their eyes glued on me as I sashayed down the hall. Even more than the last time. They were thrilled to see another one of the dresses they'd been admiring in Higgin's window on me. I had more friends at school and on Facebook now than I could count. It was like *I* was their Lydia. And it's oddly the only time I really felt like myself. But all I could think about was that new silver dress. I had to have it.

At the end of the day, I changed in the school restroom before getting on the bus home. I didn't need any questions I couldn't or wouldn't answer from Mom. I folded up the dress nicely and hid it in my backpack.

In the weeks that followed, every dress that Lydia wore appeared in my closet while I slept, starting with the silver party dress. I followed the same routine. Kept it to myself, left before Mom got home in the morning, and changed into old clothes at school every afternoon before I got on the bus. I was living my dream, and I didn't care *how* or *why* anymore.

Halloween night. Higgin's window was all decked out in menacing black cats, bats, and witches' hats. At the center of it all stood Lydia, wearing a black velvet dress with a rounded ivory collar totally appropriate for the season. I just had to see it up close.

"Happy Halloween, Miss Serling."

"You're not dressed up?" she asked.

My heart sank. I'd been found out. Busted. All she had to do was look in my backpack to see the dress.

"For Halloween," she continued. "You're not dressed up?"

"Oh, right. No, I don't want to be anything this year, actually," I said. "I'm going as myself."

"Are you sure about that?" she asked before disappearing into the back.

I proceeded to Lydia, studying her new dress carefully. Envying it. I literally couldn't wait for it to turn up in my closet. I needed to have it. *Now.*

"Closing time," Miss Serling called out from the register.

"Okay," I called back. "Happy Halloween again."

As Miss Serling put her head down to count out the register, I opened the door to sound the bell and then ducked behind a few racks. After a few minutes she walked right by me. I had to sneeze, but held it in with all my might. She turned out the store lights, stepped outside, and locked the door, leaving me alone with Lydia.

The purplish-black Halloween lights in the display window mixed with the moonlight, causing the shadows from the spooky decorations to grow in the room and cast an eerie glow on the mannequin. The wind howled outside as trash cans toppled and lights flickered and went out, just like my birthday candles.

"I'm sorry I haven't been here in a while . . . ," I said, my voice trailing off as I looked behind me. "Your dresses are a big hit with everyone at school. You're so lucky that you get to wear them firsthand."

Just then a dress fell off the rack next to me. It was teal chiffon and irresistible. I couldn't help but rush to put it on. "I'm really popular now and happy. All thanks to you," I said as I fixed my hair in an updo and checked myself out in the mirror. "I just wish it could last forever."

After admiring myself for a while, I got tired and decided it was time to go. I reached for Lydia's hand in a gesture of thanks and to say good-bye. As I grabbed hold of it, I found that I couldn't let go. I looked to see if I'd caught her sleeve on my bracelet, unable to get free.

"Let me go!" I screamed.

I was overcome with fear and felt woozy.

The last thing I heard was the bell jingle on the door and the slightest giggle fade into the wind.

The next morning I opened my eyes, relieved, thinking that last night was only a nightmare.

But I quickly realized something was terribly wrong.

I wasn't in my room.

All I could see were Halloween decorations from Higgin's window surrounding me, and the hustle and bustle of the street outside. A familiar voice was barking orders from behind me.

"Let's get these decorations down now and a new dress on the mannequin," Miss Serling said in a rushed voice. "Or we'll be here forever!"

A girl and her mother approached me from across the street.

It was MY mother.

And *ME*.

Only I was in the store window. Trapped in the mannequin.

I *am* Lydia.

"This is Lydia, Mom," the girl who used to be me said to *my* mother.

"I've never seen her up close," Mom said. "She's so beautifully dressed and lifelike, isn't she?" My mother lingered in front of the new me.

"Yes. I used to think I wanted to be just like her, but I know now I'd rather be me," Lydia said, holding tight to my mom's hand.

"And you have all those beautiful dresses that Higgin's gave to you because of *your* honesty. You *will* look just like her."

Lydia laughed. It was the exact same laugh I'd heard in the store.

It finally dawned on me that Lydia had planned this all along. She didn't give those dresses to me as gifts, to make me happy. She was putting them in my closet for herself! So she'd have nice clothes to wear when she took over my life!

And the candles on my birthday cake? She blew them out! Before I could officially wish to be like her, she wished to be me!

The happy mother-daughter duo waved good-bye to Miss Serling through the window. I tried to shout, but nothing came out.

Come back! It's me! Come back, Mother, please! I silently screamed again and again, Lydia's sweet smile now frozen across my new face for eternity. *It's MEEEEEEE!*

FEED THE BIRDS

BY STEPHEN ROSS

I SOMETIMES STILL HEAR MY AUNT and uncle screaming.

Late in the evening, when all is quiet in this large old house, I sometimes still hear their cries outside from somewhere deep in the forest; even though it has been many years since they ran out into the night, screaming with absolute terror and fear.

I don't miss them.

My mother and father drowned at sea when I was twelve, and I was left to the care of my only remaining family: Uncle Average and Aunt Zelda, two of the sourest specimens I had ever met. They had no children, and they lived here at Abercrumble House, a large, two hundred-year-old house in the middle of a forest and ten miles from the nearest town or village.

I can still remember the day I first came to live here at Abercrumble. It was the year 1872, in winter. Chubwitt, the family lawyer, a thin pencil of a man, escorted me and my two suitcases to Paddington Station in the heart of London, where he put me aboard a train bound for the village of Hertley on the edge of the Hertley Forest.

I had a first-class compartment to myself, and three small apples in my coat pocket to eat on the journey. And as I watched the city fade, and the countryside grow, I felt I was going to have a lonely life; with an aunt and uncle I had never met and of whom my mother and father had seldom spoken.

This sense of dread became concrete when my train arrived in Hertley.

"I don't care for children," my uncle announced in a gust of frosted breath when I met him on the freezing-cold station platform. "I'm only taking you in because you are the child of my wife's dead sister."

My uncle was dressed in a dark gentleman's long coat and hat. He had a mess of gray hair and a bushy gray mustache beneath his nose. He was very tall and very large. Standing in front of him on the platform, I could barely see his face for his wide chest. It was like standing in front of a large hill, with his head sitting up on the top.

We rode in his carriage, a completely black carriage drawn by two horses with a gold letter *A* on the door beneath the window: *A* for "Abercrumble." *A* for "*alone.*"

I really felt quite miserable. The driver sitting up at the front holding the reins was a short, bald-headed old man with two droopy eyes like those of an old, faithful hound. My uncle addressed him as Fulton, and as I had climbed into the carriage, Fulton had given me a smile; the only one I saw that day.

As we rode deep into Hertley Forest, my uncle said something to me, and I've never forgotten the way he said it: "Don't feed the birds." He was staring out the window of the carriage, lost in thought.

I noticed he had a large, rusty key hung about his neck on a string; I would learn that this key was always with him.

He turned to look at me. His eyes were black. "Do you understand? Do not *ever* feed the birds."

"Birds?" I inquired. I had seen none, and apart from the thud of the horses' hooves and the rumble of the carriage wheels on the dirt track, I had heard nothing, either. In fact, Hertley Forest appeared entirely empty; a deep, damp, dark entanglement of winter dead trees, with a narrow, winding pathway leading endlessly through it.

No one lived in Hertley Forest except for Average and Zelda Abercrumble; no one else wanted to live in it. Abercrumble House stood in the middle of the forest and had been the home of the Abercrumbles for over two hundred years. And with no children, Uncle Average was the last stop on the Abercrumble family line.

As the carriage rode into the clearing that contained the house, I leaned out the window to look. Abercrumble House appeared as though it had been conjured up in a nightmare: a lopsided construction of three floors, with stone walls black with moss, and windows clouded with centuries of dust. At the left front corner stood a solitary tower entwined in rotting roots. It rose up high above and seemed to threaten anyone looking up at it with a swift coming down and swatting like a fly.

My large uncle made another pronouncement: "Do not go up into the tower. It is dangerous and forbidden."

I had formed the opinion that my uncle liked to make rules. I had no idea what his occupation concerned, but he would have made for an excellent schoolmaster. He walked with a walking stick, too, and I could easily imagine him slamming it down onto school desks as he instructed you of all the things you were *not allowed to do.*

An elderly woman stood on the steps leading up to the house's front entrance. She had gray hair tied tightly back and was dressed in mourning black. She looked thoroughly unpleasant. At her feet the steps were littered with dead and rotting leaves.

"Is that Aunt Zelda?" I asked.

"No," Uncle Average answered. "That is Mrs. Fulton. She is the housekeeper."

The Fultons were the only staff at Abercrumble. Fulton (Mr.) was the groundsman and tended to everything outside the house: the grounds, the horses, and repairs to the roof; and Mrs. Fulton tended to everything inside: the cooking, the laundering, and the dust.

The front door opened into a wide, empty front hall with a checkerboard floor of black slate and white marble tiles; they looked so old and worn they had surely been laid down by the Romans.

Mrs. Fulton showed me to my room. "It was sad news to hear of your mother and father," she said.

She carried one of my suitcases, I the other. She led me upstairs to the second floor and through a maze of shadowy hallways. I had the feeling she was a woman of few words, as she said nothing else on the journey.

The inside of the house was cold, dark, and empty. There were no rugs on the bare wooden floors, no pictures hung on the walls, and nothing at all in the way of decoration. It was only the afternoon, but I felt as though I needed a candle and a priest. It was as though something had died in all the gloom.

Mrs. Fulton led me into my bedroom, dropped my suitcase on the floor, sneezed, and left.

My room was quite big and rather empty. There was a bed, a chair, a dresser, and an echo. The view from the window was of the forest, and I imagined its long, moss-mottled branches loomed large in every window of the house. I understood that one of Fulton's primary duties as groundsman was to prevent the forest from growing right up to the house and strangling it.

I unpacked, and then I went and explored, and naturally, the first place I wanted to investigate was the tower. I found the door leading to its staircase without any difficulty. It wasn't locked, and I headed up without delay. I loved a mystery, and there had to be something up at the top; why else would my uncle have told me to keep out. I certainly didn't see any danger. It was just an ordinary spiral stone staircase, and all the way up there were regular slits in the wall that let in daylight.

At the top of the stairs there was a window and a red door. Looking out the window, I could peer down into the clearing in front of the house and then out across the tops of the trees of the forest. It was like looking out across a vast barren sea of wilderness, with a gunmetal winter sky above keeping watch over it.

The red door was locked. I peered through its rusty keyhole but could see nothing of the room on the other side. I presumed the key that hung about my uncle's neck would unlock it.

I heard a rustle behind me. Two small birds sat outside on the window ledge. They were black, and each about the size of my hand. They were looking at me through the glass in a most peculiar way, as though they were studying me. I had never seen birds do that.

They flew away.

I tracked their flight down into the trees, and curious, I decided to follow them. I headed back down the tower's spiral staircase and then back up to my room, where I fetched my coat.

As I was walking out through the front door, my uncle spied me as he was coming out of the drawing room.

"Are you going outside without a scarf and a hat?" he called out.

"I'm dressed warm enough," I answered.

"Don't you catch a cold," he warned.

Another rule.

I left the house.

I followed the winding pathway through the forest for a quarter mile, until I came to about where I thought the birds might have gone to perch.

I could hear nothing, apart from a gentle breeze through the tree branches and the faint sound of the last leaves falling. *How could a forest be dead,* I wondered, *as this one certainly appeared to be?* It was as though all the color had been drained from it.

I saw movement.

One of the two birds was on the ground. It quickly hopped from sight behind the foot of a large oak tree.

"Don't be frightened," I whispered in my most reassuring tone.

The bird poked its head around the corner and peeked at me. The other bird did too; they were both behind the oak tree. Such shy birds, they were.

"You must be hungry," I said. I looked about. "And what is there to eat? I've seen no worms, snails, or spiders."

All I had in my coat pocket was a half-eaten apple left over from my train journey that morning, and I placed it on the ground near the foot of the tree.

I stood back.

The birds peeked out again. They saw the apple and looked up at me. I nodded; it was for them. They hopped out from behind the tree and started pecking away at it.

"I will bring more," I said.

The birds chirped excitedly. It had been as though they had understood my words.

* * *

I met Aunt Zelda that night at the dining table. She looked like a lighthouse. She was tall, dressed in a featureless flowing white gown with the dimensions of a cylinder, and up on top of her head sprung a tall chaos of hair the color of fire.

"It is soon your birthday," she said, staring across the table at me with a pale face and two large blue eyes.

"Yes," I answered. "I turn thirteen."

"There is a birthday present for you." She pointed at a side table, on top of which sat a square-shaped parcel wrapped in colorful striped paper.

"It was found at your house in London after your mother and father perished at sea. Chubwitt, the family lawyer, sent it on to here. There is a card with your name on it."

I looked back at my aunt.

"My sister must have purchased and wrapped it before she and your father set sail."

I had no knowledge of this birthday present. I looked back across the room at it, and for a moment, it was as though my mother and father were with me again . . . until my large uncle cleared his throat.

"Mrs. Fulton is getting a cold," he grumbled to my aunt. "She's been sniffing and sneezing all afternoon."

My aunt nodded.

For the next five minutes they discussed Mrs. Fulton's head cold, until I became quite bored listening and decided to change the subject.

"I saw some birds today," I said.

I may as well have announced that I had personally declared war on Spain, for their reaction would surely have been the same.

"There's nothing in the forest," my aunt said.

My large uncle slammed his walking stick down on the table. "If you did," he growled, "under no circumstances are you to feed them."

"Why?" I asked.

"There's nothing in the forest," my aunt repeated, shaking her head. "You only imagined you saw something."

My uncle didn't answer my question, and the next twenty minutes were devoted to his and my aunt's renewed discussion of Mrs. Fulton's cold.

In my lap lay a handkerchief, into which I had been secreting food throughout the meal. When it came time to excuse myself from the table, I hid the little package of potato, cabbage, beans, and pork behind me as I rose. I bid my aunt and uncle good night, took a candle, and went up to my room.

I waited until the late hour, then dressed warmly and crept out from my room, down the stairs, and out through the front door and into the forest.

A half-moon in a broken sky was my only light. I dared not take a candle for fear the light would have been seen from the house.

I walked carefully along the winding pathway back to the oak tree where I had last seen the birds. At the foot of the tree, I laid out my handkerchief of food in the manner of a little picnic, and I stood back and waited.

I saw nothing. The only sound was the creak of tree branches in the night. The birds appeared to be absent. I felt sad that my offering might go unnoticed.

It was frightfully cold, and a damp fog had begun to envelop everything about me. I turned to walk back to the house. I had taken no more than ten steps when I heard the faint sound of fluttering wings.

Looking back, I could see the shadows of the birds at the foot of the oak tree. They had found the food and were eating heartily. How cruel of my uncle to not want to feed the birds in the forest. These two little things were probably near starvation in this bleak wasteland.

I returned to the house.

As I approached the front steps, I smelled pipe tobacco and realized there was a man standing there in the darkness. I feared it was my uncle.

"What are you doing out here at this hour?" It was Fulton, the groundsman, out smoking his pipe. I had not heard the man's voice before, and it was surprising; it was as deep as a cave, and raspy.

"If you don't tell my uncle," I said, "I'll tell you."

He nodded and took a long drag on his pipe.

"I was feeding the birds."

In the moonlight I could see him giving me a queer look with his two droopy eyes.

"There's nothing in the forest," he rasped. "A long time ago it was full of animals, but they've all gone now."

There was a curious sound somewhere in the distance. It was like a muffled rifle shot.

"What was that?" I asked.

"Mrs. Fulton," he said.

"Is she outside in the cold?"

He shook his head.

We walked along the front of the house, and when we got to the end, I could look down the side, to where I could see a little cottage located at the rear.

We heard Mrs. Fulton again. It was an energetic sneeze.

Evidently, the Fultons lived out in the cottage and not inside the main house.

Fulton shook his head again. "Don't ever tell Mrs. Fulton you've been feeding the birds, if you really have seen any. She hates the things with every bone in her body."

"Why is that?"

"We used to have a cat."

I nodded, not that I really understood what he meant. "Where did all the animals in the forest go?" I asked.

"Never you mind. It's best for young children to not ask about it."

"I'll soon be thirteen," I informed him.

"Is that so?" he said. "I'm sixty-five. I've lived your whole lifetime of thirteen years exactly five times over, so that gives me every right to tell you not to concern yourself."

Who was I to argue with an elderly mathematician with a pipe?

"What do you do up in the tower each day?" I asked my large uncle one morning.

He didn't like this question.

Aunt Zelda let out a short burst of laughter.

My uncle stared at me from the end of the breakfast table with such inflamed intensity I feared he would melt the butter.

"He's going to make us rich," Aunt Zelda snorted. "He's been promising that for years."

There was always an undertone to everything Aunt Zelda said, as though she was secretly angry with everybody and everything. My mother had been delightful; her sister was a word I'm not old enough to use yet.

And neither my uncle nor my aunt answered my question.

I had lived at the house now for more than two weeks. Every morning after breakfast, my uncle would head off up the stairs to the top of the tower, and I wouldn't see him again until we assembled at the dinner table that evening.

I had grown accustomed to the empty house and being alone. Fulton was always outside with a garden tool or tending to the horses in the stables. Mrs. Fulton was always fussing about cooking and cleaning, and I did my best to not be underfoot. My aunt spent most of her days in the drawing room learning to play Bach's *Minuet in G major* on the harpsichord—every day, the same piece; every day, the same mistakes. I'm sure the harpsichord would have liked to have thrown itself into the fire.

I overcame my boredom by reading. I had discovered a library in the east wing of the house with more books in it than I had ever seen in my life, and plump leather chairs that swallowed you up in their comfort.

And I had continued my secret mission to feed the birds. Each day I left out a little picnic on a handkerchief in the morning after breakfast, and again at night after everyone had gone to bed. I never saw them anymore, so shy they were, but they were certainly eating what I left out. Not a crumb was ever left behind.

"Saturday is your birthday," my aunt announced. "We shall have a party for you."

"I would like that very much," I said. My attention returned to the birthday present waiting patiently for me on the side table.

My uncle's attention turned back to Mrs. Fulton and a renewed discussion with my aunt about the old woman's cold: *No*, it hadn't gotten any better. *Yes*, she was still taking her medication.

After breakfast I went outside. And as I walked away from the house, I had that *odd sensation*. I call it odd because I don't know any other way to describe it. I knew that if I looked, I would surely find someone looking back at me.

I did so.

And there was.

My uncle was staring at me. He was at the window up at the top of the tower.

What does he do behind that red door? I wondered. Did he write books, paint landscapes, play with puppets, or do nothing at all? Maybe the room at the top of the tower was empty, and all he did up there each day was sit on a cushion on the floor and think about cake.

He disappeared from the window.

I headed to the oak tree. I retrieved the handkerchief I had left out the previous evening, and I laid out a new one with that morning's feast. I heard the birds twittering. They sounded a lot happier and louder. They were full of life.

As I went back I encountered Mrs. Fulton. It was rare that I saw her outside. I wished her a good morning as we passed. She regarded me with suspicion and said nothing.

I went on to the house.

Sure enough, the next time I saw my large uncle was that night at the dinner table. And partway through the meal, he placed my handkerchief on the table. He unfolded it to reveal the food I had left out that morning.

"Who are you feeding?" he asked, staring at me as though I had driven a nail through his foot.

My aunt was also staring.

I didn't answer. I continued chewing the large piece of potato I had just shoveled into my mouth. By the rules of good table manners, I should not speak with my mouth full. My uncle knew this and was obliged to wait.

Clearly, Mrs. Fulton had brought my handkerchief and its contents to his attention. It occurred to me that I was sending a couple of handkerchiefs each day into her laundry basket, and many would have been dirtied with bark and soil from the forest floor. Had Mrs. Fulton become suspicious?

I pondered this matter.

After seven minutes of my continued chewing, my uncle slammed his walking stick down on the table in frustration. "Will you for goodness' sake finally swallow that mouthful and speak!"

I swallowed.

"I'm leaving food out for the birds," I said.

My aunt gasped.

"There's nothing else for them to eat."

My uncle's face glowed red with anger. "Do you know why there are no animals in the forest?" he roared.

I shook my head.

"Because the birds ate them all up!"

My aunt nodded in agreement.

Harsh words were spoken by adults, and I was sent to my room. The handkerchief of food I had been quietly assembling on my lap was confiscated.

* * *

Night winds swirled about the house, and my bedside candle flickered. I pulled the blankets up to my chin and stared up at the dancing shadows on the ceiling above my bed.

How could birds have eaten all the animals? It was too fanciful to imagine. It was ridiculous. Was my large uncle insane? My aunt too?

The candle died, and everything became a shadow. There was no moon outside or even stars; all was hidden under a thick blanket of cloud.

There came a rustle and a tapping. I couldn't see anything in the dark, but I knew the birds were outside at my window. They hadn't been fed that day and were surely hungry. I knew how I felt if I went a day without food.

"Don't worry," I whispered. "I will feed you."

I waited until I heard the grandfather clock downstairs in the entrance hall chime for midnight, and dressed warmly once again, I crept out of my room.

I snuck downstairs through the dark and quiet of the house to the kitchen. By the light of a candle, I found some bread and a few scraps of meat left over from that night's dinner, and I bound it up in a fresh handkerchief.

I went out through the front door and into the night.

The air had a cold bite to it, and there was a thick fog. Quick slivers of moonlight breaking through the clouds were my only moments of vision, and I navigated my way back to the oak tree more from memory than anything.

I left the food on the ground, and I put the handkerchief in my pocket; I'm sure the birds didn't mind if their dinner was served up on a tablecloth or not. Less than a minute later, I heard the eager fluttering of their wings.

"I will feed you," I said into the darkness. "I will *always* feed you. You have my promise on that."

I became aware of a light behind me, and I heard a jagged cough.

"Your uncle will hear of this," Mrs. Fulton croaked angrily.

I turned to see Mrs. Fulton holding a lantern and walking toward me with frail steps. She was as white as a bedsheet, and by her lantern's light, I could see a film of sweat on her brow. She coughed again, her eyes rolled upward in a faint, and she collapsed to the ground.

She regained consciousness within a moment, and I helped her back onto her feet and picked up her lantern. With her arm about my shoulders, and bearing her weight, I walked her back toward the house.

I called out loudly as we approached.

My uncle's bedroom window opened, and he stuck out his head.

When we got to the front steps, Fulton, no doubt having heard my cries, came around from the side. Together we helped Mrs. Fulton, coughing and sneezing, up the steps and into the house. There was an armchair inside the entrance hall beside the grandfather clock, and we navigated her to it. She collapsed into it. I set her lantern on the floor at her feet.

"What is going on here?" my uncle thundered in his nightclothes, the tip of his walking stick slamming down into each wooden step on the staircase as he descended. My aunt hurriedly followed behind, holding a candelabrum crowded with candles.

"Mrs. Fulton is dangerously ill," I reported.

Fulton spoke up, "I don't think the medicine she's been given is helping in any way."

"Well, give her *more* of it," my uncle barked, coming to a standstill in front of us.

"Look at the woman," Aunt Zelda said, poking my uncle's side with a rigid finger. "The medicine is clearly not working."

"It'll be the death of my wife, if something isn't done," Fulton pleaded.

"She should be taken into Hertley," I said. "There must surely be a doctor in the village."

Only Fulton was in agreement.

"No," my uncle said. "Potion 53 will cure her."

"You are *not* a doctor," my aunt said to him, her rigid finger repeatedly stabbing his side. "Mrs. Fulton is clearly not long for this world. I will not have her death on my conscience."

"Potion 53 will cure her," he insisted. "She just has to keep taking it."

"I could take her into Hertley," Fulton said.

"I won't allow it," my uncle barked again. "It's far too dangerous in the dark for the horses."

Something occurred to him.

"And what the dickens were you all doing outside at this time of night?"

"She followed me," I reported.

Mrs. Fulton summoned up the energy to point her finger at me. "Birds!" she cried out. "Was feeding the birds!"

If my large uncle had previously resembled a hill, he now resembled a volcano.

"WHAT?" he roared.

He swung his walking stick at me and knocked me to the floor.

"You deliberately went against my word," he thundered, towering above me, ready to strike a second blow. "Mrs. Fulton should never have gone outside. So help me, child, I will whip you!"

My aunt stepped in front of him. "It's your fault the old woman is feeling poorly. Potion 53 is clearly another failure, just like all the others."

For a brief moment the volcano hesitated, his eyes locked onto my aunt's. And in that moment, I seized my chance. I sprang back to my feet, and darting between them, I snatched the rusty key from around my uncle's neck, snapping the string as I yanked it away. I grabbed the lantern that stood on the floor, and I headed for the tower.

They followed.

As I ran up the spiral staircase, I heard my uncle's bellowing voice and the staccato beat of his walking stick on the stone steps behind me.

As I had guessed, the key unlocked the red door at the top of the tower, and I opened it. By the lantern's light, I found a room full of equipment: test tubes, burners, racks of liquids and powders, racks of empty animal cages, medical apparatus, and a microscope.

My uncle and aunt burst into the room behind me, flushed and panting from their rapid climb of the stairs.

"What is this place?" I asked.

"Your uncle is a scientist," my aunt laughed. "He thinks he's going to find a cure for the common cold."

"I will!" he barked.

"When? You've been coming up to this room every day for more than twenty years, and not one good result has ever come from it."

"I just need more time!"

"Do you want to know what happened to all the animals in the forest?" my aunt asked me. "Potion 21 killed them. Your uncle tested it on a bird, and it became ill. Not with a cold, but with something else; something that made it hungry for flesh, for anything that moved. And then its strange illness spread to the other birds in the forest, and together, they ate up all the other animals. And when there weren't any other animals left, they began to eat up one another, until there wasn't a single bird left and the forest was completely empty."

"Shut up, woman!" my uncle roared. He grabbed me by my neck and dragged me out of the room.

With my aunt following behind with the candelabrum, he dragged me back down the staircase, through the house, and up to my room. He threw me into it and locked the door.

"Your birthday is canceled!" he shouted through the keyhole. "You are going to stay in your room for the rest of your life, and from this day forward you will have no more birthdays. You are going to stay at the age of twelve *forever.*"

Fulton later told me that my uncle went and fetched my birthday present from the side table in the dining room. He took it into the entrance hall, where he and my aunt were about to set fire to it on the checkered floor tiles, when there was a knocking at the front door.

It was no ordinary knocking.

I heard it myself, locked in my room upstairs: a great, thunder-like banging on the front door. It was as though cannonballs had been fired at it.

I heard my uncle and aunt shouting.

I heard the sound of the front door being smashed open, and the sound of my uncle and aunt screaming.

I heard great animal shrieks.

And then I heard my uncle and aunt both screaming outside as they fled from the house.

I heard their screams disappear into the depths of the forest.

And then silence.

A short time later Fulton unlocked my door. He was pale and wide-eyed. "Such terrible things I've seen," he said.

"Can you drive the carriage in the dark?" I asked. "With only lantern light to guide you?"

He nodded. "The horses know the way better than I do."

"Wake them from their sleep. You have not a moment to lose."

Fulton harnessed the horses, and together we wrapped Mrs. Fulton in blankets and lifted her into the carriage. He rode off for Hertley and a doctor, and I remained at the house to await my uncle's and aunt's return.

I waited throughout the night, standing at the front entrance; it looked as though a great force of nature had ripped it open. Every so often, in the distance, I could hear my uncle and aunt screaming.

They never returned.

Fulton arrived back at the house the following morning. He reported that Mrs. Fulton was to stay with the doctor. She had bronchitis. It was expected that she would recover.

I made Fulton a strong cup of coffee and sat him down at the kitchen table. It had been with much eagerness I had awaited his explanation of what had taken place the previous evening, while I had been locked in my room. After some short reflection, he attempted to put it into words.

"We were all in the entrance hall," he said. "And there was a knocking at the door, of the likes I had never heard. Suddenly, it was as though the door had been torn apart like paper, and into the house came these two giant beasts."

"What were they?"

"Black, they were, all of seven or eight feet tall, with great black beaks and eyes."

"What were they?"

"Birds."

He stared at me. He was still terrified.

"They paid me and Mrs. Fulton no mind, but they went for your uncle and aunt, and no mistake, with a deafening squawk and caw, and they chased them right out of the house."

It has been many years since my uncle and aunt ran into the night, and I sometimes still hear their screaming. . . . Or maybe it is simply a trick of the wind in the trees; they are full of leaves now, and animals have returned to the forest.

Fulton is still my groundsman, and Mrs. Fulton still cooks and cleans. After the disappearance of my uncle and aunt, and as their only living relative, Chubwitt saw to it that I inherited Abercrumble House, where I have remained and have devoted my life to the study of ornithology (that's the study of birds).

I have never yet opened my birthday present, and it remains waiting for me on the side table in the dining room (I have always liked a mystery).

And yes, I still feed the birds. They've grown quite big now, and they're very happy.

Come and visit us. Stay for dinner.

THE PLATFORM
BY PETER LERANGIS

'D NEVER HEARD A SUBWAY train shriek until that night the orange girl fell on the track.

Seriously, imagine the driver when something like that happens. The victim falls. You slam on the brakes. Behind you, ten gigantic metal boxes full of people have been happily hurtling through the tunnel, and now the wheels are like, *What, you expect me to stop* now? It's not really a sound. It's more like someone stabbed you in both ears.

I didn't see the girl at first. Instead of going straight home after robotics, I'd gotten off at the Columbus Circle stop, and now I was listening to Christmas carols on the platform. The singers were dressed in lederhosen and peaked caps. They were probably the only group singing "Jingle Bells" with Motown choreography. Honestly, they looked like uncoordinated goatherds who took a wrong turn in Lapland and ended up at 59th Street. This level of dorkiness was normal for kids from New York City's Vanderdonck High School. They were in good company because next to them was an entire family toting shopping bags and wearing cheese hats, which are definitely *not* normal in Manhattan.

I would have been laughing my butt off, except that one of the singers was my best friend's older sister, Lucia Liberatore. Being near her fills me with glad tidings of comfort and joy. Her eyes are as deep as molten chocolate, and her smile is brighter than Christmas lights. As I watched her sing "bells on bobtails," I felt weirdly weak in the knees.

And then, a moment later, I *was* weak in the knees. Because Lucia was on top of me.

Actually, so was Jacob Schmendrick, and he's like a human fire hydrant.

This was due to the fact that a girl with orange hair and orange-framed glasses had plowed into Lucia from behind. Then Lucia plowed into Jacob, who had clomped in front of her when he should have dance-stepped in the other direction. They both lurched forward, landing on me.

The orange girl bounced off us and rammed into the strange tourist family, sending their headgear and shopping bags onto the platform. As she hurtled toward the tracks, a guy in a hoodie tried to grab her. Everyone on the platform screamed, except for a rat that was staring warily at one of the cheese hats.

Then, just like that, she went over. Onto the tracks. It was unbelievable, really. She could have stopped herself. People on the platform were stunned.

"Help her!" sang Lucia Liberatore.

And that was how I, Justin Blonsky, on that gray miserable day during the Most Wonderful Time of the Year, jumped onto the 59th Street tracks.

New Yorkers can feel when a train is coming. It creates a breeze, pushing the air out of the tunnel like a plunger. Well, down there on the tracks, it feels like a tropical wind, if you're in a part of the tropics that smells like stale pee. The girl had landed on the platform side of the tracks, but her sunglasses were on the inner side, near the electrified third rail. She was on all fours, trying to retrieve them. My second thought was that she was crazy. My first thought was *We're about to become human sushi!*

I grabbed her arm, but she shook me off. The headlights were bearing down, ballooning larger. The brakes screeched. I could see the silhouette of a driver through the front window. People were leaning over the platform, shouting. At least a dozen arms reached down toward us. I saw a baseball mitt and realized it was Jacob Schmendrick's right hand. I tried to push the girl toward salvation. But she wouldn't go. She seemed more annoyed than panicked. "Get them!" she said, gesturing toward the sunglasses.

Sunglasses!

The shriek of the train's horn was blotting out all sound. I could see the wheels, locked, sliding toward us along the rails on a bed of sparks. The lead car was emerging from the tunnel into the light of the station. We were smack in the center of the track. The train was maybe four seconds away.

"*GO!*" I tried to push her toward the platform, toward the outreached arms that could lift us up and out. But now her face was red, her eyes nearly popping out of her head. She was stronger than me. She pushed me aside and dove across the track bed. I fell in between the two rails. My brain was a panicked thicket of *Duh*, but I knew enough to lie low. People have survived being run over that way. Staying in the well between the tracks. Letting the train pass over your body. There's enough clearance. These are things every New Yorker knows.

But the crazy orange girl grabbed my arm and pulled me out of the well.

Into the light.

Into the noise.

Now she was yanking me in the direction of the platform. *Now* she wanted to be saved—*after* she'd put on her sunglasses! I wanted to kill her, but a New York City Transit's R188 was going to take care of that. I reached toward the outstretched hands—but they weren't there anymore. Even the Good Samaritans didn't want to die. People were backing off, saving their own lives.

All I could see was the blackness under the platform.

I tried to scream, but it was too late.

I think about death a lot. Partly because I'm a pretty morbid kid. Partly because I'm threatened with it on a daily basis by other classmates from the Five Corners School for the Unconventionally Abled.

My school is an official Zero Tolerance for Bullies Zone. But the zone unofficially ends about a block and a half away, just beyond the cheap sunglasses racks at the S&W Hardware and Deli. There, hidden from the school, is a battleground of wedgies, punches, lunch-money larceny, and black eyes.

If you're nerdy, unathletic, or short, you suffer. If you're all three, like I am, a walk to school is an exercise in mortal fear. In my imagination, death was an eternity of harassment, dumb insults, and ignorance.

I didn't imagine it would smell like lilacs and fresh-cut grass.

Squinting up into a bright light, I saw the outline of a girl leaning over me. "You are the luckiest little numbskull in history," came a tart, high-pitched voice.

"So, you're . . . an angel?" I said. That sounded really dumb. But I was lying on a bed of grass in a breezy field under the sun with no subway in sight. The combination of those two things made me start laughing uncontrollably.

"Not funny. There's nothing funny about what you did. I trained hard for this. You could have killed us both!" She was holding her sunglasses, shaking them at me. *"Do you think these grow on trees?"*

I sat up. My arms ached, my clothes were blackened by subway soot, and the left side of my jeans was covered in some disgusting goo that included the corner of a Snickers wrapper. Which meant I was alive, and this was all real. I had nearly died. Somehow, I was miles away now. And none of this was funny.

"Wait." I was starting to shake. It was all I could do to keep my cool. "First of all, I tried to pull you to safety. Second, those are sunglasses. Which you don't need in a subway. Especially when you're about to be bisected by a C train! And third, *what just happened*?"

She looked at me, like I was a kid reciting my times table all wrong. "Sorry, Justin. You really don't know, do you?"

"How do you know my name?"

With an exasperated sigh, she said, "Follow me."

Calm down, I told myself. *Chill.*

I thought of Lucia's face and took a deep breath. The grass beneath me was thick and cool to the touch. As I stood it sprang right back up into place. A field formed a wide circle about the length of a football field. A straight path of cedar chips ran down the center. Surrounding us were gardens erupting with flowers, their colors impossibly deep, their massive petals like a sea of hands eager for a shake. To the right I could hear a stream burbling in the woods beyond the gardens. In the distance straight ahead, a waterfall raged downward from a rocky peak, and giant hawk-like birds circled lazily overhead.

Stepping toward the path I heard a gentle voice to my right proclaim, "Clear, please, for everyone's safety."

I nearly fell back onto the grass. A group of seated people, maybe eighteen of them, was floating toward me in midair. As they drew closer I realized they weren't traveling of their own power but in an open vehicle made of some clear, glassy substance. It had seats, a floor, and side panels about shoulder height. And it was stopping in front of us.

"Geeeah!" I cried out. "What the heck is that?"

"A hoverbus." The orange girl turned and began climbing aboard. "This will save some time."

"Where is this place?" I demanded. "And who are you?"

"Right now we are at the Winged Victory statue, where West Fifty-Ninth Street bends around to meet Central Park West," she replied, standing on a clear platform in front of the passengers. "Just to our right would be the hotel with the great big globe. And in a moment we'll pass through the statue of Christopher Columbus. And I'm Hadron."

"But—but—" The passengers all smiled with a kind of bored indulgence, like I'd just performed a long, mediocre clarinet solo in the school talent show. "The future. Right? You took me through a time warp into the future. So this is where Fifty-Ninth Street used to be?"

Hadron laughed. So did some of the passengers. "It's a long story," she said.

As I stepped up and took a seat next to her, I realized the vehicle had no driver. A shoulder belt made of some clear material rose out of the seat and snapped itself shut around me. We accelerated smoothly. But instead of peaking at seventy miles an hour or whatever, we kept going. I felt my facial skin pressing back against my skull. The scenery became a wash of changing colors. I glanced at Hadron, who looked like a zombie in a wind tunnel. "Whirrrr!" she cried out, which I think was "Wheeee!" with a locked jaw.

We stopped on a wide, winding street of packed dirt. I guess you don't need pavement when vehicles hover. We were way past the gardens and the field. I could not keep my eyes off the buildings on either side of us. They rose about fifty stories, but it wasn't really the height that made me gawp. They were constructed of rectangular windowed blocks, like giant Lego castles stretching to the horizon. Where you would expect a cross street, instead vaulted archways had been constructed into the buildings at ground level. They spewed a steady stream of hovering vehicles, big and small, all traveling at breakneck speed without colliding. I realized the buildings themselves were moving too. Some of the blocks were turning slowly, their tenants standing at the windows to take in the view. Other blocks had detached and were rising upward into the air, heading for another section of the building.

"Welcome to your humble château," Hadron said.

Our seat belts were unbuckling. A deep, soothing voice called out: "The New York Transit Authority wishes Hadron and Justin a pleasant evening in Plum Hollow Ridge."

I felt numb, and a little sick from the traveling. Hadron and I climbed off the hoverbus, which whisked away into the swarm of vehicles. "This is not New York," I said. "There is no Plum Hollow Ridge in New York City."

Hadron furrowed her brow. "I think you would call this area Flushing. That's much worse."

As we walked toward the building, a solid wall that seemed to be made of brown Play-Doh began to melt. That's the only way I can describe it. An opening formed, just large enough for us to walk through. I grabbed Hadron's hand. She scared me, but a dissolving wall scared me more.

We walked through into a vast atrium. It rose above us in tiered balconies, with skylights letting in prisms of afternoon sun. On all floors, people were eating in cafés and chatting. Thick clusters of pipes snaked along the floors and up the walls. My eyes were drawn to what I thought were birds flying overhead, but they were kids flitting in midair, playing games that looked like a broomless Quidditch. Hadron was saying hi to people left and right. She stopped near a sign on a wall that said "Elevator." I didn't see any doors, just a down and up button. She stared at them and blinked. The up button glowed, and we began to rise.

As I screamed, Hadron smiled patiently and rapped her fingers three times in the air. I heard three solid knocks. "See? We're enclosed," she said. "Don't worry. Enjoy the view."

I didn't. In fact, I was shaking when she led me out onto a balcony on an upper floor. A door appeared in the middle of the wall with my name on a plaque over the top. "Welcome, Justin!" a cheerful mechanical voice greeted me.

"Thanks, Door," I muttered.

Hadron beckoned me inside. We entered a big room with pure white walls and a gigantic window looking out toward a peaceful body of water. "Long Island Sound," she said. "And if you get bored with that . . ."

She nodded at a set of buttons on the wall, and they lit up. Silently, things began sliding out of the walls—shelves full of games and books, a flat-screen TV, a big comfy-looking sofa, a trampoline, and a cabinet stocked with candy and chips.

With a deliriously happy yap, a little cocker spaniel puppy leaped up from the sofa and landed at my feet, wagging its tail. "Bruno!" Hadron said. "Say hi to Justin!"

"His name is *Bruno*?" I said.

"And he's yours," Hadron replied.

I knelt down, and Bruno began tickling my face with his tongue. He was the cutest dog I'd ever seen. He reminded me of my own dog, Pluto, who had died a month earlier. And that made me want to cry and laugh at the same time. I sat on the floor, propping my back against the sofa as Bruno whimpered and yipped and licked, like it was the best day of his whole life.

"My mom will love him," I said.

Hadron's smile disappeared. She took off her sunglasses and put them down on a snack bar, then sank down next to me. "I'm afraid," she said, "we have a lot to discuss."

I wasn't going home.

I couldn't go even if I wanted to.

From what I could understand, home would come to me. Maybe.

Hadron had explained it all, but I didn't understand a word. So she stared at a set of shelves, which vanished back into the wall. In the blank space an image appeared:

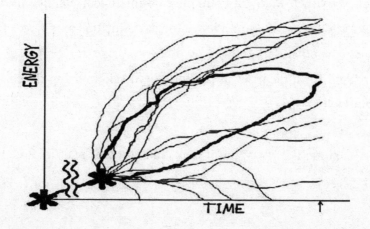

No projector, nothing.

I gasped in shock. Bruno, who had fallen asleep at my feet, let out a tiny yip and resettled.

"I know, I know, my sightwriting is so bad," Hadron said sheepishly. "Okay, the asterisk at the bottom left is what you call the Big Bang—the beginning of everything. As we go to the right, the universe expands. The single dark line that extends from the asterisk? That represents us—well, the mass of gas and elements that became Earth. The squiggly lines that look like a river, that's where billions of years go by. But if I put them in from the beginning, the graph would be too long."

"What about the second asterisk?" I asked. "And the other lines?"

"The second asterisk happened sixty-five million years ago, at the end of the dinosaurs," Hadron replied. "An asteroid hits the planet. There's a massive series of collisions on an atomic level. Quarks and bosons go wild. Matter begets antimatter. Thousands of parallel realities form—literally entire, different worlds all existing at the same time, all invisible to one another. They begin as mirror worlds, all looking the same. But little things happen in each. A mutant form of paramecium here, an odd microbe there. Tiny changes have big consequences. The realities begin to develop in different ways. Some of them are unstable and go extinct. Many of them develop intelligent life, like us. Others semi-intelligent, like you. We are the dark line that arcs across the top. You're the other dark line."

"And the little arrow at the bottom?" I said, moving closer. "Is that pointing to now?"

"Yes."

"Tell me I'm crazy, but it looks like our two realities are about to merge."

Hadron nodded. "Our quanta are converging, the particle spins aligning."

"Like I said."

"This is a good thing for your people, of course. You get the benefit of an awesome world. There are no wars. People are productive. We have always harnessed free energy from the sun. It has never occurred to anyone to mine fossil fuels. Poverty is unheard of. You have what you want, when you want it." Hadron smiled. "The secret, Justin, is that the convergence already began generations ago. Points of confluence have opened up all around the world—odd little portals between the two realities. . . ."

I felt the blood drain from my face. "Like the space under the platform at Fifty-Ninth Street."

Hadron smiled. "The portals are relatively stable, but they do move a bit, and they're invisible to the naked eye. Which is why our scientists developed a special viewing mechanism."

In my mind's eye I saw Hadron reaching for those orange sunglasses. I sank into my chair and shook my head as the reality sank in. "The glasses. That's why you wanted them. And I almost prevented you. We could have been killed because of me. . . ."

The graphic disappeared and the shelves began to emerge from the wall again. Hadron leaned closer toward me. "Over generations, there has been leakage through the portals—both ways. The first happened during the Crusades, when three gladiators from your world, brandishing spears and smelling like horse manure, appeared during a global forum on water filtration in our world. That was entertaining. Quite a few leaks to your world, too. A rather brilliant fellow called Plato. A family known as Gandhi, and a quirky soul who went by Einstein."

"We got the better deal," I said numbly.

"But there's a problem, Justin. These leaks prevent the convergence from completing. The worlds cannot merge until all the leaks have been returned to their proper reality. Which is where I come in. I am a Seeker. My job is to bring the leaks back. When our work is done, no more impediments. The worlds combine. Your New York City will look like ours."

I nodded. "So . . . no Columbus Circle. Or Times Square or Chinatown or the Statue of Liberty . . ."

"Or the Five Corners School for the Unconventionally Abled. Or the sunglasses racks at the S&W Hardware and Deli." Hadron put her hands on my shoulders. Her smile filled me with a sudden deep warmth. "You will never be ridiculed again, Justin. In no time, you'll be with your friends and family. They will have to adjust to all this. But they will. Trust me. And they'll love Bruno."

Bruno, who had fallen asleep, farted.

"But what if you don't collect all the leaks?" I asked.

Hadron shrugged. "We will be like two north pole magnets, and eventually, the lines will diverge again for another few million years. Your world will continue in exactly the way it is heading. Toward absolute, barbaric chaos."

Outside the window a kid flew by, doing a loop the loop on an invisible hoverboard. He spotted me through the window, grinned, and waved. From the wall a stove emerged, opening to reveal a pungent, steaming lasagna. My mouth began to water.

Hadron laughed. "Enjoy. And get a good sleep. Tomorrow I'll introduce you to the YE—young explorers. Our version of school. You split into topic groups—travel, tech, food, story creation, music. It's fun. You'll like it."

The door opened in the wall, and she gave me a little salute as she went through.

The lasagna was amazing. Better than my dad's, which is saying a lot. But after I'd taken a few bites Bruno awoke with a start and began yapping. "Hungry?" I said, lifting him up and offering him a forkful of lasagna. But he just kept licking my face and tickling me so that I could barely stop laughing.

As I wrestled with him on the sofa, I glanced up at the flat-screen TV. The *Guitar Hero* logo splashed on the screen, and I spotted a Stratocaster by the sofa that I hadn't noticed before. "Whoa, cool—want to dance?" I asked Bruno.

He wagged his tail and began wiggling like crazy.

I put him down and picked up the guitar. I started to play and dance, awash in the aroma of oregano and tomato sauce.

I knew I wouldn't be going to sleep anytime soon.

The voices woke me up in the middle of the night. I'd fallen asleep with Bruno and the guitar beside me on the floor. The TV screen was black.

As I staggered to my feet, I realized my clothes were still foul and stinky from the subway, and I should probably take a shower. I heard a flurry of giggles and whispering from outside, but I figured it was just some hovering kids.

I looked out the window. It was dark, but a soft light suffused the area below.

Weird. All I could see was a stretch of low trees and bushes leading to the shore. So I turned to the bathroom. But before I could shut the door, I heard the voices again.

Now I was feeling paranoid. "Did you hear that, Bruno?" I whispered.

"Yap yap," Bruno yapped. "Yap yap YAP yapyapyap!"

I took that to mean yes.

One last look.

I went to the window and peered to the right and left. I felt the entire room start to move, turning with my glance. Like it was reading my mind and wanted to help me. I lost my balance, and my hand slammed down on the candy cabinet, nearly smashing a pair of glasses.

Hadron's glasses.

As I picked them up, Bruno started growling, sinking back on his haunches.

"Dude, sorry, I didn't break them," I said.

"Grrrrrr," Bruno replied.

The orange frames were kind of cool, I had to admit. I put them on and struck a rock hero pose, but Bruno had disappeared behind the sofa.

"You are so weird," I said.

As I lifted my arm to remove the glasses, I caught a glimpse of something out the window.

My arm stiffened.

Three hairy faces were peering in. From the same body. In the midst of their foreheads were gaping toothless mouths, dripping a milky liquid. Diamond-shaped eyes radiated from the chins, shooting darts of light. When the creature saw me, it let out a squeal, waving a quartet of snakelike tentacles just below its shoulders. It rocketed backward like a frightened squid, into a floating group of similar three-headed creatures that were now chittering wildly and training their eyes on me like spotlights.

I tore off the glasses and dove after Bruno.

* * *

I don't know how long I stayed behind the sofa. My mind kind of went blank, and my body froze. I had thrown off the glasses, and now they were on the floor. Bruno had snuggled against me for a while and then wandered out into the room.

Finally, I emerged. The window was clear of monsters. Somehow Bruno had found a bowl of kibble that had materialized out of nowhere.

I stood. I gathered myself. Okay. I was tired. I hadn't slept. Leaking between quantum realities—or whatever they were called—was hard on a person. It had to be.

I was seeing things. That's all. I still needed that shower and maybe some more food.

Avoiding the window, I ran into the bathroom. Hanging on the back of the door was a pair of jeans and a T-shirt exactly my size. A pair of boxers and socks lay on top of a brand-new pair of Converse sneakers on the floor. I tossed my old clothes aside, took the shower, and then put on the new wardrobe. Everything smelled so fresh. I felt like a new person.

As I scooped all the stuff out of my old pocket, my phone rang.

I nearly dropped it. I hadn't thought of using it at all. I had assumed an alternate reality would be out of network.

The caller ID was an unreadable string of weird characters, but I answered it anyway. "Hello?"

"Justin, it's Hadron," the voice said. "Did I leave my glasses there?"

"Yeah," I replied.

"I figured. I'll be there in five. And Justin?"

"Uh-huh."

"Don't put them on, okay? Under any circumstances. They will blind you completely."

"Um . . ."

"You didn't put them on, did you?"

"No!" I lied.

"Good."

As she hung up I dumped the phone into my pocket, along with my cash and all my other stuff. I burst out of the bathroom, pushing the hair out of my eyes. Bruno came scampering up to me. His tail was wagging, and he had the sunglasses in his teeth.

"I lied to her, Bruno," I said. "But—but she lied to me. She said those things would blind me."

Bruno began yapping loudly. He was trying to tell me something. As I lifted him he extended his neck, pushing the glasses toward my face.

"YAP YAP YAP YAP YAP!"

"All right, all right." I set Bruno down and took the glasses. I was curious now. As I slipped them on, I glanced about the room. It looked darker, but the window was a rectangle of soft light. Outside was a blur of motion, black figures passing back and forth.

I went closer.

The air was thick with three-headed hairballs, with tentacles like a squid but legs like a human. They were shirtless, revealing a hairy rack of compact tubes along each side of their torsos. The tubes were the size of toilet paper rolls and throbbed as they moved, acting like jet-propulsion engines.

As I pressed my nose against the glass, I noticed two groups of the hideous creatures gathered closely on either side of the window, looking at me. As if they'd been waiting just out of sight, hiding.

I jumped back. Who were they? Stalkers? A study group? I felt like a zoo animal.

Now my eyes were taking in the entire room. I'd been so focused on the scene outside, I'd never turned inward. The smooth walls were a hodgepodge of tubes, wires, sprockets, and gears. The stove, the shelves, the TV, and a dozen other appliances were crammed together on wheeled metallic platforms. Everything that had popped in and out of sight through creamy white walls—they were all there, along with the mechanisms that moved them.

This was why she'd told me not to put on the glasses. It wasn't that they'd blind me. This was the opposite of being blinded. I was seeing everything the way it really was.

I glanced down at Bruno.

But Bruno was no longer there. In his place was a greenish insect-like creature with a segmented body, hinged arms, a beaked mouth, and two big blue eyes on stalks.

"If I were you," he said, "I would go now."

The screech was music to my ears.

My arms were tucked by my side, my back flush against the track bed between the rails. As the C train's soot-blackened chassis passed inches above my nose, I laughed.

All I could think was that Hadron was wrong.

Our people were not semi-intelligent. At least not me.

The escape had happened so fast. The last few minutes were running through my brain like a movie on fast forward. Back in the room I'd known enough to listen to Bruno. I'd drawn shades over the apartment window and snuck out the door. Running around the back of the building, I'd taken a route along the shore and finally circled back to find the hoverbus. I'd climbed aboard, looking calm and collected.

I got off at the stop in front of the gardens and raced across the field. Putting my glasses back on, I saw that the gardens were patches of steaming swampland. The field was a smoky, parched desert plain, and in the midst of it was a giant black hole.

As I prepared to jump, a three-head came jetting toward me. I knew even before hearing the voice that it was Hadron. She pleaded with me to give her back the glasses. She warned me I'd be sorry. She promised explanations. She said if I went, it was all over.

Of course I jumped.

The trip through was painful. As if my body had been vaporized and then reassembled. But when I felt myself on the track bed, I quickly tucked myself out of harm's way. And now here I was, lying in garbage and a foul pool of liquid I did not want to try to identify. My lungs felt seared by the burning metallic stink, and I didn't know if my eardrums would survive the noise.

But I would rather be here than anywhere else in the world. Or any other world.

When the train finally stopped, I heard muffled screams from the platform. People had seen my body, I guess. The train must not have made it all the way into the station because footsteps clomped overhead as passengers walked toward the front to exit. I could hear sobbing. Speculating who had died. Some claimed they saw two kids. Three. A girl and a dog. A group of Christmas carolers. A giant rat. That last one really hurt my feelings.

I finally shimmied my way up the track until I could see a gap between two of the train cars. There, I was able to sit up, grab on to a bumper, and hoist myself up.

As I rose through the gap, steadying myself on my elbows, I stared through the open door into one of the cars. I still had the glasses on. A group of people were kneeling around an older man who had fainted and was now slowly coming to. Through the glasses' lenses, everything looked exactly normal—the track, the train car interior, the people. No three heads. No optical illusions.

"Is he going to be all right?" I asked.

They all turned. A few of them gasped out loud. The old man fainted again.

Everyone else ran toward me. Several of them reached down and lifted me into the warm train car. They were shouting so loud, I couldn't understand a word. Their eyes were wide, their jaws open, like they'd just seen Santa Claus.

"Ho-ho-ho," I said.

I'm not sure anyone heard me. But I was safe. And I was home!

"Falalala . . . lalala . . ."

A week after my return, we had the biggest holiday party ever in my house—and Lucia Liberatore was singing straight at me. I hoped my face wasn't too red.

Luckily, the Vanderdonck High School Chamber Singers were dressed in normal clothes. As they caroled, our fireplace crackled behind them. The living room smelled like a pine forest. Dad had thrown out our old plastic Christmas tree and bought the biggest real tree sold by the plaid-shirted Canadians who camp out every December at our corner. When they realized he was my dad, they gave it to him for free.

People I barely knew had shown up for the party, including one of the Canadian tree people. Everyone wanted to toast and congratulate me.

The story of my miraculous survival was all over the media. I had to wear makeup for the TV interviews. As for Hadron, here's the weird thing: Even though lots of witnesses had seen her, felt her plow into them on the platform, reached down to her when she was on the track—the fact that no trace of her had been found made their claims all seem ridiculous. Police vowed to search, but the only people taking her existence seriously were conspiracy bloggers who spoke about an orange alien probably also responsible for 9/11, climate change, and human sacrifices in a secret society of corporate execs in Northern California. One by one, eyewitnesses began recanting every day— except Jacob Schmendrick, who stood by the story, but no one ever listened to him anyway.

I hadn't told anyone what really happened. To avoid questions about the glasses, I'd stuck them in my pocket as soon I was lifted into the train car. I thought about throwing them out, but I hadn't. I'd carried them around every day, including at the party. I guess I needed a reminder that the whole thing had been real. Honestly, though, the frames were pointy and beginning to feel really uncomfortable.

I slipped them out of my pocket and put them on the coffee table.

In the week since the adventure, Hadron had not returned. Which made me think that maybe the glasses were unique. Maybe by taking them through the portal, I had blocked the convergence forever. *Eventually, the lines will diverge again for another few million years,* Hadron had said. Which was fine with me. I'd take our broken reality over their idea of perfection any day.

After the party I promised myself I would throw the glasses into the fireplace.

"We bought you a present!"

The voice startled me out of my thoughts. Lucia was sitting next to me on the sofa. Another singer sat next to her, giggling. Jacob sat on the sofa arm, but it cracked, so he quickly stood back up.

As they all began singing "We Wish You a Merry Christmas," my mom entered the room carrying a guitar in a case marked *TAYLOR*. I started to cry.

"Only the best for you," Mom said.

"Play it!" someone yelled, and everyone else joined in.

I took the guitar out of the case. It was gorgeous. I couldn't really play it without an amp, but I strapped it on and struck a chord anyway, to wild applause. Lucia took the sunglasses off the coffee table and put them on my face, for effect.

I let out a yelp.

Everyone must have thought it was part of the rock-star act because they all applauded and laughed. But they weren't seeing what I was seeing. They weren't looking at Lucia Liberatore.

And a drooling, three-headed beast was not looking back at them.

"LUCIA!" I screamed, throwing the glasses onto the floor. "You—you're—"

"I'm what?" She cocked her head and smiled. She was so beautiful. Again.

But she was one of them. A leak.

Lucia!

Did she know? Did leaks into our world know they were . . . *like that*? Hadron had never explained that, and Lucia wasn't giving me any clues. She was looking at me with a big, radiant smile.

I decided in that moment that she didn't know. She couldn't have known. Here in this world she looked like a human and felt like a human. And I never wanted to see her like that again. I would definitely, unquestionably, destroy those glasses.

"Honey, where did you get these?" my mom called out from behind me.

I turned. She was bending down, picking up the sunglasses from the carpet. She rose with an amused smile and began lifting them to her face.

"*No!*" I shouted.

She put them on and struck a pose. As her friends laughed she glanced around the room.

I raced toward her. I didn't want her to see Lucia. But as she turned to us, the smile disappeared from her face. Her jaw dropped. Her skin turned a ghostly white.

I stopped in my tracks.

No. It couldn't be. It was impossible.

Out of the corner of my eye, I could see Lucia halfway across the room, leaning over a bowl of M&M's. My mom wasn't looking at her at all.

As she let out a shrill, piercing scream, she was staring directly at me.

ABOUT THE AUTHORS

RAY DANIEL is an award-winning author of Boston-based crime fiction and is the author of the Tucker Mystery series. *Hacked* is the fourth novel in the series. His short story "Give Me a Dollar" won the 2014 Derringer Award for Best Long Story, and "Driving Miss Rachel" was chosen as a 2013 distinguished short story by Otto Penzler, editor of *The Best American Mystery Stories 2013*. For more information visit him online at www.raydanielmystery.com and follow him on Twitter @raydanielmystry.

BETH FANTASKEY is the author of several novels for teens and preteens, including *Jessica's Guide to Dating on the Dark Side*; *Jekel Loves Hyde*; *Buzz Kill*; and *Isabel Feeney, Star Reporter*. She lives in rural Pennsylvania with her husband, three daughters, and an entire menagerie of pets. Her favorite ice cream flavor is chocolate chip. Visit her at www.bethfantaskeyauthor.com or on Twitter @bethfantaskey.

CHRIS GRABENSTEIN is a #1 *New York Times* bestselling author. His books for kids include *Escape from Mr. Lemoncello's Library*, *Mr. Lemoncello's Library Olympics*, *The Island of Dr. Libris*, and *Welcome to Wonderland: Home Sweet Motel*. He is also the coauthor with James Patterson of numerous fun and funny page-turners, including *I Funny*, *House of Robots*, *Treasure Hunters*, *Jacky Ha-Ha*, and *Word of Mouse*. Visit him at www.chrisgrabenstein.com or on Twitter @CGrabenstein.

New York Times and *USA Today* bestselling author **HEATHER GRAHAM** majored in theater arts at the University of South Florida. After several years in dinner theater, backup vocals, and bartending, she stayed home after the birth of her third child and began to write. Her first book was with Dell Publishing, and since then, she has written over two hundred fifty novels and novellas, including suspense, historical romance, vampire fiction, time travel, occult, and Christmas family fare. She has been published in approximately twenty languages and been honored with awards from Walden Books, B. Dalton, Georgia Romance Writers, *Affaire de Coeur*, *Romantic Times*, and more. She is the proud recipient of the Silver Bullet from International Thriller Writers, and was ThrillerMaster in 2016. Visit Heather at www.eheathergraham.com or on Twitter @heathergraham.

Edgar Award–nominated author-illustrator **BRUCE HALE** is passionate about inspiring reluctant readers to open books (and read them). He has written over forty seriously funny books for children, including the award-winning Chet Gecko Mystery series, *Snoring Beauty* (one of Oprah's Recommended Reads for Kids), and the Clark the Shark books, one of which ended up in a McDonald's Happy Meal (not the way you think). His newest, *The Curse of the Were-Hyena*, is based on a story he wrote in second grade. An actor and Fulbright Scholar in storytelling, Bruce is in demand as a speaker, having presented internationally at conferences, universities, and schools. Visit him at www.brucehale.com or on Twitter @storyguy1.

STEVE HOCKENSMITH is the author of more than a dozen mystery novels, including the Edgar Award finalists *Holmes on the Range* and

Nick and Tesla's Secret Agent Gadget Battle. His most recent books are the tarot-themed mystery *Give the Devil His Due* (with Lisa Falco) and the graphic novel *Secret Smithsonian Adventures: Claws and Effect* (with Chris Kientz). Like the trick-or-treaters in his story, he's never been fond of Whoppers. You can learn more about him, his candy preferences, and his books at www.stevehockensmith.com or on Twitter @MrHockensmith.

TONYA HURLEY is a *New York Times* and international bestselling author of the ghostgirl series and The Blessed trilogy. Her books are published in over thirty countries and in more than twenty languages around the world. She is the recipient of the Pennsylvania School Librarians Association Award, the Parents' Choice Gold Award, and is a two-time Bram Stoker Award finalist. Her books received starred reviews from such literary publications as *Publishers Weekly*, *VOYA*, *School Library Journal*, and *Kirkus Reviews*. Hurley wrote and produced two hit TV series, and wrote and directed acclaimed independent films, music videos, and video games for kids. She was a founding board member of the Morbid Anatomy Museum and is the co-host of the *Stories of Strange Women* podcast. Her much anticipated novel *Feathervein* will be published in 2019. Visit Tonya at www.tonyahurley.com and on Facebook, Instagram, and Twitter @TonyaHurley.

EMMY LAYBOURNE is a novelist and former character actress. She is the author of the Monument 14 trilogy and the novel *Sweet*. Before her life as an author, Emmy performed original comedy on Comedy Central, MTV, and VH1 and acted in the movies *Superstar*, *The In-Laws*, and *Nancy Drew*, among others. Emmy lives outside New York

City with her husband, two kids, and a flock of six nifty chickens. Sign up for her awesome newsletter at www.emmylaybourne.com or follow her on Twitter @EmmyLaybourne.

PETER LERANGIS is the author of far too many books. Nine of them have been *New York Times* bestsellers, to his parents' relief. After writing the Seven Wonders series and several The 39 Clues books, he promises his next work will not contain a number in the title. His friendship with R.L. Stine was forged over a dinner with Vladimir Putin, who kept his shirt on. Ever since, he has been very careful about emails. Peter is now locked away working on a new series called Max Tilt, and he would deeply appreciate it if you sent chocolate. Visit him at www.peterlerangis.com or on Twitter @PeterLerangis.

DOUG LEVIN's short crime fiction has appeared in *Ellery Queen Mystery Magazine, Alfred Hitchcock Mystery Magazine,* and two anthologies. He once sold a pen to a Nobel Prize winner, gave a ride to a different Nobel Prize winner, and ghostwrote for yet another Nobel Prize winner. He has also met two astronauts. A lapsed academic, former book critic, and current pug owner, Doug lives and works in Portland, Oregon. He can be found on very rare occasions blogging at www.douglevin.com.

PHIL MATHEWS used to work in an office, at a desk, behind a computer, but tired of that routine, so now he writes . . . in his house . . . at a desk . . . behind a computer. "Bloodstone" is his first published short story, but his first published work might be the book *Gumshoe,* which features the same characters from "Bloodstone." If he can finish it up and e-publish it before this anthology comes out.

ALISON McMAHAN is an award-winning screenwriter, author, and filmmaker. Her books include *The Films of Tim Burton: Animating Live Action in Hollywood*; the award-winning *Alice Guy Blaché: Lost Visionary of the Cinema*, which has been translated into Spanish and had the film rights sold; and the historical mystery novel *The Saffron Crocus*, which won the Rosemary Award for Excellence in Young Adult and New Adult Fiction in 2014 and the Florida Writers Association's Royal Palm Literary Award in 2015. Her short mystery "The New Score" appeared in *Fish Out of Water: A Guppy Anthology*, and "The Drive By" appeared in *Busted!: Arresting Stories from the Beat* anthology. She reviews for *The Big Thrill* and *Publishers Weekly*. Visit her at www.AlisonMcMahan.com or on Twitter @AlisonMcMahan.

LISA MORTON is a screenwriter, author of nonfiction books, award-winning prose writer, and Halloween expert whose work was described by the American Library Association's *Readers' Advisory Guide to Horror* as "consistently dark, unsettling, and frightening." Her most recent releases include *Ghosts: A Haunted History* and the short-story collection *Cemetery Dance Select: Lisa Morton*. Lisa lives in the San Fernando Valley and online at www.lisamorton.com or on Twitter @cinriter.

DANIEL PALMER has written eight critically acclaimed suspense novels, including two medical thrillers with Michael Palmer. He published his first novel, *Delirious*, after a decade-long career in e-commerce, where he helped build major online retailers, including www.barnesandnoble.com. A recording artist, accomplished blues harmonica player, and lifelong Red Sox fan, Daniel lives in New Hampshire with his wife and two children. Visit him at www.danielpalmerbooks.com or on Twitter @danielpalmer.

STEPHEN ROSS is a filmmaker, musician, and mystery writer. He has been nominated for an Edgar Award, a Derringer Award, an International Thriller Writers' Thriller Award for Best Short Story, and was a 2010 *Ellery Queen Mystery Magazine* Readers Award finalist. His short stories and novellas have appeared in *Ellery Queen Mystery Magazine*, *Alfred Hitchcock Mystery Magazine*, the 2013 Mystery Writers of America *Mystery Box* anthology, and many other publications. He has lived in Auckland, London, and Frankfurt, and he currently resides on the beautiful Whangaparaoa Peninsula of New Zealand, where his dog, Mycroft, takes him for walks. Visit Stephen at www.StephenRoss.net and on Twitter @_StephenRoss.

JEFF SOLOWAY won the 2014 Robert L. Fish Memorial Award from the Mystery Writers of America. His Travel Writer mystery series includes *The Travel Writer*, which takes place in Bolivia, and *The Last Descent*, which takes place in the Grand Canyon. The latest installment, *The Ex-President*, set on a cruise ship, is about a former real-estate tycoon who becomes president and then mysteriously quits halfway through his term. Jeff lives in New York City with his wife and two children, Manny and Valerie.

New York Times bestselling author **WENDY CORSI STAUB** has published more than eighty books since her first, a ghostly thriller called *Summer Lightning*, won the 1994 RWA RITA Award for Best Young Adult Romance. She is best known for psychological suspense and mysteries such as *Bone White* and *The Dead of Winter*. Her paranormal romance *Hello, It's Me*—written under her *USA Today* bestselling pseudonym Wendy Markham—aired as a Hallmark television movie starring Kellie Martin. Visit her on Twitter @WendyCorsiStaub.

R.L. STINE is one of the bestselling children's authors in history. His Goosebumps and Fear Street series have sold more than 400 million copies around the world. He has had several TV series based on his work, including the 2015 movie *Goosebumps*, which starred Jack Black as R.L. Stine himself. R.L. Stine lives in New York City with his wife, Jane, an editor and publisher. Visit him at www.rlstine.com or on Twitter @RL_Stine.

JOSEPH S. WALKER lives in Indiana, where he teaches literature courses, cheers for the St. Louis Cardinals, and frequently loses at chess. His stories have previously appeared in *Alfred Hitchcock Mystery Magazine*, *The First Line*, and other magazines. *Cinnamon's Solace* and *Cinnamon's Shadow*, the first two installments of a new ebook series of crime stories for adults, are available on Amazon. "The Only Child" is his first story for young readers, and he thanks his wife for a very productive brainstorming session. Follow him on Twitter @JSWalkerAuthor.

USA Today–bestselling thriller author **CARTER WILSON** is a two-time winner of both the Colorado Book Award and the International Book Award, and his novels have received multiple starred reviews from *Publishers Weekly*, ALA *Booklist*, and *School Library Journal*. His critically acclaimed novel inspired by the Slenderman crime, *Mister Tender's Girl*, released in February 2018. He lives in Colorado with his two children. Visit him at www.carterwilson.com.